Marry Me
in Italy

Nicky Pellegrino's Italian father moved to England after falling in love with and marrying a Liverpool girl. He brought to his new family his passion for food and instilled in them what all Italians know – that you live to eat instead of eating to live. This Italian mantra is the inspiration behind Nicky's delicious novels. When Nicky met and married a New Zealander, she moved to Auckland, where she writes books and works as a freelance magazine journalist.

Find out more at www.nickypellegrino.com.

Also by Nicky Pellegrino

Delicious
Summer at the Villa Rosa
(originally published as The Gypsy Tearoom)
The Italian Wedding
Recipe for Life
The Villa Girls
When in Rome
The Food of Love Cookery School
One Summer in Venice
Under Italian Skies
A Year at Hotel Gondola
A Dream of Italy
Tiny Pieces of Us
To Italy, With Love
P.S. Come to Italy

Nicky Pellegrino

Marry Me
in Italy

ORION

First published in Great Britain in 2024 by Orion Fiction,
an imprint of the Orion Publishing Group Ltd.,
Carmelite House, 50 Victoria Embankment
London EC4Y 0DZ

An Hachette UK Company

5 7 9 10 8 6

A CIP catalogue record for this book
is available from the British Library.

ISBN (Export Trade Paperback) 978 1 3987 1504 2
ISBN (eBook) 978 1 3987 1506 6
ISBN (Audio) 978 1 3987 1507 3

Typeset by Deltatype Ltd, Birkenhead, Merseyside

Printed in Great Britain by Clays Ltd, Elcograf S.p.A.

www.orionbooks.co.uk

For Clara De Sio, with thanks

Montenello

Augusto was sitting outside the bar in the main piazza of Montenello. He was wearing the sweater his daughter insisted he keep on unless the day was properly warm, and sipping the decaffeinated coffee his son said was best at his age. He did these things to make them happy, but very often the fuss seemed more exhausting than being elderly was.

While he tended not to think about his age very much, Augusto couldn't deny he had been alive for many years, and all of them spent living here in this same hilltop town in Southern Italy.

Life moved slowly in Montenello and each day might seem almost the same as the last, but there was always something going on if you bothered to look for it. Settled at his favourite table, a little earlier than usual, Augusto surveyed the empty piazza. He could predict when his friend would roll up in the truck that he sold vegetables from. What time his daughter would open the trattoria next door to the bar. When the street-sweeper would arrive to start cleaning up confetti.

Not that the piazza needed sweeping quite so often nowadays. Augusto could remember a time when there seemed no end of brides and grooms emerging from the town hall in a flurry of confetti and standing beside the fountain posing for photographs. What had happened? Were fewer people getting married or were they choosing other places to exchange their vows?

If Italy's most romantic town was falling out of fashion, then action must be taken. Livelihoods depended on the business the weddings brought in. How would the hotel survive without them?

Alone outside the bar, Augusto searched his mind for a solution, certain he could find one. Years ago, when he was working at the town hall, he had helped transform Montenello. It had been his idea to sell off its abandoned buildings for the bargain price of one euro. His scheme had been a great success and before long, rather than crumbling into ruins, the place began to thrive.

Augusto loved this town and the prospect of a reversal in its fortunes was unacceptable to him. Alone outside the bar, he thought long and hard about how he might be able to help.

Clearly what was needed was another bold scheme, one that that would draw publicity, and remind the world that Montenello existed. With its tangle of narrow streets, fresh mountain air and views across the valley below, it was as perfect for a wedding as any other place and likely more affordable. People only needed to hear about it. But how?

Half-closing his eyes, Augusto sensed an idea shimmering on the edges of his mind. He focused, thinking longer and harder, frowning with the effort of such concentration, before reaching for his smartphone. Smiling at the screen, he started to tap, quite slowly because he wanted to get this absolutely right. When he had finished, he had the wording of an advertisement that he hoped would run in magazines and newspapers, and be shared all over the internet, reaching people around the world, capturing their imaginations.

★

Win a dream wedding in Italy's most romantic town
Every couple that books to marry in the picturesque hilltop town
of Montenello this summer will receive a cash reward of 1,000
euro. And one lucky pair will win a dream wedding package, with
everything they need to say 'I do' in style. So, if you are in love,
why not marry in Montenello?

Reading over what he had composed, Augusto was certain this was the answer. A reward and a competition, what a good idea. Some people were bound to say the town couldn't afford it, but he would explain they couldn't afford not to. This new scheme was going to bring in more bookings and create excitement. In the end, it would be worth it.

Augusto still had some influence at the town hall, even though he was long retired. Almost every morning his friend the mayor was in the habit of meeting him at the bar so they could drink a coffee together. At times the mayor, a much younger man, might share a problem, and then Augusto would offer advice. It always pleased him to be able to do so.

Today by the time he appeared, Augusto was buzzing. He could hardly wait for his friend to settle down beside him.

'Are you OK?' asked the mayor, sensing the older man's excitement. 'Did they let you drink the real coffee for a change today?'

'No, no I have come up with a plan.' Augusto was impatient to share it. 'It is a way to reinvigorate the town, bring in more business and revenue, and I am certain it can be done. Let me tell you all about it.'

The mayor nodded. From experience he knew that Augusto was always worth listening to. It was no exaggeration to say Salvio Valentini might not still be the mayor of Montenello, without him.

'*Va bene,*' he said. 'Tell me.'

Ana

Everything about that day seemed the same as the hundreds that had gone before. There was no warning, no hint at all, that at precisely 11.58 a.m. the life Ana loved would be snatched away. All she had built and nurtured, almost everything she cared about – gone just like that. Perhaps she ought to have seen it coming, but if there were any warning signs, Ana had managed to miss them.

That morning she had woken at dawn as always, done twenty minutes of stretching exercises, drunk her coffee and spent a few moments arranging her platinum blonde hair into a chignon. Then she had dressed in tailored charcoal trousers and a matching fitted shirt and, after peering out of the window, added a rain jacket. Walking to work through the parks, whether it was wet or dry, was an important part of her routine. Ana liked routines. With her schedule rigorously planned, her mind felt free to focus on other, more creative, things.

She was thinking about Christmas as she walked through Kensington Gardens, even though it was still early April. That was the thing about working on a food magazine, you were always planning months ahead and focusing on warming soups and stews, when all you actually wanted to eat was refreshing salads. Ana had been the editor of *Culinaria* magazine for more than two decades. She had steered it through issue after issue, so to think about wintry plum puddings just as spring's daffodils and crocuses were pushing their bright heads out of the ground, didn't seem unusual.

The Christmas issue was always a particular challenge. How to make it traditional enough to please the readers and yet sufficiently different to all the festive editions that had gone before. That was what Ana was considering, as she skirted the Round Pond and headed towards the Peter Pan statue.

Culinaria's office was in Mayfair and Ana's habit was to walk there briskly, without checking her phone, even if she heard it ring or messages coming through. Nothing was so urgent that it couldn't wait until she reached her desk, where her assistant would have left the latest editions of other glossy magazines carefully fanned out beside her primrose-coloured Moleskine diary with all the day's appointments written in.

Once in the office Ana swapped her trainers for heels, checked that her chignon remained in place and reddened her lips with MAC Ruby Woo before settling down to work. From that moment on she would be busy non-stop but so long as she had managed a morning walk to clear her mind, she could cope with whatever the job threw at her. At least so Ana had always imagined.

Every day, no matter how much there was to do, she made a point of wandering through *Culinaria*'s offices, checking in with the salespeople, exchanging a few words with her editorial team, spending time in the test kitchen to taste whatever recipes they happened to be trialling. She did this partly to keep the staff on their toes – they never knew quite when she might appear – but also because she loved it, seeing all those people working away, cogs in the efficient machine that every single month produced Britain's most-loved food publication.

That April morning there was a three-hour planning meeting

in her diary, and afterwards lunch at Scott's with some advertising clients, then page proofs to clear for the next issue. A normal day, perhaps even a slightly dull one.

The planning meeting tried Ana's patience. What everyone wanted for the front cover of the Christmas issue was a spectacular cake but nobody could agree on what it should look like. They were still arguing when Lucy, her assistant, put her head around the door and caught her attention.

Ana assumed she must be running late for her lunch. 'I'll have to leave you with this for now,' she said, already on her feet and glancing at the Hermès Tank watch that had been a gift to herself eight years ago for her fiftieth birthday.

Lucy's complexion was pinker than usual. 'Your lunch has been cancelled,' she said, as Ana hurried out of the room. 'They want to see you upstairs, on the fifth floor.'

'Who wants to see me?' Ana hated plans being changed at the last minute.

'Mr Verhoeven.'

'I thought he was in the States?' Ana glanced at Lucy. 'We had a meeting scheduled for next week, didn't we? What's this about?'

'I don't really know, but I think it might have something to do with the website.' Lucy was Ana's eyes and ears in the office. If there was a rumour, she would hear it. She was plugged into a network of personal assistants.

'Oh right, the website.' Far too much of Ana's time had gone into that already. It had badly needed a refresh but as far as she was concerned, she was finished with it. They had a really good digital editor onboard now, so shouldn't she be taking care of things?

'I need two minutes,' she told Lucy. 'Tell him I'm on my way.'

In the bathroom she reapplied her MAC Ruby Woo lipstick,

the shade she had worn every single working day since 1999. She smoothed her hair and took a couple of deep breaths. Whatever the problem with the website might be, she would deal with it then get back to her magazine, which was what she really cared about.

The fifth-floor offices always felt slightly too air conditioned and yet somehow still stifling. Ana's heels sank into the deep carpet as she walked towards Christopher Verhoeven's office.

It was his father Paul who had hired her back in the late eighties. He had recognised Ana's talent and promoted her upwards, rung by rung, until she won the most glittering prize, editorship of *Culinaria*. Paul had died two years ago, felled by a heart attack, and privately Ana thought his son had been out of his depth ever since.

Glancing at her watch, before pushing open the door of his office, she saw that it wasn't yet midday. 'Good morning,' she called, striding in and Christopher seemed almost startled as he looked up from his computer screen.

Ana prided herself on being able to speak to anyone but sitting down opposite him, there was an unusually awkward silence.

'The website,' she said, taking charge. 'I was just looking at it and I'm very happy with the refresh. There are a couple of things that need fine-tuning but on the whole, I think it's working well.'

The old *Culinaria* website had been clunky and outdated. It was Ana who had pushed for a relaunch and hired the young digital editor then schooled her in all of the magazine's most important brand values.

'Tammy Wong is doing a good job, I think,' she said to Christopher now, as he stared at her. Paul had possessed a rakish charm and way too much self-confidence; his son always seemed to look half-terrified.

Ana was going to get this meeting over with and treat herself

7

to lunch, she decided. There was a little place in Soho doing a truffled macaroni cheese toasted sandwich that she had been meaning to try for ages. She wasn't sorry that the lunch at Scott's had been cancelled. It would be nice to have a little time completely to herself in the middle of the day.

'You're happy with the job that Tammy is doing?' she asked, crisply. 'The website is getting good feedback?'

'Yes, yes,' said Christopher, filling a water glass for her from a jug on his desk. Ana noticed that it had slices of fresh lemon floating in it. She hated the bitter tang of lemony water, nevertheless she took a sip, politely.

'We couldn't be more excited about the new website,' Christopher continued, as if reading from a script. 'It's helping us to reach our readers in a more relevant way. We're covering more categories, connecting with them like never before and they are loving the access to daily content.'

'That's great,' said Ana, wondering if she should just eat a light salad for lunch as, later this evening, she was meant to be attending a degustation dinner.

'We're excited about the growth and opportunity this brings,' Christopher continued. 'We love the printed magazine, of course, but paper costs are up, advertising revenue is down, and so the timing seems right.'

'I'm sorry, the timing for what?' asked Ana, wondering if she had missed something important when her attention had wandered.

'To stop publishing the monthly magazine,' he said, slowly and carefully.

'I'm sorry?' Ana asked again, assuming she must have misheard.

'We're going to stop printing physical copies of *Culinaria* and focus all our resources on developing the website,' Christopher confirmed.

'You can't do that,' she said, and her voice sounded odd, far away and very faint.

'The decision has been made.'

'But readers love *Culinaria*.' She was outraged. 'It's been publishing for over ninety years, it didn't even miss an issue during the Second World War.'

'Times are changing and we have to move with them. The future is digital.'

Ana wasn't prepared to accept that. 'The magazine is still making money, isn't it?'

'For now, yes.' Christopher sat back in his chair and gave a resigned shrug. 'But the projected figures aren't good.'

'What if I bought it from you?' As she said the words, Ana was already thinking about how she might pull that off.

Christopher was quick to dash any hopes. 'It's not for sale. As I said, we're committed to the website.'

'You'll be keeping staff on ... the test kitchen crew, the sub-editors, designers?'

He shook his head. 'Almost everyone will go, aside from a very small digital team that Tammy Wong will lead.'

'You're firing me too,' Ana realised, so shocked that the words came out as a whisper.

'Not firing,' Christopher said. 'You're hugely valued by this company but unfortunately there isn't a role here for you anymore so it's time for you to pursue other opportunities.'

'When ... when do you intend to do this?' Ana managed to stammer.

'The change is effective immediately.'

'But we're about to go to press with the next issue,' Ana told him.

'Any material from that can be passed on to the website team. There won't be another magazine.'

'But ...' she tried to object.

'The rest of your staff should stop work,' he said firmly. 'Right away.'

The most recent edition of *Culinaria* was on his desk, a glorious springtime issue with a bouquet of white asparagus and purple chive flowers on the cover. Ana stared at it; the last magazine ever; it seemed impossible.

'I'm sending out a company-wide email at 1 p.m. but thought you'd want the chance to tell the team yourself,' Christopher continued.

Ana closed her eyes for a few seconds, and focused on her breathing. When she opened them again, it was to find Christopher on his feet, a signal that it was time for her to leave. She wanted to scream, to sweep everything from his oversized desk and onto the floor, to slap his face. Tempting as it was, she didn't do any of those things.

'For what it's worth, I think you'll regret this,' she said calmly, before walking out of the room and wading through the too-soft carpet towards the lifts.

In the few moments it took to reach Culinaria's floor, Ana tried to gather her thoughts. She had an hour to break the news, to call any members of staff who were off sick or on maternity leave, to decide what to say to them. An hour was all the notice Christopher Verhoeven had thought it worth giving her. As the lift doors opened, she struggled to contain her fury.

Striding out, deep in thought, she almost walked right into Sara the Art Director, who was pacing the corridor, a folder clutched to her chest.

'Oh, Ana good, you're still here,' she said, thrusting a piece of A4 paper towards her. 'This is our Christmas cover. It's elegant but still festive enough; I know it will work.'

Ana found herself examining an image of an elaborate cake, automatically giving it her careful consideration, before realising with a jolt that it didn't matter anymore because there wasn't going to be a Christmas issue.

'It was created by The Lost Cakery,' continued Sara. 'This woman in deepest Somerset that I've discovered. She's a genius and I'd love to highlight her work.'

'Forget the cake,' Ana told her. 'I want to see everyone in the test kitchen. Ask Lucy to help you round them up.'

'What, all of us?' Sarah sounded taken aback.

'Anyone who works for *Culinaria* yes, come to the test kitchen, immediately.'

The kitchen was at the heart of the magazine, where every single recipe they published was trialled over and over again until it was foolproof and perfect. It was like an ordinary home kitchen, only bigger, and there was almost always a smell of warm sugar and melting butter wafting from its open door and down the hallways.

If you were having a bad day you came to the kitchen. If you were hungry or sad, stressed or tired you found refuge there, knowing they would give you something good to eat, fresh baking or runny cheese, perhaps even pour you a glass of wine.

As Ana strode in the cooks barely looked up. They were used to her appearing without any warning.

'Everybody, can I have your attention,' she called. 'Stop what you're doing. Put your tools down, turn the ovens off.'

They looked surprised, but no one argued, not even Tessa the usually stroppy food editor. There must have been something about Ana's face or in her tone of voice. Then the rest of the staff started filing in and before long the room was crammed with people, all of them silent, all of them waiting.

Ana opened her mouth and heard her own voice, steadier now, authoritative even.

'It is with a very heavy heart that I have to pass on some bad news that I have literally only just heard myself. A decision has been made to stop publishing *Culinaria* magazine. Only the website will remain. As of today, the rest of us are finishing work.'

Several voices gasped 'No' and 'What?'. Somebody let out a cry of distress. Ana waited for them to settle.

'This has come as a huge shock. I'm devastated for all of us and for our readers. It makes no sense to me at all, but there's nothing I can do. Mr Verhoeven has said that he will be letting the whole company know very shortly and I'm sure afterwards Human Resources will be available to answer any questions.' Ana stared at them all, at their pale faces and wide eyes. 'For now, I don't know what else to say. This is … this is …'

Her assistant touched her shoulder and Ana realised that her cheeks were wet with tears. As Lucy steered her towards a chair, people's voices rose around her. Why was this happening? How could it be? When was such a thing decided? Ana had no answers.

She watched as the wine editor unlocked the walk-in cupboard that served as a cellar and started pulling out bottles. Tessa and her team handed out glasses and soon everyone had a full one in their hand and they were opening the fridges, emptying them of anything that was ready to eat, their faces growing redder and voices louder as they repeated over and over again that they couldn't believe this was happening.

'Ana, I'm so sorry.' It was Tammy Wong, the digital editor she had gone to such lengths to encourage and train.

'You already knew,' Ana realised. 'He told you before me.'

Tammy screwed up her face. 'I'm sorry,' she repeated.

'I can't imagine that it's going to be much fun, your job now,' Ana couldn't resist saying. 'Just a lot of hard work.'

'Yeah, I know,' said Tammy. 'You had the best of it – the lunches and the events, the travel.'

'I did,' Ana agreed, looking round the room at her team, all handpicked, many that she counted as good friends as well as colleagues.

'When will you be leaving?' Tammy wanted to know.

'You know what ...' Ana took a sip of her wine, dimly registering that it was something special. 'I have absolutely no idea.'

Once they had drunk every drop of wine in the cellar, her staff decided to move on to the pub. Ana didn't go with them in case her being there made everyone feel awkward. Instead, she stayed in the office as small groups of them left. When it had emptied out completely, she went through, looking at abandoned desks cluttered with cookery books, at scrawled Post-it notes reminding people of the things they had needed to do, at banks of computers with darkened screens. She looked at her world, the place she had been happy to come to every single working day since her career began. It almost broke her.

Ana blinked and shook her head. Then she eased off her heels and laced up her trainers, before leaving the building with only the briefest backwards glance and walking through the parks, past the Peter Pan statue and the Round Pond, just as she had a few hours earlier when this day had seemed set to be the same as any other.

Skye

Sometimes it feels like I'm made of sugar. Like it's filling my lungs and my veins, seeping out of my pores, and I might just dissolve into a sticky, syrupy puddle of it. So much sugar. Powder fine icing sugar for glazes and creamy fillings, soft dark brown for caramels, caster for light cakes, coconut for the illusion of health. I tell myself that it's an act of love baking all these sweet treats which are mostly for people I'll never meet.

I've always been a baker. As a little kid I made apple pies and Victoria sponges with my nana and in my teens I made tray-loads of biscuits for school fairs and village fetes. Later, working in an office, I was always the one bringing in home-made treats. And after I had kids, I got into cake decorating and became the mum who made amazing creations every birthday.

It was because of Tim that I turned my hobby into a career. I'm no entrepreneur; he is the one with the bold visions. We wouldn't be here now, living in Lost Cottage, if he hadn't fallen in love with the little cedar house in a clearing on the edge of a woodland. I might have been deterred by practicalities – the size of the mortgage, the secluded location – but once Tim had seen Lost Cottage we absolutely had to have it, even if the conservatory was shabby and the garage in bad shape.

'We'll borrow more money, extend the conservatory, turn

the garage into an annexe,' said Tim, already envisaging what it would look like. As usual he was unstoppable.

To make extra cash, I started taking commissions for celebration cakes, mostly from friends and other mums at Becky and Josh's school. All my weekends and evenings were spent in the kitchen but I loved to see the joy on people's faces when I delivered a towering wedding cake covered in rosebuds or a pink unicorn cake for a little girl. And it satisfied this urge to be creative that I'd always had.

I wasn't prepared for how quickly things grew. People shared photos of my cake creations on their social media pages and the orders doubled, then tripled. I used up all my annual leave and when that ran out, I had to take sick days to meet all my commitments.

Tim did some sums and worked out that if I became a full-time baker, and turned the annexe into a commercial kitchen, there was the potential to make more than I could in my job.

And so, the Lost Cakery was launched and my little business flourished just as Tim had promised it would. To begin with I tried to do everything myself, until unsurprisingly I burnt out completely. That's when I hired Meera to help.

She turned up to an interview and the very first thing she said was, 'I hate cakes.'

'What, all cakes?' I asked, looking at this apparition covered in flower tattoos and diamond studs.

'I don't eat sugar at all,' she told me. 'I think it's toxic.'

'You don't have to eat the cakes you just have to help me make and deliver them. Would that be a problem?'

'No, of course not.'

'And you might not want to mention the whole sugar-is-toxic thing to customers,' I said, pretty sure that Meera wasn't the right person for the job, but forced to hire her anyway because she was the only one who had bothered applying.

Sometimes now I wake up in the night and panic about what I'll do when Meera leaves me. She does more than help bake cakes and deliver them. She keeps me sane.

It can get lonely here at Lost Cottage when the kids are at school or off with their friends, and Tim is caught up in whatever his latest obsession might be. For a while it was pottery and we still have a kiln and potter's wheel stored in one of the sheds. There's a sailing dinghy in the other and the spare room has been taken over by a screen-printing press. I wouldn't mind having some of that space for storage and Tim keeps promising a clear out but it never happens.

Meera can't stand Tim, which is odd because he's one of those people that everybody tends to love, a life-and-soul-of-the-party type. She took a strong dislike to him the very first time they met. I think he'd tried to explain something to her, a theory about recycling the cake boxes that was entirely impractical and would have created more work. Tim has lots of ideas and not all of them are good ones. Meera doesn't have any time for him at all. Whenever he's around, she tends to stay quiet. But if we're alone, she'll chat as we're working and tell me about whatever guy or girl she's dating, or a new tattoo she's thinking of having, or her father's distress that she isn't ever planning on returning to her law degree.

Then Meera will disappear with a tray of passionfruit cup-cakes for a café in Clifton or a fudge brownie cake shaped like a spaceship for some little boy's birthday and I'll be on my own with my view of the trees and strangers walking their dogs or riding horses along the bridle path behind the willow fence that skirts our property.

If they happen to glance through the lace of branches, and their eyes drift across the wildflower meadow and beyond the cottage garden, they might glimpse me red-faced and wearing the mesh hairnet I keep on at all times for hygiene reasons. It's literally the ugliest headgear ever invented and, unfortunately, I'm one of those people that really needs some hair around their face to look good. My eyes are deep-set, my nose is a little too wide and my cheeks are plump. I have quite nice hair, shoulder-length and a coppery chestnut but when I remove the hairnet-of-shame at the end of the day it always looks limp and defeated, which is pretty much how I feel by then too.

Meera isn't the only one who doesn't eat cake. I hardly ever touch it myself these days unless I'm testing a new recipe and even the kids tend to ask for savoury treats. All of us are drowning in sugar – we've had enough sweetness to last a lifetime.

Meanwhile Tim has ideas to expand the business. He wants us to open a cake boutique somewhere in Bristol and is always driving into town to check out possible premises. He thinks I should develop a range of at-home baking kits. And he has a list of celebrities we could reach out to for endorsements. He means well. But just making cakes is as much as I can cope with. The cakes and fudges, the cookies and slices. And the thought occurs to me now and then, what if Meera is right, and sugar is toxic?

Ana

Ana stared into her wardrobe at the charcoal-coloured tailoring she always wore to work and the soft washed denim and slouchy knits that were her weekend uniform. It was a Thursday and she didn't know which to choose.

There was no reason to leave her apartment. No meetings, no lunch, no deadlines. Ana considered the more formal outfits she should have been wearing and wondered if perhaps she should give them away since she didn't have a job anymore. She couldn't imagine ever needing them again.

Still dressed in the cashmere pyjamas she had slept in, she caught sight of her reflection in the mirror. Perhaps it was the light, but suddenly Ana thought she looked much older, her forehead creasing as she frowned and a jowly fold softening her jawline.

In her forties she had made a decision to age gracefully, no Botox or fillers for her, and now she found herself regretting it. Ana stretched her skin with her fingers until it almost looked taut again. Was it too late? Did she need surgery? Someone on *Fashionaria* magazine could probably advise her. But she wouldn't be seeing those people again, wasn't returning to the office, had nowhere to go at all.

The future belonged to people like Tammy Wong, young

and bright, digitally savvy. Jobs like Ana's old one barely existed anymore. She was kidding herself if she thought a facelift would make her more employable. Her career was over.

She sat down on the bed, slumped sideways, and pulled her knees up to her chest. Five minutes, that was what she needed, just to lie here. Or ten minutes, maybe fifteen. What she was feeling seemed very much like grief, which was ridiculous because no one had died, only a magazine.

After half an hour curled on top of the bedcovers, Ana gave in to the urge to climb beneath them. She never took sick days; they were a waste of time for a busy person. But she wasn't busy anymore. There were messages pinging through on her phone, people expressing their shock and asking what had happened. All Ana wanted was to lie there, swathed in Frette linen bedsheets, and she couldn't bring herself to respond.

Half dozing, caught between dreams and memories, she saw herself all those years ago arriving at the *Culinaria* offices, fair hair worn long, skin smooth, jawline firm. Her first job had been to update a dining-out guide. For three months she had rung restaurants to check their listings were correct and then when she finished, and the guide was sent off to the printers, Ana had started the whole process again. It was the dreariest work, sitting on the phone all day, repeating the same things, but still she was excited to come into the office. She was taking the first steps of a career and if she worked hard then she would get ahead, Ana was sure of it. From time to time, she would glimpse the editor, striding down a corridor or hurrying out of a meeting. She was a tiny woman with a reputation for being fiery and Ana was too intimidated to speak to her. She never dreamed that, some day, she would be her successor.

How had she gone from there to where she was now, with everything behind her? Ana could probably measure out the months and years in magazines. All those issues of *Culinaria*, all the recipes that readers wrote in to say they treasured, the photo shoots and tastings.

With a supreme effort, Ana forced herself into a sitting position and put her feet on the floor. Lying in bed all morning was a route to depression. She would take a shower, get dressed then decide what to do with the day, and with tomorrow, and the day after that.

Ana felt a shade better once she was clean and had moisturised from top to toe. What she needed was to establish some sort of routine. She started with a coffee.

Boiling the kettle to heat the cup, she took the Nespresso pods from the kitchen drawer that had been specially designed to hold them then filled the milk frother; movements so familiar they were almost reassuring. A few moments later, sitting at the kitchen counter with her flat white, she was aware how quiet her apartment seemed. All Ana could hear were distant things, a siren, a rumble of traffic, a plane overhead.

Moving to the window she looked down onto the street, at people rushing places, or walking dogs or jogging past. She felt like the only person with nowhere to go.

Ana had always liked being single. While other people were filling their worlds with husbands and children, pets that were a responsibility and gardens that needed tending, she valued her freedom. And, of course, she had her job, her fabulous job, and that seemed more than enough.

Her apartment was fabulous too, with pale wooden floors and high ceilings, filled with light and decorated mostly in white. For Ana it had always been a place she liked to retreat to for quiet and solitude at the end of a busy day. Now the silence felt oppressive, the rooms empty and stark.

She would go for a walk and get some fresh air, she decided, and that solved the dilemma of what to wear. Pushing aside her work clothes, she paired leggings with a Stella McCartney hoodie, and laced up her trainers.

Avoiding the park and her old route to work, Ana set off in the opposite direction, through bustling streets and past shop windows. Everything seemed too loud and bright, clashing with the thoughts that were still noisy in her head. She hadn't gone far when she spotted a black cab with its 'For Hire' sign illuminated, and impulsively hailed it.

'Kew Gardens please,' she told the driver.

Ana was a member at Kew and often visited on weekends. There was a regular walk she took through the vegetable plots and glasshouses, past the giant waterlilies and cactus gardens and down between the Broad Walk borders. It was quieter now on the pathways than on weekends when she usually visited, but otherwise everything felt the same and Ana completed two brisk laps of her preferred circuit, ignoring the phone vibrating in her pocket.

Afterwards, feeling more like herself, she caught the Tube back, stopping on her way home for a few supplies, crusty sourdough bread and organic eggs, fresh pasta, heirloom tomatoes, a bunch of herbs and a couple of cheeses. She was in her kitchen, putting everything in the fridge, when she heard the buzzer. Someone was downstairs at the front door and whoever it was kept pressing it insistently.

'Yes?' Ana asked, over the intercom. 'Who is it?'

'It's me, Lucy. Can I come up? I've brought your personal items.'

'Lucy, sorry yes, of course.'

Ana had been so shattered that she hadn't taken any belongings when she left the office for the final time. There would be books that were hers, gifts she had received over the years, a few pieces of clothing and some make-up for when she went straight from work to a function. Now she felt bad about leaving her assistant to deal with it.

'I couldn't get hold of you and wasn't sure what you'd want to keep,' said Lucy, arriving on the doorstep with an assortment of boxes and bags that she had ferried up to the second-floor in the lift. 'So, I've packed it all. I can help you go through and sort everything if you like.'

'No, it's fine, just leave it. I've got plenty of time to do that myself.'

'Are you sure?' Lucy asked.

'You shouldn't have to; you don't work for me anymore,' Ana reminded her.

'Actually, they've asked me to stay on to clear out the offices. There's quite a lot to do.'

Ana couldn't imagine anything worse than dismembering *Culinaria* magazine bit-by-bit but at least it might mean a few more weeks of work for Lucy she supposed.

'Let me make you a coffee before you head back,' she offered, flicking the switch on the Nespresso machine.

'Seems really odd, you making me coffee.' Lucy perched on a stool at the kitchen counter.

'Everything seems odd though, doesn't it?' replied Ana, reaching for some coffee capsules and the milk frother.

'Are you OK?' asked Lucy.

'I feel as if I've let everyone down, that's the worst thing,' admitted Ana, her back turned to Lucy, as she set about making coffee.

'But you didn't; it wasn't your fault.'

'All those people … losing their jobs … what will they do?'

Ana overfilled the frother, slopping milk on the counter and she fumbled with a roll of paper towels trying to soak it up.

'Here let me,' said Lucy, slipping from the stool. 'You sit down.'

Watching as her former assistant made the coffee, Ana was

aware that she was going to miss this young woman. She was smart and full of potential, very like she had been herself at that age. Ana had been planning to develop her career and guide her up through the ranks at *Culinaria*. That wouldn't happen now.

'The thing is,' said Lucy, placing the coffee in front of her, 'you only ever hired really talented people, didn't you? Everyone that worked for you was brilliant at what they did.'

'That's true,' Ana agreed.

'So, you don't need to worry because they'll find other jobs. I think Tessa and a couple of the test kitchen team have already had approaches actually. Sara is going to freelance on *Fashionaria* for a while. One of the other designers has been taken on by the digital team.'

'What about you?' wondered Ana. 'What will you do once the office has been cleared out?'

'To be honest I wasn't planning on staying at *Culinaria* for much longer anyway. I've been saving for a big surfing trip; Bali, Australia, maybe Hawaii and now I've got a redundancy payment, so that's a bonus.'

'You were going to walk away from your job?' Ana stared at her. Suddenly it felt like she didn't know Lucy very well.

'My boyfriend surfs too. We're going to travel together.'

'What about your career?' asked Ana, who had never been a fan of gap years or sabbaticals.

Lucy shrugged. 'I'll worry about that later. There's more to life than work, right? If I need cash then it shouldn't be hard to find some sort of job.'

Ana worried that her assistant was making a mistake. 'How long will you be away for?'

'We're not really sure.'

'Perhaps you should update your CV and put some feelers out before you go, make a plan for your return.'

'No.' Lucy shook her head. 'We want to feel completely free. That's the whole point.'

'Yes but ...'

'My nana ran a corner shop and always worked really hard ... Nana was lovely,' Lucy interrupted, pulling out her phone to show Ana a photo of a smiling older woman. 'While she was dying, me and Mum were sitting with her and, at one point, she opened her eyes and asked, "Have I had my life?". When we said yes, she looked devastated and I always wondered if there were things she regretted not doing.'

'That's why you're going surfing,' supposed Ana.

'Yeah, my plan is not to have any regrets, if at all possible.'

Ana couldn't imagine regretting the passion she had poured into *Culinaria*, only the way things had ended. She watched Lucy rinse the cups, then dry them with a clean tea towel and put them away in the cupboard, lining them up carefully with the others. The younger woman had such attention to detail. Privately Ana had always thought that one day she might step into her own shoes.

'It's been so great working for you. I've learnt such a lot,' Lucy added. 'But now I'm ready for new things.'

'When do you think you'll head off?' asked Ana.

'In the next couple of months or so. Before I go, I'd like to take you out for lunch.'

'That's very kind. But you should save your money for your trip.'

'You've been such a great boss, Ana. Some of the other editors don't treat their staff so well. I've heard plenty of stories about what goes on at *Fashionaria*.'

Ana had heard those stories too. 'You've been a great assistant, Lucy. I'm not quite sure how I'm going to run my life without you.'

'What will you do next?' the younger woman asked.

'Something will come along,' murmured Ana. 'I'll take a bit of a break before I decide on my next move.'

'Plenty of time to join me for lunch then,' said Lucy. 'Let's go somewhere fancy. Where's your favourite?'

Ana didn't want the girl blowing her budget. 'Actually, my favourite isn't fancy at all. It's a trattoria in Clerkenwell called Little Italy.'

It was where Ana had often eaten when she was flatting in the area, one of those friendly little places you could drop into for a coffee and pastry in the morning and return to later on for a bowl of spaghetti and meatballs. There was better food to be found in London, but still nowhere else that left Ana feeling quite so well fed.

'We'll go to Little Italy then,' said Lucy, picking up her bag and turning for the door. 'Would a Friday work for you? If so, I'll make a reservation.'

Once she had left, Ana glanced at the boxes and bags filled with remnants of her office life. Later she would take a proper look at whatever they contained although most likely a lot of it would end up going to the charity shop on Kensington Church Street. Ana hated clutter. She was amused when people got so excited about Marie Kondo, as she had been living that way forever.

Perhaps Lucy was right, she thought, turning away from the bags and boxes. Maybe everyone was going to find a new job and it would all be fine. Ana very much hoped so. But she didn't hold out the same hopes for herself. An editor-in-chief, nearing sixty, a woman who could only do one thing which was make a beautiful magazine in return for an inflated annual salary. Ana didn't want to work on something inferior and earn less.

Have I had my life? The question echoed in Ana's mind as

she chopped tomatoes for a salad and put water on to boil for the goat's cheese tortelloni. It worried her that she didn't have an answer.

Skye

The hairnet goes on before dawn and I'm in my kitchen shortly afterwards to start baking. The first people I see are the kids, coming to the door to say goodbye before biking off to school.

'Did you have breakfast?' I ask, trying to be a decent mother while I cream butter and sugar. 'Have you remembered your sports kits? What are you doing this evening?'

Josh mumbles his replies; he's at that stage of boyhood. Becky ignores the hairnet rules and comes in to give me a hug. Then they are gone.

Meera arrives next to help with the first batch of baking, the cupcakes and cookies she will deliver later on to cafés and farm shops. She isn't a morning person, especially if she's been out partying the night before, so her communication skills at this point are often very much like Josh's and suboptimal. She'll warm up eventually though.

Some mornings Tim might remember to bring us cups of tea but today he's busy balloon chasing. It's one of his random jobs. He follows the tourist hot air balloons and, when they land, delivers champagne and pastries to the exhilarated passengers. Tim is actually a business coach but he started balloon chasing as a favour to a friend. He also works a couple of nights in a local pub and has other jobs that come and go. I'm not sure there's very much business coaching happening these days, but he does spend a lot of time staring at his computer screen.

'What's Tim even for?' asks Meera, more talkative now. 'You don't need him. Why not cut him loose?'

She says that kind of thing quite often. Meera reckons I do all the work and Tim is just an extra weight I have to carry, and she isn't shy of mentioning it.

'You'd be better off on your own,' she tells me.

'Relationships take work,' I say, because I believe it's true. 'You have to push through the tough times in the hope better ones are coming.'

'Sounds like a really good reason to stay single to me,' mutters Meera.

'But you're still in your twenties, I'm in my forties; it's different. Some day if you have kids and a mortgage, then you'll understand.'

The mortgage on Lost Cottage is huge and Tim's income tends to be unreliable. My little Cakery is what pays the bills and puts food on the table.

Meera makes coffee and I sit down to drink mine, groaning like a much older person as I take the weight off my feet.

'Have you eaten?' she says, mothering me. 'Should I make you some toast?'

'No, I'll go and grab something in a minute.'

'Make sure you do, OK?'

What I love most about my job is creating the special occasion cakes. Turning out trays of cupcakes isn't so much fun anymore, but spectacular one-offs still give me a real buzz. The process of coming up with ideas, then the focus it takes to get an entire 360 degrees of perfection; that is my happy place.

'Did you hear *Culinaria* magazine has folded?' Meera asks now.

'No!' I'm shocked at this news.

'It's gone website-only but that's the kiss of death, right?'

I love *Culinaria*. I've been buying it for years and at night, in bed, it's what I flick through to relax before trying to sleep. Also, recently I've been in touch with the art director to pitch an idea for the Christmas cover that she seemed really excited about.

'How could they close it?' I say, disappointed on so many levels.

'No one is buying magazines, because everyone is on their phones all the time,' says Meera, who has a phone in her hand and is scrolling as she speaks.

I wonder if the art director, Sara, has lost her job and hope not as she seemed so nice. I'm going to miss *Culinaria*. And I'm sad about the missed opportunity of that front cover as it would have been a thrill and might have led to more interesting work.

'Maybe they'll still need your cake, for the website,' says Meera.

'Yes, maybe,' I agree, although I doubt it.

Meera helps me to box up some cakes and then I help her carry them out to the delivery van, and watch her driving away down the narrow lane very carefully because she is aware, just as I am, that at any moment Tim might come whipping along in the opposite direction.

Tim drives too fast. For someone who doesn't do very much, he always seems in a hurry. I worry that he'll knock a child off their bike or collide with a tractor. But there's no point in nagging because he never listens.

I stand in the garden and pull off my hairnet, get some sun on my face and breathe the fresh air. What I should do now is start scrubbing the kitchen. After a session baking it's a mess in there. But I need a break and to look at something other than the same four walls, so I decide to go for a walk and deal with the cleaning later.

I whistle for Happy, my greyhound, and he ignores me as always. He's still curled up on his divan in the living room, eyes wide open, tongue lolling out of his mouth, deep in sleep. It's a disturbing sight until you're used to it. He looks a bit dead.

'Happy,' I say, and he doesn't even blink.

I wave his lead at him and he yawns.

'Please come. Don't make me walk alone. Happy, come on, Happy!'

Looking slightly resentful, he stands up and stretches, and I clip on the lead before he can lie down again.

The woodlands where we live are networked in pathways so I always take a slightly different route. It's muddy at the moment and I have to pick my way carefully through the puddles but the ground is carpeted with bluebells and wild garlic and as we wander along beside the brook it's so pretty that my spirits lift. When I reach the meadows, I unclip Happy and let him run. There's something about watching a greyhound at full tilt. They look faintly alarmed as if they are speeding in spite of themselves. Happy tires quickly though and after he's done a few zoomies around the meadow I clip him back on the lead again and we carry on walking.

We reach the pond where Becky and I like to take a dip on hot summer days, ignoring the sign that says 'No Swimming' and I stop for a chat with another regular dog walker whose kids go to school with mine. She's excited because she has just booked a summer holiday in Portugal.

'Are you guys going anywhere exciting,' she wants to know.

'Not sure yet,' I reply, and, as I walk on, I'm feeling bad for Becky and Josh. It's difficult for me to take time off work and since I started the Lost Cakery eight years ago they've not really had a proper holiday. This summer we have to manage at least a few days at a beach, maybe a long weekend in London. Becky is interested in art and would love to visit some galleries and Josh needs coaxing out of his shell because he spends far too much time playing computer games. I start thinking about how I might manage it. I could leave the café baking to Meera perhaps and block a space in my diary to keep free of celebration cake orders.

I'm still thinking as I head up the narrow lane towards the Far Orchard. We used to own this sunny slope and its rows of apple trees. We bought it a few years ago when Tim decided to become a cider maker. At the time it didn't seem like a whim; he wrote a proper business plan and was set on making it his new career. When Tim's mood is up, it's like he can do almost anything, but if his mood is down, then it's a different story. I'm well aware of that, as we've been together since our late-twenties, but occasionally I'm so desperate to have faith in him that I agree to something rash. And I really loved the idea of picnics under the apple trees with our own cider to drink.

There was never any cider made. The first crop of apples would have rotted on the ground if I hadn't organised a bunch of locals to pick them and then practically given them away. After that Meera rang around and found an actual cidermaker who wanted to lease the Far Orchard and a short while later he ended up buying it, which was a relief all round.

I don't walk here very often anymore, but today the trees are starting to blossom and the air is scented with their honeysuckle-like sweetness. It's so pretty that I stand and gaze over the fence for a few moments.

Tim has an ability to turn his back on mistakes and let other people clear up any mess he has made. It's incredible really, a superpower. He's never seemed especially upset that the orchard doesn't belong to us anymore. But looking at it now, at the shadows in the long grass between the trees and the pale pink-tinged blossoms against the blue of an April sky, I feel regrets nudging at me. And I find myself wondering if perhaps Meera might be right about a lot of things.

Ana

Ana was beginning to realise how far *Culinaria* had reached into every corner of her life. Without the magazine there was no personal assistant to do a hundred different things each day, no IT department to sort niggles with her laptop, and perhaps most unexpectedly no social life to speak of. Before, when she was working long hours and had a diary filled with business lunches and cocktail parties, there hadn't been much time for friends and so it had never really occurred to Ana that she didn't have many. Over the years she had lost touch with schoolmates, only very occasionally had the neighbours round for drinks and after her parents died and her sister moved to Australia, barely bothered with family.

Most of the people that Ana thought of as friends were actually colleagues. She had spoken to everyone from her team at least once, checking in on how they were doing, and finally got round to returning all the kind messages that people had sent. But everything was about *Culinaria*, it coloured their conversations, as if there was nothing else about her life worth discussing.

Food was the other thing that had changed. As the editor of *Culinaria*, Ana was obliged to eat a lot of rich meals so in her own time ate very little. Years ago, her famously slender predecessor had told her that if she cared about her figure, then she would have to be disciplined and Ana had taken the advice seriously. If there were no gala dinners or degustation menus requiring her attention, she might take home a meal from the test kitchen, but very often she skipped supper altogether. The Italian granite kitchen in her apartment never needed much attention when the cleaner made her weekly visit.

Now Ana was becoming a regular visitor to Waitrose and Tesco Express. It was a part of the new routine she was trying to establish. She still started the day with coffee and a session of stretches, still took a brisk walk, tethering herself to as much of the old schedule as possible. After that it was planning what to cook and eat, then shopping for ingredients, that took up most of her morning. Ana pulled out her recipe books and day-by-day what she made became more complex and time-consuming. Most evenings she invited someone to share whatever she had cooked. Tessa her old food editor, the woman in the flat below, a cousin that lived in Islington who had sent her a lovely message after the magazine closed. Everyone asked the same question. What are you going to do now? And Ana stuck to the same story; she was doing all the things she had always been too busy for.

'What sorts of things?' they wanted to know.

'Cooking, having people for supper, going to the theatre,' said Ana.

Most people smiled and nodded politely, only Tessa snorted derisively.

'That's going to get old pretty fast,' she said, eating a first course of tuna tartare on a crisp shell of pastry that Ana had made herself.

'What do you mean?'

'You're bored already, aren't you? Admit it. You're a worker Ana. It's what you do. That big brain of yours needs to be firing and keeping you occupied otherwise you're going to get into trouble.'

'Trouble?' Ana was indignant.

'Mark my words, you'll do something crazy,' Tessa warned her.

'Don't be ridiculous, I've never done anything crazy in my life,' said Ana, dismissively.

'Your life had a magazine in it. Now it doesn't.'

'I don't need reminding of that.'

Ana cleared the empty plates and went to finish the main course. She was serving pan-seared sea bass in a light bisque with crushed potatoes and in the fridge were ramekins of lemon pannacotta for dessert. Mentally she totted up the extra calories. She might have to order one of those Peloton bikes.

'What does the former editor of *Culinaria* magazine do?' she asked Tessa, returning with the plated-up fish. 'You're in demand. But no cookbook publishers are asking me to test recipes. It's not that I don't want to work, it's that work doesn't want me.'

'Oh Ana,' Tessa's voice throbbed with unwanted sympathy.

'Honestly, I needed a break,' she added, hurriedly. 'I'm reading novels again and I've even started Duolingo Italian; I've been trying to learn forever.'

In her late teens, Ana had spent a summer at a language school in Perugia. She remembered it as a happy time, although she never really got to grips with the language. Since then, she had tried Teach Yourself tapes and CDs, listened to Italian music and watched movies and it always faintly irritated her that she had never become fluent. It seemed like a failing.

'Why don't you spend a few weeks there; that's the best way to learn,' suggested Tessa.

'I suppose I could.'

'You have some contacts in Italy surely. There's that chef we were always featuring. And what about the couple that make the cheese?'

Ana nodded although she wasn't sure how warm a welcome she would get from any of those people, not now she didn't have a magazine.

'Intelligent people need something to occupy them; they need a purpose,' insisted Tessa.

'Funny ... that's exactly what my dad always used to tell us.'

'Well then,' said Tessa, as if that settled everything.

Her father wasn't referring to Ana though; he was talking about her mother who never worked a day in her life. Her aim had been to become the matriarch of a large family, but instead she'd had several miscarriages and there was a decade between Ana and her older sister Rachel. In some ways her mother was equipped to be a corporate wife. Ana still remembered her signature dinner party menu – prawn cocktail, chicken Tettrazini and chocolate mousse to finish. The table was always beautifully set and her mum looked glamorous in a little black dress and long pearl necklace. But very often by the end of those evenings she would be so drunk that Ana's father had to carry her to bed. And she could be more badly behaved than charming, stirring up trouble, setting people against each other, creating dramas where life seemed dull.

Intelligent people need something to occupy them, her father would observe, after a skillet was aimed at his head in the midst of a high-volume argument.

Ana had never forgotten his words and always made sure she had plenty to do. Even now she kept her days full and her diary marked with engagements. There were exhibitions to see and concerts to attend, she had joined a gym and started lifting weights, was making an effort to connect with people she hadn't seen in a while and taking a greater interest in the portfolio of shares her father had left her.

'I'm really busy,' she told Tessa. 'I don't know how I ever managed to find time to edit a magazine.'

The truth was she tried not to think too much about *Culinaria*. There was no point in being angry or sad because that wouldn't change anything. Instead, she blocked it all off in a far corner of her mind where she stored the other things it was better not to dwell on. Her sadness at losing her parents – Dad to bowel cancer far too young, Mum to a stroke a few years later – as well as the hurt of any betrayals or failures. Ana managed to discipline her thoughts much as she did her body.

For that reason, she considered cancelling her lunch with Lucy. Fond as Ana was of her young assistant, she worried that, after spending the past few weeks dismantling *Culinaria*, it would be all she could talk about. Ana didn't want to know what had happened to the decades-worth of files or how Tammy Wong and the digital team was coping. She hadn't so much as glanced at the website since the day she walked away.

But when Lucy rang to confirm, saying how much she was looking forward to their lunch, she sounded rather flat, and Ana didn't like to let her down.

It was a pleasant enough spring day so she walked to Little Italy, carrying a pair of heels in her apple-green Bottega Veneta tote bag. Reaching Clerkenwell, she stopped for a bottle of water and to change her shoes. When she walked into the restaurant, she wanted to be the version of herself that Lucy would recognise, tailored charcoal clothes, hair in a chignon, bold red lip.

Her assistant was seated in a corner near the bathrooms, but when the head waiter realised it was Ana joining her, he hurried over and moved them to a better table.

'We haven't seen you for a while. How have you been?' he asked, bringing over menus and a carafe of water.

'I'm great thanks,' Ana told him. 'Is Addolorata in the kitchen today?'

'No, she is in Venice at the moment.'

Ana had featured Addolorata Martinelli, the owner of Little Italy, in a Venice-themed edition of *Culinaria* so was aware she spent some of her time there these days. All the same she was disappointed not to find her cooking.

'The food will be good, I promise. We have a new chef.'

The waiter might not have known that Ana had no magazine these days and for a moment she half forgot it herself, nodding her agreement then listening carefully as he ran through the day's specials, describing each dish almost lovingly.

'So,' she said to Lucy, once he had finished 'How have you been?'

'Oh, fine really, I mean I shouldn't complain.'

'Busy planning your trip?' asked Ana.

Lucy's face lightened. 'We've booked our flights to Australia and now we're looking at accommodation in Byron Bay so it's starting to seem more real. What about you? How's it been going?'

'I can't complain either. I'm busy doing lots of fun things.'

Lucy's eyes widened fractionally. 'That's great.'

Ana looked back at her. 'You can't imagine me having fun, can you?'

'I can't imagine you without *Culinaria*,' Lucy admitted. 'Even when you took a holiday, you went somewhere to learn about food. You were always so dedicated to your job.'

'That's true,' said Ana.

'I've been worried about you to be honest,' said Lucy. 'A few of us have.'

'Worried?' Ana realised that everyone must be discussing her. 'Am I the current topic of office gossip?'

'Not gossip,' Lucy was quick to assure her. 'People care

about you, that's all. You were a great person to work for. I mean demanding, yes, and you never suffered fools gladly but you were always really fair and everyone could see how hard you worked yourself. So, we were a bit concerned about how you're doing now without any work and that you might be a bit ... well ... lonely.'

'Lonely?' Ana was taken aback. This smooth-skinned twenty-something was worried about her. Did the girl imagine she wasn't resilient enough to cope with the odd setback? 'There's really no need to worry,' she said briskly, picking up the menu to take charge of the ordering. 'I'm fine; couldn't be better.'

The dishes she chose were Venetian classics. Ana had eaten them on previous visits to the restaurant and also in the city itself, so was familiar with the earthiness of the squid ink risotto and the acid bite of fried sardines marinated in sweetened vinegar. Today the flavours were rich and clear, every mouthful bringing memories of other meals and a time when she was younger and more carefree, taking her back to what she realised now must have been her heyday.

Still, it was a pleasant enough lunch, once she had steered the conversation onto safer ground. Ana kept Lucy talking about her travel plans and shared advice about things she should be sure to experience in various countries if she had the chance.

She insisted on paying the bill, although Lucy tried to argue, and hugged her former assistant goodbye, thinking they were unlikely ever to meet again, as one of them headed towards adventure and the other went home.

Once she started walking away, Ana's mood plunged. People were feeling sorry for her, the team she had led with such success and confidence, her own employees, and they had been discussing it. They thought she might be lonely. The idea was appalling. Loneliness wasn't something that happened to people like her.

She walked home rather than taking a taxi as she had planned, hoping the exercise would help steady her. On the way she stopped to buy a large bunch of white flowers she would arrange in her Jasper Conran Waterford vase. Once back in her apartment she made herself a cup of Earl Grey tea and sat down for her daily session of Duolingo. But rather than distracting her, the language app only made her more on edge and disgruntled.

She would find a tutor and take a couple of Italian lessons every week, decided Ana, purposefully. Putting aside her iPad, she went to fiddle with the flowers in the crystal vase again. For some reason she couldn't seem to position the stems in a way that pleased her eye. Ana was meticulous and the unruly blossoms bothered her. She moved them to a sideboard, out of her line of sight.

Sitting in the middle of her large open-plan room a feeling of dissatisfaction settled over her. Was the shade of white she had chosen so carefully for the walls actually a little too creamy? Was the sheet of granite she had picked out for her kitchen dominating the space? Had the parquet floors begun to discolour a little near the window where the light touched them? She had designed this interior herself, deliberating over every detail, aiming for perfection, but now nothing looked quite right. Perhaps it was time to make some changes.

Fetching a roll of bin liners from a kitchen drawer, she stood in front of her wardrobe staring at the neat rows of tailored charcoal-coloured workwear that she had absolutely no use for anymore. Pulling a wool crêpe dress from its hanger, she folded it quickly before she could change her mind, and placed it at the very bottom of the first bag. All of this would have to go.

Skye

Flour and sugar always manage to find their way into the furthest corners of the kitchen, shrouding everything in a gritty, sticky layer, stubbornly clinging on. After I've finished making cakes, the baking tins need to be scrubbed, the mixers and bowls cleaned, the stainless-steel counters wiped and the polished concrete floor mopped. I'm good at the clean-up; I've honed my skills. And the faster I finish, the sooner I can get out into my garden.

In the conservatory there are tomato seedlings sprouting and my dahlia tubers are being cosseted in pots until there is no danger of a late frost and I can start planting them out. Every year I dig up more of the lawn and let a tangle of herbs, climbing roses and leggy hollyhocks take over. I like a romantic garden but Tim complains. He prefers the ride-on mower, the leaf blower and weed-eater, anything that makes a loud noise. If it was up to him, we'd have nothing but trees and grass around Lost Cottage. But I have made a chaotically beautiful garden, and very often I'll stay out there until the light fades.

It used to be that my evenings were for being with the kids, watching nonsense on TV, taking twilight walks, toasting marshmallows over the fire in winter. Becky and Josh still like doing those things, but they have their own lives now and are too busy to hang out with me as much. I'm pleased they've got friends and are independent, still it can be lonely sitting on the sofa with Tim as he juggles his screens – usually he's on at least two – laughing at clips from *Fawlty Towers* and *Monty Python* that he must have watched a thousand times. So, I stay out in the garden for as long as I can, even when there's a soft rain falling or it's cold enough to see my breath.

Today I want to dig out a section of turf then layer on lots of compost and well-rotted horse manure. This is where I'll plant my dahlias and, over summer, I'll be able to glance out and enjoy them as I'm working. It's an effort digging, as Happy my greyhound lies beside me in the evening sunshine, but I know it will be worth it.

When Tim appears, he doesn't seem to notice what I'm up to. He's distracted by his phone.

'Have you seen this?' he asks.

'Seen what?' I reply, busy sinking my spade into the soft earth.

'We should definitely have a go,' he says. 'Wouldn't it be amazing to win.'

I'm guessing that this must be about his latest obsession, entering competitions. It doesn't really matter what the prize is – free passes to a movie or a music festival, meals for two, cookware, jewellery – Tim is enthused about the possibility of winning. He's signed up to special competition websites and subscribed to newspapers and newsletters, but is yet to get lucky.

'Amazing to win what?' I ask.

'Loads of people will enter,' says Tim, still distracted. 'But you don't get anything if you don't have a go, right?'

'Right,' I agree, wishing he'd go and enter whatever it is rather than standing there talking about it.

The competitions are keeping Tim occupied. They're not

costing us much, at least I don't think so, and he might actually score a prize at some point – hopefully something we want, not a hand-held garment steamer or a year's supply of nappies.

Tim's mood tends to be either all the way up or all the way down. He doesn't seem to have a halfway point. If he's very low then he can be silent, lying on the sofa with a cushion over his head, and that's grim, especially for the kids. Sometimes he'll get anxious and needy, wanting reassurance, mostly from me. But when he's up, buoyant with energy and confidence, that's when Tim is at his most dangerous, that's when the spending happens, the dreaming up of grand plans.

Don't get me wrong, he's done some amazing things. One Christmas he festooned the whole of Lost Cottage and most of our trees with fairy lights. People came from miles around just to have a look and on Christmas Eve the church choir sang carols in the garden and Tim did mulled wine for everyone. He loves to orchestrate surprises, birthday parties and mystery trips, and he made Josh and Becky's childhoods magical with the stunts he pulled. Now they're teenagers, and not quite so into having fun with us, I think he's struggling more than I am.

'A holiday in Italy,' he says, waving his phone at me. 'The kids would love it. I'm going to enter.'

'Good idea,' I say, as he walks away.

I'm out there tearing up lawn until a sliver of moon has risen above the trees and the sky has turned inky blue. Becky is sleeping over at a friend's place and Josh has texted to say he'll be late so I'm not worried about cooking dinner. Tim prefers snacks anyway, corn chips and dip, those individual slices of processed cheese, cold frankfurters and tinned pineapple chunks. Children's party food, as Meera always says.

I make myself some cheese and tomato on toast, which is what I had for lunch as well, so I add an apple for variety. Tim is in the living room, laughing at something he's watching on

TV and as I'm pottering round the kitchen, I remind myself how much I have. This house, a husband who loves his family, a business that supports us. I need to be more grateful.

Taking my makeshift supper, I go and join Tim who is sitting on the sofa surrounded by his snacks and screens.

'Did you enter that competition?' I wonder, because I've been thinking about Italy and how lovely it would be if Tim got lucky at last and all of us could go there.

'Which competition?' he asks, glancing at me. 'I've entered a few today.'

'To win a holiday in Italy.'

'Oh yeah.' The confusion lifts. 'Not a holiday in Italy though, a wedding.'

'A wedding?' Now it's my turn to be baffled.

'Yes, a wedding in Montenello, Italy's most romantic town. You get a dress and a cake and a celebrant, a venue and a party, the whole package. Plus, flights and accommodation in a hotel. How cool would that be?'

Tim and I always meant to get married but our ideas were bigger than our budget. The castle in Scotland, the island in Fiji, even the Las Vegas wedding chapel; they were never going to happen. I'm aware that the bride's parents are meant to foot the bill but my mum and dad don't have much. Dad was a painter/decorator and Mum a teaching assistant, and they needed their savings for retirement. If I'd asked then they'd have been pleased to foot the bill for a church ceremony and a party in the pub, which is their idea of a proper wedding, but that didn't match Tim's expectations. For a while we put money aside but it kept being channelled into other things. Then we had the kids and bought Lost Cottage and both of us stopped talking about weddings. We haven't brought up the subject in years.

It occurs to me that I'm not sure whether I want to marry

44

Tim anymore, even if we won a package, and the whole thing was free and no effort at all. It's not like I could ever leave him; the business, the kids, we share too much. Still, I'm not keen to stand at an altar and take vows with him either. I hadn't realised that till now and it unsettles me.

Thankfully, Tim has no idea about the thoughts going through my head. He's busy listing competitions and the potential prizes. Minibreaks at country hotels, air fryers, duvet cover sets, BBQs.

'I have to win something sooner or later.' He slumps lower on the sofa and I wonder if perhaps his mood is turning and we're heading for a low.

'You're bound to eventually,' I reassure him.

And I really hope he does. Give me a weekend glamping, or a VIP experience, an ocean cruise, kitchen equipment. Just not a wedding, even if it's in Italy.

Ana

The urge for change had taken hold of Ana. It started with thoughts of giving her apartment a makeover, then she realised that she didn't need to be in London at all, it was possible to live anywhere now and that's when the house-hunting started. She launched into it by looking at properties online, listing all the features she might want in a fresh Moleskine notebook. A place with a small garden and some privacy from neighbours. Plenty of light and period features, the potential to be transformed. Then she set about trying to find it.

Ana enjoyed visiting different homes, picturing how she would change or fill the spaces, imagining the life she might lead there. Back when she was buying her apartment, she had been rushing. Her parents' house had recently sold and she wanted to reinvest her share of the money as quickly as possible. Now there were no time pressures, still it became the thing she threw all of her energy into.

At first, she went by train, exploring the south-east – a Jacobean house in Hastings, a waterside cottage in the Norfolk Broads, a country estate in Suffolk that she couldn't really afford. After deciding to get a car, she widened her search, driving the powder-blue BMW as far north as Scotland, looking at houses by lakes and in the shadows of mountains, at cosy cottages and elegant mansions, discussing their features with a series of estate agents, always keeping careful records about what she had seen.

Sometimes Ana would arrive back at her own apartment, exhausted and glad to be home, then wonder if perhaps the shade of white on her walls was exactly the right one after all and so what if her parquet floor had signs of wear and tear. More importantly, did she really want to leave the city?

Intelligent people need something to occupy them, Ana reminded herself, as she applied for a job as an editor at a London publishing company known for its beautiful cookbooks. The money on offer wasn't amazing but the work sounded appealing and Ana was shocked when the publishers didn't even give her an interview, only sending a very polite email expressing their admiration and wishing her the very best for the future.

Stung by the rejection, Ana went back to house-hunting. The south-west beckoned next. Bristol was appealing so she started her search in hilly Clifton then headed over the suspension bridge exploring beyond it. There were hills and valleys with sweet little villages, the city was nearby, the sea not far away. Ana rented a cottage and spent a few days getting to know the area. She bought an excellent sourdough loaf in Chipping Sodbury and enjoyed fresh oysters by a lake in the Chew Valley.

On the final morning, she stopped at a farm shop to pick up a takeaway coffee for the drive home. The assistant was a woman of about her age, and Ana engaged her in conversation while the milk was being frothed, since local knowledge could be invaluable. Were there any interesting properties she knew of? Houses with owners that might be open to selling?

'Actually, I might know of a place,' mused the shop assistant, before they were interrupted by another woman rushing in, face flushed and coppery hair in a frizz, carrying a trayload of baking.

'Sorry, sorry running late,' she gasped, depositing it on the counter. 'Delivery driver let me down.'

'Take it easy Skye,' said the shop assistant. 'No one is going to fall apart if they don't get a flapjack.'

The redhead grinned, turning to leave. 'I hope not.'

'Where's that husband of yours anyway?' the assistant wondered.

'Busy balloon chasing this morning,' the woman called, on her way out of the door.

'Busy being a waste of space, more like,' the assistant muttered, not quite under her breath, then added in a more normal voice, 'You were asking about a house.'

'Never mind,' said Ana, hurriedly taking her coffee. 'It doesn't matter.'

'What about one of these flapjacks then? They're very good,' the assistant promised.

'Thank you but no,' she said, firmly. Living here suddenly seemed much less appealing. Ana didn't want people knowing every little detail about her. She hated gossip, and most sweet little English villages would be full of it. Grateful to the shop assistant for reminding her of that, she drove back to the anonymity of city life without a flutter of regret. The southwest hadn't been right after all.

For the next week Ana kept busy. She went to an art history talk at the National Gallery, took several long walks and considered volunteering at the charity shop that had taken her old clothes. Those were the sorts of things that retired people did, and she might as well accept it.

Whenever she was out walking, Ana was careful to steer clear of the *Culinaria* offices. She put a large circle around it on the map of London she carried in her head and never strayed inside because she didn't want to bump into other editors, the ones whose glossy magazines hadn't been cancelled. It was difficult to think of them still leading the life Ana had loved, so she tried not to.

Often her routes were designed to take her past a new restaurant she had been meaning to visit or an old favourite when she was craving a particular dish. If she had eaten a decent lunch then her evening meal need only be an apple and a wedge of cheese, perhaps a handful of walnuts. As the editor of *Culinaria*, Ana had often held forth on the importance of home cooking. It was a privilege to create a meal, she would declare; and once had written those very words in her editorial. She winced at the memory. How insufferable she must have seemed to anyone who knew that top chefs vied to feed her and that Ana's idea of food shopping was to drift round Borough Market on weekends with a basket over her arm.

Now she understood that producing meals every single day could be more a chore than a privilege. And so, she walked to Notting Hill for a kedgeree and Chinatown for pork dumplings and Soho for a particularly good Peruvian ceviche.

One Sunday lunchtime she made her way to her old favourite, Little Italy, planning to revisit the dishes that had been so good when she had eaten there with Lucy.

Ana had forgotten how busy the place was on weekends, with old Italian men sitting at the tables outside to play cards and noisy families gathered in groups. She hesitated on the pavement, but the waiter had already spotted her and was smiling a greeting.

'How good to see you again so soon,' he said smoothly, ushering her inside to a quieter table. 'Would you like to start with a cocktail? Perhaps a spritz?'

'Yes, a spritz,' agreed Ana. 'No need for the menu. I know what I want to eat.'

'Addolorata is in the kitchen today,' he told her, once she had finished ordering. 'I'll let her know you're here.'

Ana had known Little Italy's owner since she was a little girl and her father was running this place. She remembered her taking over the restaurant years ago, when she was still quite young. Now as she came striding across the dining room, Ana could see the evidence of all the time that had passed since then etched on Addolorata's face. They were both getting old.

'I haven't seen you in ages,' Addolorata said, after greeting her warmly. 'How's life on the magazine?'

Ana had assumed most people would have noticed by now that *Culinaria* was missing from the newsstands but, apparently, Addolorata had no idea.

'Oh, I've left the magazine,' she said, quickly. 'It was time for a change.'

'Gosh I can't imagine it without you. What are you up to instead?'

'There are a few projects bubbling away,' lied Ana. 'Nothing I can talk about yet though. And actually, I'm taking a bit of a break right now.'

'Well, it's always lovely to see you. I heard you came in not long ago when I was away in Italy.'

'You had a new chef in the kitchen,' said Ana. 'Is he here today?'

'You must mean Dante. That was a trial run but he'll be back. He's going to look after this place over the summer and I'll be guest chef at his restaurant in Venice.'

'A whole summer in Venice, how wonderful,' said Ana.

'We love it there; it feels like our second home now and I'm always trying to find ways to get back. So, I'm thrilled Dante has agreed to this.'

'You aren't worried that he will change things here, stamp his own influence on the menu?' To Ana that seemed like a risk.

'I'd prefer it if he didn't but ...' Addolorata gave an easy shrug. 'Sometimes it's good to shake things up.'

Later, as she was settling the bill and starting on the walk home, Addolorata stayed in Ana's mind. It would take guts to pack up a family and leave a business, even only for a few months. The reward would be getting to know somewhere so well that you almost felt like a local, really immersing yourself in the life there. Still Ana wasn't sure that she would choose to spend a summer in Venice. It was a city she had always preferred in the misty, shadowy winter months when it was less likely to be packed with tourists picnicking on bridges, leaving litter and muting its magic. Also, if you were going to take the leap then you may as well be bold and travel somewhere you had never visited before then get to know it piece by piece, like putting a jigsaw puzzle together when you didn't have a picture on the box to guide you. At least that is what Ana imagined.

Lost in her thoughts, she kept walking, avoiding the shoppers on Oxford Street and sticking to the quieter streets that ran parallel. Her mind was on Italy. She had travelled extensively, visiting many different countries, but it was Italy that kept drawing her back. Maybe it was the simplicity of the food and how much the way they ate seemed to matter to Italians. Perhaps it was the warmth of those people and their sunshine. After her father died, she had spent a whole month in Tuscany, mostly alone, and it had been a place to remember and let go, far better than any therapy. Since then, she had holidayed there with friends, popped over for work trips, made the most of any reason to go back. Ana loved Italy; for some reason she always felt lighter and freer when she was there.

Why not go now? There were still parts of the country she hadn't seen, particularly further south. Ana was picturing herself behind the wheel of her powder blue BMW, speeding down an oleander-fringed highway when she heard someone calling her name in an instantly recognisable drawl.

'Ana, daahling.'

A stiletto-heeled woman was advancing towards her, with hair fiercely blunt-cut, face smooth, outfit on point. Lorelei Hope, editor of *Fashionaria* magazine and absolutely top of the list of people Ana least wanted to bump into.

'Daahling, how wonderful,' Lorelei gushed, stooping to kiss Ana's cheek, her dark hair falling into both of their faces. 'I've been meaning to reach out to you. How absolutely bloody it's been, I had no idea they were going to do that to your magazine, I'd have fought for you darling, you know that.'

All Ana knew was that Lorelei was almost certainly the most insincere person in London. What she said and what she meant were never the same thing. Also she was wearing too much scent, and it was overwhelming.

'We need to have a lunch, catch up properly. Darling, you look wonderful, not having a job must suit you.' Lorelei glanced at the gold Rolex Oyster Perpetual watch worn loose on her wrist. 'I'm so sorry but I have to run. We'll diary that lunch, I'll have my assistant get in touch, I can't wait to hear all your news.'

She held up a manicured hand to flag down a passing taxi, and Ana watched as she climbed inside, blowing a kiss in her direction.

Lorelei Hope was legendarily awful. Everybody had a story about her and Ana couldn't recall ever visiting the bathrooms on the *Fashionaria* floor and not hearing someone sobbing in a cubicle. Right from the beginning the pair of them had been adversaries, fighting for the biggest slice of the budgets, the plushest office and the largest team, the most extravagant advertiser events. They were fashion versus food, and now fashion had won; how Lorelei must have gloated.

Walking on through Cavendish Square Ana's head buzzed with new suspicions. Had Lorelei somehow been behind

Culinaria's demise? She was in and out of Christopher Verhoeven's office, effortlessly flirting and flattering and, while it wasn't known for sure if they were having an affair, no one would be surprised. Everything about the woman made Ana grit her teeth. If Lorelei behaved one way, she had been sure to behave in quite another. Still, look where that had got her.

Reaching Hyde Park, she slowed her pace. Seeing Lorelei had stirred up thoughts she had been trying to keep damped down. She was a failure, her career was over, she was irrelevant. Pushing past some dog walkers, Ana sank down onto a park bench and put her face in her hands. She needed a moment.

Half an hour later when she managed to continue on her way, her mind was made up. There would be no lunch with Lorelei, not even a coffee. If her assistant did call with a date for their diaries, Ana would be unavailable. She was leaving town, going someplace far away and quite possibly that place would be in Italy.

The moment she was home, she started planning her escape.

Skye

Sunday is the worst day of the week, mainly because I don't have Meera. Café owners still want their sweet treats delivered, people throw parties and hold weddings, cakes are needed, but it's Meera's day off so I have to find someone else to deliver them.

You might think that Tim would be the obvious option but there's always some reason he can't help. I need someone I can rely on, like I do Meera. The two school mums I hired to do alternate Sundays have proved to be utterly unreliable and keep letting me down. This morning one of them claimed she had a sore throat and the other refused to cover for her because she wanted to watch her son play basketball. That meant I had to do two jobs which would have been impossible if it hadn't been for Becky and Josh pitching in.

Josh is an excellent baker, although I have to curb his experimental streak, while Becky has a flare for decoration and loves making cupcakes. I wouldn't encourage either of them to do this for a living but I love it when they come and help out on weekends. My kids are great company, we always have a laugh when we're working together. Today though I'm darting in and out, leaving them in the kitchen to follow my instructions while I drive the Lost Cakery van all over the countryside and into Clifton, slightly late with everything.

By the time I get back from the final delivery, they've almost finished the clean-up and I'm so grateful that I get a bit teary. Josh looks horrified and leaves Becky to comfort me, but then he comes back five minutes later with a cup of tea.

'You should fire that stupid woman, what's her name?' Becky tells me.

'Which one?' I ask.

'I dunno, fire both of them.'

'Then I'll have to find someone else.'

'Couldn't you pay Meera extra?' suggests Josh.

'She needs to have some time off,' I tell him. 'Besides I'm not sure she actually goes to bed on a Saturday night. Driving a van full of cakes wouldn't be the best idea.'

'Dad should do it then,' says Josh.

'Yes,' agrees Becky. 'Why not?'

'He's busy,' I say, because with the kids I'm always defending Tim. I don't want them to pick up on any friction between us. Home should be a calm and contented place; that's the most important thing to me.

Meera, of course, has opinions about this. She says the kids aren't stupid, they must have noticed what their father is like, because it's pretty obvious. But she's wrong, they love him and in lots of ways he's a really good dad.

Since it's Tim, there always tends to be some sort of grand gesture involved. Like Becky's sixteenth birthday a few weeks ago, when we couldn't afford to take her friends out to dinner so Tim turned Lost Cottage into a restaurant instead. He spent hours and hours following recipes, carefully rolling out dough for wafer-thin lavash crackers, marinating olives, whizzing up hummus, grilling aubergine for baba ganoush. He lit candles, printed up menus and even borrowed chef's whites to wear.

'Your dad is so much fun,' Becky's mates told her and I'm pretty sure Josh's friends thought the same thing the weekend

Tim organised a computer game tournament and hired a wood-fired oven to make them proper pizza. In comparison to him, I must seem quite boring.

'I don't suppose either of you wants to come for a walk with me and the dog after lunch?' I ask now, expecting the kids will both have other plans.

Josh is heading out to catch up with friends, but Becky's not doing anything so we snack on cheese toasties, then put on our walking boots. The woods are muddy this time of year and, although the sun is bright, it isn't hot enough to penetrate the canopy of trees and dry out the paths beneath them.

Becky may be sixteen now but with the breeze making her cheeks glow and tousling her glossy brown hair, she still looks like my little girl. It's difficult to believe that in a couple of years she'll be heading off to university. I want her and Josh to have their own lives, I've raised my kids to be independent, and yet the thought of them leaving almost seems to make my heart stop beating. Once they've gone, it'll just be Tim and me at home.

'Dad said something about us going to Italy,' Becky tells me.

'It's the prize in one of his competitions,' I explain.

'OMG really?' Becky rolls her eyes. 'Isn't he bored with them yet?'

'Apparently not.'

'If he doesn't win something soon, he will be though, right?'

I'm busy navigating some stepping stones across a little stream and don't respond. Besides it's difficult to know what to say. Becky is eighteen months older than Josh and, while I'm pretty sure he still sees his father as a supplier of unexpected fun and happy times, it sounds like she might be starting to think differently.

'I'd like to go to Italy,' she says. 'All that art and amazing old buildings, imagine it.'

'Not the pasta and pizza?' I tease.

'Those too, obviously.'

Becky loves anything to do with art and design and I feel guilty for not feeding that passion more than I do. I ought to be taking her places and showing her things.

'What if we spend some time in London over the summer holidays? There's art and architecture there too,' I say, as we're walking up towards the meadow.

'Actually, me and Issie were thinking of going for a day trip soon. There's this Frida Kahlo thing we want to see,' she tells me.

Again, I don't know what to say. Becky and her friend Issie are both smart kids so it's not that I wouldn't trust them to catch a train to London then get home again safely, but the world is full of creepy people who like to prey on pretty young girls, and I'm not sure if they know that yet.

'You could come with us,' Becky suggests. 'Issie's mum might like to as well, although I think she'd be more into shopping.'

'Perhaps we should do that, then,' I agree, relieved. 'You girls can go to your exhibition and we'll check out the shops.'

'You're not a shopper though, Mum,' says Becky, looking pointedly at my worn cotton leggings and hoodie.

'I wouldn't mind a browse,' I say, although she is right.

When we reach the meadow, I unclip the dog. Greyhounds are fast and also very clumsy so I only ever let Happy off the lead when there is space for him to run about at high speed without crashing into a tree. Watching him now zooming across the grass, I realise this is my job, helping them all run free but also keeping them safe, and it's a tricky balance.

'Happy, Happy,' calls my daughter. She's chasing the dog, arms outstretched, and she does look full of joy. Adopting a greyhound was one of Tim's better ideas, even if he did quickly lose interest in feeding and walking him, let alone cleaning up poo from the garden.

Back on the woodland paths, Happy is restrained again for his own good. Becky and I walk side-by-side as he trots along between us, still panting.

'What are you up to tomorrow?' Becky asks. 'Lunch with Meera as usual?'

Monday is my one day off and, although there is always admin to sort, I try to make time for a catch up with Meera.

'Yes, we're going to a vegan place,' I say, and Becky laughs.

'You two are co-dependant,' she tells me.

'Probably,' I agree.

During the average working day there is hardly ever time for me and Meera to have a proper chat. So usually, we do that on Mondays. She's a window on a world that's very different to mine. I'm not really sure why Meera wants to hang out with me. She says it's so she can make sure I have at least one proper meal a week ('You can't live on cheese, Skye') and usually insists on us going somewhere that serves lentils and fresh vegetables.

Becky starts telling me about one of her teachers, something they did or didn't say, and how everyone was upset. It's a long and dramatic story, that I'm only semi listening to, because I'm looking at my daughter and thinking how lovely she is and wondering what she'll be like when she's in her twenties and whether we'll still be close.

Much as I love my own parents, they seem like a different species. The things that concern them, their conversation, their attitudes; none of it matches mine. That's one of the reasons why I like talking to Meera. She's preparing me for who Becky might become one day, so we always speak the same language.

Becky breaks off from her story. 'Has Meera gone vegan then?' she wonders.

'No, she's an ethical omnivore.' I know this because Meera

changes her food philosophy constantly and keeps me updated. 'It involves foraging and nose-to-tail eating, and there's talk of applying for a firearms licence so she can shoot rabbits.'

'Wow really.'

The idea of Meera brandishing a shotgun is alarming but I'm confident she'll have swapped to some new eating style before she ever gets her licence.

'Is she dating anyone at the moment?' Becky is fascinated with Meera and looks up to her, which is fine by me as she's mostly a pretty good role model. 'Did she break up with that girl she was seeing?'

'Yes, and apparently now she's into single positivity.' Last time we had lunch I heard all about this and was left with the strong impression that Meera thought I should be into single positivity too.

'I want to come for lunch with you tomorrow and eat vegan food. Can I miss school?'

'No, of course not.'

'Dad would let me,' says Becky, and she isn't wrong. Tim thinks education is society's way of controlling young minds. He wanted to enrol the kids in an experimental school but we couldn't afford it.

'It's just one day ... and we never go out for lunch to-gether ... will you at least think about it?' Becky wheedles.

'You can't skip school,' I tell her, although I'm sure that her future life is unlikely to be derailed by one missed day of learning.

'It's boring,' she complains.

'You like seeing your friends,' I point out. 'And you enjoy music, and art, and writing lessons.'

Becky is very like I was at that age. Maths and science were dull, all I wanted was to be creative, and I couldn't wait to leave school behind and go to art college. My parents were concerned about me ending up with a huge student loan so encouraged me to get a sensible office job to save a bit first. Somehow, I got stuck in that office until I met Tim on an evening out with friends and was completely dazzled by him. And here I am now, creating cakes instead of paintings or sculptures.

'I'd enjoy having lunch with you and Meera more than any lessons,' says Becky, refusing to give up.

My daughter is more determined than I ever was. I can't imagine her being railroaded into a job she doesn't really want. And I'm not my parents; I'd much rather she lived her dreams than got stuck with being sensible.

'OK then, come for lunch,' I say recklessly, and am rewarded with a smile.

'Really?'

'Yes, although I don't know what we'll say if we bump into one of your teachers.'

'Mum, none of my teachers are going to be eating lunch in a vegan restaurant.'

'What makes you so sure?' I ask.

'They're not that interesting.'

Adults must seem desperately boring when you're sixteen. Becky probably thinks that all I care about is turning off lights to keep the electricity bill down, and paying the mortgage on time, because those are the parts of me that she gets to see. I do have a bit more going on; I'm sure her teachers must too.

'Well, we'll risk it,' I say.

The path is looping back towards Lost Cottage. It's narrow here and Becky is walking slightly in front. Soon she'll be racing ahead of me, finding her own route, leading her life. I want that for her. Still, I need to make the most of every single moment we have together before then.

'If you come for lunch with me and Meera, then can I come along to the Frida Kahlo exhibition with you and Issie?' I ask.

'Of course.' Becky glances back at me. 'But it's not just an exhibition, Mum, it's a fully immersive experience and it sounds amazing ...'

And then she's off again, talking about virtual reality and how we're going to feel as though we've stepped through the canvas and into a painting, while showing me things on her phone. And I love listening to her.

Ana

For once Ana didn't bother making a list. She launched straight into googling, sitting on the sofa, her bare feet up on the coffee table. First, she looked at places she might like to be, medieval villages and baroque towns, dramatic coastlines, landscapes dotted with tall cypress or sprawling rows of espaliered lemon trees. Then she needed to think about the apartment that she would be leaving behind and what she was going to do with it.

Ana started googling letting agents. She decided to rent out the place fully furnished because she wasn't going to be bothered with putting things in storage. It might mean some of her belongings would get damaged by her tenants but she had a strange, floaty feeling, as though she didn't really need many of the things that were around her anymore.

Most of her clothes she would keep, of course, as well as family photographs and a few favourite cookbooks. What else did she need? Ana cast a critical eye over her apartment. She loved the vintage copper moulds decorating her kitchen walls, her pale blue Le Creuset casserole, and her birchwood-handled Japanese kitchen knife. These were things she looked at or touched every day and it was hard to imagine leaving them behind. But she was planning to take only what would fit in her car.

Ana started telling people about her plans to leave, partly because she was excited, but also as it seemed like a way of committing herself. She broke the news to her downstairs neighbour the following evening when she came over for a bowl of butternut squash soup and mentioned it to her cousin the next morning when they caught up for coffee. If either was surprised then they hid it. Mostly they were encouraging.

The one person she felt close to nervous about telling was her sister. Generally, she and Rachel talked on Sundays, when it was morning in London and evening in Melbourne. The call was never particularly long because they didn't have much in common. But Ana always sent gifts to Rachel's children and grandchildren on birthdays or Christmas. Maintaining the connection seemed important.

'This is later than usual, have you been out brunching?' asked Rachel, when she called.

'Sorry, were you in bed already?' Ana tucked the phone beneath her chin and filled the kettle to make tea.

'No, I'm wide awake. Everyone came over for a Sunday roast today. It was fun but I may never finish the dishes.'

Rachel had an Australian accent these days and her life revolved around family. Growing up she had been so much older than Ana that they were never especially close, and now a huge physical distance lay between them too. Still, there was something reassuring about speaking to her week after week, and Rachel had been particularly kind since Ana lost her job.

'How are things with you?' her sister wondered now. 'Are you doing OK?'

'If you'd asked me that a few days ago, I might have said no, but actually I've got news.' Ana poured hot water over Earl Grey tea leaves and draped a linen cloth over the pot to keep it warm, before outlining her still alarmingly sketchy plan.

'Italy,' Rachel said, when she had finished. 'Good on you, that sounds great.'

'You don't think I'm being capricious and crazy?' asked Ana, settling on the sofa with her pot of tea.

Rachel laughed. 'Those are not words I would ever use to describe you.'

'What would they think, do you reckon, Mum and Dad?' Ana often silently asked herself that question, but had never said it out loud.

'They were so proud of you, especially Dad. I think he would have supported anything you did.'

'Would he have thought that I've failed though?' Ana said it very softly so her voice wouldn't catch on the words.

'Bloody hell, Ana you're the most successful person I know.'

'Not anymore, I'm not.'

Rachel paused for a moment. 'Can I tell you what I really think?'

'Please do.'

'You've worked hard, given everything to that job and now you're almost sixty. The thing is in about ten minutes you'll be almost seventy, like me. By then where do you want to be? Not working all the time surely? Maybe not in Italy either, but make one change and other changes will follow.'

'You've never really understood it have you, my career?' Ana dared ask, since they were being honest with each other.

'It wasn't what I'd have chosen but I could tell it made you happy.' Rachel paused again. 'And I'm proud of you too, I show off about you to friends; my amazing clever sister.'

'You don't.'

'Yeah, I do. There's a stack of your magazines on my coffee table. So, I'm not saying you shouldn't have given your all to *Culinaria*, just that now it's time for you to be amazing somewhere else.'

'Like Italy?'

'I'm really excited for you,' said Rachel. 'I'm going to give you one more piece of advice though. Don't plan it all too much. Let things happen. Make it an adventure.'

Ana had always been a planner, even as a child she liked to help make shopping lists. She remembered herself as a neat, quiet kid who looked up to her more adventurous older sister. Rachel was the one who spent months backpacking in exotic places then moved all the way to Australia, while Ana stayed in London worked hard and took minibreaks. She might have admired her sister but had never wanted to be her.

Ana planned, she couldn't help herself. She made lists in her Moleskine notebook: what to take and what to sell or give away, lists of routes and places she might like to visit, restaurants worth eating at. She pored over maps and websites. She even did a trial pack up of the car to establish that it really wasn't too small and she could take her vintage copper moulds if she wanted to. The more she planned, the calmer she felt.

It all seemed fairly theoretical until the apartment was rented out. The moment a stranger took a lease was when Ana sensed there was no going back. That Sunday morning, she had an extra-long call with Rachel, firing questions at her. What if this was a mistake, what if something went wrong, what if she got lonely and lost?

'Of course, you're nervous, but that's no reason not to do it,' Rachel replied in a no-nonsense tone that still felt familiar from Ana's childhood. 'Things probably will go wrong but if anyone can cope, it's you.'

'Right so I'm going then,' said Ana, gazing round at her already barer-looking apartment. 'This is happening.'

'Yes, it is.'

Ana's downstairs neighbour found space on her walls for the paintings she couldn't bear to sell. Her cousin took some of the recipe books and the rest she distributed around charity shops, along with a few more clothes. Bedding and most of her kitchen equipment went to a women's refuge. Every day that went by she owned less and felt lighter.

When Ana emailed her former assistant Lucy with the news that she was leaving, along with several of the *Culinaria* team that she had been especially close to, there was a flurry of replies suggesting farewell parties, lunches and drinks. Ana said no, she didn't have time. There was really only one person she needed to say goodbye to and that was her old self.

On her final morning in London, she dressed in some slouchy grey linen pants and a loose-knit cotton sweater, left her hair round her face, put on sunglasses and a scarf, and didn't bother applying her trademark red lipstick. Glancing at herself in the mirror, she looked unremarkable, not much like Ana the editor at all.

Walking towards the *Culinaria* offices, following her old route through the park, even nodding at a couple of dog walkers that looked familiar, Ana felt nostalgic. This had been her life for so long; now it was all behind her.

Reaching the building, she kept her head down, and stayed on the opposite side of the road. She leant against a wall, with her phone in her hand so it seemed as though she was scrolling, when actually she was looking at the doorway that she used to walk through every day and up at the windows on the second floor where her office had been.

Ana recalled herself on the very first day, arriving in clothes she had spent ages carefully ironing, wanting so much to impress and do well. She thought of the many late nights and early mornings, the long hours at her desk, and how it had all seemed worth it when she got the job she was aiming for. Ana couldn't be sorry about a single moment of being editor of *Culinaria*. She had loved making a magazine. It was a privilege.

Standing there now, staring up at the blank windows, not knowing who lay behind them anymore, Ana realised that for a person who was such a planner, she hadn't given much thought to the far future. What if the magazine hadn't folded? Might she have been there ten years down the track, clinging to her job, refusing to make way for someone new? It was always going to end sooner or later, but she had never formed a strategy for that.

It was nearly lunchtime and people were heading in and out of the building: a stylist that she recognised from *Fashionaria*, women from accounts, a couple of sub-editors. If Ana stayed there too long somebody was going to notice her and she wanted to avoid any awkward encounters.

She straightened and put away her phone, turned away from the building and started walking, slowly at first, then more briskly as she rounded a corner.

Ana wasn't going to look back anymore.

Skye

Tim is planning to spring some sort of surprise. I recognise the signs by now. He is buzzing with excitement, smiling for no reason, he talks faster, and moves a lot. Something about his energy reminds me of the Tim that I met for the first time at the Nova Scotia pub all those years ago.

We were at a dockside table that evening, me and a group of friends, drinking beer and eating crisps, getting a bit raucous. Tim was there with this short-legged little dog he had, which he always refused to put on a lead. The dog had been sniffing round our table begging for crisps and a few moments later I saw it wandering off towards the main road. Since Tim didn't seem to have noticed, I jumped up to grab it by the collar and lead it back to him.

'Oh, Flossie you clever dog, you've brought me a beautiful girl,' he said.

'I was worried she might get run over,' I told him.

Tim smiled down at his hairy brown dog. 'Not my Flossie.'

I was instantly drawn to him. He was tall and lean; his dark hair was a mess of curls and his eyes glittered with mischief. I could tell he would be fun to be around.

I never rejoined my friends that evening. Tim kept talking, made me laugh and bought me drinks till the Nova Scotia closed. The next day, we took Flossie for a walk in the country park up at Ashton Court and went to another pub for lunch. That was it, we were together.

Tim's hair is still all floppy curls and he is as lean as ever. I think it's me who has changed the most. His flair for the un-expected always used to seem charming. I loved his surprises. Now when I sense one coming, I tense. What will it be this time? What will it cost us?

Sometimes I can guess what Tim's planning, but very often I have no idea at all. I need to wait until he gets tired of dropping cryptic hints and keeping his secret.

This time it has been building for a few days and Tim seems especially pleased with himself. When Becky and I get back from our vegan lunch with Meera in the city, he's so keyed up that I'm sure the big reveal can't be far away.

Becky goes upstairs to her room to do some homework and Josh is still at school, so Tim and I are alone together. For once I have a couple of spare hours and, since the sun is shining, I decide to spend them in the garden. But Tim wants to talk, so he follows me out to the shed as I go to fetch my tools. He still seems obsessed with the competition he entered, the one to win a wedding in Italy, and has been googling the town so needs to tell me all about it.

'Wouldn't it be cool to have a wedding?' he says, as I'm kneeling beside one of the flower borders planting a mass of zinnia seedlings that I hope will become a sea of orange.

Suddenly Tim is plunging down on his knees right beside me. He is pulling out something from his pocket, a small jewellery box and beaming as he opens it with a flourish.

'Skye, will you marry me?' he asks.

I stare at the ring, my brain freezing. I can't seem to speak or move.

'It's an emerald,' says Tim. 'Green is your colour; it looks good with your hair.'

Taking the ring from the box, he slips it onto my finger. 'If we don't win a wedding, we can still have one,' he says, brightly.

'Tim ...' I look down at the emerald on my finger, then up at his face. He leans in to kiss me and I'm sure we must look ridiculous, kneeling together on the lawn, a middle-aged couple in an embrace.

'We've been together so long, why do we need to get married?' I ask, pulling away.

'Because it will be fun,' Tim tells me. 'We'll have a party.'

'We could have a party anyway, if we wanted.'

'You'll have a gorgeous dress and I'll get a new suit. We could even do it here, put up a marquee in the garden.' Tim doesn't seem to notice that I'm not saying yes.

The ring stays on my finger. Tim shows it off proudly to Becky and then to Josh when he gets home. Both our kids are excited. They like the idea of us being married. Becky starts googling bridal gowns and Josh wants to know if he can be the best man.

I don't ever wear jewellery because my hands are always busy baking or gardening. This emerald ring is going to be something else I need to think about. I'll be forever taking it off and putting it on, worried about losing it. And I can't imagine where Tim found the money to buy it because balloon chasing doesn't pay that well. Has he managed to take out a new loan that he hasn't told me about?

Money is the last thing on Tim's mind right now. The engagement ring is all he can think about. He keeps catching my hand to admire it.

'It will be a family heirloom,' he tells me. 'You'll pass it onto Becky some day and then she'll give it to her daughter and they'll always remember you when they see it on their fingers.'

That idea does appeal to me. And I like the ring actually,

it's what it represents that I'm not sure about. Marriage isn't something that's been on my radar for a long while. Why would we bother? So, while Tim and the kids are entertaining themselves with increasingly ambitious schemes for our dream wedding – horse-drawn carriages, fields full of sunflowers – I comfort myself with the knowledge that it will never happen.

Sure, I'll wear the ring from time to time to please Tim, and he'll talk up a good game about our wedding but then he'll let it slide as other ideas come along and are more exciting. That's how it tends to go with him.

Tuesday is a working day. I leave the emerald ring in a little dish – which is probably where it will spend most of its time – and put on my hairnet. I like to ease into the week, I can't bear to be rushed and stressed. So, I get up early and Tim is still sleeping as I slip out of our room and tiptoe down the creaky stairs to make a pot of coffee.

The coffee has gone cold by the time the van comes up the driveway. I hear the slam of its door and go out to help because I know Meera's bringing ingredients: sack-loads of flour and sugar, cartons of cacao, eggs and butter, lemons for us to zest. As we're carrying it all in, I can tell she's in one of her darker moods. Meera's hangovers are legendary and at first, I assume she's had a big night.

'Where is it then?' she asks, looking pointedly at my hand. 'The ring of doom?'

'Becky told you,' I guess.

Meera nods. 'She texted last night. She must assume I want to congratulate you.'

'I've put the ring away. I'm not going to wear it for work. It's just a bit of jewellery, Meera,' I say wearily, because I know exactly what she thinks about Tim and there's no need for her to keep reminding me.

'You're officially engaged?'

71

'Maybe. Yes, I suppose so but it doesn't change anything.' As I'm speaking, a glint in Meera's nostril catches my eye. 'Do you have some new jewellery too? Is that another piercing?'

She tilts her face to the window so I can see a sliver of diamond catching the morning light.

'Didn't you have another tattoo last week? You'll be all holes and ink at this rate,' I observe.

'It's my body,' she replies.

Meera helps me make a batch of pastries filled with sweet vanilla bean custard and topped with crunchy salted caramel. Personally, I think they're too rich but there's a café that can't get enough of them. We decorate cupcakes and ice a lot of biscuits shaped like unicorns and dinosaurs, mostly in silence.

Then I help her pack the van and for once I'm relieved as she drives away. It's not that I think Meera is wrong. If life was as straightforward as she imagines then I'd tell Tim that I don't want a wedding and to take his ring back to the shop. But I've got his feelings to consider, and Becky and Josh's too. It's easier for Meera; she gets to live the way she wants with no compromises. I'm part of a family and my life often feels like nothing but.

By the time Meera makes it back, her dark mood seems to have lifted. She doesn't mention the engagement ring again. Instead, she tells me that she's thinking of signing up for a weekend animation workshop.

'That's a good plan,' I say, hoping she isn't going to ask for loads of time off over summer, as that's our busiest part of the year with weddings and parties ramping up.

Meera is a restless person; it's why this job suits her. She likes driving round from place to place and seeing different people. Animation might suit her too though, and the idea of her resigning makes me want to lie down on the flour-dusty floor, because how could I manage without her?

After she leaves for the second delivery of the day, I try not worry about any of it. Worry is a wasted emotion, that's what my mother always says, and for once I'm in complete agreement. But I look at my fingers, long and lightly freckled, scarred by burns and knife cuts, nails trimmed short. Already I can almost sense the missing weight of Tim's ring.

I've finished with baking and am about to start cleaning up when Tim comes to find me.

'Did you bring me a cup of tea?' I ask, hopefully.

'Sorry, no.' He shows me his empty hands. 'I thought you might want to take the dog for a walk.'

I look around at the state of the kitchen. 'Much as I'd love to, there's too much to do.'

'Leave it for now,' Tim urges. 'I'll help you sort it out later.'

'The woods are muddy,' I warn, because I know he doesn't enjoy puddles and slippery slopes.

'Let's go somewhere different for a change.'

'Where,' I ask, untying the strings of my apron and slipping free of the hairnet.

'You'll see,' Tim tells me.

'A surprise then,' I observe.

'Just a little one,' he twinkles back at me.

Apparently, I won't be needing sturdy boots, so I put on trainers and, since the sky is hung with low clouds, grab a rain jacket.

Happy is delighted to be going somewhere by car, leaping gracefully onto the back seat and settling down. I turn round to pat him as Tim is barrelling down our narrow lane. He really is the sweetest dog.

Reaching the main road, Tim turns left.

'We're going to Ashton Court,' I guess. 'For a walk in the country park then a coffee at the Courtyard Café.'

73

He only smiles, and keeps driving past Ashton Court and on towards the city.

We leave the car in a side road by the city docks, close to where they meet the River Avon. Years ago, I used to live nearby and I love this part of town but hardly ever make the time to come back nowadays.

Walking the path that loops round the harbour, past moored houseboats and barges, feels like a real nostalgia trip. The clouds are clearing and Happy strides along between us, with plenty of stops to sniff at lamp posts and walls, while Tim peers into the boats to glimpse how the people who own them live.

'I always wanted one of these,' he tells me. 'Look, this one is for sale. Isn't it gorgeous?'

'No,' I say, and Tim laughs.

'Admit it, you think it's cute. How could you not?'

It is a particularly nice little barge, painted green-and-white, with a deck at the rear covered in pot plants and a wrought iron table for two.

'OK, it's cute,' I agree. 'But I wouldn't want it for a home.'

'Maybe one day though, when the kids have left home and we're semi-retired. We could have a boat and take off for adventures, canal trips, England ... France even.'

It's a nice fantasy and I let Tim run with it as we head across the bridge and walk back along the wharves. I'm desperate for a cup of tea by now but he won't stop at any of the cafés we pass so I assume he must have something else in mind.

The Nova Scotia, the pub where we first met, I should have guessed it. We sit at the same dockside table and Tim goes inside to fetch pints of cider and packets of salt and vinegar crisps.

'It's such a long time ago, that evening,' I say, sipping my cider. 'This pub has hardly changed though; not like we have.'

'We're not so different,' Tim assures me. 'The odd wrinkle

74

or grey hair maybe, but we're still the same people.'

He stretches his arm across the table, and takes my hand. Overhead, seagulls shriek. The cider tastes the same as it always did, sharp and crisp.

'What if you hadn't come here with your friends that night,' says Tim. 'We may never have met. Our lives would be totally different now.'

'There'd be no Becky and Josh,' I say, struggling to imagine it. 'No Lost Cakery.'

'You'd have done something interesting with your life,' says Tim, sounding certain.

'Maybe,' I say, thinking of myself back then, drifting along, not really knowing who I was or what I wanted. My world was more colourful once Tim was in it, full of excitement and new possibilities.

'But we did meet,' adds Tim. 'I was sitting right here and watching you, surrounded by all those girls, wondering how on earth I could get your attention.'

'Why me and not one of the others?' I ask, because I wasn't the prettiest of the group nor the most vivacious. 'What made you notice me?'

'There was just this spark, a sort of energy that drew me to you.'

I felt it too, that spark, I remember it so vividly.

'I knew in those very first moments that we were going to be important to each other,' says Tim.

'And here we are,' I say. 'All these years later.'

With a thumb, Tim strokes the back of my finger. 'You're not wearing your engagement ring,' he observes.

'I meant to put it on when I finished work.'

'I should have got you one ages ago,' he says. 'I meant to.'

'I've got one now,' I say lightly. 'I just need to get used to wearing it.'

Tim squeezes my hand, then releases it and clinks his glass against mine. 'Here's to us,' he says. 'And to our perfect timing, both being here on the same evening.'

'Me and my friends used to come to the Nova Scotia quite a lot,' I tell him. 'It was our local.'

'I was a regular too,' says Tim. 'I liked to pop in for a pint.'

'Most likely we'd have met each other sooner or later then.'

'I think you're right.' Tim reaches for my hand again. 'We were meant to be.'

And who am I to argue with that? Since I can't imagine where I'd be today without him.

Ana

Ana was still a woman who had lost her career and magazine. But now she was also a woman who was packing everything else that mattered into a car and driving to Italy. The plan was to explore until she found somewhere she liked then stop for a while to see if she could live there. It seemed like a good plan, one that allowed for enough of an adventure like her sister had suggested.

She left London with a minimum of fuss. Her neighbour came out to wave her goodbye and Ana pretended she hadn't noticed the tears glistening in her eyes because she couldn't afford to get emotional too. Ahead were miles and miles of roads to travel. Ana just had to settle into them.

Music kept her company, soul classics and disco hits. Singing along, she sensed her spirits lifting. It felt good to be right at the beginning of something.

Her journey was well organised up to a point. She had booked and paid for the car ferry from Dover to Calais and reserved rooms in hotels along the way. The ferry crossing was rougher than she expected, some of the roads were busier, one of the hotels didn't live up to the hype on its website and she ate as many disappointing meals as good ones. But even a planner couldn't control everything. Ana was prepared for minor setbacks.

What she wasn't prepared for was the way she felt on reaching the end of the course she had plotted. South of Naples, there was nothing to guide her. No email confirmations on her phone, no one expecting her at all. This was where the real adventure was meant to begin.

Once she had navigated the traffic, and Vesuvius was in her rear-view mirror, Ana had to pull off the road and get out of the car. She sat on a plastic chair at an Autogrill, heart racing and mouth dry, watching groups of people enter and leave. They must all know where they were heading. She seemed like the only one who didn't.

Ana allowed herself this one panic attack, although she hadn't planned for it. For an hour she stayed in the Autogrill, sipping mineral water, as traffic blurred by on the motorway. If anyone else had behaved this way, she would have been impatient, thinking they needed to pull themselves together. But now it was happening to her.

Somehow, she managed to get back in the car and point it south again. In her head there had always been the idea of going to Puglia. To the heel of Italy's boot, as far south-east as you could be, to baroque towns carved out of limestone and to sun-kissed sandy beaches. Helen Mirren had a place there apparently. Meryl Streep too.

Ana might not be a Hollywood star but couldn't she buy a house in Puglia, somewhere modest and in need of renovation? As she was driving, the idea played through her mind.

She knew that property was cheaper in many parts of Italy and, in some places, they seemed to be practically giving it away. Like almost everyone else, Ana had read the newspaper stories about Italian towns selling off abandoned buildings for as little as one euro. There was sure to be some sort of catch, still she kept thinking that if she bought a real bargain then she would be able to hang onto her apartment which would give her a route back to London when and if she needed it.

Ana drove for over four hours without a break, on high-ways that wound between spring-green hills and along roads fringed with wild flowers, thinking she would stop at the next town then the next, but driving on instead, stealing glimpses of the sea as she sped along. Heading down straight lengths of highway punctuated by roundabouts, it was only hunger that brought Ana to a halt. She had barely eaten any breakfast and skipped lunch altogether.

Ahead she spotted a town crowning a hilltop, dazzlingly white against the blue sky. Locorotondo according to the sign-posts. It seemed as good a place as any to spend a night.

Ana followed the signs and found a place to park the car that was only a short walk from the centre of town. She took a small bag packed with a few things and left everything else locked in the boot for now. What she needed was budget-friendly accommodation, a decent meal and an early night. But first she wanted to stretch her legs and get her bearings.

This town was all narrow alleyways that seemed to take her in circles. Ana walked over polished stone, past white-washed buildings with pointed tiled roofs and balconies filled with bright flowers, until she found a small hotel.

Up until now everyone she had encountered had spoken some English, but here the old nonna who answered the door only shrugged uncomprehendingly when Ana asked if she had any rooms available. She switched to her halting Duolingo Italian and somehow managed to make herself understood.

The room she was shown was charming, with pale exposed stone walls and sloping ceilings. Ana longed to stretch out on the bed and close her eyes. She felt a little shaky still, possibly more from lack of food than panic now.

In the bathroom she tidied her hair and put on some red lipstick. She had done it; Ana reminded her reflection; she had followed her plan and it had brought her here. A stranger would be in her apartment by now, perhaps scratching up the parquet floors and ruining her granite kitchen countertops. It didn't seem to matter as much now that Ana was in Italy.

She had visited enough small Italian towns to know there was always a piazza, with a bar and perhaps a restaurant. Ana had come across one earlier while she was exploring and so retraced her steps. What she wanted was proper food, rather than a snack, but to ask for a meal at this early hour would mark her out as a tourist.

Instead, she ordered an aperitivo at a bar beside the arched gateway that led into the old town. Sitting alone at a table, Ana's thoughts kept her company. She was still unsettled by that episode at the Autogrill. It wasn't as though she had never experienced a moment's anxiety before. Walking into a room full of strangers, giving a speech or presentation, appearing on television, those were things that made her edgy. Over the years she had developed a technique to control any unhelpful nerves. First Ana would pause and remind herself of who she was. A top magazine editor, a woman in control, someone who had succeeded. Then she would stride into a room or up onto the stage, and be that person.

At the Autogrill, exactly who she was seemed less certain. She had felt hollow and directionless. Now, as the waiter set down her Aperol spritz and she smiled her thanks, Ana was set on making sure she didn't feel that way again. What she needed was a plan, better still, a project.

Sipping her drink, she alternated between people watching and googling on her phone, browsing through articles about towns that were selling vacant houses for one euro. There seemed to be no shortage of them. One municipality was offering a former monastery that needed restoring. Another was actually giving people money if they would commit to living there. They must be desperate to revive these places that were slowly crumbling to dust. What sort of state would a one-euro house be in? Ana envisaged buckling walls and caved-in roofs, buildings that were no more than derelict shells.

Not that she was afraid of taking on a renovation; if anything, the idea excited her. Pulling out her notebook, Ana started making a neat list of possible locations, then switched to trimming it down, discounting places that were too far north, villages that seemed very remote, a sprawling industrial town, a settlement where the dwellings had been very badly damaged by an earthquake. Even so there were plenty left to choose from.

Mindlessly grazing on olives and crispy things, she lost herself in articles about foreigners who had restored derelict houses, then she managed to find a website with a fairly uninspiring selection of them for sale. Ana put away her phone for long enough to pay her bill and find the nearest restaurant. Once she had run through the menu with a waiter and chosen a dish involving a chickpea broth and strips of fried pasta, along with a side of baked fennel drenched in butter and Parmesan cheese she returned to her research, filling more pages of the notebook with ideas and observations.

'Can I tempt you to a gelato, Signora?' the waiter asked, when he came to clear her dinner plates. Reflexively Ana shook her head. She tried to avoid sugar, and besides she had already eaten more than she intended.

Intent on gathering local knowledge, she took her chance to ask the waiter a few questions about the one euro house scheme. Were there any empty places that he knew of in Locorotondo? Or other towns in the Valle d'Itria that might be considering selling off vacant buildings?

'This story of houses for one euro, it is only for the publicity,' the waiter said, dismissively. 'Thousands of people apply, then they auction the buildings for much higher prices. It is a kind of scam, you understand?'

'Surely some of them are genuine?' Ana had seen a map of Italy flagged along almost the whole of its length with towns that were participating.

He shrugged. 'Myself, I wouldn't bother.'

His words didn't deter Ana. All those years in journalism had taught her the value of finding out things for herself. She would pick one of those towns and drive there.

Walking back towards the hotel, she reminded herself who she was. A woman that had left her failures behind, who was unafraid and resilient; or at least a woman who knew how to act that way.

Skye

Time doesn't make much sense. How can the days drag but then the weeks and months seem to speed by? Perhaps it's because mostly I do the same things and see the same people. My life is an unchanging landscape; at least it would be if Tim wasn't in it.

That's what I liked about him at first; he made everything more interesting. If some of my friends weren't so sure, I was happy to leave them by the wayside as he swept me along. Those early years were a blur of never knowing what to expect, of surprise trips to Paris, and midnight swims in the sea, and theme park rollercoasters.

Tim never cared about rules and regulations, they didn't apply to him. He also reckoned that any fool could get a job, the real skill was avoiding it. With his encouragement and a heady feeling of freedom, I handed in my notice at work. My parents were horrified as we started burning through my savings. But I was sick of being responsible and entirely convinced that Tim was right. Why stay in a dull job when there was money in the bank? Wasn't this our chance to have a good time?

When we ran out of cash, we turned our hands to different things – house-painting and picture hanging, bar work, gardening – and something always seemed to come along. People paid us to stay in their houses and look after their pets while they were on holiday. For a while we got into foraging and dumpster diving which meant we hardly paid for food. Just like Tim's little dog Flossie, I was off my lead and roaming free. I had never been happier.

Mum and Dad kept telling me I couldn't carry on like that, I was ruining my life, destroying my future, but of course I didn't listen.

'Why can't they see that I don't want to be like them?' I said to Tim, frustrated. 'They just don't seem to get it.'

'It's not their fault,' he told me. 'They think their way is the only way. If they're upsetting you, just don't speak to them.'

At that point we were into wild camping. Me, Tim and the dog would head off with this tiny tent and a Primus stove in our backpacks. We'd have a couple of sleeping bags and I'd bake flapjacks and a dense nutty fruitcake to keep us going. We always hitch-hiked and we'd go wherever the rides took us. Neither of us had a mobile phone; Tim refused to carry one so I didn't either. It was easy to lose touch with the world as we disappeared into woodland glades, or onto moorlands and mountains, pitching our tent wherever we wanted, staying away for as long as we liked.

Once a farmer tried to chase us off his land and Tim pretended to be French until the guy gave up and went away, then we held each other and laughed till tears ran down our faces. Another time we put up the tent in the dark and woke to find we were right beside the most beautiful lake so we went skinny dipping in the clear, icy water. Then there was a night in Scotland when the rain became torrential and we found a church that had been left open and slept between the pews our bodies curled around each other. Of all the years that Tim and I have spent together, those memories are the brightest and I'm glad I lived that way for a while. I'd never want to change it.

But my parents were right, we couldn't carry on like that forever. I think the first change was when Tim decided to become an entrepreneur. He started by organising a series of parties and raves in empty warehouses. I used to find wads of cash in his pockets or pushed to the back of a drawer, money he hadn't mentioned and I never asked about.

Then Tim opened a cider bar on a river barge and a night-club in town up near St Nicholas Market. He never kept a business for long. He would set up something, sell and move on to the next thing. Eventually he got a reputation for having a magic touch so that's when he started being a business coach.

While all that was going on, I got pregnant, once by mistake and the second time because we didn't want Becky to be an only child. Also, I loved being a mum. Even when the kids were really little and we were awash with dirty nappies, half deafened by crying and dealing with sleepless nights. I had made these little humans and I was crazy about them.

As things shifted, we changed too. We took on the mortgage for Lost Cottage, even though it was more debt than we could comfortably afford. There were other things, like a digital start-up Tim put money into and a rundown country inn he thought he could turn into a gastropub. When both businesses failed, he was convinced that he had lost his magic touch. Tim's lows got lower, and the highs seemed to go higher to make up for it. And suddenly we weren't young anymore, we were middle aged.

Time is so confusing. Our years of living irresponsibly seem ages ago and yet also close enough to touch. I know Meera sees me as this hopeless case, ground down by life, stuck in a relationship rut. But she didn't know Tim back when his eyes glittered, and you knew he was about to take you somewhere that you really wanted to go.

Right now, Tim is following me round the house, into the kitchen where I put the kettle on, out to the garden when I go to pick bluebells, he's following me and talking. Often, he's like this after a morning spent alone, full of pent-up energy and a torrent of thoughts he has to speak out loud.

Tim is aware that Meera doesn't like him much. For a while he tried to win her over, using all his considerable charm, but eventually he gave up. Now they edge around each other, speaking as little as possible, and if Meera is at work in the Cakery, then Tim is generally somewhere else. The moment he hears the delivery van driving away, that is his cue to come and find me.

I have no shortage of things to do. A bride is coming in later with her fiancé for a consultation and I need to set up a table in my little wisteria-covered bower. There is a cake to decorate and tons of admin to do. But Tim is talking and I'm trying to make time to listen.

'If we decide to go for a marquee wedding, then do you think we should buy a tent rather than hire one?' he is asking. 'Then we can rent it out for village fetes and things, and we'll make the money back.'

'Where would we keep a marquee though?' I want to know,

'Once I've had a clear-out, there'll be plenty of space to store it in one of the sheds.'

Tim's long promised clear-out would mean coming face-to-face with too many of his failures: the screen-printing business he never got off the ground, the dinghy he never learnt to sail properly. I can't see it ever happening.

'We'll have loads of festoon lights, flares and maybe a fire pit,' he continues, enthusiastic about his vision. 'The roses will be blooming and scenting the air. If it's a fine day, it will be perfect.'

'What if it rains?' I can't help asking.

'If the weather's bad then everyone will cram into the

marquee and there'll be music and dancing so we'll have a good time anyway.'

Tim trails after me as I head to the conservatory, where I cover the table with a linen cloth and set down a vase of bluebells, along with some vintage plates and cake forks. Still talking, he follows me into my Cakery and settles on a stool.

'If you're going to be here, then you have to wear a hairnet,' I remind him for about the millionth time.

He frowns, irritated by the interruption, but covers his curls with the hairnet I offer.

'I was thinking we'd have a harpist for the ceremony itself and then a party band for afterwards,' he says. 'I've still got a few contacts, so I'm sure I can get us mate's rates.'

I make a start on decorating a baby shower cake. I'm frosting it with meringue buttercream and, as I work, I'm half-listening to Tim and half-wondering if this wedding obsession is ever going to run its course.

'We need to get onto organising this. August isn't that far away,' he says.

I look up and frown in his direction. 'This August?'

Tim is smiling and nodding.

'That's much too soon,' I say. 'And anyway, it's such a busy time for me.'

'You're always busy,' he points out. 'And also, you're always making other people's wedding cakes. It's time you had your own.'

'No,' I say. 'August is impossible.'

'I reckon I can make it happen.' He sounds bullish.

'Next year. Let's plan for then.' I say, hoping that a long delay will give Tim enough time to lose his enthusiasm.

'We don't want to wait that long surely?'

'We do,' I insist. 'Then we can get the band we want and I'll have the garden looking wonderful.'

'Your garden always looks great.'

'Next year,' I repeat, firmly.

'Ah well,' He gives a resigned shrug. 'You never know, we might win that wedding in Italy.'

'They'll have had thousands and thousands of entries,' I remind him.

'I wrote a pretty compelling one.'

I look up again to see that Tim won't meet my eyes, which makes me immediately suspicious. 'Did you get creative?'

'I might have,' he admits, and an odd expression flits across his face, he almost looks ashamed.

Tim has always been a teller of tall tales. He exaggerates to make things more interesting, which can be funny but more often than not I find infuriating.

'How creative? What did you say exactly?' I ask.

'It doesn't matter really. Like you pointed out, there'll be thousands of entries, won't there?'

'If you win then you'll have to tell me.'

Tim slips from the stool and pulls off his hairnet. 'If I win then we'll have to get married this summer,' he says, before striding out of the door.

After he's gone, I'm so distracted that I make a mess of piping a buttercream border and have to scrape it all off the baby shower cake and start again, which puts me behind with everything else. There isn't enough time in my day for Tim and his big dreams. I don't have enough energy for them either. As I'm piping, more carefully this time, I'm thinking that life might be calmer and easier without him.

Ana

The windows of Ana's hotel room were open and she was following her routine of morning stretches, breathing air scented with coffee beans and looking out over the steeply pitched rooftops.

She had been doing this same series of body stretches for decades now and it had become a time to think, as well as move. In the old days, what used to occupy her mind was mostly work related. Who she might commission to write an article, ideas for food themes, niggles with the *Culinaria* team. Now all of that had been wiped clean, like words from a whiteboard, and Ana was free to think about herself.

She stood on one leg and focused on lowering her shoulder blades, keeping her breathing steady. As she held the pose, Ana was wondering if she might have arrived in Italy with unnecessary stealth. She did have a few contacts here, but hadn't been in touch with any of them because she wanted to avoid having that same conversation. Yes, it was terrible that *Culinaria* had closed. No, she didn't know what she would do next. True, it was important to embrace change.

Ana switched to balancing on the other leg. She thought about the people she knew who might live within driving distance of Locorotondo. There was an American writer who had married an Italian and now wrote books about their life together. All Ana could remember was that she lived somewhere near a town called Martina Franca.

She finished her exercises with a few deep belly breaths, careful to take in the air through her nose, smelling coffee again, along with the sweet, yeasty smell of baking. Most likely it was drifting through the window of a house somewhere down below, and here at the hotel all Ana would be offered was long-ago boiled eggs and curling slices of cheese. She dressed in slouchy grey linen pants and a loose white shirt, and went to check anyway.

In the breakfast room, she found the old nonna wearing a floral apron but no sign of the dispiriting buffet she had expected. There was a tiled table with eight wicker-bottomed chairs arranged around it and, as Ana took a seat, the nonna disappeared. When she returned it was with a wooden board that she placed on the table. A large puff of pastry sat alongside two small golden ovals of shortcrust pies and a scattering of tiny wild strawberries.

'*Buon appetito*,' said the nonna, before leaving her to eat.

As Ana bit into the flaky pastry, she found the flavours of peppery béchamel sauce, warm mozzarella, a fresh tang of tomato, and an intense butteriness too.

The miniature golden pies were filled with sweet custard and the strawberries had a pleasantly acidic bite. Before Ana knew it, she had eaten everything. She would have to miss lunch, walk off her rich breakfast, eat a light dinner.

The nonna removed the wooden board, bare of all but crumbs now, and replaced it with a tiny Moka pot of steaming coffee. Ana sipped, searching her mind for the name of that American writer who had made her home in Italy. She had attended her book launch then later published a couple of her travel stories and once they had lunched together. She could still picture her face, unnaturally smooth from Botox and fillers, and recall her story of falling for an Italian man and his way of life. If you ever come to Puglia, be sure to look me up, the woman had repeated and now Ana was here and very well might, if she could only remember her name.

She reached for her phone and typed a few words into Google. *American, writer, Puglia, autobiography, love story.* Her search yielded a lot of unhelpful results. Other names came up, but definitely not the right one.

The only other option was to check the *Culinaria* website. Ana hesitated. She had purposely avoided doing that, not wanting to deal with the feelings it might bring up, and now she asked herself if she really needed to see this woman she barely knew. But Martina Franca was such a short drive away, and she had rather enjoyed her company that day over lunch and besides, wasn't her husband something to do with houses, an architect or a real estate agent? Ana couldn't quite remember that either but there was only one way to find out. She double-clicked on the *Culinaria* website.

Straight away she saw that her old digital editor Tammy Wong had given it yet another redesign. With some satisfaction Ana noted that, while it looked very pretty, it was clumsy to navigate. Still, she managed to find the archive and, scanning through the travel stories, found the one she was looking for. *Love, Life and Cucina Povera: an American in Puglia* by Carina Mondadori.

Ana found herself re-reading the article. It was full of atmosphere and colour, with descriptions of food that would have made her mouth water if she wasn't already full of breakfast. Carina really was a lovely writer.

Armed with a name now, she managed to find an email address. Ana composed a short message, explaining that she was in the area for a while and would love to catch up for a drink or coffee, adding her phone number before sending it off. Carina might be away overseas of course, she recalled her saying that she still lived for part of the year in New York, or maybe it was California. Briefly Ana wondered if her memory was worsening now that her brain wasn't put through the rigorous daily workouts of editing a magazine.

She went upstairs to pack up the small bag that she had brought from the car. The rest of her stuff was still stowed in the boot, at least Ana hoped so. She didn't like leaving her things behind and the sooner she found a base – even a single room where she could put books on a shelf and clothes in a cupboard – the happier she would feel.

Her phone rang as she was zipping up her bag. Seeing an Italian number, Ana assumed it must be Carina.

'Hello, Ana King speaking,' she said, answering as she always did although there was no longer any need to be so formal.

'Ana, are you really here?' The warm, accented voice was immediately familiar.

'Carina, hello, yes, I'm in Locorotondo actually.'

'Where are you staying?'

'I've just spent the night in a little hotel, and now I'm thinking I might head further south.' The moment the words were out of Ana's mouth, she regretted them. Now it would be obvious that she didn't have any accommodation arranged and Carina might feel obliged to offer her a room.

'You must come and stay with us,' she proved her right by saying. 'At least for a couple of nights while you plan your route.'

'Oh no, I don't want to put you to any trouble,' said Ana, who never felt the least bit comfortable staying in other people's houses no matter how hospitable they might be.

'You wouldn't be,' Carina replied. 'We've got plenty of space and we'd love to have you.'

'Thanks but no, I ... .'

'Ana what you have to realise is that Mauro and I have been together now for thirty years. We're bored with ourselves and each other. Please come, and make life more interesting. You'd be doing us a favour.'

Ana laughed. 'Just for a couple of nights then,' she agreed, thinking it might not be such a bad idea after all. 'If that's OK.'

'I'm going to put flowers in the guest room and take you to my favourite place for lunch.' Carina sounded excited. 'I can't wait to see you.'

Ending the call, Ana looked round at the small hotel room. She preferred her own space. That was why in London she rarely invited people to stay and certainly not acquaintances she had met once or twice. She liked to close her front door and feel the freedom of it, to cleanse her face and undo her chignon.

Years ago, she had tried living with a boyfriend but everything about him had driven her crazy. He left his shoes in the middle of the floor, and piles of things trickled from his pockets onto almost every surface. And he always seemed to be there, in her way, wherever she didn't want him to be. After they broke up, she hadn't tried it again. While Ana welcomed dinner guests, friends for drinks, and the occasional lover who spent the night, she was never sorry when they left her alone again.

Still, it seemed as though Carina genuinely did want her to stay and it was only a couple of nights, Ana reminded herself as she glanced at her reflection, paused to tidy a stray hair and apply some lipstick then went to find the old nonna so she could pay the bill.

Carina lived near Martina Franca, down a long dirt road that wound through olive groves. Assuming that all this land must belong to her friend, Ana was impressed with the Mondadori estate, and then she saw the house. A two-storey *masseria* with cherry-pink walls and arched windows, it was set in a flagged courtyard beside towering palms and drystone-walled gardens.

'Welcome, welcome.' Carina hurried over to greet her, arms outstretched and smiling. It was at least a couple of years since their last meeting but she didn't seem to have changed. Her hair was still streaked with blonde and her skin flawlessly smooth thanks to whatever was being injected into it. Ana felt yet again that she may have missed a trick by deciding to age gracefully.

'This place is gorgeous,' she said, once they had touched cheek-to-cheek. 'Absolutely stunning.'

Carina smiled again. 'Wait till you see inside.'

She led Ana through the main doorway and into a spacious hall with vaulted ceilings then onto a large room lined with windows that looked out over a garden filled with blossoming lemon trees. It all looked very grand but still lived-in, with piles of books and magazines, urns filled with houseplants and vases brimming with flowers.

They passed through a series of smaller rooms, one with a television, another a library, until they reached a *loggia* and beyond that a saltwater pool.

'Wow,' said Ana, who had reached the conclusion that if it were less cluttered then this might be her dream house. 'What an amazing place.'

'It's too big for us really, a lot of work to maintain.'

'Did you do the restoration yourselves?' Ana thought she remembered Carina saying so.

'Oh yes,' Carina nodded. 'The place was almost a ruin. There were months and months with an army of builders, then we had to landscape the gardens and put in the pool. If I'd known how stressful it was going to be ...'

'Isn't your husband a property developer?'

'Mauro? No he's a lawyer. But his brother used to be in construction, and I suppose that may have made things easier, although it didn't feel like it at the time.'

They kept walking through to the kitchen, where an oak dresser was stacked with mismatched plates, an armoury of pans hung from ceiling hooks and the worn granite countertops were etched with the damage made by generations of women who must have cooked here.

'Coffee?' Carina asked. 'We're going out for lunch in an hour, so I won't offer you food.'

'I'm absolutely fine,' Ana assured her.

'In that case, I'll show you to your room. Don't worry about your bags, I'll have them brought up. And Ana?' Carina paused in the doorway. 'I'm not going to go on about how sad the whole business with *Culinaria* is, because I imagine that you're sick of talking about it.'

'Thank you.' Ana nodded, gratefully. 'Yes, I am.'

'Also, I want you to make yourself at home here. Use this place as a base, if you like, while you're in the area exploring. Don't feel like you're going to outstay your welcome, because I promise you, I'm very glad of the company.'

'What if I turn out to be a terrible house guest?' Ana asked her.

Carina laughed. 'Somehow I doubt that's going to happen.'

Ana followed her upstairs to a large chamber at the far end of a corridor. An immense curtained bed lay at its centre and a chaise piled with cushions was set beside a window with a view of the olive groves.

'I'll go and organise your bags and you can settle in,' said Carina. 'I made a reservation for lunch at one of my most favourite local places.'

After she had gone, Ana stood at the window, gazing out

95

over acres of red earth and rows of silvery green olive trees. This felt like the Italy she had come to find.

She only had a few moments alone. Carina soon returned, followed by a gardener carrying her bags. Then she was back again with coffee and before very long it was time for lunch.

After such a large breakfast, Ana wasn't hungry but could hardly say no, since Carina seemed so excited about taking her out.

'Your books and articles make the food here sound so wonderful,' Ana remarked, as they were driving the short distance to Martina Franca in her car which was now filled with a sharp citrusy fragrance the older woman was wearing.

'There is bad cooking to be found in Puglia, just like everywhere else,' Carina said, with a shrug. 'It's certainly not the kind of high-end dining out that you'll be used to in London.'

Ana had eaten a lot of meals all over the world. She had been served a seven-course supper made almost entirely from the edible blossoms of foraged plants in Copenhagen, been offered a series of dishes designed to look like a Japanese forest floor, eaten food prepared with Patagonian rainwater. Even though she appreciated the cleverness of those chefs, and their obsessive dedication, food as art always left her feeling slightly emptier.

'The food of Puglia has come from poverty,' Carina added, as if Ana needed reminding. 'It is mostly very humble.'

'I'm happy with humble,' Ana promised.

Martina Franca was another bleached town perched on a hilltop, with baroque churches carved from pale stone and a cluster of whitewashed houses. As they passed beneath an arched gateway, Ana slowed her pace to match Carina's shorter stride. Dressed in layers of pale linen, with a Hermès scarf knotted at her throat and eyes covered by large-lensed sunglasses, Carina might have been any age. But the careful way she walked over the slippery flagstones, made Ana long to offer an arm, and there was something about the stoop in her shoulders that suggested frailty.

'You've arrived here at the right time, before too many tourists swarm in,' remarked Carina, as they made their way into a small piazza dominated by a dazzlingly white basilica.

The restaurant she had chosen looked more like a butcher's shop, with cuts of meat on display in a glass cabinet and wait-staff in striped aprons. There was a handful of outdoor tables beneath a canopy of sun umbrellas and they were ushered to one.

Ana left the ordering up to Carina as she seemed to know the menu well, chatting to the waiter in Italian as she made choices. They ate bombettes, grilled meaty cheesy rolls, that she explained were so named because they almost exploded with flavour. There was the promised puree of fava beans topped with wilted wild chicory and a plate of baby artichokes fried until they were crisp.

'Are you writing at the moment?' Ana wondered, unable to resist a second serving of the artichokes. 'Another memoir?'

'I've been working on a new project, a novel, but it's not going well.' Carina gave a heavy sigh. 'That's one of the reasons I was so happy to hear from you. It's given me an excuse to escape my desk.'

'It's brave of you to try something different.' Ana helped herself to a couple more bombettes – they were too good not to.

'Or maybe it's foolish, I don't know anymore,' Carina sounded dejected. 'I sit there, day after day, and often delete more words than I manage to type. Mauro says I should give up, but who am I, if I'm not a writer?'

Ana thought she understood how Carina must feel. 'Will you keep trying then?'

'I suppose I must. But I'm glad today to have you to distract me.' Her voice brightened. 'So, tell me, why are you here? How long are you staying? Tell me everything.'

'Like you I decided to try something different,' Ana explained. 'Actually, I've been considering buying a place here. I've been reading about all these properties being sold off for one euro but someone told me it's a scam.'

'I'm not sure if that's entirely true,' mused Carina. 'You do have to commit to spending a certain sum of money on the house or live in it for an agreed period of time though.'

'That sounds fair enough,' said Ana, feeling more encouraged. 'I may pursue it then.'

'There's no shortage of properties in Southern Italy waiting to be restored but if I were you, I wouldn't rush into anything. It might be better to rent for a while.' Carina hesitated. 'In my books and articles, I give a certain impression of life here. What I don't say is that it can be very lonely, that in winter a cold wind sweeps across Puglia and in summer it's brutally hot, and if you stay for any length of time, you get very tired of eating fava bean puree and bitter wild greens.'

Ana smiled. As good as that dish had been, she might not feel the need to order it again any time soon.

'I only ever tell a part of the story, the bit readers want,' Carina admitted. 'In a way it's a fantasy version of my real life.'

'You're not unhappy here, though?'

'No, but I've always had an escape. There's a tiny apartment in New York that used to belong to my parents and I go there when I need a change of pace. For years I've been leading a double life. Now I have a birthday coming up, a milestone.' She mouthed a number.

'Eighty?' Ana had known that Carina was older than she looked, but not so much older.

'Shhh.' She held a finger to her plumped-up lips.

'You don't look it.'

'Mauro is much younger than me, of course, so I've spent a lot of time and money on not looking my age. Unfortunately, that hasn't stopped me starting to feel it. Sooner or later, I'll have to stop travelling and choose one of my lives over the other.'

'Italy or New York?'

Carina stared down at her plate and sighed. 'Mauro says he will never leave Puglia, but I'm not so certain if I want to be here for the rest of my days; no wonder I have writer's block. You know how it is when your mind is busy; it's impossible to concentrate on putting words together.'

'I don't do any writing at all these days,' Ana admitted.

'Nothing?' Carina sounded surprised. 'A blog or a news-letter, no? Not even social media?'

'None of those things.'

Carina widened her eyes. 'How charmingly old-fashioned.'

'I certainly couldn't conjure up a story out of my life, not like you have. But then my life is a lot less interesting than yours has been.'

'Now that you are here you might meet your own Mauro, a charming Italian man.' Carina's tone wasn't teasing, she was presenting this as a real possibility

'I don't think so,' Ana said, dismissively. 'I'm very happily single. The last thing I want is a relationship.'

'That's what I thought too, before my husband came along and changed my mind.'

Ana remembered the story, or at least the version of it she had read in Carina's book. She had been at a supermarket, shopping for artichokes. A handsome, dark-eyed stranger shook his head as she filled her basket, whispering that at the stall down the road, they were much fresher and cheaper too. Then he escorted her there, helped her carry the full basket home, demonstrated his mother's method of trimming artichokes and stayed to eat them. It was a foodie romance, and the age difference had never been an issue. Or so Carina had written.

'I'm not going to change my mind,' Ana promised, because she never entirely trusted in other people's love stories and didn't aspire to have one herself. 'I'm looking for a charming house to fall in love with, not a charming man.'

Skye

I love bluebell season. I pick bunches of them in the woods and fill jugs that I put all over the house. Tim is always complaining that the bell-shaped flowers shrivel and the water gets stinky, but I keep bringing them home anyway. Bluebell season doesn't last long and I need to make the most of it.

'You can't use bluebells on the cakes,' says Tim, as if I didn't know. 'They're toxic.'

I nod, but don't say anything, as I arrange the stems in a pottery jug that I found in a Clifton charity shop. It's home-made and misshapen but the shade of the glaze matches the flowers almost exactly.

Tim has been following me about again. I try to hide my relief when he announces that he won't be at home for dinner.

'I'm doing a shift at the pub.'

'Oh great.' It's been a while since Tim's worked there and I had assumed he had given it up.

'You should come in and have a drink later,' he suggests.

'Maybe,' I say, knowing I won't. Already I'm thinking about what I might do with the evening ahead. Take a long bath, watch a romcom, pot up some plants.

'They're going to be having a quiz night on Tuesdays,' Tim tells me. 'We should get a team together.'

I feel about quiz nights much the same way that I do about fancy-dress parties; far too much work and why would you bother? Naturally Tim is wildly enthusiastic about both.

'It'll be fun,' he promises, and I wonder when our ideas of what constitutes a good time diverged so drastically. Maybe young me would have enjoyed having general knowledge questions fired my way. Am I getting old and boring? Have I turned into the sort of person I always swore I wouldn't be? Am I actually my parents now?

I put the jug of bluebells on the window ledge and try to mindfully experience the moment of joy they are meant to be giving me. Even that feels like hard work.

'Who else could we get to be in our team?' Tim asks.

'I don't know,' I say, wishing he'd stop distracting me. 'What about the kids?'

'Yes, yes,' cries Tim as if I've come up with an idea that never would have occurred to anyone else. 'They'll be great at all the pop culture questions and I can cover history and sport, probably politics too.'

Tim does know a lot of stuff. He's got one of those retentive brains and is always online reading. He'll be in his element at a pub quiz and I try to muster some enthusiasm.

'Sign us up then,' I say. 'Tuesday evenings, right?'

'If we're as good as I think we'll be then there's a league, inter-pub tournaments.'

'Seriously? A league?'

'There'll be stiff competition, of course,' Tim sounds excited. 'And the quizmaster is meant to be tough.'

I tell myself that it'll be nice to have an evening at the pub with the kids. We haven't done anything like that together in ages. Most nights we don't even watch the same shows on television. And perhaps this will be Tim's new thing, a replacement for entering competitions and planning our dream wedding. A few beers and a packet of crisps; that has to be a cheap night out.

Once he has taken himself off to work, I think about all the things I should be doing. Paperwork, life maintenance, cooking, sweeping and scrubbing; there seems no end to the chores I can list in my head. But I'm also thinking about how dull I've become. Is my best self behind me? I really hope not.

I run a bath, scented with lots of rose geranium oil, and sink into it with a sigh. When the kids get home, they'll find food in the fridge and can cook themselves dinner. I'm making space for self-care, like Meera's always suggesting. More importantly, I'm carving out some thinking time.

Who do I want future me to be? Not my father reading the *Daily Telegraph* and endlessly complaining that the world is going to hell in a handcart. And, much as I love her, not my mother, who mostly nods along. Who will I be when the kids leave home and I get the whole of my life back? Will collecting bluebells in the woods and planting dahlia tubers be enough? And will Tim be there, following me around and talking while I do it?

Lately I've been thinking more and more about how it would be to break free. Scenarios play through my mind when I'm alone, doing something monotonous like decorating identical cupcakes or piping cream into a batch of doughnuts. We would have to sell Lost Cottage, which would be hard but I'd find a way to cope. I could rent a commercial kitchen and keep baking, find a flat with enough space for the kids to stay whenever they wanted, carve out a life of my own. Tim though, he might struggle and, if he was lonely and sad, that would make me feel awful. Tim needs me, he always has. Almost right from the beginning I've looked after him and I can't stop doing that just because I find him difficult to live with at times. I couldn't ever leave him, it's impossible.

And so, those thoughts will stay in my head; I won't share them with anyone. I'll go to the pub quiz and even compete in the league if I have to. Tim's ring will be on my finger, and he'll know the answers to at least half the questions, and all of that will make him happy. Isn't that what I want, for everyone to be happy?

I'm in bed by the time Tim comes home but I can tell by the way he slams the front door and stumbles up the stairs, that he's had too much to drink. That's not like Tim. Usually he makes cocktails for everyone else at a party, then only has a couple of low-alcohol beers himself.

Tonight though, I think he's drunk much more than that. He falls onto the bed fully dressed. 'Skye? Are you awake?' he asks, breathing whisky fumes over me.

'I am now,' I reply, gruffly. 'Please tell me you didn't drive home.'

'Cory wouldn't let me. Said I was drunk. He dropped me off.'

Cory, the pub manager, probably got him drunk in the first place. Still at least he hadn't let Tim behind the wheel of his car.

He rolls closer. 'Skye, I'm sorry.'

'You don't have to apologise for having a few drinks.'

'No, that's not why.'

'Get undressed, come to bed,' I tell him.

His head is on the pillow next to mine and he wraps an arm around me. I sense myself tensing. Surely, he isn't going to want drunk sex? I'm definitely not up for that.

'Tim ...'

'I just want to hold you Skye, I want to hold my fiancée.'

He's slurring his words. I've known him get tipsy but never sloppy drunk. This isn't like him at all.

'What's wrong?' I ask.

'You'll be cross if I tell you.'

'Tim, what have you done?' Now I'm fully awake and worried.

'I shouldn't have said what I did and I feel like I'm wishing it on you.' He's pushing his face into my shoulder and his voice is half muffled.

'I've got no idea what you're talking about.'

'I wanted to win it so much. I thought that might get us across the line. I'm so sorry, Skye.'

Tim tries to press closer to me, and I push him away. 'What's going on?'

I reach over to the bedside table and switch on the lamp. His face is crumpled and he blinks in the brighter light. He looks like a very middle-aged small boy.

'Tim? Stop being so cryptic.'

'What I wrote, in that competition entry, I shouldn't have.' His words come out in a rush.

I say nothing, just listen to his breathing, whisky-laced and ragged, waiting for him to fill the silence with words,

'I told them that you're sick, that you've got cancer,' he half whispers. 'I said that winning a wedding in Italy would be a dream come true for us.'

Now I can't speak. At first, I don't believe it then I'm angry beyond words. Cancer is everywhere. My mother has had it twice, a good friend died of it, lots more have been through treatment.

'It was just a story Skye, a fiction.'

Tim has always been an embroiderer of the truth, but this was a proper lie. And what if we did happen to win? Did he imagine I'd go along with it? I don't bother to ask. Even if he was sober there wouldn't be any point.

He's saying that he loves me, that I'm everything to him, but his voice is unwanted noise. What I'd like is to sleep somewhere else, the living room sofa or the old chaise in the conservatory but I can't risk having the kids finding me like that so instead, I roll over and turn off the light. 'Please stop talking Tim, I have to sleep.'

'But Skye ...'

I try to tug the duvet up over my shoulders, but he is weighing it down. 'Stop talking,' I repeat.

He falls asleep before I do, fully dressed and on top of the covers. I hear his breathing slowing and deepening, and before long he's starting to snore.

Tomorrow, I have to be up early. There is a cake to decorate. Right now, I'm too blurry to remember if it's for a wedding anniversary or a baby shower but either way, there are people celebrating, and it's my job to make their day a little sweeter. I have to get some rest. Instead, I lie awake, eyes open in the darkness.

Tim stirs and moves closer, breath warm on my neck. 'I love you, Skye,' he murmurs but I don't bother to reply. Shuffling away towards the edge of the bed, I'm thinking about life without him again. Now all those scenarios, they feel comforting if anything, not quite so impossible as they seemed before.

How could Tim tell a lie like that?

Ana

Ana was beginning to dislike Mauro. At first it wasn't because of anything he had said or done – possibly this was him trying to be charming – it was more the effect his appearance had on Carina. He arrived home at cocktail hour and she was there ready with his Aperol spritz. Dishes of snacks had been arranged in the *loggia* and Carina had changed out of loose linen and into pleated Issey Miyake. She seemed different to the woman Ana had eaten lunch with, deferring to Mauro, falling silent if he showed signs of wanting to speak and watching for his reaction whenever she did say something.

'Mauro's family is an important one in this area,' Carina was explaining, adding swiftly, 'Of course, as the town's lawyer, he is very important too.'

'This is why it is difficult for me to retire, you understand,' Mauro said, spritz in one hand, unlit cigarillo in the other. 'Many people rely on my guidance.'

With Ana his manner was mildly flirtatious, in a way that made her wonder what he might be like had his wife not been sitting there.

'You are retired now, yes?' he asked her.

'Well, I ...' Ana still didn't really think of herself as finished with work.

'I am curious. What has made you pack up your life and drive to Italy?'

That question was much easier to answer. 'Everything was changing, so I had to change too.'

'And you are planning to stay here?'

'For a while, at least.'

'I wonder if you will find it, whatever you are looking for,' he mused, waving his cigarillo, expressively. 'What is it exactly? Inner peace, contentment, romance?'

Ana wondered where the gardener might have parked her car after they had returned from lunch. It had been whisked away somewhere out of sight and she had the urge to find it and drive away from this man with his insistent questions, and his wife, fluttering about lighting his cigarillo and pushing a dish of fennel *taralli* biscuits closer to his elbow.

'Who says I'm looking for anything?' she said, leaning to reach one of the baked dough biscuits and biting into it with a crunch.

'Everybody is looking for something.'

Mauro's gaze held hers. His eyes were dark and deep, his hair unnaturally black, his skin clean-shaven and lightly tanned.

'Obviously you are trying to find yourself,' he decided.

It wasn't entirely untrue, but Ana didn't want to admit it.

'Why Italy though? Why not go to an ashram in India or walk the Camino trail?' he wondered.

Carina had disappeared into the kitchen with his empty glass, and Ana heard the pop of a cork as she opened another bottle of Prosecco.

'I suppose I could have done any number of things,' she said, lightly.

'But you came here.' He held the cigarillo between two fingers and smoke curled towards her. 'Just like my wife did all those years ago.'

When she returned with his freshened drink, Ana assumed that Carina would rejoin them, but now there was dinner to prepare.

'Can I help at all?' she asked, hopefully.

Carina was quick to refuse the offer. 'No, no, stay here, enjoy your drink, entertain Mauro.'

Ana would rather not be alone with him. He was the kind of man who assumed every woman found him attractive.

'Expatriate life in Italy is not for the faint-hearted,' he was telling her now. 'I am sure Carina would say the same. You come to a new place but you are still the same person, you know?'

'Yes, I know,' Ana replied.

'Whatever you were carrying with you, you have brought here. It was not packed up and put in storage or given away.'

'I know that too.'

'But Carina and I, we are here for you. Whatever we can do, we will be happy to help. And you must stay with us for as long as you like.'

'That's very kind,' murmured Ana, feeling increasingly trapped.

Dinner was served in the dining room, a light meal thankfully. For most of the time Mauro regaled them with a long story about a legal dispute, two brothers battling over a piece of land, and Carina listened with rapt attention although Ana suspected she may have heard the entire tale before.

Then they moved to the living room to drink a *digestivo*, and he talked some more. Ana's thoughts turned to how she might arrange an escape first thing in the morning.

'Tourism is killing Puglia,' Mauro was saying. 'The crowds on the beaches and in the towns are worse each summer. Where will it end?'

'I suppose it brings income and employment,' said Ana.

'Money is all anyone cares about. What about our way of life? Our traditions?' Mauro's voice was growing louder and he was brandishing another cigarillo.

'Do you really think those things are threatened by foreign visitors?' asked Ana.

'Mauro is right,' put in Carina. 'In the time that I have lived in Puglia, it has changed so much. In some places you barely hear an Italian voice.'

'But you're a foreigner,' Ana couldn't resist pointing out.

Mauro responded, and at length. They were married and she had made every effort to embrace the culture and tradition, she cared about Puglia, she belonged here now.

'It is not that I dislike foreigners. I only worry that, with too many, the real Italy, the very thing they have come here looking for, bit by bit it will be overwhelmed,' he finished, at last.

'Where would you go then, to find the real Italy?' wondered Ana, turning to Carina, hoping to bring her back into the conversation.

Again, it was Mauro who replied. 'This is a good question. Where is the real Italy, untouched, pure? In my opinion there are pockets of it everywhere. Even in those places that tourism is crushing – Venice, the Amalfi Coast. But if I was going to choose a region that has been overlooked by visitors, it would be mountainous and remote, perhaps somewhere like Basilicata.'

He went to the library to fetch a map, placing it on a long, low table and tracing with a finger. Basilicata touched the sole of Italy's boot, a slice of land with two short stretches that faced the sea.

'Here there are towns and villages whose names you won't read in guidebooks, space that is wild and empty, people whose lives don't change. This is a region you should visit if you want to discover a version of our country that is not being tainted by too much tourism,' he told her.

'You really think Puglia is being spoilt?' What Ana had seen of it so far hadn't seemed too bad.

'Not spoilt,' Carina assured her. 'There are still corners that visitors never find and restaurants like the one we ate at today. But it is true, as Mauro says, that some places are becoming crowded.'

'More crowds are coming,' he warned, folding the map and passing it to Ana. 'Go to Basilicata, that is my advice. There you might find what you are looking for.'

'On your advice, that's what I'll do then,' said Ana, lightly. 'Thank you.'

Carina darted a glance at her. 'You will see more of Puglia first? You said that was your plan.'

'My plan isn't fixed; it can always be changed. If Mauro recommends that I check out Basilicata then I might head there in the morning.'

'Tomorrow?' Carina seemed disappointed. 'But I was so looking forward to showing you more of my favourite places.'

Ana thought Carina must be lonely, here on this vast estate by herself every day, struggling with her writing and fretting about her future, while Mauro was off somewhere being self-important. Still, there was nothing to be done about any of that. Ana needed to extricate herself.

'I've had such a lovely day and evening,' she said, with an air of finality. 'It's been so nice having the chance to get to know you better.'

'You're sure I can't persuade you to stay a little longer?' Carina asked.

'We'll stay in touch,' Ana promised. 'I want to hear how

your novel goes and what you decide in the end, a life in New York or Italy.'

Glancing at Mauro's expression, Ana thought it seemed very likely that Carina would be staying right here, in this grand house hidden away in a sea of olive trees. The decision had been made for her.

Early the next morning, driving away from the Mondadori estate, Ana fought the urge to throw the map out of the window. Mauro had insisted that she take it, although it was one of those huge fold-out ones and completely useless when you were driving. Now it was sitting on her passenger seat looking untidy.

At the end of the dirt road there was a choice to make. Turn left towards Basilicata as her host had advised or in the opposite direction. Ana didn't hesitate. She didn't need a man making up her mind.

Heading deeper into Puglia, she swore not to repeat her mistake. From now on Ana would turn down any offers of hospitality, no matter how much she happened to like a person or a place. She was finished with being a house guest.

Travelling from town to town, keeping an eye out, as how awkward would it be to bump into them, it seemed as though Carina and Mauro had taken up residence in her head.

Standing in Polignano a Mare, watching divers hurling themselves from the towering cliffs and into the topaz blue sea below, she wondered what Carina's life might be like if she hadn't fallen in love with a handsome Italian man at least fifteen years her junior. Would she have been freer or lonelier without him? And would she still have written those books?

Who am I, if I'm not a writer? That was the question Carina had asked over lunch. Now Ana applied it to herself. If she no longer had a job, did that actually mean she was retired? Her parents had both died not long after retirement. No wonder Ana resisted that idea.

She found herself thinking about Carina and Mauro more often than she wanted. They came sneaking into her thoughts during moments of quiet reflection. Sitting and drinking iced coffee in a piazza in Lecce, walking beside the sea wall in Gallipoli, eating lunch on a terrace in Ostuni. There they were back again, inside her head, uninvited.

She suspected Mauro had niggled partly because he had a point. What was she hoping to achieve by coming here? And why Italy anyway?

Of course, there had never been any question of yoga and meditation in an Indian ashram. Or walking for miles through Spain in search of spiritual fulfilment. If Mauro had known Ana at all, he would have realised that.

As she circled through Puglia, each new day offered something to delight her. The ornate façade of a baroque building or a simple pasta meal. Her first swim in the sea that was cool and crystal clear. The sight of several generations at a long lunch table, with babies being passed from arm-to-arm and noisy conversation. Clustered conical roofs of trulli houses punctuating the landscape. Church bells ringing for a wedding.

Why not Italy?

The map of Southern Italy was still in her car, cluttering the passenger seat. Ana kept meaning to throw it away. But then she edged over the border into Basilicata to visit the cave houses of Matera. From there it seemed to make sense to keep moving. Not because anyone had told her to. Certainly not following Mauro's instructions. And as she drove further into Basilicata, she left him and Carina behind.

Skye

There is a *froideur* between me and Tim. That's what his mother would have called it as if a French word makes things more sophisticated than two people not speaking to each other unless they really have to. The chilliness continues as the bluebells fade from the woods, as blossom rains from the trees, as the days lengthen and warm. It feels like this is how we live now.

'What's Dad done this time?' Becky wants to know, but I can't talk about it and especially not with her.

'Oh nothing, really,' I say, hoping she'll be so caught up with school work and friends that she won't notice how bad things are and how long it's lasting.

Josh doesn't say anything but he must have noticed too. Tim keeps moping around the house, and hasn't sprung a surprise on us or come up with a crazy plan for ages. Usually when he's falling into one of these lows, I'll do whatever I can to pull him out. I'll cook his favourite foods and coax him to eat properly, make sure he gets some exercise. Now though, I leave him to it. I let him fall.

I'm busy brooding about his lie and the more I think about it, the uglier it seems. That I have cancer. A made-up story for a competition entry. Who would do that?

I hope those Italians are overwhelmed with responses, that

they never get round to reading what Tim said, that the lie gets deleted. But in the meantime, I can hardly bear to look at him. I feel the hurt, a heavy weight in the pit of my stomach, I take it everywhere I go.

During the day I do my best to put myself wherever Tim is not. At night in bed, I can't escape him. That's when he talks, by turns sad, contrite and needy, saying he's sorry, repeating that he loves me, begging to be forgiven. Mostly I pretend to be asleep.

All this is going on as wedding season arrives, my busiest time of the year. Today I'm holding a consultation in the flower-covered bower that on finer days is the perfect backdrop for sugar and love. Fresh samples are arranged beside a folder filled with my designs. The cakes pictured in it are elegant towers in pale shades topped with fresh flowers. That's my style and what I love to make. But increasingly it's not what couples are asking for.

I did the first giant glitter cake, against a soundscape of Meera's complaints, because edible glitter gets everywhere, in your hair, eyebrows, skin; and both of us shimmered for days afterwards. The bride really wanted it, she was a blingy person and I have to say that my finished creation was spectacular. It was Instagrammed by scores of wedding guests and #glitter-cake went viral. Now everyone is demanding an element of sparkle and, much to Meera's dismay, we go through tubs of iridescent dust.

'Is it really edible?' she keeps wondering, and honestly who would know but plenty of people are eating it.

The moment that today's bride and groom step out of their car, I know glitter is what they'll ask for. She's dressed like a Kardashian and her stiletto heels sink into the gravel driveway as she walks towards the conservatory. He seems taken aback by its rustic interior and the table covered in vintage lace doilies.

'We want something really glamorous,' the bride tells me, taking a seat.

'A showstopper,' the groom agrees.

'Our theme is Hollywood glitz.' The bride pulls out her phone to show me an image, and there it is, my original glitter cake. 'We're going to dazzle our guests.'

For a while I tried to steer my couples towards a touch of sparkle, a subtle hint of bling, telling them that they should be the centre of attention, not their cake. But no one ever listens. People love glitter, so that's what I give them.

I notice this bride is tasting only the tiniest slivers of cake. It's not uncommon, actually. She'll be on a diet, to fit some figure-hugging gown, even though she's already quite slender and very lovely. The groom eats more, making appreciative sounds as he tries the coconut lime, and wonders if they might consider a layer of raspberry and white chocolate too.

'Whatever you want, babe,' the bride says, gazing at him.

They sit hand-in-hand, describing their vision. Glitter, glitter, glitter. Everything, from the bridesmaids' fingernails to the tablescapes are to be covered in crystals. I agree that it sounds amazing and make notes about the cake I'm going to create for them.

I used to enjoy spending time with couples at these consultations. My little bower would seem full of hope and love as they tasted samples. Their future might hold any number of disappointments, but no one was looking too far beyond the happiest day of their lives.

Lately consultations make me edgy and I can't wait for the couples to leave. I want to believe their lives will be as perfect as their wedding day but I know that sparkle fades.

'Red velvet cake looks so dramatic when you cut into it,' says the bride, dreamily.

'Why not have a tier of that then,' I suggest, trying to move things along. 'Then the raspberry and white chocolate. And something plainer, like lemon.'

'Is lemon boring?' the bride asks her husband. 'Would we prefer coconut lime?'

'Yes, we would,' he says, decisively.

'Great, that's settled then.' I make a careful note. 'Three large tiers it is.'

'Will you come to the venue and set up the finished cake?' the groom wants to know.

'Either myself or my assistant Meera will be there.' All of the local wedding venues are familiar to me by now. We talk about where the cake will be situated, the stand it is to be displayed on, the knife that will cut it. A wedding means endless little details and this groom seems more engaged in the decisions being made than many. It might be a good sign that he isn't leaving everything to her, or it could be that he is controlling. No one really knows what goes on inside someone else's relationship, do they?

I send them away clutching small boxes packed with more samples of their chosen flavours. There's time to change their minds, I remind, them walking out to their car. They want to be sure this is the right decision.

'Thank you so much.' The bride hugs me goodbye. 'I'm excited that we're going to have one of your fabulous cakes.'

Meera is in the kitchen, looking through the window as the couple drive away.

'Glitter?' she asks.

I nod my head. 'Maximum glitter.'

Meera sighs. 'Will it ever go out of fashion?'

Even the children's birthday cakes, the unicorns and rainbows, have to sparkle nowadays. 'I think we'll be glittery for the foreseeable future,' I tell her.

Meera sighs again. Like me she must be thinking about the clean-up. Wherever there is glitter, there is also a price to pay.

I wonder if maybe it is time to stop doing celebration cakes altogether. It's always been my passion, but they are a huge amount of work. If I gave them up then that would mean all the love and glitter gone in one fell swoop. The idea is so appealing that I suggest it to Meera.

'Would we pick up more café baking instead?' she asks, sounding surprised.

'Hmm maybe.' I haven't thought that far.

'You wouldn't miss it, doing the creative work?'

'A bit, yes,' I admit.

'Because you love it, right? And it would be boring turning out cupcakes and cookies,' she points out.

'We could expand the range. Lemon tarts, doughnuts, and what about macarons?' I say, improvising a plan.

'Is it the cakes you're sick of or the people?' Meera wonders. 'Because I don't mind doing the consultations for a bit if it's any help.'

Sometimes it's like Meera can see what I need way before I realise it.

'Really?' I ask. 'You wouldn't be tempted to tell them all their ideas are boring and unoriginal.'

'Oh, I'll definitely be tempted,' she admits, with a grin.

Meera doesn't smile often but when she does, it changes her face.

'You won't roll your eyes?'

'I will roll them like crazy but not until after they've left.'

'OK then, what if I do the birthday and baby cake consultations, and you do the weddings and anniversaries.'

'Sure,' she agrees.

I wonder what the Kardashian brides are going to make of Meera, with her undercut hair, chunky boots paired with retro

Liberty prints, vibrant tattoos and multiple piercings. They'll probably adore her.

'It's a deal,' I say, instantly cheered. No more happy couples, holding hands and glowing with love. If I don't have to deal with that then I can cope with a surfeit of edible glitter surely?

Ana

Ana had found a use for Mauro's annoying map of Southern Italy. She was plotting her course on it in red biro. As she circled and detoured through the lower regions of Italy, the line zigzagged crazily, like bad abstract art. It amused Ana to look at it.

There were places she didn't bother stopping. Towns that blotted the landscape with unfinished buildings, stretches of Calabrian coastline given over to holiday apartments and amusement parks. The real Italy wasn't always all that beautiful, she noted at times as she was heading south-west.

Looping back, she started to think more seriously about finding somewhere to settle. Ana was tired of the nerve-wrackingly short *autostrada* on-ramps and the speeding drivers. She was tiring of newness too and never knowing what to expect. It was time to find a town where she could have a favourite café for coffee and a usual table at a restaurant, some small place where things were familiar and she might not always be a stranger. If the red line on the map kept wiggling around, that was never going to happen.

She came across a pretty village with a tall white statue of Christ high on the mountain above, and stayed for a while, thinking this might be it, her place in Italy. She loved the sweeping views of the sea and found a restaurant hidden in a back street where the menu was only in Italian. But there were souvenir shops in the piazza alongside overpriced boutiques, and when Ana looked at the adverts for houses in an estate agent's window, her eyes widened at the prices. If this was her place, then she would be living in a cramped apartment with no view to speak of, as it was all she could afford.

There was always the option of selling her home in London to free up some funds but that meant casting herself adrift completely. Ana needed to be sensible.

Settling down for a lazy afternoon on a lounger beside the hotel pool, she stared at her screen, checking out the possibilities. Mostly her searches took her over the same ground as last time but finally she clicked on an article that she hadn't seen before. It was about an English woman who had bought a tiny jasmine-covered house in the Southern Italian town of Montenello for a single euro, and now was married to the mayor and working as a wedding planner. The woman was very attractive, so was her husband and the child they held between them. Ana stared at the photographs of these people and their town and re-read the text more carefully. Things had worked out for them; but they were young.

As soon as the thought crossed her mind, she dismissed it. Ana wasn't afraid of hard work and, perhaps more importantly, thanks to her father, she could plaster a wall or paint a ceiling. It was how the two of them had spent much of their time together, busy on little projects to spruce up the house and keep her mother happy. Always patient and very practical, he had shown her how to hang wallpaper and grout tiles. Once they spent their Easter holiday restoring an old wooden cabinet together.

All those skills, Ana hadn't needed in years, but they must still be there. And as she was picking up a paintbrush or mixing plaster, it might even feel like her father was near, encouraging her in that quiet way he had, saying 'Nice job Ana, well done'.

Looking at the photographs of Montenello, she thought it seemed much the same as any number of mountaintop towns she had passed. One image showed a cluster of stony buildings fighting for space on a rocky outcrop, and another was of a bridal party in front of a fountain. To reach it would send the red ink on Mauro's map scoring straight through Basilicata again. Ana imagined his face as he made it clear that this was where she should have stayed in the first place. Then she dismissed all thoughts of him too.

Ana went to Montenello because it was the closest thing to a plan that she had. She typed the name into Google Maps and followed the directions. By now she knew the wisest course of action was to find a parking space somewhere on the outskirts of a town and continue on foot to the centre in case the roads became pedestrian zones or sent her off into one-way systems.

Montenello though, foxed her. There was a causeway across a ravine and the moment Ana was over it she found herself locked in a labyrinth of winding lanes and heading towards the main piazza as the lanes narrowed, then narrowed again, and her car beeped every time she steered too close to a wall or another vehicle, which was almost all the time. Nothing she had come across online had warned her of this.

'Shit, shit, shit,' Ana muttered under her breath, but there was no going back or even pulling over so she could check the map for alternate routes.

She was moving so slowly that the driver of the car behind kept hooting his horn. Glancing in the rear-view mirror Ana assumed he was a local and was sorry, because this must be frustrating, but she couldn't speed up. The next moment, turning a corner, she glimpsed the piazza ahead, and realised in the same moment that she appeared to be completely stuck.

If she went forwards, then surely Ana would scrape at least one parked car, if she reversed then the corner of a building was waiting, and it was already covered in smudges of paint. The hooting behind grew more insistent and her own car's sensors beeped plaintively, in response.

'Shit,' Ana said, louder this time.

She took a couple of deep breaths and tried to calm herself. But being calmer didn't help Ana to identify a way out. There wasn't even room to open the car door. She wound down the window and peered at the sliver of space between her and disaster, at a loss for what to do.

A man in a doorway was gesturing and yelling something in Italian that Ana didn't understand. Two younger guys on a scaffold started shouting instructions too. Then an older woman joined in, waving a broom in the air to illustrate whatever point she was trying to make. Ana could have cried. None of them were any help.

She edged forwards slowly, trying to ignore all the beeping and hooting, and at one stage might have closed her eyes, bracing herself for the soft crunch of an impact. Instead, a cheer went up. The men on the scaffold were whistling, the man in the doorway clapping his hands, the older woman waved her broom more approvingly; somehow Ana had done it.

As soon as she was in the piazza, she could see that her problems weren't over. Ahead was the fountain she had noticed in the photographs, jets of water arcing prettily in the air. Nearby was a flatbed truck loaded with vegetables, and beside it another vehicle that must have been selling food because the smell of something deep-fried was drifting in through the car window. People were milling about everywhere, queuing at the trucks and gathering round the fountain, and it wasn't even clear where she was supposed to drive. As for finding a parking space, there were no signs to guide her, and as she slowed the powder-blue BMW to a standstill again, the car horn behind her started up again.

'Oh, shut up,' she screamed out of the open window at whoever was hooting, irritated beyond her limits, because what good was all this noise doing. Yelling made Ana feel marginally better and she eased her foot off the brake again. This town had absolutely nothing to recommend it and if she could work out how to navigate her way out of its too-narrow streets, she would escape and never return.

There was an elderly man waving at her, beckoning actually. Ana thought he might have come from one of the tables outside the bar and now he was on his feet and issuing instructions. He was pointing towards a spot near a bench where a couple were enjoying the sunshine. Ana didn't think this was a parking space at all, in fact there were people standing in her way, but he was gesticulating at them with one hand and continuing to beckon her forwards with the other.

'Really?' she said, as the driver behind leant on his horn and the very old man smiled and nodded, and the pedestrians obediently moved. 'OK then.'

Perhaps this old guy would demand money to watch her car. Or he would try to escort her to some tacky souvenir shop. Frankly Ana didn't care. She pulled into the parking space and silenced the engine. Montenello had been a mistake but she needed a break before dicing with more of these roads that seemed to have been built with donkeys in mind rather than cars.

The old man beamed as she stepped out of the car. He was a frail figure with only a few wisps of grey left on his head but he was dressed in a neatly-pressed pink shirt and had a turquoise sweater worn knotted around his shoulders.

'Are you sure parking is allowed here?' asked Ana, in her stiff Italian.

'Of course, of course,' he replied in English.

'Is there a parking meter.' Ana's gaze swept the piazza, but she couldn't see one.

'There is no need, Signora,' he assured her. 'Stay for as long as you like. Perhaps you would like to enjoy a meal in my daughter's trattoria or take a drink in my son's bar.'

So that was it, Ana realised, he was a very elderly tout and stationed here to pull in customers to his family's businesses.

'Thank you but no,' she said.

He wasn't easy to brush off. 'My daughter is an excellent cook, everyone says so.'

'I'm fine,' she insisted.

'You are hungry?'

Ana hesitated. She had skipped breakfast again and now it was well past lunchtime. Also, the trattoria he was trying to usher her towards did look charming. It was small with rough plastered walls covered in bright ceramics and in the doorway leant a woman with salt-and-pepper hair and a plain white apron covering her round body. She shook her head at the old man and he threw his hands in the air.

'*Chiuso*,' the woman said, firmly. 'Closed.'

'No, no!' The old man sounded genuinely outraged.

'*Si, si*,' the woman insisted, and an argument ensued, in Italian and at a rapid pace that Ana couldn't hope to follow.

'Really, it's fine,' she tried to insist, but now the woman seemed to be relenting and the elderly man was beaming again and urging her inside.

There were a few people at the handful of tables, but they looked to be finishing their meals and Ana felt awkward.

'My father likes to help people,' the woman told her in

English, sending her eyes heavenward. 'Sometimes it is easier to do what he wants. And you need to eat, yes?'

'Well, I do, but if you're about to close …'

'No menu, you eat what I cook,' the woman said brusquely, and when Ana nodded, she showed her to a table.

It was one of those restaurants that felt like it might not have changed in decades. From where she was seated near the kitchen, Ana could see into a small space with dented saucepans hanging from hooks and shelves lined with carafes and wine glasses. The woman seemed to be both chef and waitress. She filled a basket with bread and poured red wine into a glass, bringing both to Ana, before returning to her kitchen, and the sound of clattering pans was soon followed by the smell of good things cooking.

In Ana's considerable experience, the very first mouthful of any dish was generally the best. Flavours tended to dull bite by bite and people only kept eating out of hunger or habit. That was why the best chefs served the tiniest portions. They wanted to offer a sensation of taste, a perfect moment, rather than nourish or feed you.

But Ana was properly hungry. She craved a deep bowl of something warm and comforting, and as she breathed the steam from whatever was being simmered, the craving intensified. It smelt like home.

Neither of her parents had been all that interested in food. Her mother was always counting calories and her father too busy to spend much time in the kitchen. Often, their dinners might be beans on toast or something with chips. The exception was Sundays. Her father expected them all to have a meal round the table together and he was the one who cooked. Usually, it was something that had slowly simmered or braised. All afternoon the air in the house would seem almost soupy with the smell of it and Ana would get hungrier and hungrier until the moment they sat down and her father served whatever he had made. A gluey ragu of beef and tomatoes, an oniony stew of chicken and wine, a soup of split peas and smoky pork hock blanketed in grated cheddar cheese. Her father would raise a glass, her mother would complain about the amount of food he expected her to eat, and to Ana every single mouthful always tasted amazing.

This little trattoria took her back there. As she breathed air layered with flavours, tears sprang to her eyes and she wiped them away hurriedly as the woman approached, a bowl in her hand.

It was a pasta dish, flat ribbons uneven enough to have been made by hand and puddled in a tomato sauce so silky and rich that it must have been simmered for hours.

Ana spooned up a little of the sauce, then tried the pasta. She ate very slowly, savouring each bite, which tasted as good as the one before. When she looked up, the woman was watching.

'It's delicious,' said Ana. 'Is it a family recipe?'

'There are no recipes,' the woman replied, then her expression softened a little. 'But yes, I make it the way my nonna taught me.'

If Ana still had *Culinaria* magazine she would have written about this place, an authentic taste of Italy, a hidden gem, and she might have tried to coax a few secrets from the cook. Instead, out of habit, she asked more questions.

'There is no menu at all, not even a blackboard?' she checked.

'If you want to read a menu, go to the hotel,' the woman said, gruffly.

'So, you serve what you feel like cooking, as if we were eating in your home?'

The woman gave a brisk nod of confirmation.

'And you do it all, you have no help?'

'Sometimes I have help. But they leave, they fall in love,

127

have babies. In the end who can you rely on? Only yourself.'

Ana had much the same philosophy. It didn't pay to expect too much of people. Better to be self-contained, to demand more of yourself than you did of others.

'At the moment, I open only for lunch,' the woman told her. 'When there is no food left, I close, so it pays to come early.'

'I was lucky then that you still had enough for me.' A thought occurred to Ana. 'Or have I just eaten your lunch?'

'No problem.' The woman shrugged. 'Usually, my father appears with someone. Today it was you.'

Ana ate a second course – the lemony dark meat of a chicken and a sweet-sour caponata of aubergine and capers – then paid the bill which was scrawled in pencil on a scrap of yellowing paper and very reasonable. Almost reluctant to end what had been a very good lunch, she stood in the doorway for a few moments before stepping out into the piazza. A bridal party was heading towards the fountain and people were parting to let them through, calling out their congratulations, '*Auguri, auguri*', as confetti rained down. At the bar next door, a few men were grouped around an outdoor table, noisily playing cards. In front of her two women stood, baskets over their arms and heads close together, deep in conversation. The sun shone and there was music playing, some Italian tenor, quite possibly Pavarotti.

Ana turned back to the woman, who was now busy cleaning her kitchen. 'Did you say there is a hotel?'

Skye

I'm making a divorce cake. Don't ask me when they became a thing, but it's the third I've done. This one is to be heart-shaped, covered in black fondant icing and fringed with red roses. Meera thinks it's completely ridiculous.

'Why would anyone want a big, fancy cake for their divorce?' she asks.

'Why have a cake for a wedding? If you think about it, that doesn't make much sense either.'

Meera has her phone out and is scrolling already. 'Apparently, it's been going on for ages. It says here that the ancient Romans used to break some sort of scone over the bride's head to sym-bolise her purity.'

'Which makes no sense at all,' I point out.

'In the Middle Ages they got into huge stacks of spiced buns,' she continues. 'Newlyweds would try to kiss over them ... do you think that's even true?'

I'm busy smoothing down dark chocolate ganache with a palette knife, to create a nice smooth base for my fondant.

'It's probably true,' decides Meera. 'People love traditions don't they ... rules to follow ... especially for weddings.'

I happen to know that Meera isn't interested in following rules. She shaves her hair and inks her skin. She works with me instead of getting a university degree like her older sister.

'Rituals can be comforting,' I say, putting the divorce cake in the fridge so that it's nicely set before I start on the fondant icing. 'I think that's the point of them.'

'Did you know that forty-two per cent of marriages end in divorce?' counters Meera, still googling.

'If they all ended in cake as well, that would keep us busy,' I reply.

Meera is shrugging off her apron and removing the hairnet. It's time for her to head off in the van to do deliveries.

'Bring me back some lunch,' I ask. 'One of those asparagus quiches from that little deli in Clifton.'

She gives me a quick sidelong glance. 'Did you hear that someone hurled a brick through the window of the butcher's shop next door to that deli?'

Immediately I'm suspicious. 'Might that someone have been you, by any chance?'

She smiles impishly in response. 'Now why would you think that?'

Animal activism is big with Meera at the moment. She will only eat meat if she's hunted it herself. I'm not sure if she's actually killed anything yet but there's been a lot of talk about it.

'Anyway, I'm avoiding that street for the time being,' she admits. 'So, no asparagus quiche, sorry. I'll bring you back a sourdough loaf from that artisan bakery you like instead.'

When she has gone, I retrieve the divorce cake from the fridge. Working with fondant icing is quite lovely once you have the hang of it. I find it peaceful, meditative even and so when I hear Tim calling my name as I'm about to begin rolling out, I feel a flare of irritation.

'Skye, Skye where are you?'

'Exactly where I always am at this time of day,' I call back.

He comes rushing into the Cakery and skids to a halt.

'Hairnet,' I tell him.

'Yes, yes,' Tim says impatiently, still not bothering to put one on.

'Nobody wants to find one of your hairs stuck to their cake.'

'I've got news,' he says, and I can tell he's bursting with excitement. 'Big news. You're going to want to hear it.'

'Hairnet,' I insist, and Tim sighs, but reaches for one anyway.

'It's the perfect opportunity,' he tells me, tugging it over his unruly curls. 'Exactly what we've been wanting to do. We'd be crazy not to say yes.'

'Say yes to what?'

'You know that bicycle shop up in town, the hipster one that sells all the really cool e-bikes?'

'Bicycle Junction?' I guess. During the period when Tim thought that we all needed e-bikes he spent quite a bit of time in there.

'They're planning to open a little café in the corner of the store,' he explains. 'Great coffee, a few cakes and savouries, very simple. And they'd like us to set up and run it.'

Tim's eyes are shining. It must have given him a boost being asked for help. He used to get these sorts of approaches all the time, but not so much these days.

'What do you think?' he wants to know.

As usual it's going to be my job to provide the reality check. 'Running a café would be a lot of extra work, we'd need to hire more people, manage them, pay wages.'

'It wouldn't be that big a deal,' he insists. 'And no one is suggesting it would be all up to you.'

I don't want a fight, but neither do I want to run a café with Tim. And he isn't in any state to be reasoned with.

'What could go wrong?' He's pacing around, working himself up. 'The space is right there waiting. All we need is a commercial espresso machine; a retro one in a cool colour would be good. We'll pick up furniture second-hand and I know a guy who can make a counter. I'll do a business plan obviously, but I don't see how we can lose.'

Tim is great at starting things, so that wouldn't be the problem. Keeping them going is always the issue. Maybe it will be different this time. A small café might keep him occupied and bring in some income. I tell myself to give him a chance.

'Do a business plan then,' I agree.

'Right yes, I'm on it.' Still wearing the hairnet, he goes haring off, back to his desk. As I return to working on the cake, my head is buzzing with frustration. I've been in this exact same place before with Tim. I've read his business plans and marketing strategies, and the thought of going through it all again is exhausting.

I drape the divorce cake in glossy black fondant icing, trimming and smoothing it carefully, so the finish is flawless. Then I wind a length of black satin ribbon round the bottom and secure it with a pearl-head pin. The client has asked for three words to be handwritten on it in gold. She emailed them to me to be sure I didn't get it wrong. *Freedom, joy, forever.*

I find myself wondering what sort of marriage she is breaking away from. Was he an abusive and cruel man? Or did she simply decide that life would be better without him. *Freedom, joy, forever.* I'll paint the words in careful calligraphy before I add a trim of red roses and three cake sparklers to send out jets of gold when she lights them.

Freedom, joy, forever. Doesn't everyone want that?

I hear Tim's voice again. 'Skye, Skye, Skye, Skye.'

He rushes in and starts jumping up and down on the spot so haphazardly that I'm concerned for the safety of the divorce cake and reach out, trying to stop him.

'Skye, Skye, I did it, finally I did it.'

I'm assuming this has something to do with the café project

we were talking about earlier. 'You spoke to the people at Bicycle Junction?'

'No, no, I won ... the big prize ... it's all ours.'

I stiffen. Everything seems to slow. 'What prize? What have we won?' I ask, even though deep down I already know.

'The wedding in Italy, we won it, they chose us!'

Tim is dancing laps round the room and whooping now, waving his hairnet in the air; I don't think I've ever seen him so happy. Right in the middle of all this, Meera appears. She must have come back for something that she left behind, and standing in the doorway, staring at Tim, her expression moves between confusion and disapproval.

'What's going on?' she asks, eventually.

'One of the competitions; Tim won a prize,' I say, unsteadily.

At my side, he stops dancing and wraps an arm round my waist. 'We've won a dream wedding,' he tells Meera, breathlessly.

She stares at me, eyes widening almost imperceptibly, and I stare back at her.

'Skye and me are getting married.' Tim is pulling me closer. 'We're getting married in Italy.'

For a few moments Meera is very still. Then she gives a long, slow shake of her head and I look back at her, helplessly, not knowing what to say or do.

'Wait till the kids hear we're all going to Italy.' Tim is still fizzing. 'How shall we tell them?'

Meera gives me a final hard look, before turning on her heel and storming out.

Tim hardly seems to notice. 'Let's surprise them with the news this evening. I've got a great idea.'

Then he's on the move again, leaving me alone in the stillness and silence. Perhaps I'm in shock because I don't do anything except stand there, propped against my workbench, head spinning.

Freedom, joy, forever. Words on a cake don't mean anything really. I should know that better than anyone.

Ana

If her lunch in the trattoria had made Ana think that Montenello might deserve a second chance, it was the hotel that convinced her. It was smarter than anything she had expected to find in this hilltop town, with a carved wooden reception desk and a function room glittering with chandeliers and filled with well-dressed people holding flutes of bubbly.

From the moment she stepped through the door, everything went more smoothly. The manager, who sounded Australian, had an air about him that made Ana feel as if nothing she demanded would be too much trouble.

'My car is parked in the piazza,' she explained. 'An Italian man said it would be OK to leave it there but I'd hate for it to be towed away; all my bags are still in it.'

'No worries,' he assured her. 'We'll fetch your bags and provide parking for your car. Just leave me the key and I'll sort it.'

'Thanks so much.' Ana was relieved. 'It was a nightmare driving into town. All the roads are so narrow.'

'Yeah, yeah.' He sounded sympathetic. 'For some reason the navigation systems seem to send people via the most difficult route. When it's time to leave, I'll show you a better way. But hopefully you'll be staying with us for a while.'

'Maybe a couple of nights.' Ana traced the smooth whorls

of the wooden desk with her fingers. It was an extraordinary piece. 'Is there much to do around here?'

'People have weddings.' He nodded towards the packed function room. 'But I think our best-kept secret is our food. We have an amazing *pasticceria* in town, formal dining in our hotel restaurant, a thriving street food scene and an excellent trattoria in the main piazza.'

'Actually, I ate lunch at the trattoria,' Ana told him. 'The very elderly man who parked my car insisted that I should.'

'Ah I think you must have met Augusto then.' He smiled. 'That guy's a character. Anything you want to know about this town, he'll be able to tell you.'

What Ana liked most about the hotel, was that she wouldn't actually be staying in it. The suites were all situated in restored houses dotted about the town to give guests a real sense of being part of the community.

'We're pretty booked up but there's still one little place you can have to yourself,' the man on reception told her.

'Perfect,' Ana decided.

'I'll show you the way; you definitely don't want to drive.'

'If you could just mark it on a map,' suggested Ana.

'I'll do that too, so you can find your way back. I'm Edward by the way. Co-owner of the hotel and general dogsbody.'

Even though it was only a ten-minute walk, Ana was glad to have Edward guiding her through the maze of backstreets, up hidden stairways and down narrow passageways. As they walked, she asked questions. How long had he been living in Montenello? Did he like it?

'We came on the one-euro house scheme,' he told her. 'That's a few years ago now.'

Ana's ears pricked. 'You got a house? So, it's not a scam then? I heard it was.'

'In this town, definitely not,' said Edward, as they were passing a row of unloved buildings, their cracked windows dulled by dust, weeds springing from broken guttering. 'There's a few of us who have decided to make a life here. We all know each other, of course. It's kind of nice.'

'And the locals don't mind?'

'A few might have resisted the change at first but now they can see what it's done for the town.' He gestured back towards the semi-derelict houses. 'A lot of Montenello was in that state when I first arrived.'

'Is the one-euro scheme still running?'

'They keep saying it's finished but the best person to ask is Augusto.'

'You mean the elderly man I met earlier?' Ana confirmed.

'Yeah, if they're going to release any more houses, he'll be the first to hear about it. The whole scheme was his idea in the first place I think.'

Ana fell behind as they reached a steep, narrow flight of steps. Looking upwards had set her head spinning, and she leant into the wall for support. At the top, she steadied herself and drew alongside Edward again.

'Are you looking to buy in Italy?' he asked.

'I'm only flirting with the idea at the moment,' said Ana, unsettled by the moment of dizziness.

He turned and smiled at her. 'That's generally how it starts.'

The house where Ana was to stay was on the upper terrace of the town but any view was obscured by taller buildings tightly tucked around it. Stepping inside, she found pale limewashed walls and a wood-beamed ceiling, a fireplace it would be too warm to use and a deep bathtub she intended to make the most of.

'My husband Gino took charge of the restoration,' Edward

explained. 'He's fanatical about using authentic materials and hiding all technology. The effect is meant to be simple but luxurious.'

Ana glanced around in approval. 'It's really lovely,'

'Yeah, it's just rustic enough and peaceful too. I hope you enjoy your stay here.'

Once he had gone, Ana tested the bed, which was pleasingly firm, and opened all the windows to let in some air. Then she investigated the cupboards, finding a coffee machine and kettle in one, then a larger space where she could stow her bags so they wouldn't spoil the uncluttered look of the room, and a low ottoman filled with books and magazines that may have been left behind by previous guests.

Rifling through, she found an old copy of *Culinaria*. It was a spring issue with a bouquet of feathery fennel and chive fronds on a pale green background and a coverline that promised fresh new season flavours. Ana could remember how long it had taken for the stylist to tease the herbs into exactly that shape and a long debate about the inclusion of sage flowers.

Turning the pages, she found her own face smiling out from the top of the editor's letter. Hair pulled into a severe chignon, bright slash of Ruby Woo lipstick, sharp charcoal jacket. It was like looking at someone she used to know.

Before long, her suitcases arrived as promised, delivered alongside a cloth bag filled with tiny apples with wrinkled russet skins, freshly-ground coffee, paper-wrapped waxy cheese, and hard-crusted bread.

Ana put away the copy of *Culinaria* and closed the ottoman. She thought about making coffee but instead ran a bath, adding a rose petal sachet she found in a cabinet. Stripping off her clothes, she sank into the warm water.

Long afternoon soaks weren't something her past self would have indulged in. Even on weekends she was always too busy ploughing through some sort of to-do list. Now there was no list, only silence and steam scented with rose petals.

The water had almost chilled by the time she climbed out of the bath and towelled herself dry. An apple and a piece of cheese might have sufficed for her evening meal, but Ana decided to head out for a walk and see if she could get a feel for this town. She dressed in loose linen pants and a white broderie-anglaise top, tucking the map Edward had given her into the apple-green Bottega Veneta tote bag that was the last present she had bought for herself before the loss of her regular salary.

Leaving the house, Ana climbed a steep incline towards an old tower that might have offered views over the surrounding countryside except its door was padlocked shut. Continuing along the road as it sloped downwards, she walked into a maze of narrow lanes winding between houses with drying laundry fluttering from balconies, the sounds and smells of people's lives drifting through their unshuttered windows.

Only when every street looked very much like the next, did Ana consult the map, and by then it seemed almost as bewildering as the maze that surrounded her. Uncertain if she could even retrace her steps at this point, she kept on walking.

Somehow, she managed to arrive back in the piazza. Her car had disappeared – presumably someone from the hotel had come to collect it – and there was a different couple sitting on the bench and no bridal party in sight. Still, as Ana glanced around, she was sure she could see some of the same faces she had noticed earlier on.

In a town this size, life must be repetitive, with little to do except mill around and have an afternoon siesta then take a drink in the bar. Days would drift by and time would pass slowly, nothing much would happen, until finally you were like the elderly man who had helped her find a parking spot earlier. Ana spotted him now outside the bar, wearing his turquoise sweater, surrounded by a group that were playing cards, smoking cigarettes and sipping dark liquid out of small glasses. As she stood watching, the old man glanced up in her direction.

'Signora,' he called. 'You enjoyed your lunch?'

'Yes thank you,' Ana called back. 'It was very good.'

'Of course.' His face lit up with a smile. 'But you are here on your own? Please join us.'

'Actually, I was just out for a walk.'

'Take a rest, sit down for a moment, enjoy a drink.' He was on his feet and pulling over a chair from a nearby table, apparently determined.

Usually, Ana didn't have a problem saying no to people. She had used the word, politely but firmly, day after day in her working life. Here in Italy, though, it seemed harder. This man, clutching the chair back for balance, gesturing for her to sit with his other hand, face wreathed in smiles and wrinkles, Ana found herself unable to say no to him.

She sat between a woman with vibrantly red dyed hair and a man with almost no teeth; both of them ancient. With a brief nod in her direction, they continued with the argument they had been having, and Ana tried to follow their rapid Italian but all she understood was something about a wedding.

The friendly man, Augusto, seemed the only one among them who spoke English with any degree of fluency.

'Every night the same discussion,' he told Ana, shouting to be heard from the opposite side of the table. 'They never tire of it.'

'What are they saying?' Ana called back.

'They are talking about the competition,' Augusto explained, and at her blank look he continued. 'To win a dream wedding. It was in an English newspaper, surely you must have seen it?

Teodoro thinks if you give something away for free then no one values it. Giovanni complains it is always him that sweeps up the confetti. Francesco is sick of being asked to move his vegetable truck when they are taking their photographs in the piazza; why should he? And so it goes, even though it doesn't matter what they say because weddings are what we are famous for now, here in Montenello.'

'I thought you were known best for your one-euro houses?'

'In the past, yes, but that is finished now,' Augusto told her. 'Always in life you must be moving forwards, making progress. This is what I tell all my friends, but no one ever listens.'

The red-haired woman raised her voice and drowned him out. She seemed especially impassioned about the point she was making, waving a hand in the face of the man beside her. Was he Francesco or Teodoro, there was no way of knowing, but Ana sat back in her seat, watching and listening, understanding only snatches of the conversation.

Eventually the barman brought out a clean glass and Augusto poured some of the black liquid from a bottle with a colourful label and passed the drink to Ana. It tasted bitter and herbaceous.

'You are here in Italy on holiday?' he called, as the argument lulled a little.

'I'm travelling around, thinking I might find a place to settle down for a while. That's why I was interested in the one-euro house scheme. I was planning to ask at the town hall tomorrow, check whether they are thinking about releasing any more houses.'

Augusto's hand was cupped round his ear and he was frowning. Then he shook his head, emphatically. 'Don't waste your time, Signora. As I told you, it is finished now.'

'It's always worth asking though, isn't it?'

'They will tell you the same thing as I do. If you want a house in Montenello, there are some for sale, but you will need to pay much more than one euro.'

'Perhaps another town then,' said Ana, not prepared to give up.

Augusto nodded, thoughtfully. 'It is true that many have copied our idea. But you must be careful Signora, find out exactly what is expected of you, read the contract carefully, make sure the dream of Italy doesn't turn into a nightmare.'

He sounded genuinely concerned, and Ana was quite touched. 'I'll be careful,' she promised.

'Who knows with those other towns.' He gave an expressive shrug of his bony shoulders. 'This is the only place I can be sure about.'

As dusk settled over the piazza, silvery lights made the water in the fountain sparkle. There was a busker playing his guitar and singing Italian love songs for the queue at the food truck which had lengthened. Whatever was being served, people were taking it away in large paper cones, some sitting on the steps of the fountain and others on the benches that were dotted around.

'This truck, it sells *fritti*,' Augusto said, his eyes following hers. 'Tomorrow there will be one that has pizza. Every day it is different. It is a new thing and very good, although my daughter doesn't think so.'

'Because they're competing for business with her trattoria?' guessed Ana.

'No, because she says the *fritti* are bad for my cholesterol, and the pizza I like has too much cheese, and at my age I shouldn't consume anything that tastes good.' He grinned at her. 'So, what do you say, Signora, shall we have some?'

Ana had been breathing in savoury-scented clouds of air and watching people eat the food that steamed in the cones.

She wondered what it was. Little arancini balls? Tentacles of octopus?

'It will taste very good,' Augusto promised, and again she couldn't seem to say no to him.

The old man had a walking stick, which mainly he seemed to use for pointing things out. Over there was the window of the office in the town hall where he used to work. Over here was where they always put the stage for musicians to perform during the festa that was held every year. That was the way to the house where he used to live before his daughter insisted that he move in with her.

He waved his stick at Ana. 'Don't tell her about the *fritti*.'

'No,' she promised, thinking that a little deep-fried food surely couldn't do him any harm. 'I won't.'

It appeared there was no need for Augusto to queue. He nodded at the man behind the counter who moments later held out two large cones that the people in the long line passed back to him.

'*Fritto misto*,' Augusto sighed happily, his nose almost in the paper cone.

Briefly Ana wondered if her old work wardrobe of tailored charcoal clothes would even fit her anymore. Freed by loose linen, she was skipping fewer meals and could feel an extra kilo or two settling around her middle. But the cone was warm in her hand and she could see the pleasure on the old man's face as he tried a lightly battered morsel.

'*Baccala*,' he told Ana, swallowing a mouthful. 'Salted fish. Try some, try.'

She bit into one of the crisp parcels, hot mozzarella spilling out like lava. A stuffed pumpkin flower, guessed Ana, creamy and salty, tinged with the flavour of sage. The busker was strumming his guitar, singing 'Volare' in a reedy voice. A slight

143

breeze was freshening the evening air. Beside her the old man gave a soft sigh of enjoyment.

'What could be better than this?' he asked Ana.

And she searched her mind, but couldn't come up with a single thing.

Skye

I can't get out of bed, even though when I open my eyes, I can see fingers of light reaching through the curtains. Meera will be here soon and I'm trapped beneath the duvet. It's not that I've slept particularly well, only that I can't seem to move. Beside me, Tim is snoring gently.

As I lie, arms wrapped tightly round my own body, I'm thinking about last night and what I could have done to change the way things played out. This was Tim at his most excited. By the time I'd finished work there was Italian opera playing loudly in the house and pizza warming in the oven. Like me, the kids recognise the signs that a surprise is coming, so they were hyped up too. Instead of struggling to smile as Tim broke the news about us winning the wedding in Italy, I should have spoken up. But I didn't.

It was the joy on the kids' faces, and how Becky talked about the art we would see and the way Josh seemed to know all sorts of random history facts about the Coliseum and the Pantheon.

'We'll be able to visit Rome, won't we?' Becky asked, anxiously.

'Rome is a must-see,' agreed Josh.

And Tim said yes, of course, we'll make it happen and I

didn't contradict him because how could I ruin this for every-one?

The three of them sat round a laptop, researching Rome and its attractions. Tim is one of those people who knows all sorts of random facts about unexpected things and it turns out that he's always been fascinated with the Pantheon.

'No one understands quite how they constructed the dome, it's an architectural miracle,' he explained, as the kids listened rapt. 'And it's about two thousand years old.'

'We have to see it,' breathed Josh.

'I can't believe we're going.' Becky's eyes were shining.

Then Tim insisted that we should all watch *Roman Holiday* and, although I was certain they'd be bored by a black-and-white film from the fifties, everybody seemed to love it. There was hardly any scrolling on their phones and no one suggested looking for something better on Netflix. All of us crammed together on the sofa like we used to when the kids were little, and watched Audrey Hepburn running away from her respon-sibilities to eat gelato on the Spanish Steps, ride a Vespa with Gregory Peck, and have a day of freedom.

Every now and then I glanced away from the screen and at the faces of my family, pale in its flickering light – Tim starting to show signs of age; Josh not quite a man yet; Becky blossoming into such a beauty. I wished I could keep things exactly as they were, hold onto the moment. I didn't want the film to finish.

But then the words 'The End' appeared on the screen, sending Becky to her room and Josh off to make himself a snack. Me and Tim stayed where we were, his arm round my shoulders, both with our feet up on the coffee table. There have been so many nights when we've sat exactly like that. All those years when the kids were little, and we'd put them to bed then have the rest of the evening to ourselves. We'd watch

TV, drink cups of tea and somehow always end up right in the middle of the sofa, close together, a part of me touching a part of him. When did we stop sitting like that? I wished I could remember.

'That's such a lovely film,' I said, not moving from the curve of his arm. 'I'm glad you thought to watch it.'

'And that'll be us soon, running away to eat gelato on the Spanish Steps, seeing all the sights together,' Tim said happily.

In *Roman Holiday* there's a scene where Gregory Peck puts his hand inside a monument called the Mouth of Truth and pretends that it's been bitten off. He's lying to Audrey Hepburn, of course, that's the point of the scene, he's not entirely the good guy he's pretending to be, even if he manages to do the right thing in the end.

Is Tim a good guy? I've always thought so. He has his flaws, like everyone, but all he really wants is for his family to be happy. That's what I care about too, more than anything. I want Becky and Josh to have an amazing trip, and for us to be in Italy together making memories. I want to do the right thing.

My biggest problem is the fact that Tim lied; I can't get my head around how we're going to deal with that and I don't know if I can forgive him.

Those are the thoughts circling around my head as I watch the daylight slowly brighten, and lie beneath the duvet, wishing I could stay there.

Forcing myself up, I throw on the clothes I left on the floor the night before, and head downstairs for a quick coffee, regretting all the wine I drank last night. Now my head aches.

By the time I appear, Meera is already at work in the kitchen setting up for the first bake. Almond croissants and sweet custard brioche for the farm shop up the road, Nutella-stuffed chocolate chunk cookies for one café in town, lemon sprinkle for another. She stares at me as I walk in, but doesn't speak, and I get on with making cookie dough while she rolls croissants, without a word between us.

'Well?' she asks eventually, putting a tray of croissants into the oven.

'Apparently we're going to Italy,' I tell her, and Meera closes the oven door with a disapproving slam.

'That's great then isn't it,' she says, voice loaded with sarcasm.

Everything is so clear-cut for her. She has such strong and certain beliefs. Maybe I was like that at her age, but now life seems more complicated and I hardly know what I think a lot of the time.

'Tim needs me,' I say.

She gives me a hard look. 'Have you ever thought maybe it's you that needs him?'

I consider the idea as, around me, the air fills with the warm, yeasty smell of baking croissants and then dismiss it; aren't I the one who holds everything together?

Meera has retreated back into her silence which is fine because my head is still aching and I don't want to talk any more either. I'm her boss and more than twenty years older than her; how did we ever get to the stage where she thought it was OK to tell me what to do? I suppose it was all those Monday lunches, me confiding in her, even venting about Tim at times, treating her like my best friend, not an employee.

When Meera heads off in the delivery van, I go back to the house to make another coffee and take Tim a croissant for his breakfast. He's sitting on the sofa with his laptop on his knee and I can tell from the way he's jabbing at the keyboard that his excitement hasn't subsided.

'Have a look at this,' he calls. 'I've found the coolest little boutique hotel near Piazza Navona.'

'Tim.' My voice sounds with a note of warning.

'I know what you're going to say, we can't afford it, but we'll find a way.'

Last night I didn't want to argue with him in front of the kids, and I was too drunk and exhausted to start a fight as we were falling into bed. Now though, we need to have that talk.

I give him the almond croissant, wrapped in a paper serviette. 'Actually, that's not what I'm going to say.'

'Oh?' Tim looks up, taking the croissant from me and setting it aside, because he's too hyped up to eat. He barely touched any pizza last night, either.

'How are we going to handle the fact that you lied to win the competition?' I ask him.

'Oh God, you're still furious about that aren't you?' He sounds impatient.

'Yes, I am.'

'It was a strategy,' he tells me, bullish now. 'The reality is sometimes you have to take risks to get the result you want.'

'It wasn't a risk, it was a lie,' I'm trying to make him understand. 'And now you're going to turn me into a liar too. We have to tell them the truth.'

'No,' says Tim. 'Absolutely not.'

'We have no other choice,' I insist.

'Yes, we do, just let me think about it, I'll figure something out.'

I can't imagine how Tim is going to fix this situation. There is the truth and there is a lie; nothing in between.

'Whatever happens we can't jeopardise Italy,' he says. 'It means too much to all of us. Did you see how happy the kids are?'

'Yes,' I say, helplessly, because there's no arguing with that.

'I'm happy too.' Tim stares at me, eyes wide, his gaze holding mine. 'Aren't you?'

'Not about the lie.'

'Stop worrying, it's not your problem, I'll come up with something,' he promises.

I can't stand here getting nowhere with Tim any longer. There's a cupcake tower to make for a christening. A hundred or so cupcakes, frosted in white and covered in silver sprinkles. I need to get on with them. Turning away, I head back to my Cakery.

Usually, I don't struggle to focus on work but today my stomach is churning and the smell of baking sugar makes me feel faintly nauseous. At least it's an easy day and cupcakes are all I need to produce.

The cakes are cooling on a wire rack and I'm mixing up snowy white buttercream, when I start crying. The tears flood down my cheeks and I back away from the bowl in case I contaminate its contents. I'm not a crier. It isn't a useful thing to do and I'm a practical person. But now, if anything, I'm sobbing harder than before and, as my face falls into my hands, it registers that I'm also making an odd noise, a sort of moaning and wailing.

That's when Meera arrives, hurrying in and wrapping her arms round me as I fall onto her shoulder. She smells of cedarwood and magnolia, some natural fragrance she uses. Breathing it in calms me a little and the sobs start to settle.

'What is it, what's happened?' Meera sounds panicked and, holding my shoulders, she stares into my face. 'Was it me? Did I upset you? Shit, I'm sorry. Please don't cry.'

'It's fine, it's fine,' I hiccup.

'No, it isn't, I made you feel bad.' She looks stricken.

'Lots of stuff is making me feel bad right now. It's not your fault.'

'Ignore me,' she says, squeezing my shoulder. 'You do what you've got to do, OK?'

I take a deep breath. 'What I need to do is frost a hundred cupcakes and pack them into boxes.'

'I'll handle it,' says Meera.

'Then I have to drive them to the venue, put them in paper lace wrappers and stack them on the tower.'

'I'll look after that too. Why don't you get into the garden for a bit or take the dog for a walk?'

'Actually, you know what, I've got some tax stuff to sort.'

'Argh Skye.' She gives a groan of frustration. 'I'm trying not to be bossy, but you're making it really difficult.'

I find myself smiling blearily at the expression on Meera's face. 'Maybe I'm just a hopeless case.'

'No, you're fantastic, kind, strong, always looking out for everyone, you're just not that nice to yourself sometimes.'

Now the tears are coming again. Impatiently, I wipe them away.

'The sun is shining,' Meera tells me. 'Take a break, you deserve it.'

Walking through the woods with my greyhound, who seems pleased by this unexpected outing, it's good to be surrounded by greenery. I try to think more calmly about the problem that I'm facing. When Tim gets us into situations, generally it's me who gets us out of them. There's always a solution in the end.

At Abbot's Pool I stop and sit on the rocks, looking out at the still water, stroking Happy who is lying beside me. I think about a lot of things, including what my mother said the day I told her that I was serious about Tim.

'Your life is going to be interesting then.' Her words were accompanied by raised eyebrows.

'I hope so,' I replied, confident that an interesting life was what I wanted.

What Mum must have realised is that never knowing what

to expect is much less fun when you get older. Sometimes my friends will complain about husbands who are boring and stuck in a rut. They always want to do the same things, holiday in the same places, eat the same meals. These days boring seems a safer and easier option to me, and I struggle to sympathise. Boring means you sleep better at night.

Giving my dog one last pat, I climb to my feet and set off again. The ground is drying out now that summer has arrived, although it's still muddy and slippery in places, and I'm walking carefully as I'm thinking.

I have so many good things; if I could focus on that then I might stop worrying. I have two amazing kids and, for now at least, I also have Meera who knows that the cupcakes need to go into specially designed boxes and will be careful not to drop them. Lots of people don't have anyone they can rely on.

I hope Meera and I are still friends in twenty years' time, because it will be interesting to see the woman she becomes. Will she still be hurling bricks through the windows of butchers' shops? Will she have regrets about inking and piercing so many parts of her body? Will she be married to a man or a woman? Even though I know her well, it's impossible to say.

As I'm thinking about Meera, I realise that she knows me well too. What she said, earlier, was spot on. This whole business with Tim, with Italy and the wedding, even the lie ... I'm going to do what I have to do.

Ana

Ana's sense of wellbeing was still intact the next morning when she woke in Montenello. Propped up on pillows in bed, sipping her first coffee of the day, she smiled at the thought of her impromptu dinner of street food with Augusto. He was a character, that was for sure. Ana's smile faded a little as she remembered her empty, grease-spattered paper cone. She would have to skip more meals and take longer walks; loose linen was only so forgiving.

She completed her routine of morning stretches thinking about the day ahead. First, a stroll back to the piazza, trying to retrace her steps from the night before to see if she could shake off the feeling of disorientation this town seemed to give her. Then a visit to the town hall to make enquiries about one-euro houses. Not that Ana was convinced that she wanted to settle here, but it was worth considering all opportunities.

Any place she bought would need to have a view. Space and light were important. Also, Ana didn't want to feel hemmed in by neighbours so it would be nice if there was a little land, although definitely not a vast estate that she would struggle to maintain.

After she had showered, she couldn't find a hairdryer, so had to let her hair air-dry into loose ringlets. There seemed to be no iron either and the white cotton shirtwaister dress that Ana put on was creased. She matched it with some now-scuffed silver Veja trainers. Once she had checked all the essentials were in her Bottega Veneta bag – sunscreen, packet of tissues, paper face mask just in case, phone of course – she skipped applying lipstick and stepped out into the sunny day, without needing a glance in the mirror to know she didn't look her best. Nobody here would notice or care, still Ana missed the feeling of being properly put together.

Walking up towards the tower, she noticed its heavy wooden door seemed slightly ajar and at first assumed it must be a trick of the light. As she drew closer, Ana realised someone must have smashed off the padlock.

Grasping the rusted metal handle, she pushed the door and it opened with a creak. In the dim light, she could make out a stone spiral staircase winding temptingly upwards. Could it hurt to climb it? This was probably private property, but Ana wanted to find a lookout point to get a real sense of how Montenello fitted into the surrounding landscape and the tower seemed her best option. Glancing back over her shoulder, not seeing anyone else around, she slipped inside.

The space smelt musty and the steps were uneven. In places the handrail was missing and, as she edged upwards in the half-light, her footsteps echoed. Hadn't her sister told her to have an adventure? Ana wondered if this counted.

At the top, she stepped onto the ramparts and was rewarded with the view she had been hoping for. Over the low parapet she saw a valley criss-crossed by roads and beyond it blue-grey hills set against a wide sky. This must have been a watchtower during the years when Montenello's citizens had to guard against marauding bandits. Seeing a patch of stone scorched black by fire, along with discarded cigarette stubs and a collection of dented old beer cans, Ana guessed that now it was used by young people who came to party.

It was breezy enough to make her eyes water and she was chilly in her light cotton dress. As she tilted her head upwards to look at the sky, she experienced another dizzy spell, like the one she'd had the day before. It was disconcerting and she stepped back from the parapet, suddenly aware of the danger and less interested in the view.

Carefully navigating the steps downwards, and leaving the door as she had found it, Ana walked through streets she couldn't be sure if she remembered. Perhaps all roads led to the piazza because eventually it was where she found herself again. The town hall lay at one end, a grand building, two storeys high with a row of flags flying from a balcony and the word *Municipio* carved into the stone above the entranceway. Trying the door, she found it locked, so Ana decided to wait in the bar and have another coffee.

The entire piazza was deserted, a breeze whipping across it, ruffling the water jets of the fountain and eddying through pools of confetti still not swept up from the day before. Inside the bar, the waiter was chatting to the cook from the trattoria, who was smoking a cigarette, which surely was against the law indoors. Ana ordered a caffè macchiato, with a splash of foamy milk, and sat as far away as possible from the curls of cigarette smoke, checking her phone for emails and casting an eye over the day's news headlines. From her seat she could see through a window towards the entrance of the town hall which still appeared to be closed. She was getting impatient. What time did people start work in this town?

Finally, a scruffy-looking man arrived, unlocked the door and went inside. Ana wondered if there was a back entrance that other staff used or if he was the only worker in there because, if so, she may as well have another coffee, and three was her limit for the day.

As she was considering it, Augusto appeared. He was accompanied by a younger man whose face seemed familiar although she couldn't possibly have met him before.

'Buongiorno Signora,' Augusto greeted her, as he approached the table. 'I am glad to find you here this morning. You must meet my very good friend, Salvio Valentini, the mayor of our town.'

Now Ana realised why she recognised this man. Hadn't his photograph accompanied an article she had read about the one-euro houses? He was relatively young and very good-looking and, as he shook her hand, offered a charming smile.

'Welcome to Montenello, I hope you are enjoying your visit. Are you here with friends?' the mayor asked.

This was a stroke of luck, thought Ana. No need to queue at the town hall and talk to some lowly official who might not know what was going on. Here was the man in charge.

'Actually, I'm alone. I was just going to have another coffee. I'd love to hear about your town. Would you join me?'

The younger man glanced at the older one, who nodded and smiled. 'Of course.'

Settling down seemed quite a procedure, Augusto taking off his sweater and knotting it round his shoulders, the mayor removing his suit jacket and hanging it over the back of his chair, both of them putting their phones on the table and checking for messages before turning their attention back to Ana.

'Augusto and I meet to drink a coffee together most mornings,' the mayor explained. 'He worked for the *comune* for many years and has been an important part of the changes we have made to this town, eh my friend?'

The old man smiled in agreement. 'Of course.'

'Do you mean the one-euro house scheme?' Ana seized her

chance to introduce the topic. 'I was reading about that. It sounds like a great success.'

'Indeed,' agreed the mayor. 'That was the beginning of a new era for this town.'

He started to talk about Montenello's revival. The tourists who had come, the destination weddings business that his wife now ran, the festa they held every year, the dream wedding competition that he was sure she must have heard about. He talked on and on as Ana listened politely, waiting for her moment.

'Is there any likelihood of more one-euro houses becoming available?' she managed to ask, as he reached the end of his monologue.

The mayor shook his head, then immediately shrugged his shoulders. Ana wasn't sure whether this was meant to convey a 'no' or a 'maybe'.

'I've noticed a few places that still look abandoned,' she added.

'Unfortunately, yes, especially in the upper parts of the town,' he agreed. 'But every house has a different story. Perhaps the owner wants to keep a connection with Montenello, they hope to come back some day or believe their building is worth much more. So, they pay their taxes and they keep it.'

'The scheme is finished then?' checked Ana.

'For now, at least.'

'I was hoping for a place with a view and a garden. Could you suggest anywhere else I might try?'

The two men exchanged a glance, then they both shrugged.

'Should I try in the north maybe? Or what about Sicily?' Ana persisted.

'Who can say,' the mayor replied.

Glancing at her, Augusto frowned then held up a finger. 'There must be a way to help you, Signora. Wait, I am thinking.'

He froze, finger still aloft, deep in concentration for a few moments. Then he threw up both his hands, excitedly. 'Of course, of course. The Di Goldi *masseria*. How long has it been for sale? Many years surely. A good price could be negotiated.'

The mayor seemed unconvinced. 'Isn't it over twenty kilometres away?'

'It has a view,' Augusto reminded him.

'Won't it be in a very bad state of repair?' the mayor countered.

'It is magnificent.' Augusto was undeterred. 'But wait, I will show you.'

He picked up his smartphone and holding it close to his face, gave a dazzling smile. Watching him, the mayor's lips twitched.

'This is the expression he has to make for his new phone to recognise him,' he explained to Ana. 'Augusto always likes to have the latest *telefonino*. He stays up-to-date.'

'Of course,' the old man said, shuffling his chair closer so Ana could see his screen. 'Now this *masseria* belongs to the Di Goldi family who used to be rich and important until there was some problem, gambling maybe, and now the money is gone and the *masseria* is empty.'

Ana squinted at the photograph he was showing her. There was a tower not unlike the one she had just climbed. It had ramparts at the top, and beneath it was a cluster of lower buildings, all the same pale honey-coloured stone.

'It looks huge,' she said, as Augusto's shaky finger flicked across the screen and the image was replaced with an interior shot of a room with an arched ceiling and mottled whitewashed walls.

'See the view, Signora.' Augusto's finger was flicking again, revealing to Ana that the *masseria* was set on a slope with a grove of trees beneath it.

'Do not even think about this place, Signora.' The mayor sounded certain. 'It is too large and I am sure very rundown because no one has lived in it for a long time.'

Ana gave him a sideways glance. When she had asked this man for advice, he hadn't been prepared to give it. Now apparently, he was full of opinions.

'I might contact the estate agent anyway,' she said, mostly to be contrary. 'See if I can go and take a look tomorrow on my way out of town.'

'You are leaving?' Augusto sounded surprised. 'But you have only just arrived. Where are you going?'

'I'm not sure,' admitted Ana. 'I'll possibly head north.'

'Wait.' He held up his finger once more. 'I am thinking again. An idea is coming.'

She and the mayor both watched as his face reflected his thinking process, first the effort he was making then excitement.

'Of course! We must go together today to take a look at the Di Goldi *masseria*. Then we can eat lunch at a restaurant that is owned by the mayor's mother. It is very, very ...' His eyes flicked towards the woman still sitting at her table in the far corner and smoking another cigarette. 'It is almost as good as my daughter's trattoria.'

'I wasn't planning on driving anywhere today,' Ana told him.

Augusto's face fell. 'And I cannot drive us. They say I am too old and don't see well enough these days. It is difficult for me to go anywhere at all.'

'I'll take you for a ride at the weekend,' the mayor promised.

Augusto rallied, smiling again. 'You are good to me Salvio.'

'But right now, I must go to work or I will be late for a meeting.' The mayor stood, removing his jacket from the chair back and putting it on, picking up his laptop bag, tucking his phone in his pocket. 'It was good to meet you, Signora. I hope that your travels in Italy go well.'

As he left, the waiter came over with a plate of plain pastries and Augusto took one, wrapped the end of it in a paper serviette, and stared at it dolefully.

'I will stay here for the day,' he said. 'My friends will arrive and we will have the same conversation we had yesterday. And you Signora, what are you busy with?'

Ana hadn't thought beyond the visit to the town hall that she didn't need to make anymore because apparently it would be a waste of time. 'I'm not sure.' She felt sorry for Augusto stuck in this bar day after day, which she suspected was what he intended. 'I suppose we could go for a drive, but I don't actually know where they've taken my car.'

'If I call the hotel, they will send someone with it.' He looked at her, hopefully. 'Yes?'

A drive in the countryside would be fine and she might not want to live in an abandoned *masseria* but still Ana was curious enough to take a look inside. 'OK,' she agreed.

Before long she saw her car pull up outside and, with the engine running and the hazard lights blinking, a young woman climbed out, waved at Augusto through the window, and walked away. Ana didn't like the idea of leaving her car out there with the keys in the ignition but it seemed impossible to hurry Augusto. He had to finish his pastry and use the bathroom. Then his daughter insisted he put on his sweater and they bickered about it until he agreed. The waiter retrieved his walking stick, warning him not to go too far and overdo it, and they both insisted on taking Ana's phone number, the cook scrawling it in a notebook she took from her pocket, the waiter putting it into his own phone.

Finally, they were outside and Augusto turned to her. 'What

you must realise, Signora, is that, once you are older, everyone that you love starts to treat you like a child.'

Following his directions, Ana drove a ribbon of road that wound its way around the outside of the town, a far less alarming route than the one she had taken when she arrived. Then they were crossing the causeway and reaching a wider, straighter highway and after that the driving was relatively easy.

'Shall we listen to some music, Signora? What do you like?' Augusto was holding his smartphone and smiling at the screen again. 'My nephew showed me how to make the music I have on my phone play on the car stereo. Let me see if I can remember. No, that is wrong, *uno momento*, I will try this ... and this ... *eccolo!*'

Ana had been expecting some Italian classic, instead a track by the Rolling Stones blared and he turned up the volume.

'You like this?' Augusto raised his voice. 'I have lots more music, if you prefer something else.'

'This is fine,' Ana shouted back.

By the time they pulled up outside the gates of the Di Goldi *masseria*, they were listening to Bruce Springsteen, louder than Ana might have liked but the elderly man was probably a bit deaf and he seemed to be enjoying himself.

The gates were impressive, tall and made of decoratively twisted metal, but the walls either side were crumbling. Beyond them Ana could see a gentle slope covered in trees and the tower of the *masseria* rising above them.

'Should we have contacted the estate agent?' she asked Augusto, who was unbuckling his seatbelt. 'Let someone know we're here?'

'Why?'

'Won't we need a key?'

'Who is going to bother locking the place when there is nothing inside?' asked Augusto.

As he had promised, the gates were easily opened and, driving up towards the farmhouse, Ana thought the olive grove seemed well-tended. The *masseria* though looked abandoned, its windows shuttered and weeds springing up between the flagstones of the courtyard where she parked.

Still, she could imagine the place when it was full of people, the parties they must have held in this courtyard, with long tables set beneath the trees and candles flickering and music playing. What a shame it had been abandoned.

'Shall we take a look inside?' asked Augusto, opening the front door which was unlocked as he had promised.

'Of course,' Ana replied, and stepping inside the dim, empty space, her head was filled with possibilities.

Skye

I'm on my way to a wedding reception. It's a showy affair, in a marquee pitched at a country venue about half an hour away. I'm delivering the cake and even though my van is kitted out with special racks, foam mats and insulated cool boxes, I'm driving very carefully. Disasters happen, but not to me and Meera, and I don't want that to change.

Meera has been really great lately, taking care of all the bridal commitments. She offered to miss her animation workshop today but I couldn't let her. Of all the weddings though, I wish I wasn't stuck with this one. The order is for a towering cake and the venue has poor access, so I'm going to have to stack the tiers once I'm there, when I'd prefer to get in and out as fast as possible. The less I have to do with weddings the better. I don't even want to think about them.

The venue is a hive of activity. A catering team is busy and a string quartet is tuning up their instruments. Soon 150 people will be partying here but for now everything looks perfect, tulle on chair backs, flower arrangements on tables, fairy lights strung up ready for when dusk falls.

Several people greet me as I appear, carrying the first cake box, but nobody offers to help, because they know I'd rather they didn't. The only one I trust aside from myself is Meera. Weddings are high stakes. Everything has to be perfect.

Soon I'll be getting married.

I try to push the thought out of my mind, as I head towards a table that's been set aside for my cake. There are more boxes to ferry in from the car as well as a cooler bag full of white roses. Then I have to unpack each tier, position it carefully, wind ribbon, arrange flowers.

I'm getting married.

I feel like I'm on a bus that's careening past the stops and refusing to let me off. There seems to be nothing I can do to change the course we're on. While I'm busy working, it's easier not to think about it. But at night, when I wake at 3 a.m., I feel chilled by the idea of standing beside Tim, holding a bridal bouquet. And here in the marquee, surrounded by all things wedding, I have to steel myself.

'Hello Skye, how are you?'

I glance up and see Chrissie, the venue manager. She and I were part of the same crowd, back when I first met Tim, and although we don't catch up very often, I still think of her as a friend.

'I'm fine, what about you?' I ask.

'Oh, you know, stressed, exhausted, the usual. This bride has been a total ...' Chrissie mouths the word, then adds unnecessarily, 'a total you-know-what. I'll be glad when the day is over.'

'I don't know how you do it,' I say, wishing she hadn't chosen right this moment to come over, because I'm about to start stacking the tiers.

'Hey, I heard that you and Tim are getting married. After all this time ... congratulations.'

Tim must have told every single person he's ever known. Wherever I go I'm congratulated by someone.

'You won a dream wedding, right?' says Chrissie. 'Amazing.'

'In Italy,' I tell her. 'The kids are coming, so it's more of a family holiday really. The wedding's not a huge deal.'

'No five-tier cake for you then?' she asks.

'No string quartet,' I tell her.

'Not even a firework display? What sort of wedding is it?'

'A very small one,' I say. 'No fuss at all. I definitely won't be a you-know-what of a bride.'

'Yes, you say that now but they're all fine at first. It's as the big day gets closer that people tend to turn.'

'Mine is not going to be a big day,' I say, firmly.

'The kids must be excited.'

'Beside themselves,' I agree. 'They haven't had a proper holiday in years.'

One of the catering team approaches, with some problem that she needs Chrissie to fix. I'm relieved, because I need to focus on finishing the cake and making my escape.

'We'll have to catch up for a wine some time,' says Chrissie. 'Then you can tell me all about your wedding plans.'

'Lovely, yes, see you soon,' I call, as she heads away.

I'm getting married and I really don't want to.

I keep telling myself it won't change anything, but of course it's bound to. If getting married didn't matter then people wouldn't keep on doing it. All this fuss with cakes, frocks and flowers, it's about binding couples closer, declaring to the world that they belong together.

Once the cake is finished it looks spectacular and I take a few photographs for Meera to use on the website, before packing up. Hopefully the you-know-what bride will be satisfied and I won't end up getting cake-shamed on social media.

Back in the van I sit for a few moments. Then I start the engine and drive home. I'm planning to spend the rest of the day walking the dog and pottering in the garden. Tim won't be around. He's trying to earn some cash to cover any extra expenses of our trip to Italy. This wedding isn't really for me, it's for him and the kids, that's what I keep telling myself. We all need a holiday and now we're getting one, with a party thrown in.

I'm doing what I've got to do.

When I get home I find Becky at the kitchen table, doing homework on her laptop. I can tell by the set of her shoulders that it's a subject she doesn't like, maths or one of the sciences, and she uses my arrival as an excuse to take a break.

'Mum come over here and sit down. We need to finalise our wedding gowns.' Becky says those last words in a singsong voice and does a chair dance. She's never had a proper gown before.

'I was going to take Happy for a walk,' I tell her. 'Can't it wait?'

'They need to know today,' Becky insists.

We are picking out gowns from an Italian designer's capsule collection and have been discussing it for days because Becky doesn't agree with my choice.

'Not the one with the long sleeves, Mum,' she reminds me, opening the designer's website. 'You've got great arms and shoulders; why not show them off?'

'Not the strapless dress either though,' I say, settling down beside her. 'It's too young for me.'

'It has to be this then.' Becky clicks on a frock and we examine it from all angles. It's creamy white, with long lace sleeves and a high neckline.

'Yes OK, that one,' I agree, wanting the decision to be made.

'I know you don't care about clothes Mum, but you need to be sure. Are you?'

'Absolutely.'

'You don't seem very excited,' says Becky, looking at me, eyes narrowed.

'I am. This is me excited.'

Becky smiles at that. 'I suppose if both my parents got as worked up as Dad does, then I'd be in trouble.'

Lately Tim has been on such a high that he's exhausting to live with. Fortunately, between doing extra shifts at the pub and some new job he seems to have picked up, he's not at home very often.

'There's not as much choice for the guys,' I observe. 'A suit is a suit.'

'Dad's planning something different though,' Becky tells me.

Of course, he is. Maybe it's going to be a kilt in a bold plaid or a jaunty waistcoat, anything to make him the centre of attention.

Becky has turned to bridesmaid's gowns. She knows which design she prefers, but can't decide on the colour. Hot pink or coppery gold? We've already spent a lot of time considering the two options and now, as we get into it again, I try to enjoy this mother-daughter moment.

'I like the hot pink,' I say, leaning in.

'Me too, but if I wore the coppery one then I could dye my hair red to match yours. Wouldn't that look cool?'

'Don't dye your hair,' I tell her. 'Your natural shade is lovely.'

'Do you think?' Becky pushes her fingers through her glossy brown curls.

'Not the copper dress,' I tell her.

'But it's an autumn wedding.'

'Wear the pink.'

Next, we have to take our measurements. They've sent us a list of the designer's requirements and Becky follows it carefully, holding the tape round my waist and hips, then checking how long the fall of the gown will need to be and noting everything down.

I start doing the same for her, taking a few seconds to admire the perfection of my daughter's figure and thinking how good she will look in a hot pink bridesmaid's dress with a ruffled hemline.

'I still can't believe we're going to Italy,' Becky says, as I'm winding the tape round her waist. 'I won't believe it's real till I'm there.'

I'm doing the right thing, really, I am.

Becky appears to have forgotten about her homework. Once we've finished with the measurements, she starts talking about making an appointment with a local hairdresser, to trial some different looks.

'You might want an up-do,' she explains. 'Or there's this style called a half-up that's meant to be great when you have curly hair. Hold on, I'll show you.'

She's tapping on her laptop, showing me different options. Then she starts fretting about pedicures and manicures, and where we should have them. Definitely not in Rome as it would waste a morning when we could be seeing the Sistine Chapel, but there doesn't seem to be a nail salon in Montenello.

'Since when are we into all this girly stuff?' I ask.

'Mum seriously?' Becky rolls her eyes, theatrically. 'We've got to be well groomed.'

'Do we though?'

'Yes! We have to look good in the pictures. Who knows where they'll end up being used.'

'What do you mean?' I genuinely haven't given any thought at all to the wedding photographs.

'They'll appear on social media and in marketing campaigns,' points out Becky. 'That's the whole reason why they're giving away a wedding, right? It's a promotion, to try and encourage more bookings.'

Simultaneously I realise that my daughter is right and I'm a total idiot. Of course, Tim will have signed over permission to use our images. And what about our story, the fake one, the lie he told? Will that become marketing content? I shiver a little and hunch my shoulders.

'Are you OK, Mum?' asks Becky.

'Just a bit cold,' I tell her.

'It's not cold. This is summer.'

Outside in the garden the hollyhocks are towering and the roses are in bloom. Soon the first of the dahlias will show their faces. I love summer but it never lasts long enough. Autumn is always here before I know it.

'I need to get out for a walk,' I tell Becky. 'Will you email over all the details they need?'

'I'll take care of it,' she promises.

I should probably double-check that everything seems accurate. But I don't care if my gown is too tight or the wrong length. All I can think about are the worries racing though my head.

How am I going to do this?

I find my greyhound asleep on the sofa and coax him out for a walk. Heading along familiar paths, taking deep breaths of woodland air warmed by early summer sunshine, I'm in a complete fury with Tim. I tug the lead impatiently whenever Happy stops to sniff something, because I have to keep moving, and use up some of my tense, restless energy as I think about what I'm going to say to my husband the next time I set eyes on him.

Tim won't be home until much later, as he's working a

double shift at the pub. He'll expect me to be in bed by then, I imagine. And it strikes me that, while I've been feeling pleased that he's not been around much, maybe Tim has been just as keen to avoid me.

Ana

The moment that Ana stepped inside the *masseria*, she started dreaming about living there. Paint peeled from the walls, plaster was crumbling, but the fact its grandeur was so faded seemed to make it more magical. When she flung open the shutters, light poured in revealing cobwebbed ceilings, mounds of dead flies and mouse droppings, but Ana could picture the place with all of that swept away. This house needed to be rescued.

Augusto called out from another room and she was enchanted to find it floored with decorative tiles worn down from perhaps a couple of centuries of feet passing over them and a ceiling covered in pale frescoes. Always a few steps ahead, next he came across a chamber still hung with three massive wrought iron chandeliers. And it was him that encouraged her to climb the stairs leading up to the tower.

'Do you think they're safe?' asked Ana, doubtfully.

'Of course,' he replied. 'But you go, I will stay here.'

And so, she investigated, deciding that the stairs seemed sturdy enough, but not relying on the handrail which no longer seemed properly attached to the bare stone wall.

This could be a study, she thought, reaching a second storey room with views for miles and miles. Ana pictured herself in there, sitting at a vintage wooden desk and working on something, taking inspiration from her surroundings. Or it could be a bedroom, although there didn't seem to be a bathroom up there so that was a problem.

All of the bathrooms were problems. Downstairs, there were three of them, but the water must have been turned off ages ago and each had a distinctive and unpleasant smell. In the kitchen a few pieces of furniture had been left behind, a huge dresser and a heavy marble-topped table, and there was an enamel cooking range that might still work but badly needed cleaning.

'Did you ever visit when the Di Goldi family were here?' she asked Augusto.

'If I did then I don't remember,' he replied. 'And surely I would remember a place like this.'

Could she live here? Ana couldn't help considering the possibility. In her head she was already arranging furniture, overstuffed sofas and antique cabinetry. Houses like these were often fairly cheap to buy, because the cost of maintaining them was high. This one had good bones, plenty of character, a beautiful location. And it had something else that Ana hadn't known she was looking for; splendour.

'What about the olive groves?' she wondered. 'Do they come with the house?'

'They will be leased out to a farmer, almost certainly,' Augusto replied. 'This is good land.'

Some of the outer buildings must have been storage barns or places where animals were kept. There were no windows, only arched open entranceways and the floors were flagged with stone. Passing through these cavernous, empty spaces, Ana's head filled with ideas for them.

'A lot of work would need to be done,' she observed. 'Just to make it habitable.'

'Of course,' Augusto agreed.

Ana was never going to live here. It would hardly be sensible. And she had always been a person who made sensible choices.

'The plumbing would have to be checked. And is there even any heating?' she wondered.

They were on the point of leaving when a flatbed truck rattled into the courtyard and a burly man climbed out. He and Augusto launched into a long conversation, speaking in a dialect that Ana couldn't understand, and she tried to contain her impatience, waiting for them to finish. Occasionally it seemed like they were on the point of saying goodbye, then something would occur to one of them, and off they would go again; talking rapidly, hands waving in the air.

At last Augusto started shuffling towards the car. Thinking he seemed tired, Ana suggested they should drive directly back to Montenello, rather than stopping for lunch as planned. But Augusto wouldn't hear of it, assuring her that all he needed was a short rest and he would be fine.

He supervised the typing of the restaurant's address into Ana's phone, then instructed her to wake him if she got lost, before closing his eyes. He seemed asleep by the time she pulled out of the gates. Listening to his deep, even breaths, she wondered how old Augusto was. In his eighties, or possibly even his next decade? And what was she doing driving around the southern Italian countryside with him? Ana wasn't quite sure how it had happened.

Nearing the restaurant, she might have been confused by the dusty lanes cross-hatching fields of red earth and rows of olive trees, but by then there were signposts to follow, hand-painted onto splintering wood, hammered onto gate posts and fastened to walls – *Ristorante di Donna Carmela*. A short stretch further on, she found the narrow gateway of the restaurant.

Augusto's eyes fluttered open as she pulled into a car parking area. 'We are here?'

'Are you OK?' checked Ana.

'This is what my daughter asks me a hundred times a day.' He sounded irritable, perhaps because he had just woken. 'Of course, I am OK. Why wouldn't I be?'

Ana looked around. Ahead was a large stone barn, its walls ablaze with bougainvillea, and a garden of prickly pears. Surrounding it, olive groves stretched to the horizon.

'Should we have made a reservation?' she wondered, noticing that the car park was almost full.

Augusto seemed not to have heard. He climbed out of the car and, as he made slow progress towards the barn, Ana kept a careful eye on him, so wasn't aware of the woman until she was right beside them and sweeping the elderly man into an embrace. She was tiny, with long silvering hair, glowing olive skin and thick gold hoops in her ears. Leading Augusto onwards, she talked excitedly to him in Italian, glancing back to smile at Ana as if she were an afterthought.

The barn was laid out as a dining room. Almost every table was taken and it was noisy. Holding onto Augusto's arm, the silvery-haired woman ushered them through and out into a garden where she showed them to a small table set beneath a striped awning. One waitress was summoned to bring an extra cushion, another to supply iced water and menus. The woman whirled away again.

'That is Donna Carmela,' said Augusto, as she disappeared. 'She is the mother of our mayor; did I tell you that?'

'I think you did,' said Ana.

'Sometimes I forget things,' he admitted.

Ana had been marvelling at how sharp his mind seemed to be and hoping hers would be the same if she ever reached that age.

'All of us forget things,' she reassured him.

'But here is an example,' continued Augusto, after taking a sip of water. 'I cannot remember if I told you what the olive farmer said to me.'

'You fell asleep, before you could.'

'Of course, of course.'

He launched into a long, complicated story about the lives of the Di Goldi family ever since they left their *masseria*, listing disaster after disaster, barely pausing for breath and apparently recalling every detail the olive farmer had shared without any trouble at all.

'... then the father died and now the sons are fighting over what will happen to the house,' Augusto finished. 'That man I spoke to, he leases only the land and isn't interested in taking on the *masseria*. Sometimes he uses one of the barns, but if you allowed that to continue then he would pay you in olive oil.'

Ana realised he must be under the impression that she was seriously interested in the place. 'I'm not going to buy the *masseria*. I have to be practical.'

'But you seemed to like it very much.'

'Oh, I love it, but it needs too much work,' she explained.

Augusto paused for a moment, fingers pinching the bridge of his nose, deep in thought. 'Of course! My nephew will help. He lives quite near.'

'Is he a builder? Or a plumber?'

'Yes, yes,' the old man replied, vaguely.

Ana's mind was drifting back to the *masseria*. The trick would be to introduce enough modernity to be liveable without robbing the building of all its character. In the wrong hands a property like that could be ruined completely.

Donna Carmela returned to take their order herself. As she launched into an explanation of which menu items were no longer available and what had been introduced in their place, she spoke in English, but still mainly to Augusto. For years, whenever she went out to eat as the editor of *Culinaria*, she had been fawned and fussed over, treated like she was very important. Now it felt strange not to matter.

'Perhaps the braised octopus,' Ana suggested, taking charge. 'And the baked peppers, a fennel salad and some meatballs. If we share will that be enough?'

'I will also bring a little of the *tiella*. It is a gratin of salt cod and vegetables and very good.' Donna Carmela didn't wait for Ana's agreement. She was moving again, heading down a path that wound its way between the thick trunks of two ancient olive trees.

'Donna Carmela is ... how do you say ... a force of nature.' Augusto explained. 'She made all of this, from almost nothing.'

'It's a beautiful spot,' remarked Ana.

'The barn was a ruin and the house was rundown. She made it beautiful.'

Donna Carmela's food was as wonderful as the setting she had created. She brought each dish to their table personally and presented it with a flourish. Ana found herself dreaming up ways she might feature this rather overpowering woman in a magazine and was flooded by a rush of regret because she didn't have one anymore.

As she was gazing at the shaved fennel salad, trying to settle her thoughts, Augusto stared at her, expectantly. 'You want to take a photograph? For the Instagram?' he checked.

'I'm not on Instagram,' Ana told him, with a shake of her head.

'For the Facebook then? No? What about that new one, I can never remember what it is called.'

'None of them.'

'You are like my daughter,' he said, ladling onto his plate shards of crisp fennel mixed with finely sliced orange. 'Always

I am saying the Instagram would be good for her business, and she tells me I should stop interfering.'

Ana could imagine it. She stifled a smile.

'But I am her father. If I don't interfere then who will?' he continued with a shrug.

Ana wished her own father was still around to offer un- wanted advice. Right now, would he tell her to hurry home to England and find a proper job? For some reason she didn't think so. This restaurant would have intrigued him, particularly the pathways that led through the trees to who knew where. Halfway through the meal his curiosity might have got the better of him. Then he would have jumped up to go exploring and her mother would have frowned and drunk wine furiously.

Extra dishes arrived, tastes of things that Donna Carmela wanted them to try. Sardines wrapped round little balls of herbs, cheese and breadcrumbs, sweet pale-purple aubergines marinated in olive oil, a plate of wild asparagus drizzled with shallot vinegar, more food than an elderly man and a woman watching her figure could possibly manage, even if they had all afternoon to spend slowly grazing on it.

'*Dottore!*' A man was bearing down on them and Augusto levered himself up from the chair, so they could shake hands and clap each other on the back. There was some excitable chatter, before he went on his way.

The same thing happened a little later with a slightly younger man. '*Dottore, salve ...*'

'*Dottore* means doctor,' observed Ana, once he had gone. 'Was that your job?'

'It is only a mark of respect that they call me that,' Augusto explained. 'I worked in the *municipio* – the town hall – from the day I left school to the moment I retired. So, I cannot heal you if you are sick. But if you want to buy a house then maybe

I can help because I still have many connections.'

Ana was touched by how kind he was. There was bound to be some red tape to deal with if she were to buy in Italy and the advice of a local would be useful, especially one that had some sway with the bureaucrats.

'I like helping people,' he explained, interrupting her thoughts. 'Or as my daughter would say, interfering.'

They were brought a dessert they hadn't asked for, a tart of chocolate and almonds sprinkled with candied vanilla. Ana only meant to try a mouthful but found herself enjoying several more. When the bill arrived, it seemed half what it should have been and Augusto insisted on taking care of it, waving away Ana's attempt to offer her card.

'Please, let me get it,' Ana said.

'Your money is no good here,' Augusto insisted, pulling out cash from a creased leather wallet, and again she couldn't seem to argue.

On the drive back to Montenello, Augusto drifted off to sleep and Ana waited till they reached the causeway, before waking him. Blinking and yawning, he directed her along the easiest route to the piazza.

'Wouldn't you prefer me to take you straight home?' Ana checked, hoping he didn't live down one of the narrower streets.

'No, no we go to the bar, my son will be expecting me. You will join me there for a spritz?'

Pulling into the piazza, Ana noticed that his group of friends were gathered at their usual table. 'Thanks, but maybe not this evening.'

'Tomorrow then,' he said, climbing from the car and, before she could remind him that she planned to leave the next morning, he was on his way, waving his walking stick in a greeting as he went carefully across the cobbles towards his friends who were calling out to him enthusiastically, as if they hadn't seen each other for years.

Sitting in the car and watching the scene for a few moments more, it occurred to Ana that Montenello might be a pleasant place to grow old in. Perhaps she wouldn't rush away just yet but stay and get to know it like a local might. Wasn't that why she had come to Italy in the first place?

Skye

So much of what I love about my life is thanks to Tim. I have to keep reminding myself that – whatever Meera might think – he isn't all bad. But one undeniable flaw is that he avoids anything he doesn't want to face. It's taken me all week to force him into this conversation. Now I've managed to surprise him hiding away with his laptop in the conservatory, obviously thinking he wouldn't be disturbed there, and I've brought a coffee and a salted chocolate chunk cookie to make it harder for him to find an excuse to slip away.

I get straight to my concerns. How will we deal with this prize-winning lie he's told? What exactly are our publicity commitments for the wedding? Is there a way to handle any of this?

'Stop worrying, Skye,' he says, when I finish. 'If you only see the problems then you'll never do anything.'

Tim trots out this sort of thing all the time. It's a mantra when he's business coaching. I suppose his clients might find it inspiring, but I never have.

'Yes, but if you pretend the problems don't exist then you'll run into trouble,' I counter.

He stares out of the window towards my garden, which is looking particularly lovely because I thought ahead and planted flowers that are blooming now.

'So, what's the plan, Tim?'

'It's fine,' he tells me. 'I'll let them know we don't want to talk about any issues to do with your health, that we're focusing on enjoying the moment, making the most of it.'

'We have to tell the truth.'

'No,' he says, sounding very certain. 'That's a terrible idea.'

'But we have to, Tim.'

'We can distance ourselves from what I wrote in the competition entry. It doesn't have to be a big deal. Sure, we'll do publicity but all they need is some lovely photographs with a few quotes about how dreamy the wedding has been and what a perfect location Montenello is.'

I stare at him. Tim has always had a fairly relaxed relationship with the truth, but he's gone too far this time.

'Effective people know how to walk away from their mistakes and move on,' he tells me.

'Does anyone ever buy this nonsense?'

Tim looks like I've slapped him. 'Yes, actually a lot of people find my approach very helpful.'

'Lying isn't helpful,' I say.

'It was a mistake, I've apologised to you already countless times, what else am I supposed to do?'

'You need to apologise to them ... the people in Montenello ... the wedding planner ... what's her name again?' I can't remember because I've had as little as possible to do with any communication.

'Elise Valentini,' he reminds me.

'Let's email her now.'

He snaps his laptop shut. 'Let's not.'

'Tim please ...'

'What you have to realise Skye, is that they won't care. This wedding planner is running a business. The hotel where we're having the reception, the bridal designer, everyone, all they're interested in is getting coverage, and we'll give them plenty of that. We're an attractive family, the pictures will be gorgeous and we'll tell a nice story.'

He's right, we do look good together. But this is about more than how things look.

'The angle they'll want from the story is that I'm sick,' I point out.

'It's our story, we'll tell it the way we want.'

It's impossible arguing with Tim. He has an answer to everything.

'Trust me, Skye. I'm not going to let anything bad happen. I never do.' And there is the boyish smile again, the charm he relies on to keep things going his way.

'I don't even look sick,' I say, exasperated. 'It's quite obvious I'm not having cancer treatment.'

'Not everyone loses their hair these days,' he tells me. 'They've got new techniques. But maybe you could cut yours a bit shorter?'

'Shit Tim, seriously? You expect me to make myself look like I'm sick?' I'm reeling at the idea.

'I didn't say that,' he's quick to assure me. 'I'm just trying to get you to stop over-complicating things, otherwise, you'll ruin the whole trip. And everyone else is looking forward to it, in case you hadn't noticed.'

How could I not have noticed? Josh is taking his best man duties very seriously and working on a speech. Becky has drawn up an itinerary of exactly where we're going and loaded it into a new app she has on her phone. When we're together, it's almost all we talk about. Tomorrow we're meant to be going shoe shopping.

Tim has opened his laptop again and is staring at the screen. He must be aware that I'm still there, staring at him, but is trying to tune me out.

'No,' I say, and reluctantly he lifts his eyes to mine. 'I can't tell a lie. I refuse to.'

'I'll make sure everyone knows not to mention it to you,' he promises.

'My fake illness?'

'Darling, darling.' His tone is wheedling now. 'I know it was wrong, but I did it because I love you so much and I want us to have this dream trip together and make memories with our kids. We won it didn't we? How amazing is that?'

Another unwelcome thought has occurred to me. 'You didn't actually say that I'm dying though, did you? That's not why they picked us?'

'Of course not.' His eyes have shifted back to the screen and I'm not sure if he's telling me the truth.

'Tim ... ?'

'Skye, stop worrying, everything will be fine, I'll make sure it is.' He picks up his cookie and takes a bite. 'Mmm that's good,' he murmurs, through a mouthful of crumbs.

Everything will be fine; that right there is Tim on an up-swing. If he starts sliding into one of his lows then nothing will be fine at all. I know which state he must have been in when he lied on that competition entry. His moods are extreme and easily identified. Watching him now, phone in one hand, cookie in the other, focusing on the laptop sitting on his knee, I'm feeling pity ... exasperation ... even a little tenderness. And I'm unbalanced by it, off-kilter, just like Tim seems to be so much of the time. I can't marry this man but I can't not marry him either.

'What am I going to do?' I murmur.

Tim glances at me again. 'You're going shoe shopping with Becky, aren't you?'

I'm frowning and Tim must assume that I'm worrying about the expense because he smiles and waves the half-eaten cookie at me. 'Buy something nice, you both deserve it. I want my gorgeous girls to feel good.'

Shoe shopping has never been my idea of a good time. I've spent years clad in sensible footwear. At work I wear clogs and often forget to take them off until I go walking in the woods and need to change into sturdy boots. Maybe my feet have spread or something because the stilettos I'm wearing now are already pinching and I only put them on a few moments ago. They're champagne-coloured satin with slender heels and straps that wrap tightly round my ankles.

The shop assistant wrinkles her nose. Sorry not an assistant, she's a style concierge and part of a bridal team at this luxury department store.

'Stand up Mum, let's see you walk in them,' Becky encourages me.

I think that I'm doing a fairly good job of stepping gracefully across the stretch of shiny white floor, even so my daughter seems concerned.

'We'll be going from the ceremony in the town hall, down to the piazza for photographs and then onto the hotel. Most of that means walking on cobbles.' Becky must have been looking at Google Earth.

'Where are you getting married?' the style concierge wants to know. She's dressed like a bridal guest herself, in a cream suit worn with high heels that lengthen her slim brown legs.

'Italy,' Becky says, excitedly.

'Amazing! I was there last summer; we went to Puglia.'

'The town where we're staying isn't all that far from Puglia,' Becky tells her.

'You'll fall in love with the place,' the style concierge promises.

She goes off to fetch a shoe that is perfect for a wedding in

Italy. It has a pointy toe, a more manageable heel, a subtler blingy detail.

'This brand is known for great attention to comfort and ergonomics,' she explains, as I'm trying on a pair.

When she tells me the price, I blanch. 'That seems a bit much.'

'Shoes are a statement, they make you feel special, especially when you're walking down the aisle,' she says, airily. 'Beside you'll get lots of future wear because they're perfect for parties and balls.'

My social life revolves around summer barbecues and the occasional evening at a pub. These shoes will have one solitary outing then live forever in a cupboard. But when I try walking in them, I see she is right. They are more comfortable.

'I love them, Mum. They'll look great with your dress,' Becky tells me.

'I'll think about it.'

Becky sighs. 'That always means no.'

My daughter's feet are narrow and she has polished her toe-nails in iridescent pink. Every shoe she tries on looks perfect and I wonder how she'll make a choice. However, Becky has already given this a lot of thought and knows exactly what she likes – a pair of transparent crystal sandals with an elegant heel.

'I'm not sure if I'll be able to dance in them, but I can always slip them off,' she decides, examining her reflection in the mirror.

What has made Becky think there will be dancing? There aren't even going to be any guests at this wedding. I've dissuaded my parents from attending, playing down the whole affair. Dad's never liked Tim and my mum thinks it's silly getting married at my age, even if it is mostly free; they weren't too hard to convince. As for Tim, his parents are long gone and, while he's got a ton of mates, they are mainly people he bumps into at a pub, spends the night hanging out with, then doesn't see again for ages. I'm pretty sure this isn't going to be a wedding party with a dance floor.

'I'll take them,' decides Becky, turning in front of the mirror. 'I've been saving and I think I have enough.'

She has a Saturday job at the farm shop down the road, but doesn't earn much and I don't want her blowing the lot on one pair of shoes.

'Put some of your money towards them and I'll make up the rest,' I tell her.

'Then you won't be able to afford to buy a pair for yourself.'

'Yes, I will. Pretty much everything else the whole day is free, remember.'

'We've won a dream wedding in a competition,' Becky explains to the style concierge, who squeals in delight.

'Amazing!'

We're in the car on the way home, driving over the Clifton Suspension Bridge, and Becky is hugging the shoebox to her chest. 'I'll be able to wear them to my school ball as well. I'll keep them forever,' she is saying.

'Forever is a long time.' I smile to see her so happy. 'Some day you might not be the kind of person who wears those shoes.'

'You mean I'll be more like you; practical?' It doesn't sound like my daughter thinks being practical is the greatest characteristic.

'I'm creative too,' I remind her, jumping to my own defence.

'You make a spectacular cake, then people eat it and it's gone,' Becky observes, 'all your skill and artistry, just like that.'

'I always take photographs of the best ones,' I remind her.

'Even so.'

'I didn't always want to make cakes.' I don't think I've ever told Becky this before. 'At your age I was hoping to go to art school.'

'What happened?' she wants to know.

'I guess life got in the way.' That is more or less the truth.

'It's not too late for you to make art. If it's what you dream of doing.'

'When would I have time for that?'

Becky isn't going to let this go. 'You could clear out one of the sheds. Turn it into a studio.'

'The sheds are completely full of your dad's stuff,' I remind her. 'Have you ever known him clear out anything?'

'No,' she admits. 'All those things he never uses. The potter's wheel, the sailing dinghy. Dad's a hoarder really, isn't he?'

'Oh well,' I say, not wanting it to seem like we're criticising Tim. 'I'm fine creating my cakes. It's art that people get to eat, that seems pretty good to me.'

'Cake makes people happy I suppose,' says Becky.

'It pays for our lives,' I remind her, not wanting my daughter to think of me as having failed somehow. 'Cake just bought us these shoes. It also covers the bills and puts food on the table. Cake is doing pretty well right now actually.'

Becky is silent for a while after that, still hugging the shoe-box, looking out of the window at the woodland and fields flashing past. I assume she's thinking about the conversation we've just had but as we're pulling into the narrow country lane that leads to Lost Cottage, she surprises me by asking, 'Mum, you're happy with Dad, aren't you?'

'Of course, I am darling,' I'm quick to reply, wondering again where Becky is getting her ideas from.

Ana

Montenello had held onto Ana for longer than she meant to stay. After only a few days, it almost felt as if people here were expecting to see her. The man in the *salumeria* who offered tastes of his sharp cheeses and smoky cured meats, the cook in the trattoria where she ate another excellent lunch, the regulars at the bar particularly Augusto who very often was there at his usual table.

At the end of the week, she would absolutely have to move on since the hotel was fully booked. Ana might be sorry to leave this town but not the house where she was staying. She kept coming across new things not to like about it. There wasn't enough light, no matter how bright the day might be. The bathroom was awkwardly small, its fittings scaled down to match. And any keen cook would find the kitchen ill-equipped.

Ana couldn't seem to get the Di Goldi *masseria* out of her head. Its space and light, the length of its reception rooms, the breadth of its kitchen, the views. Everything about the house seemed to make a grand gesture and Ana was tempted to take one more look, not for any reason other than that she liked being there.

This time she went alone, listening to classical music as she drove. The gates were still unlocked as was the front door, and she pushed it open, calling out a greeting in English then in Italian in case anyone was there and hearing her voice echo back at her.

On this second visit, Ana noticed things she had missed before: cracked plaster, broken shutters, holes in the walls, what might have been dried manure and oil stains on the stone-flagged floors of the barns. Someone with vision and resources could do so much with this place. The kitchen had a beamed fireplace studded with the iron hooks that once must have held pots of simmering soups and stews. The dining area offered space to feed a crowd. There were business opportunities here. Ana was thinking about cooking classes, maybe even a boutique bed and breakfast, when her phone rang. Seeing it was Tessa, her old food editor from *Culinaria*, she answered straight away.

'You'll never guess where I am,' said Ana, warmly.

'Tell me,' Tessa replied, and it was good to hear her voice.

'In Italy, in an extraordinary house that's been abandoned and needs someone to save it from crumbling away into a ruin.'

'Are you that person?'

'I wish, but I think it's too much for me.'

'Nothing is too much for you,' Tessa told her.

Moving to the window, Ana looked down over the rows of olive trees. 'It's kind of you to say so, but I'm not sure that's true. How are you, anyway? What's been happening.'

'Actually, that's why I'm calling.' Tessa hesitated for a moment. 'I really wanted you to hear the news from me.'

'What news?' Immediately Ana jumped to the conclusion something was wrong, perhaps Tessa was ill or a friend had died.

'There has been a reader outcry and they've done a U-turn ...' Tessa began.

Now Ana guessed what she was about to say, although she

couldn't quite believe it. 'Are you telling me they're bringing *Culinaria* back?'

'Only as a quarterly, but yes that's what they're about to announce.'

Ana leant against the window frame and felt her heart thumping. 'Who's the editor?'

There was the sound of a heavy sigh. 'I hear Tammy Wong and the digital team will produce the content and Lorelei Hope will be editor-in-chief.'

Ana struggled to take in the news. Lorelei Hope, editor of *Fashionaria*, must have been scheming all this time to get control of her magazine. Now she had managed it.

'The woman isn't even interested in food,' Tessa complained. 'I don't think she's consumed anything but dust and water since 1994.'

Ana felt shaky. She needed to sit down, but there wasn't a chair. Half-sliding down the wall, she slumped on the floor in the spot where she had been standing.

'It's the dumbest decision ever and no one can believe it. I'm so sorry Ana ... are you OK?'

'Perhaps Lorelei will do a good enough job though,' she replied, in a smaller voice than before.

Tessa snorted in reply. 'Are you kidding me? Who are you and what have you done with Ana King?'

'I hope she does ... for everyone's sake ... for the readers especially.'

'What the readers want is the magazine you made, your vision, your brilliance,' said Tessa, fiercely.

'I've got another life now though,' said Ana, trying her best to make it sound true. 'I think my future may be here.'

'Is it wonderful in Italy?' Tessa asked. 'Where are you exactly?'

'I'm in Basilicata, it's the real Italy, almost undiscovered still, and let me tell you about the food ...' Grateful for the change of subject, Ana launched into a description of the meals she had eaten, the authentic trattoria, the restaurant in the olive groves, the *pasticceria* she was yet to try that everyone said was exceptional.

'It all tastes fresher and better here. You really have to come,' she enthused.

'If you buy a house there then nothing will stop me,' Tessa promised.

Ana was determined not to cry because this wasn't worth getting upset about. It was only a magazine. But bloody Lorelei Hope. Picturing her smooth, smug face, she was grateful to be far away in a place where she was unlikely ever to bump into her. Lorelei's visits to Italy were all about air-kissing designers at fashion week in Milan. Venturing this far south wouldn't appeal to her.

Still on the floor, Ana stared at her phone. Tessa may have been first with the news, but more people would soon want to share it and she would be caught up in the same conversations, with everyone endlessly wanting to know if she was OK. Ana remembered how much the question had irritated Augusto. Deciding he had a point; she switched her phone onto silent.

The floor tiles she was sitting on were beautiful. With her hand, Ana swept away the dust to better see the pattern in faded shades of blue and yellow. Tilting her head, she looked up at the frescoes that covered the soaring ceiling. This space should be filled with well-dressed people sitting round a banquet table, eating good food and having interesting conversations. Picturing the scene, for a few moments it almost seemed real, and Ana wasn't a sad woman sitting on the floor of an empty room wondering what had become of her.

Hauling herself to her feet, she brushed the dirt from her

clothes. In her pocket the phone was vibrating and she wondered who it was this time. Probably another member of her old team but sooner or later Lorelei Hope herself was going to call, she wouldn't be able to resist. On the surface the woman might be all charm, still Ana knew how much she would be gloating. The thought of her planning the next issue of *Culinaria*, briefing Tammy Wong and the team on her vision for the magazine, lunching with advertisers. All alone in the empty room Ana gave a scream of rage and her voice bounced off the bare walls and high ceilings. It made her feel slightly better, so she did it again.

What she needed was to show all those people that her life had moved on. If they were discussing her, then her old colleagues shouldn't be wondering if she was OK. Ana wanted to give them something better to talk about.

Pulling the Moleskine notebook from her bag, she started listing everything that would be required to make this abandoned house into a beautiful home again. Tradespeople to check the thick masonry walls and mend the roof, to restore water and electricity, a gardener to tame the overgrown grounds. Ana's notebook was almost filled with small, neat writing and surely there was more she hadn't thought of. Still, she felt a rising sense of excitement. All of it was possible.

On the drive back to Montenello her resolve grew firmer and by the time she crossed the causeway, Ana was almost convinced. She was never going back to her London life again. What she had said to Tessa was the truth. Her future was here in Italy.

It was aperitivo hour, and Ana drove directly to the piazza, parking the car at a rakish angle, half-on-and-off the kerb then rushing into the bar, impatient to find Augusto and tell him all about her new plan to sell her apartment, buy the Di Goldi *masseria* then bring it to life again.

192

All of his friends were at their table, enjoying the late afternoon sunshine, but Augusto wasn't with them. There was no sign of him inside, either, and Ana realised she hadn't spotted him earlier on this morning, when she stopped in for coffee.

The barman glanced at her with a questioning raise of his eyebrows, tilting the empty glass he was polishing, checking if she wanted a drink.

'Augusto?' Ana asked, assuming he didn't speak any English.

'*Lui non c'e.* Not here. *Un raffreddore*,' the barman replied, adding more words in Italian as Ana fumbled for her phone to find Google Translate since it seemed she wasn't equipped for this conversation.

'Augusto has a cold,' the man sitting on the bar stool beside her explained. He had an Australian accent but looked Italian, in a dark-eyed, square-jawed way.

'Is he OK?' asked Ana, thinking that at Augusto's age even a cold could have consequences.

'I believe so,' the man told her. 'Apparently, they've insisted he stays home to rest, and Augusto isn't happy about it. You're a friend of his?'

'Yes,' replied Ana. 'Actually, not really, we've only just met but he's been helping me house-hunt and I wanted to let him know that I've made a decision.'

The Australian shifted in his seat, so he was facing Ana, apparently more interested now. 'Are you buying here in Montenello?'

'Out in the countryside. The Di Goldi *masseria*. Do you know it?'

The Australian nodded, slowly. 'Huge crumbling old pile on an olive estate, empty for years?'

'That's it,' said Ana.

'To be fair that description fits any number of places round here, but I think I know the one you mean. I'm Gino, by the way.'

'I'm Ana King and I'm about to do something that I may live to regret,' she told him.

Gino laughed. 'You'd better have a drink then. Negroni?'

'Why not?'

'You're the second Australian I've met in Montenello,' remarked Ana, watching the barman mixing her drink.

'I'm guessing the first one was Edward, my husband, and you're staying at our hotel?'

'That's right.'

'What brought you to Montenello?' asked Gino. 'We're known as a wedding destination.'

'I'm definitely not getting married,' said Ana, accepting her negroni and taking a sip. 'Mmm that's good.'

'Yeah, our barman Renzo makes an excellent cocktail.'

'I came to investigate the one-euro house scheme,' she explained. 'But apparently that's not happening anymore so Augusto put me onto this other place.'

Ana told him about it and at length, with Gino listening intently and commenting every now and then about the importance of choosing the correct paint and preserving original details.

'Are you an architect?' wondered Ana.

'Actually no, I'm a furniture maker. If you're staying at the hotel then you've seen my work. I made the reception desk.'

'Ah yes, that's beautiful.' Ana had been struck by its craftsmanship and design. 'If I buy the *masseria* I'm going to need a banquet table.'

'You mean when you buy the *masseria*,' said Gino, with a smile.

'There's a lot to be done,' Ana had been making another list in her mind. 'I have to negotiate a price, deal with no end of red tape I imagine, and then find tradespeople, builders, plumbers ...'

194

'It will be a challenge,' Gino agreed.

Challenges were to be faced head on, that was what Ana had always believed and now she didn't feel any different. Sipping her second negroni on a stomach empty of anything but a few crisp *taralli* biscuits and a handful of piquant black olives, she had a rising sense of excitement. It had been a long time since she had felt like this about anything.

Waking early the next morning, Ana tested her mood. Had she changed her mind about the dilapidated *masseria*, come to her senses? Had the potential pitfalls Gino had outlined put her off at all? If she was going to commit to this project it would be all consuming, and she needed to be sure it was the right thing to do.

Sitting up in bed, she checked her phone and noted how many calls she had missed. It seemed as if everyone she ever worked with had tried to get hold of her or sent a supportive message. Reading their words, hearing how angry and disappointed they were on her behalf, and how they hoped she was OK, Ana knew she wouldn't be contacting any of them until she had something positive to say.

She was going to buy the Di Goldi *masseria* and bring it back to life. Lorelei Hope could keep her magazines, Ana was ready for a new challenge.

Reaching for her notebook, she embarked on a fresh list of things she needed to get on with. Put her apartment on the market and let the tenant know. Find out who to contact about the *masseria*. See if she could discover what similar places in the area had sold for and settle on a fair price. Find out what sort of visa or permits she might need. Still propped up on pillows in bed, she did sums, estimating how much money she would have to spend and what her costs were likely to be.

When she couldn't ignore her empty stomach rumbling with

hunger, she stopped jotting and went to take a quick shower. Throwing on yesterday's creased linen, she gave her hair a cursory brush and didn't bother with make-up. Ana needed food and coffee.

By the time she reached the piazza, it was starting to bustle. The vegetable truck was parked in its usual spot and a man was sweeping up confetti. Outside the bar, Ana was pleased to see a familiar figure with a silk scarf wrapped round his throat despite the summer heat of the morning.

'Augusto,' she called.

'Signora, do not come too close,' he warned in a voice that sounded frailer than usual. 'I have the cold. I do not wish to give it to you.'

'I never catch colds.' It was true that Ana tended to be robust, also she was keen to tell him her news.

'Of course,' he said, as she was on the brink of launching into it. 'You are buying the Di Goldi *masseria*. I have heard this already.'

That paused Ana's excitement for a moment. She had been in this small town a matter of days and already people here knew her business. Was that really what she wanted? But Augusto was beaming now and, forgetting his concerns about passing on germs, patting the chair beside him, encouraging her to sit.

'We must talk about how I can help. Although ...' He cast a glance through the window of the bar. 'They say I mustn't interfere unless you want me to.'

'You're not interfering,' Ana promised. 'Actually, I thought I might go back to the *masseria* later on, if you'd like to join me.'

With another look through the window of the bar, he gave a regretful shake of his head. 'There was a fuss about me even coming here today. But I cannot stay at home. I will die of boredom and do they want that?'

'I'm sure they don't,' said Ana, although she could understand why his children were protective. In their place she might be too.

'I will make some calls and find out who you must talk to about the *masseria*,' Augusto promised, sounding more energised. 'Also, I will ask my nephew to visit and report on what needs to be done. But first coffee.'

'I'm ravenous,' Ana admitted. 'Do you think I could buy some food at the *pasticceria* and eat it here or would that cause a problem?'

'Why would there be a problem?' Augusto seemed confused by the question. 'It is a very good *pasticceria*. My granddaughter owns it.'

Ana smiled. 'Are you related to everyone in Montenello?'

The old man reflected her smile. 'Of course.'

Stepping through the door of the *pasticceria* Ana was struck by the array of sweet things and the long glass-fronted cabinet they were displayed in. Whimsical and rustic, its legs were twisting spirals. Ana's thoughts turned to the style of furnishings that would work best in the setting of the *masseria*. Pieces that were more solid than this, in wood polished to a high shine, elegant sideboards and dressers, and a long banquet table that would seat at least twelve people. She held the image in her mind, as if it existed already.

Still, all that lay in the future and there was much to achieve before then. Choosing some sweet little tarts filled with ricotta and pistachio paste that she hoped Augusto might also like, Ana returned to the bar, where she found him already busy on his phone, sending messages.

They sat together in the sunshine, people stopping by their table every now and then to say hello, Augusto regaling them with her news, insisting they sit down, cutting up the tarts and offering them round. There seemed no end to the advice they were given in return. Almost everyone was encouraging and their excitement fuelled hers until Ana couldn't wait to go back and see the house again.

At this rate she was going to run out of notebooks. On her third visit to the *masseria* Ana was determined to look behind every door and inside every cupboard to determine exactly what she was taking on. Cobwebbed corners and dim spaces littered with mouse droppings were thoroughly investigated. In one of the barns Ana found a desiccated rat and shivered as she wondered how many living ones might be scrabbling around out of sight.

She was halfway up the stairs to the tower when she heard the sound of a male voice, echoing below.

'Signora, are you here?'

'Yes, hello?' she called, making her way back down again.

A mountain of a man was waiting in the entranceway, tall and heavyset, clad in pale blue overalls, with a thatch of white hair and an aquiline nose.

'I am Rocco.' His dark eyes met hers, and the lines around them crinkled as he smiled. 'Augusto sent me.'

'You're his nephew?' asked Ana.

'So, Augusto tells me. He says I am to help.'

'You're the builder?' she checked.

He made a movement of his head, neither a shake nor a nod, shrugging his shoulders at the same time. It was the sort of non-committal response Italian men seemed to specialise in and Ana found infuriating.

'What I need is someone to check the structure for any major issues,' she instructed him. 'Also, I want to know how difficult it will be to connect the electricity and water.'

'I can take a look but …' Rocco put a hand to his head and

made a sweeping motion, ' … you have something in your hair.'

Cobwebs, Ana realised, trying to brush them away. Her clothes were filthy too. At one point she had been on her hands and knees trying to look up a chimney, so it was hardly surprising.

'You are buying this place?' Rocco was staring through an archway that led to a large reception room.

'Yes, I am.'

'OK, show me.'

As she walked him through the house, Rocco didn't speak much, raising his eyebrows occasionally, grimacing at the state of one of the bathrooms, knocking his fist against a wall here and there, poking a finger into softening plaster.

'Am I crazy?' wondered Ana, arriving back in the entrance-way. 'Is that what you're thinking? That no one sane would buy this place?'

Rocco shrugged again then nodded towards the stairs leading to the tower, 'Are they safe?'

'I was hoping you could tell me.'

He smiled as if Ana had been making a joke, which she most definitely wasn't.

'Why don't we find out then?' he suggested.

She followed him upwards, hearing the stairs creak more loudly beneath his sturdy boots than they did under her now ruined silver Veja trainers. At the top, he turned back to her.

'It seems they are safe.'

Ana stared at him. It was very kind of Augusto to send his nephew to help but she didn't think she would be hiring this man to manage her restoration project.

'What would you do with a room like this?' Rocco asked, staring out of the window at the view she had already fallen in love with.

'I thought perhaps a study.'

He considered the idea, and made another non-committal gesture, this time showing the work-roughened palms of his hands as he shrugged.

'You don't think I should buy it do you?' asked Ana.

'The decision isn't mine, Signora. But since you are interested in my opinion what I will say is that houses like this fall into ruin if they are abandoned for too long. With some work this one could still be saved. The structure seems sound enough as far as I can tell at this point,' Rocco paused for a moment. 'But are you sure you want to be here? That is the most important thing. Is this where you want to spend your life?'

Ana considered the question, realising that she had been so caught up in planning a renovation, very little thought had been given to the reality of waking up here every day once it was finished. What would that be like? Her mind went to Carina, and the empty life she led in her beautiful house; that wasn't what she wanted at all.

'I think so ...' she said, an edge of doubt in her voice. 'I think I'll be happy here but it's impossible to know for sure.'

'This *masseria* belonged to a landowner,' Rocco told her, as he prodded at the rotten wood of a window frame. 'The people who lived here must have had servants to look after the place. It may be hard work for you to manage it without help.'

Hard work had never bothered Ana. She told him so.

'You will be isolated,' Rocco added. 'In town you can walk out of your door, visit a bar for your morning coffee, say hello to the people you know. Here there are only olive trees.'

Ana had always been content with her own company. Besides she could get in her car and be in Montenello before too long. 'Loneliness is not my thing. That won't be a problem,' she told him.

Rocco studied her for a moment. 'Then what is worrying you?'

Ana gave the question some thought and realised that mainly it was Carina and the idea of following in the older woman's footsteps, then finding herself marooned in a life she didn't want anymore, unable to escape it. She couldn't quite shake the image of her, a woman tied to a place by a man.

'In Puglia I met a woman who had restored a *masseria*,' she found herself confiding. 'The house was wonderful, still I got the feeling that she was unhappy, that she had started to feel trapped there and wanted to leave.'

'In that case why didn't she sell it?' he wanted to know.

'Her husband insisted on staying.'

'Do you have a husband?' Rocco glanced at her bare finger.

'No,' Ana replied.

He shrugged. 'Well, then.'

As she walked with Rocco down the driveway, towards the dented van he had left parked outside the gates, Ana decided she would be doing her own research about builders. She needed someone reliable and professional. While this man seemed perfectly pleasant, she was pretty sure he didn't fit that description.

'How exactly are you related to Augusto?' she wondered, thinking that the two men weren't remotely alike.

'Who would know?' Rocco replied, with another of his casual shrugs. 'It remains a mystery, but he insists that I am.'

'Well thanks for coming to take a look at the place,' she said, as Rocco was opening the car door. 'I really do appreciate it.'

Rocco paused, turning back to her. 'Signora, may I give you one piece of advice?'

'Sure,' said Ana, expecting that now he was going to tell her the place was too much for her to take on.

'If you do buy this house then Augusto is sure to want to help. My advice is you should let him. You are an independent woman, I can see that, but this is Italy.'

With that, Rocco reached out to brush the last shreds of cobweb from her hair, then climbed in the van, offered a wave of his broad hand in farewell and drove away, raising clouds of dust from the tinder-dry dirt road as he went. Ana didn't expect to see him again.

Skye

I was planning to spend an hour in Bicycle Junction, checking out the site where they want to have a café and meeting the owner, Victor. We've been here far longer than that already and Tim is thoroughly distracted by the latest e-bikes, deep in discussions about speed and battery power. I can tell he's itching to take one for a test ride. It's time for me to interrupt.

'When were you thinking you'd want the café to open?' I ask Victor, a chatty younger guy with a bushy beard who is passionate about bikes. 'Only we're going away for a couple of weeks in September so wouldn't be able to make much progress before then.'

'Where are you off to?' Victor asks, politely.

'Just Italy,' I say, not wanting to sidetrack us any further.

'We won a wedding,' Tim puts in, because he can't miss an opportunity to show off about it. 'The whole package, plus flights and accommodation.'

'Wow, seriously?'

'Yeah, I entered this competition I saw in the *Daily Post*,' Tim explains. 'We're going to a little place called Montenello that you've probably never heard of.'

'Wait!' Victor sounds excited. 'Montenello, yes, I think I might know the competition you mean. My girlfriend read about it on Facebook. She was going to give it a go.'

Tim's eyes pop in surprise. We haven't come across anyone else who entered.

'But then she checked the small print,' adds Victor, 'and you had to actually book a wedding to be in to win, right? That's why we didn't bother.'

'No,' I say. 'It can't have been the same competition. You didn't have to book anything to enter the one that we've won. That's right isn't it, Tim?'

But Tim has gone quiet. He's looking out of the window and, when he does speak, changes the subject.

'I know it'll be mostly a takeaway place but do you think we could put a few café tables and chairs on the pavement?' he asks Victor.

'Yeah, hopefully,' Victor replies. 'We'll want some stools in the window too. The whole idea is to attract more people into the store and keep them here longer.'

Now they're back on topic and I don't interrupt. As they're talking about the logistics of window seating, I pull out my phone and find the *Daily Post* website. It doesn't take too long for me to find an article with the original advert. I discover that Victor is right. It must have been the same competition. And yes, there were fishhooks.

Win a dream wedding in Italy's most romantic town
Every couple that books to marry in the picturesque hilltop town of Montenello this summer will receive a cash reward of 1,000 euro. And one lucky pair will win a dream wedding package, with everything they need to say 'I do' in style. So, if you are in love, why not marry in Montenello?

I've stopped listening to what Tim is saying. Who knows what rash promises he is making. With one hand over my mouth, I'm re-reading, more carefully this time. Tim gives me an uneasy glance but doesn't break off his conversation and I stay quiet for now.

'Great.' Tim is wrapping up the discussion. 'I'll have my lawyer put together a draft agreement and look into what permissions are needed these days for outdoor tables. And we'll stay in touch, OK.'

Victor claps him on the shoulder. 'Good man,' he says. 'And hey, congratulations.'

Once we're outside, walking back to where we parked the car, Tim turns to me. 'Don't say it, just don't.'

I'm too furious to speak.

'Don't give me a hard time.' He's taking long strides and I'm having to half run to keep up.

'What the hell were you thinking, Tim?' I've found my voice. 'You actually booked a wedding? Seriously? If we hadn't won, what was your plan then?'

'Obviously I'd have cancelled the booking,' he says. 'You wouldn't have wanted to pay for a wedding or a foreign holiday, I know that.'

The pavement is crowded, and I knock into a middle-aged man who gives me a dark look, even though I'm quick to apologise.

'Did you pay them a deposit?' I ask, catching up again. 'Would we have lost money if we'd cancelled?'

'It wasn't all that much; some people probably spend more than that in a year on lottery tickets. And the point is Skye, the gamble paid off. So, it was worth taking, wasn't it?'

We've reached the car and Tim is getting inside. By the time I'm sitting beside him he's already turned on the engine and started indicating.

'How many more lies have you told?' I ask.

Tim edges out into the traffic and points the car towards the bridge. 'If you had any interest in me at all, you'd have got involved and then you'd have known.'

'I'm really busy,' I say, defensively, although I know he's right; I'm not that interested in what he does and didn't bother looking properly at the competition before now.

'Yeah, yeah, whatever,' Tim replies.

We're crossing the Clifton Suspension Bridge, over the river flowing through the gorge dizzyingly low beneath us, when Tim clears his throat.

'I hope our kids don't turn out like this,' he says, softly.

'Like what?' I turn and stare at his profile. 'What do you mean?'

'I've done my best to make sure they don't have life limiting beliefs,' he says, matter-of-factly. 'I've tried to show them that it's OK to take risks, the sky won't fall on their heads. I want them to have the courage to follow their dreams.'

'I want that too,' I say, outraged. 'Obviously.'

'Then why go through life as if disaster is looming round every corner? You act like you're the one holding everything together when actually, we're doing fine. We live in a beautiful place, we've never missed a mortgage payment, we have enough money to live on. But you never give me any credit for that. It's all down to you, isn't it? You're the one standing between us and a catastrophe.'

'No,' I say, in a smaller voice, although it's true that it's how I feel a lot of the time.

'Now this amazing thing has happened. We've won a competition. And all you can do is look for problems,' Tim finishes. 'Can't you think positively, for once?'

We drive the rest of the way in silence. I'm shocked by Tim's words. In the heat of an argument all couples say things to each other that they don't mean. But Tim sounded like he meant it. Is this how he sees me, as an over-cautious killjoy?

It's not how I see myself. I feel like he's pulled back a curtain on another view of me, one I hadn't known was there. I can't help wondering if there's at least some truth in what he just said and I don't much like it.

Tim's words have cut so deep that I can barely sleep. I'm worrying that he's right and I'm raising our kids to be anxious people. I want them to have adventures; that's what being young is all about. But I also want them to work hard and be responsible people. Is it possible to have both, to be the best of me and Tim rolled together, or do you have to choose?

I start the new day exhausted by those questions and must look terrible because when Meera arrives at work, she gives me a worried glance.

'It's all going to be OK, you know,' she says. 'I'll look after things.'

'What sorry?' I'm cutting up a coffee and walnut traybake into neat slices.

'I'll manage while you're away, I won't be too busy smashing the patriarchy,' she says.

While we're in Italy, Meera is going to be taking care of the café baking and deliveries, with the help of a school mum who I hope will be more reliable than the last two. She'll tackle a couple of birthday cakes but they're reasonably straightforward and she's confident she can manage. Plus, she'll be house-sitting and looking after the dog. It's a lot of responsibility.

'I know you'll do a great job,' I tell Meera, because I'm determined not to be the negative, anxious person that Tim described.

'You'll be too busy sunning yourself to care,' she says. 'It's really hot in Italy at the moment.'

She's right that they're having a heatwave. The high temperatures have been among the many concerns on my mind.

'It will have cooled down by the time we get there.' I'm trying to be more positive. 'And the hotel in Rome has a pool. It looks really lovely.'

We're staying on the Gianicolo Hill. Becky found us a surprisingly cheap boutique hotel and we've booked in for several nights. Between them, she and Josh have been planning our whole itinerary. Tim urged me to leave them to it.

'You sound like you're starting to look forward to this trip,' says Meera, who disapproves, not only of the wedding, but the environmental impact of four people travelling.

'Art galleries, architecture, good food ... there's a lot to look forward to.'

'The kids must be super-excited,' she says.

'They really are,' I agree.

Watching Becky and Josh researching hotels and tours, seeing how sensible and capable they are, has made me proud. Whatever Tim says, those things are important. I can't have done such a bad job of raising them.

'Do you want one of these?' I ask Meera, as I'm boxing up the coffee and walnut slices. 'They're vegan.'

'Hmm tempting,' she says.

'I used organic maple syrup not refined sugar,' I add.

For once she can't say no. 'Go on then.'

Meera makes us coffee and we take a five-minute break out in the garden, because the sun is shining. I resist the urge to start running through any of the details I've been worrying that she won't remember. Where to order various supplies from or how the invoicing system works. She'll cope, I remind myself, and can contact me if there's a problem.

'This is really good,' she says, munching the sweet slice. 'Although maple syrup still counts as sugar, you know.'

'It can't do any harm to have a little now and then can it?'

Meera hardly ever eats what we bake. Her views about sugar

are among the reasons this job is only a stopgap measure while she works out what she really wants. It may turn out to be animation as she enjoyed the workshop she took. Or activism as that's her passion. Sooner or later, she'll leave though. She'll have the courage to follow her dreams.

'Sugar rots your teeth and causes inflammation,' she reminds me. 'It's toxic.'

'Yeah, I know. There's a downside to everything though isn't there?'

Meera might not be entirely convinced that it's OK to take a break from your principles, but she finishes her last bite. 'I'm pleased more cafés are ordering the plant-based options. It shows things are starting to change,' she says.

I hide a smile as the café has no idea that they'll be getting vegan baking. My coffee and walnut cake slices are so good, the customers never know the difference. I don't tell Meera that but perhaps she suspects.

'Or did you make these just for me?'

'Of course not,' I lie but, when we go back indoors, I set another slice aside for her. Everyone deserves a few treats and it makes me happy to provide them.

Ana

Ana hurried through her routine of morning stretches accompanied by the sound of church bells ringing. Her mind was filled with thoughts of the new life she was planning and, as soon as she had finished, she ran her eyes over her latest to-do list. It was time to begin ticking things off.

Around twenty minutes later she was sitting with Augusto outside the bar in the piazza, drinking her first coffee of the day.

'I need somewhere to live,' she said, hoping he might know of a place nearby that she could rent for a while.

'But surely you will live in the *masseria*?'

'I'll still need somewhere to stay while the sale goes through and I believe that might take at least a couple of months.' Ana had been doing some research.

Augusto frowned, tilting his head from side to side.

'Longer than that?' guessed Ana.

'If there is an issue with the documents then it may be six months, or even more. This is Italy,' he told her.

'Six months,' Ana was dismayed.

'Don't worry, Signora, I have an idea. It may be possible to lease the *masseria* from the Di Goldi family until the sale is complete. I am sure we could negotiate a very low rent.'

Instantly, Ana could see how this would have its advantages. Living in the farmhouse, seeing the way the light changed and getting a proper feel for the place, would help guide the changes she made. And if the purchase progressed slowly, it would at least mean she didn't have to rush through the sale of her London apartment. Then she remembered the bathrooms.

'The house is in too bad a state. I couldn't possibly live there at the moment.'

'My nephew Rocco will fix things. He came as I asked him to, yes?'

Ana wasn't convinced. Nothing about Rocco had inspired confidence.

'The plumbing,' she reminded him. 'The fittings, the floors, it's all a mess. And what about furniture ... heating ... ?'

'Rocco will fix everything,' Augusto promised.

She looked at his face, brightened by morning sunlight. He was smiling at her encouragingly, the wrinkles pleating at the corners of his eyes. His wispy white hair was cropped short and his ears seemed too large for his head which drooped on frail shoulders. Augusto was a very elderly man, and Ana shouldn't be burdening him.

'Perhaps I'll contact him then,' she agreed, thinking that she probably wouldn't.

Wherever Ana went in Montenello she came across signs of the bridal parties that seemed to be the business that kept half the town employed. There was the streetsweeper who grumbled as he cleared away drifts of confetti around the fountain, the tiny store crammed with tulle at the far end of the piazza, the hotel where they always seemed to be setting up or clearing away a wedding reception, the *pasticceria* where a glass cabinet displayed a model of a wedding cake.

Today even Augusto seemed distracted by the idea of people

getting married. When the mayor, Salvio Valentini, arrived to join them for his morning coffee, it was all he could talk about.

'This is the gown she has chosen,' Augusto said, waving his phone under her nose.

Ana glanced at the picture with a vague smile, her mind still on her own affairs.

'I think it is too plain,' Augusto added, regretfully. 'And she is so beautiful. What a pity.'

'I'm sorry, who is getting married?' asked Ana, more attentive now. 'A family member?'

'No, no it is the competition ... win a dream wedding in Italy's most romantic town ... you must have heard of it.' The old man sounded impatient. 'Surely we told you?'

'Our competition, the one that was Augusto's idea,' Salvio put in. 'Another initiative to help Montenello prosper. We are very excited that our winners will be arriving here soon. At the town hall we have been making plans for an official welcome.'

Weddings didn't interest Ana. Long speeches and uninspired food had been features of most she had attended and several of those happy couples were divorced by now. 'How lovely,' she murmured, since the two men seemed so energised by it.

'You must come to the cocktail party we are holding for our winning couple,' added the mayor. 'I will make sure you get an invitation. It will be nice for them to have some other English people there.'

Ana couldn't imagine wanting to go. She smiled and nodded, anyway.

'Skye and Tim Olsen, with their children Becky and Josh, they are from Bristol,' Augusto told her, reading the names from his screen. 'A lovely family.'

'There will be no other family members at the wedding, no guests at all, so the whole town will be making an effort to make their time here special,' added Salvio.

They slipped in and out of Italian as they talked on. Ana heard them discussing music and the menu. At one point there was a short argument, but it ended in laughter.

'It is important for the town, this wedding,' the mayor explained, turning to her, as if he thought she should care as much as they did. 'We have to be sure everything is completely perfect. My wife Elise is the wedding planner but, as well as the welcome party, we are organising a lunch in the olive groves at my mother's restaurant.'

Briefly Ana wondered about this English couple and their children, hoping they were ready for the fuss the town was going to make. If they were shy, retiring types that might be tricky. As her mind started drifting back to her own plans, she was fairly sure the two men were discussing the possibility of putting on a firework display.

Ana spent the day tackling her to-do list, working her way through it methodically. She contacted the estate agent who would manage the sale of her London apartment, then let her tenant know about the changing situation and even managed to find an English-speaking property lawyer to guide her through the purchase of the *masseria*. It was satisfying to have made so much progress and, by the time she had finished, her mood was celebratory. She decided to take herself out for dinner.

The hotel restaurant seemed her closest option and, glancing at the menu online, Ana thought it looked promising. Assuming there would be no need to make a booking, she pulled out the nicest dress she had packed, attempted to tidy her wayward hair and put on bright lipstick.

Walking through the town, the evening light turned pinky-gold and the stones of the old buildings seemed to glow in reflection. Ana passed a woman sitting beside her front door-step, shelling borlotti beans. She overtook an elderly couple walking slowly arm-in-arm, as a Vespa sped past ridden by two teenage girls, helmetless, hair streaming out behind. The air was scented with the meals being prepared beyond people's open windows; garlic and onions warming in oil, tomato-rich sauces slowly simmering.

By the time she reached the hotel, Ana was hungry. The restaurant was surprisingly busy, possibly with part of a bridal party, still they rustled up a table and she ordered an Aperol Spritz to sip while she studied the menu more carefully.

She liked what she saw. Small plates might be designed for sharing but Ana had always thought them ideal when eating out alone. You could sample different dishes and choose whatever you pleased without needing to account for another person's likes or eating habits.

Once she had ordered, Ana sat back to take in her surroundings. The restaurant ranged through several spaces, its furniture was rustic and on a sideboard was a clutter of vases filled with wildflowers that might have been picked at the roadside.

At the far end of the room, she noticed the hotel's two Australian owners, Edward and Gino. They were sitting with another man whose back was turned to her and something about the broad set of his shoulders seemed familiar. She was fairly sure this was Rocco. Watching for a few moments, she wondered if it was a business meeting or a gathering of friends. They seemed to be sharing a meal and were deep in conversation. Then her own food arrived and she turned away from them.

The meal was very good. Seared flank steak had been married to a creamy pesto of gorgonzola and hazelnuts, a dish of buttery cannellini beans was spiked with smoked caviar, sweet Padron peppers were scorched by fire and then there was her favourite dish of all, a crisp pastry shell filled with tart sheep's curd and a tumble of oven-softened cherry tomatoes. Ana was impressed. She hadn't thought to eat like this in a small town on a hilltop in the middle of nowhere and wanted to congratulate Edward and Gino on their choice of chef, but they were still locked in conversation with the man, whose face angled more towards her now, was definitely Rocco.

Waiting for the bill, her attention was caught by the three men at the far end of the room. There was a bottle of limoncello being delivered to their table, and she observed it being poured and their glasses clinking together. Perhaps a deal had been struck, thought Ana, as Rocco threw back his head and laughed at something Gino had said. They seemed unlikely friends, the stylish Australian hoteliers and the burly builder, who had shed his overalls and was dressed now in worn jeans and a white linen shirt, the cuffs rolled up his wide forearms.

Ana hadn't intended to intrude on them but, as she settled the bill and stood to leave, Rocco turned and smiled in her direction, then Gino beckoned her over.

'Ana, there is good news, we hear. Would you like to join us for a celebratory glass of limoncello?' he called, as she moved towards their table.

Ana assumed he must be referring to her decision to buy the *masseria*. 'Actually, nothing is settled yet.'

'According to Augusto you are moving in. He tells me you are renting the place until the sale goes through.'

'Well yes, we did talk about that when I saw him this morning,' conceded Ana.

'Since this morning it seems that he has spoken to someone from the Di Goldi family and an arrangement has been made,' Gino told her.

Ana stiffened. She was unnerved by the idea of a stranger knowing her business before she did. 'Really? And how much rent will I be paying?' she asked, a little tartly.

'That information I don't have, but I'm sure he'll have

bargained hard for you,' responded Gino, seeming not to pick up on the acid tone in her voice.

'No, no.' Ana shook her head. 'It's impossible ... the place isn't liveable ... there's no furniture ... I haven't even agreed to rent it yet.'

She heard her voice rising and saw Rocco's lips twitch into a wry half-smile. He reached out, resting one of his strong, square hands very lightly on her arm and Ana, who wasn't the most tactile person, found his touch unexpectedly comforting.

'As I told you Signora, our old friend likes to help people.' Rocco said, gently. 'And today he has been helping you. But sit, have a drink with us, and we will explain.'

He pulled out a chair, and Ana agreed to sit as another glass was fetched and more limoncello poured. Having someone else slip into the driving seat of her life was unsettling, even if it was an elderly and very sweet man who had the best intentions. Ana had made a point of not asking for his help. And she wasn't sure if she liked it being given anyway.

'When Augusto gets an idea in his head it is almost impossible to stop him,' Rocco told her. 'Trust us, we know this from experience.'

'It's true,' agreed Gino. 'Edward and I wouldn't be here without him. His one-euro house scheme changed our lives.'

Ana didn't touch the limoncello, which she had always thought tasted too much like washing-up liquid. She looked at the builder leaning back in a chair that seemed too small for him, his hair rumpled, shirt half-unbuttoned.

'Your uncle is very kind but really I don't think he should be doing so much,' she told him.

Gino turned to Rocco. 'Wait, Augusto is your uncle now?'

'Apparently.' Rocco shrugged. 'He can be infuriating Signora, I am not denying that, and he interferes too much sometimes but on this occasion he has been helpful. First of all, there is the question of furniture. Edward and Gino have some in storage and he has had the idea you could lease it.'

'Look you can borrow our stuff, no need to pay,' said Edward. 'Just cover the cost of transporting it.'

'That's very generous.' Ana was surprised by the offer. Absent-mindedly she took a sip of limoncello, then frowned at the flavour and set the glass aside.

'Not really; it's only gathering dust in a barn and we'd rather it was used than rats got into it. It might not be to your taste, of course,' warned Gino.

If this man had chosen the furnishings there would be nothing to dislike about them; that wasn't what worried Ana. 'You're very generous,' she repeated. 'But there's no water at the house, no power, and the bathrooms are all in a terrible state so I don't see how ...'

Now Rocco spoke again. Nothing was a problem. He would return to the *masseria* first thing in the morning, check the plumbing and see about restoring power and water. There was a local woman who could clean any rooms she wanted to use. And he owned a truck that was large enough to carry furniture.

'Leave it all to me, Signora. You will be living there in no time.'

Ana felt slightly dizzied. She was reluctant to agree to these arrangements that had been made. But wasn't it all exactly what she wanted? Everything had been on her to-do lists, waiting to be ticked off. It would be churlish to complain when other people had been kind enough to do the ticking for her.

'In a few months' time when the sale goes through you can embark on your restoration project and make the house exactly how you want it,' finished Rocco.

Ana had a vision so clear that it might have already existed, her *masseria* the way it would look once she had finished, its grandeur less weary, its shutters thrown open and the rooms full of people, a meal being cooked in the kitchen.

'What time shall I meet you there tomorrow morning?' she asked Rocco.

'As early as you can Signora, if you are going to do this.'

'I'm doing it,' she said. 'No doubt about that.'

'Then this calls for a proper celebration,' Rocco decided. 'Champagne yes, not limoncello?'

'Champagne once I'm in the house. An early night now I think,' Ana replied.

'As you wish.' Rocco's gaze held hers, and the corners of his mouth lifted into that same wry half-smile. 'I will see you tomorrow once you have had your morning coffee with Augusto. He will be pleased to hear that everything is progressing.'

Ana nodded in agreement. She ought to thank Augusto while at the same making it clear that no more help was necessary. She could handle things herself from now on.

Dusk deepened into inky darkness as she walked up the steep incline towards her hotel rooms. She was almost there when she heard a bang then a whoosh and a sky rocket lit up the night, an explosion of golden hearts. Someone must have let it off from the top of the tower. Perhaps they were testing fireworks for the wedding party that the town was soon to be hosting. Tilting her head, Ana watched sparkles of gold shower over the rooftops. Looking down again, her head started spinning and she gripped a nearby wall until the dizzy spell had passed.

It occurred to Ana that perhaps she ought to see a doctor.

Skye

Summer is almost over and this year mostly it has been cold and wet. But today I wake to sunshine and spend half an hour picking blackberries from the brambles that are running rampant on the fringes of our property, whilst dodging stings from the nettles that also seem to be thriving. I ought to pull out the whole lot, but I kind of like the wildness. Besides today the undergrowth has rewarded me with a bowl of glossy, plump blackberries that I'll turn into bramble jelly later.

While I've been out foraging, I've missed a text from Meera. She's going for a swim and wants me to join her. Usually, I take a dip in Abbot's Pool, as that's only a few minutes away, but Meera suggests we drive to the little seaside town of Clevedon and have a coffee on the pier afterwards.

I ought to start packing for our trip. But the sky is a cloudless blue and the thought of the sea too tempting, so for once I procrastinate, putting on my swimming costume beneath my clothes and calling out to Tim that I'm taking the car. He's staring at his screen and doesn't bother replying. We're semi not speaking to one another at the moment. I'm still hurt about what he said the other day, and he's pretending not to care.

The air conditioning in the car isn't working and I get stuck in traffic on the way so arrive overheated and flustered. Meera is already in the water and waves at me as I stand on the edge peeling off my clothes.

'It's cold when you first get in,' she warns, then strikes out towards the rim where the proper swimmers thrash up and down. Clevedon has a marine pool. It isn't very deep and the seawater that tops the wall on a very high tide is from an estuary so looks opaque and dark. It does feel good though. I ease in and shiver with pleasure as the chill envelopes me, then set off at a sedate breaststroke, steering clear of the paddle boarders.

I churn up and down for a few lengths, and as I swim my mind seems to clear. The longer I think about it, the more I can see that I'm pretty unexciting. Left to my own devices I wouldn't go very far. Walks in the woods, swims in the out-doors, hours in the garden, that's me nowadays. I don't even go into the city unless I have to. Meanwhile Tim continues to live for excitement and novelty. It's never really occurred to me before now that we're becoming entirely incompatible.

'I didn't think it would actually happen,' says Meera half an hour later as we're sitting in the sunshine letting the saltwater dry on our skin. 'I thought you'd change your mind you know, about the wedding.'

Every day I ask myself if getting married is the right thing to do. I don't say that to Meera though. How can I explain how much responsibility I feel to my kids and Tim? How could I ever describe what it's like to keep on loving someone for decades of your life, as a thousand little things chip away at that love, quietly and almost without you noticing, until it's a hurt and hollow thing that might not survive.

Staring out at my view of the mouth of the Severn River, the long finger of the pier stretching out elegantly into the water, I keep all that to myself.

'Coffee then?' I ask Meera, instead.

'Coffee,' she agrees, and we both tug on our clothes over sticky-salty skin and our still damp swimming costumes.

Normally there is an entry fee for the pier, but Meera delivers cakes to the café twice a week and they greet her like an old friend. We stroll down together, past all the many plaques engraved with names that are dotted down its length, looking down at glimpses of muddy brown water through the gaps in the wooden boards.

This pier has a story that I particularly like. Years ago, one of its struts collapsed and the whole structure fell into the sea. The locals rushed out in their boats and salvaged whatever they could then worked together to raise the funds and rebuild it. A pier isn't a necessity, it's a beautiful folly, but this little seaside town wouldn't be the same without it. And now here it is again, thanks to all those people. It was their love that remade it.

We order coffee from the café in the pretty Victorian pavilion at the furthest end and sit outside to drink it. Meera is staring back towards the marine pool. She clears her throat.

'I need to talk to you,' she says, 'about my future.'

My heart is sinking, but I try not to show it. 'You're going to try for a career in animation?' I say, brightly.

'Definitely not. I mean I enjoyed that course but wouldn't want to do it all the time, too much sitting at a computer.'

'What then?' I ask.

'I want to be like you and have my own business, do work I'm really passionate about but I don't know what it is yet,' explains Meera. 'I was kind of hoping you might help me find out.'

I'm touched that she seems to be inspired by me, and, also, I can remember how it feels to be her age and not quite sure how to begin. 'That's something you have to work out for yourself, I'm afraid.'

'I knew you'd say that.' Meera screws up her eyes against the bright sun and takes a sip of her coffee.

'I do have an idea though,' I tell her. 'Tim and I are meant to be opening a small café at Bicycle Junction up in Clifton. You could run it, if you like.'

'Really?' She sounds keen. 'So, I'd be like, the manager.'

I haven't spoken to Tim about this, because I've only just had the thought myself, but I can't see why he'd object. 'Yes really.'

'Then who would do my job?'

'I'd have to find someone new. You could help train them.'

'They won't be as good as me,' she teases.

'Obviously not,' I agree.

'Do you think I'm up to it though? Running a café?' Now Meera sounds young and uncertain.

'There are things you'll need to learn but me and Tim will be there to help.'

'Tim?' she says, doubtfully.

'He does know a lot about running a business. You could learn from him.'

'I'd rather learn from you.'

I send her a fond smile. In many ways Meera feels like a second daughter. 'Yeah, I know. But, even if Tim was involved, would you be keen?'

'I would,' she agrees. 'Massively.'

Tim is still hovering over his laptop when I get home. He's unexpectedly enthusiastic about the prospect of Meera running our café. Perhaps he'll be glad to see less of her at Lost Cottage because he doesn't even argue with my intention to give her a pay rise. Tim's already talking about recruiting someone to take her place in the Cakery. Then he moves on to his plans for us to produce at-home baking kits.

'This may be an opportunity to push ahead with that.' He sounds eager.

'One thing at a time,' I tell him, putting the brakes on as always. 'Let's get the café going first.'

I leave Tim with his laptop and climb the stairs to the loft to pull down our suitcases. They're dusty and need an airing as we hardly ever use them. I know Becky will sort her own bag but my son and Tim can't be trusted to pack everything they need, so I start looking through cupboards and organising clothes in piles on the spare bed.

My own pile is brighter and more stylish thanks to my daughter who has been supervising the online purchase of what she calls resort-wear. There's a floaty garment for me to wear beside the pool at our hotel in Rome and some colourful frocks.

Then there are the wedding accessories: shoes, a blingy comb to put in my hair, earrings. I can't imagine myself in them, standing next to Tim, saying vows. Whenever I try to picture it, my mind blanks. Is this the way a bride is meant to feel? Somehow, I doubt it.

I round up my make-up and toiletries. Tim's fancy after-shave and the lotion that Josh has started putting on his skin, the radiance-boosting foundation Becky advised me to buy, the mascara Meera promises won't run when I cry. I'm not sure whether she is expecting tears of joy or sadness. At this point either seems possible.

I fetch our passports and print off the tickets even though I know everyone will laugh at me because these days you only need your phone. What if the phone goes flat though? What if you drop or lose it? It's me who thinks about these things and makes sure there's a back-up.

Which trainers will Josh want to take; he has a collection. Does Tim need a sweater in case the evenings are cold? Am I

223

really going to wear that green off-the-shoulder top? It takes me ages to organise everything and as I start packing our stuff into the cases my stomach tightens. Just like Meera, I didn't think any of this would actually happen.

Once I've finished as much as I can, I sit on the edge of the bed and stare at the stack of bags, trying to decide what task needs my attention next. Every single day there is so much for me to do. Running our lives takes everything. If I've become boring and negative, like Tim claims, then that's the reason why.

Standing up, I glimpse myself in the mirror. My hair is all saltwater ringlets, my skin glows and I look more carefree than I feel. It strikes me that I need this week in Italy, just as much as the others. Maybe it will make some sort of difference. I really want to hope so.

Ana

It was unheard of for Ana to skip her routine of morning exercises but today she had neither the time nor patience for the slow stretching of her muscles. She wanted to catch Augusto at the bar then hurry to the *masseria* to supervise whatever Rocco might be getting up to there.

Arriving early in Montenello's piazza, she found the whole sweep of it deserted. Even the fountain wasn't running yet and drifts of white confetti still covered the cobbles. At the bar her usual table was still littered with last night's glasses and, as Ana drew closer, the barman hurried out to clear them.

'Coffee?' he asked.

'Yes, please ... *caffè*,' If she was going to be living here then Ana needed to make more effort to improve her Italian.

She was checking through her to-do list when she glanced up to see Augusto making his way across the piazza. The barman must have spotted him as well because, as the elderly man sat down beside Ana, a cup of decaffeinated coffee appeared at his elbow.

'Renzo, *mio figlio*, just one good espresso macchiato to start the day,' he pleaded with the barman who waggled a finger in response.

'Ouf,' complained Augusto. 'Always my son thinks he knows best.'

Ana couldn't drink as much coffee herself these days but was resisting the move to decaffeinated. 'It doesn't taste quite the same does it,' she sympathised.

'What can I do?' The elderly man raised the cup to his lips, sipped then grimaced. 'It isn't only my coffee they are interfering with; it carries on all day: take a nap Augusto, wear a jacket, eat less salt, rest your feet. And every few moments there is someone asking me the same question, are you OK Augusto?'

Ana needed to interrupt. She had come here to thank him, not sit listening as he aired his frustrations.

'Wasn't it me that came up with the idea of the wedding competition?' Augusto continued, in full flow. 'I did this by myself, without anyone's assistance so why do they believe I need help deciding what to wear or how to eat and drink?'

At last, Ana managed to get in a few words. 'You've been such a huge help to me.'

'I have?' Augusto beamed a smile; his mood shifting like light over water.

'I didn't have the slightest idea who to contact about renting the *masseria*. Without you I wouldn't have found it in the first place. Then there's all the furniture from the hotel that you've arranged for me to borrow. You've done so much. I'm not sure how to thank you.'

'No need for thanks, I am happy to help, very happy,' he assured her, cheeks pinking. 'If there is anything else I can do ...?'

'I'm hoping to move in before too much longer, unless there are problems getting the power and water switched back on,' Ana told him.

'My nephew Rocco will look after that. He is a good man. If he says he will do something then he does it.' Augusto nodded, sagely.

Ana's best guess was that Rocco must be some sort of general handyman, able to turn his hand to all sorts of little jobs but not properly qualified for any of them.

'Once you move into the *masseria*, you will invite me to take another look at the place?' asked Augusto.

'You'll be my first visitor,' she promised.

'You will make me a very good coffee? Not like this.' Augusto pushed aside his cup.

'I'll do my best.'

'Then I will be sure my nephew knows it is important for you to be living there very soon, Signora.'

Rocco's van was already parked outside the gates by the time Ana arrived at the *masseria*. She noted with approval that he wasn't one of those tradesmen who arrived late or didn't turn up at all.

Calling out '*Buongiorno*', she wandered down the hallway and found him standing in one of the bathrooms, arms crossed, staring at a pipe. Turning to her, he held a finger to his lips and they stood together in silence for several minutes.

'What are we listening for?' asked Ana, finally.

'Dripping sounds, gurgling noises, anything to suggest a pipe might need attention,' he told her.

'Has the water been switched back on already?' Ana was surprised.

'That wasn't too difficult.' Rocco turned a tap and brownish water gushed into the washbasin. 'It comes from a well and, at least for now, you should drink bottled water, OK?'

'I think I'll be brushing my teeth with bottled water too,' observed Ana, not liking what she saw.

'The power will take a little longer to organise,' Rocco told her, turning off the tap so she no longer had to look at the distressingly soupy water. 'Today all there is for you to do is

227

choose which of the rooms you would like to have cleaned for your use.'

'This bathroom is probably the best one,' Ana screwed up her face, 'or rather the least terrible. I'll need the kitchen obviously, as well as a room to live in and another to sleep. That should be enough for now.'

Until the days cooled, Ana envisaged herself staying mostly outdoors, beneath the shade of the olive trees. She wondered how cold it would get once winter arrived. This house didn't seem to have any form of heating which meant the most sensible choice for living areas would be a couple of the smaller rooms. And yet, Ana was drawn to light-filled spaces with elegant dimensions and the place she wanted to be was the room with the tiled floor and painted ceiling.

Head flung back and lost in thought, she was gazing up at the fresco of naked cherubs playing with garlands of flowers against a sky of faded blue, trying to decide whether it ought to be professionally restored or left exactly as it was, when Rocco's deep voice startled her.

'They had a great deal of money this family, I think, or at least they liked spending it.'

Ana glanced down and, as she did so, her head started spinning. She reached for Rocco's arm to steady herself then immediately pulled it away, apologising. 'Sorry, but I'm having these strange dizzy spells at the moment. I don't know what's wrong with me.'

'Vertigo,' he said, matter-of-factly. 'I have the same problem too sometimes.'

'Vertigo? What would cause that to start happening all of a sudden?'

Rocco threw up his hands and the corners of his mouth turned down.

'You're not going to say it's my age, are you?' asked Ana, dismayed.

'I would never suggest such a thing.'

Ana had always been in favour of thinking positively about getting older. She was fit and healthy, past the many inconveniences of menopause and aiming to be an active elderly person one day just like Augusto. Vertigo was definitely not in any of her plans.

'If you have vertigo, how are you managing to go up and down ladders?' she wanted to know.

'I make it go away by doing the exercise,' Rocco explained.

'There's an exercise?'

'Yes, wait I will show you.'

She watched as Rocco sat on the tiled floor, put his head to one side, then lay down and turned his head very quickly in the opposite direction. He rested that way, flat on his back, for twenty seconds, counting them out.

'Augusto tells me the problem has to do with crystals that are floating in your ear and you have to send them back to the proper place,' he explained from his prone position. 'He suggested I try this and it works for me.'

'I suppose I should give it a go some time.'

'Why not now?'

Staring down at him, Ana hesitated. Rocco's eyes were deep-set and she noticed for the first time that they were a soft brown. His skin was tanned to butterscotch and the fingers that were beckoning her to join him on the dusty floor had neatly-squared nails. Deciding that she may as well see if this worked, Ana lowered herself carefully to a seated position, copying the same manoeuvre, moving her head sharply from one side to the other once she was lying on her back beside him.

'Well?' he asked, when she had finished counting out her twenty seconds.

'I don't feel any different.'

'Try it again, but turn your head the other way,' advised Rocco, still on the floor, propped up on one elbow.

Ana did as he suggested and, this time, the movement of her head set it spinning more fiercely than ever before. 'OK yes, that's weird ... very unpleasant actually.'

'If it makes you feel dizzy, then it is working. At least so Augusto tells me.'

'I felt dizzy all right.' Ana lay there, staring up at the blurring frescoed ceiling, waiting for the sensation to pass. 'Is that it then? Fixed?'

'If it happens again, then you repeat the exercise.'

Ana thought about incorporating this manoeuvre into her series of morning stretches. She ought to do some research about it. There may be a better solution. 'Thanks,' she said, turning to look at Rocco.

'No problem,' he replied, lips twitching with the hint of a smile.

Ana smiled back, a little awkwardly. 'Well, here we are, lying on the floor together,' she observed.

'It seemed a good idea at the time.'

'We should get up.'

'Oh, I don't know the view is good. Your fresco is very beautiful.'

'It is, isn't it?' Ana gazed upwards and thought what an amazing find the place had been.

'Will this be your living room?' Rocco wondered. 'With the cherubs looking down at you?'

'I think it has to be. Although it probably isn't very practical.'

'This place is your dream, isn't it?' Rocco was still stretched out beside her, apparently at ease. 'Dreams aren't always practical.'

★

Ana spent the morning with Rocco going through the *masseria* discussing in more detail everything that might need to be done. She found he was of the same mind as her and understood how important it was for as many original features as possible to be preserved even as modern comforts were introduced.

'Part of its charm is that it's not perfect,' said Ana. 'But all those rotting window frames and shutters aren't charming and the bathrooms definitely aren't.'

It was Rocco who suggested that she consider putting a swimming pool on a flat piece of land beyond the courtyard. The idea hadn't occurred to Ana but, as soon as he mentioned it, she imagined herself sitting beneath the shade of an olive tree looking at a cooling rectangle of blue water on a searingly hot summer's day.

'If my budget stretches that far, maybe I will,' Ana mused. 'I won't know how much I've got to work with until I've sold up everything in England.'

'You are not keeping a home there?' Rocco sounded surprised.

'No, this will be my home.'

'You will live here alone.' It seemed more a statement than a question. Ana couldn't help wondering what this rather enigmatic Italian man thought of her. Perhaps he only cared about the money he might make.

'Once the renovation is finished, I'll think about starting some sort of business. It would be a shame not to share the place with other people.' She was considering gastronomic retreats, bringing in guest chefs, holding cooking classes. The potential of the house was what occupied her mind when she wasn't thinking about how it could be improved.

Rocco shook his head, but apparently not in response to what she had said. He was poking at a rotten window frame. 'All of these will need to be replaced.'

Ana frowned. 'With modern windows? That would be such a shame.'

'Perhaps there will be something more authentic to be found at a demolition yard. Leave it with me for now.'

He moved towards the door and Ana assumed he must be finished with her for the day.

'You're sure the bathroom is OK?' she called. 'No leaks to worry about?'

As Rocco turned back to her, his face was shadowed against the bright light pouring through the open doorway. 'I will take another look but right now it is time to eat. You will join me?'

This was unexpected and Ana felt taken aback. Did he mean that they should go and have lunch together at a restaurant somewhere? She couldn't make out his expression and wasn't sure how to respond.

'You are hungry?' Rocco asked. 'I brought plenty of food. And it is lunchtime, yes?'

'Well yes,' she agreed. 'It is.'

Following him outside, Ana's eyes widened as he produced a wooden folding table and two chairs from his van, setting them up in the courtyard beneath a pergola covered in leafy wisteria. The table was dressed in a bright blue cloth and napkins, yellow cushions were placed on the chairs and, gesturing for her to sit, Rocco fetched a large cooler bag.

'Do you do this for all your clients?' asked Ana, as he passed over a plate and some cutlery.

There was the trace of a smile on his face and he began unpacking the bag, covering the small table with packages and tubs, two glass tumblers and a bottle of sparkling water.

'*Buon appetito*,' he said, unwrapping a panino for her.

The sandwich was a flat disc of woodfired bread, split in two and filled with a soft chilli-spiked spread of Calabrian sausage and red onions oven roasted until they were jammy.

There was a salad of tender artichoke hearts and earthy shavings of pecorino cheese, another of yellow tomatoes and torn basil leaves, along with a rustic tart of baked egg and smoky pancetta.

Augusto must have insisted he provide her with lunch, thought Ana as she tore into the panino, savouring the sweetness of Tropea onions. Or perhaps he had nothing to do with this, and rather it was a bid from Rocco to win her over and secure her business.

She looked towards the old stone walls of the *masseria*, the view from here all layered rooftops and sharp corners. The air smelt of wild fennel warming in the midday sun and the only sound was the hum of bees. Red earth and silvery-leaved olive trees stretched away in every direction. Ana took another bite of panino and watched Rocco do the same, holding the woodfired bread in both hands, tearing into it with his teeth. For a few moments they ate together in silence. Ana wondered if he had prepared the lunch himself or had his wife make it. Whoever it was understood seasoning.

'My first meal at my new home,' she said, between mouthfuls. 'Thank you, it's delicious.'

Rocco gave her a slow, easy smile. 'The first of many meals, I hope.'

Skye

I'm experiencing Rome through the expressions on my children's faces. Josh's wonder when we turn a corner and find ourselves right in front of the Pantheon, Becky's joy when we stand at a balustrade on the Gianicolo Hill, looking down on domes and a mosaic of rooftops. If I'm honest, this city is too intense for me, overcrowded and hot. There always seems to be an ambulance racing past with its siren blaring loudly. The Spanish Steps are plastered with tourists and we have to push through people to stand beside the Trevi Fountain. It's another reminder of how small and quiet my life has become, and how I prefer it that way. I don't say that to my family though. The kids aren't daunted by Rome's pace or noise, and Tim seems so at home in this place where people talk more loudly and smile more often.

Today we have come to somewhere less frantic. The Tivoli Gardens lie up in the hills, half an hour beyond Rome and here it is cooler and quite peaceful. First, we walk through the empty rooms of the Villa d'Este, our voices echoing as we marvel at its frescoed floors and ceilings. Then we are outside, descending worn stone steps into a formal garden where we drift away in different directions to explore its green-walled pathways.

The air here smells damp and mossy, the sound of rushing water is everywhere. I come across a whole avenue lined with fountains and an awe-inspiring cascade. What I like most though are the half-hidden places, the stone alcoves where a statue stands guard over a still pool, the smaller fountain of Mother Nature almost forgotten behind some shrubs at the far end of the gardens. I like the clipped hedges, slender spires of cypress trees and the sense of calm. It's the first time in days that I've been alone and I sit for a while in a shady spot on the rim of a fountain.

It's so peaceful here that my mind seems to empty. Thoughts rush in and fill the space, of course – I've never got the hang of mindfulness and meditation – but these thoughts are different. I've got the urge to paint the way this place makes me feel. To pick up a brush and bring its watery calm and cool to an empty stretch of canvas. It's the first time in ages that I've thought about painting. I assumed I'd left that part of myself behind somewhere but, apparently, it's still in there.

I'm sitting lost in thought, still making art in my head, when Becky comes to find me.

'Thank you for suggesting that we come here, it's perfect,' I tell her.

'Actually, this was Dad's idea,' says Becky. 'He said you'd like it.'

I'm surprised because I didn't think Tim paid that much attention to what I do or don't like. But he's right, this place is me completely.

When he appears, Tim is full of talk about installing a water feature in the garden of Lost Cottage, or at least a statue. For once I let him run on, instead of forcing him back to reality.

'Imagine living here,' he says, gazing up towards the Renaissance villa standing high above its gardens. 'Imagine the parties they must have had.'

I nod at him, knowing that, if it were mine, I wouldn't need to fill this place with other people to enjoy it.

'Montenello tomorrow,' Tim reminds me.

I'm anxious about the long drive south, although he'll be the one behind the wheel. This morning's shorter trip to Tivoli has proved that Tim isn't daunted by chaotic traffic or hooting horns. Hitting the *autostrada*, he put his foot down and drove like a real Italian.

'If you're not confident on the road, that's what gets you into trouble,' he said, as I eyed the speedometer nervously.

When I misread the satnav, and we ended up semi-lost in the narrow back streets of old Tivoli, squeezing through a narrow tunnel then navigating past parked cars and pedestrians, I was the one clenching my jaw with tension while Tim seemed to find the whole thing a hoot.

'Yes, Montenello tomorrow,' I repeat now, thinking of the many kilometres of motorway we'll need to cover to reach it.

'A small hilltop town where life moves slowly, that's what the guides say,' Tim tells me. 'It should be peaceful there too. I think you're going to love it.'

Neither of us mentions the wedding. We haven't talked about it much since we arrived in Italy. Tim has been distracted by other things and I have nothing left to say. I keep telling myself that it's just one day out of several and I'm doing it for my family. Watching our children, Becky scanning the guide book, and telling Josh something about the fountain they are looking at, seeing them together in this beautiful place, I hope I can get through it, that one day.

I'm surprised by how mountainous Italy is. Tim and the kids roll their eyes when I tell them that. Haven't I followed our route online, they want to know? Didn't I do any research at all? We're speeding south down the *autostrada* towards

Basilicata. Becky is in the passenger seat navigating and I'm in the back with Josh who is pointing out places of interest. Monte Cassino high on a hill to our left. A while later Vesuvius on our right dominating the skyline above Naples.

Tim is all for taking a detour and finding an interesting hilltop town in Campania where we can have lunch. I'm not convinced it's the best idea.

'Let's eat at a motorway service station, when we stop for petrol,' I suggest. 'Isn't that what we planned?'

'Yeah, you're probably right,' he concedes. 'We don't want to arrive late in Montenello and miss the welcome party.'

'I'm sorry, what welcome party?' I ask the back of Tim's head.

'Cocktails with the mayor and other local dignitaries. Sounds dull but it would be rude not to show up,' he says, casually.

'You didn't tell me about this,' I say, accusingly.

'Yes, I did, I mentioned it.'

'He did Mum,' the kids chorus in support.

'That's why we got you the orange dress,' adds Becky. 'And I thought you could wear the green one for lunch in the olive groves the day after the wedding.'

'I didn't know about this lunch either.'

'Dad told you,' Josh insists. 'We were all talking about it. You can't have been paying attention.'

It's entirely possible that I may tune out Tim a lot of the time. When you've been with someone for years you already know most of what they're likely to say; listening doesn't seem as necessary. But surely, I'd never tune out my kids in the same way? They must have had the conversation while I wasn't in the room.

'We all talked? Really?' I ask, not believing it.

'You were probably distracted, thinking about work,' says

237

Tim, hooting at a car that is straddling two lanes then speeding past as it drifts sideways.

'No more surprises, OK,' I tell Tim.

'Fine.' Gripping the steering wheel, he shrugs. 'There's also going to be a firework display on our wedding night. It's probably not a big deal though. I'm sure they're always letting off skyrockets.'

I'm seeing now that my one day is going to seep into the others, filling them with wedding glitter, with people I don't know, speeches and forced conversations.

Lost in thought I'm slow to notice that we're pulling into a motorway service station. The heat hits us as we get out of the car and go to investigate what there might be for us to eat.

No one there speaks any English but Tim doesn't need language to communicate. Soon he's got the cashier smiling as he's miming what he wants, pointing at things and most likely mispronouncing the few Italian words he does know. We buy far too much. Panini filled with buffalo mozzarella and prosciutto, pastries that look like crisp shells and are filled with a dense ricotta custard, pizza breads and a salad of fresh green leaves, gorgonzola and walnuts. It all tastes good and I'm particularly taken with the flaky, layered sweet pastry. I've never come across anything like it at home. Could the Lost Cakery try producing a version?

Tim goes back to the counter and has them write down its name. *Sfogliatella.* Josh looks it up on his phone and I pore over the recipe. Getting the layered effect with the pastry seems a bit fiddly.

'You should give it a go,' Tim encourages me. 'It would be great to have something totally different to offer when we open the café.'

'You're right,' I agree. 'It would.'

'Maybe we can find someone who'll share their secret

recipe. Worth asking right,' adds Tim, before darting back to the counter to order tiny cups of fiercely strong espresso.

Despite the coffee, I fall asleep in the car after lunch. When I open my eyes again, we've left the *autostrada* behind and are winding our way through the mountains, through tunnels and round hairpin bends. Noticing that I'm awake, Josh puts on some Italian pop music. Soon he and Becky are complaining about how cheesy it is, while Tim insists that actually we like it.

Then Tim launches into one of his stories. The kids must have heard it a hundred times before. He's describing a hike we went on years and years ago and his determination to take a shortcut across a field through a herd of what he insisted were cows.

'Your mum and I had an iPod back then. They were the latest thing. We used to walk hand in hand, wearing one earbud each, so we could hear the same music. We were listening to a terrible cheesy pop song very like this one, enjoying our walk and the sunshine. Then we got a bit closer and your mum realised the cows were actually bulls. They started following us and she said we shouldn't run, in case they chased us, but like an idiot I panicked, dropped everything and raced off. And guess what, they did chase me. I only just made it over the gate. Meanwhile your mum very calmly picked up everything I'd dropped and climbed the fence to safety.'

'You're an idiot, Dad,' says Becky, fondly.

'I totally am,' Tim agrees.

He has so many of these stories. Sometimes he'll remember things that I've completely forgotten. Mostly they don't show him in the greatest light. Tim never seems to mind.

He's telling another one now and the kids are already laughing. As the car speeds on, he keeps talking.

Finally, we have our first glimpse of Montenello, a cluster of buildings clinging to a steep-sided hill with a tall tower at its highest point. Tim pulls over to take photographs and, when another motorist does the same, he asks him to take a family shot; the four of us lined up in front of the town where we'll be spending the next week.

From there it's a short drive across a causeway and along a road that skirts upwards, Becky expertly guiding us towards the hotel's parking garage. Everything happens so smoothly. Our luggage is spirited away and we're transported to our accommodation, to freshen up and change our clothes, ready for the cocktail party.

We're staying in a grand palazzo. It has soft gold walls and rows of shuttered windows and inside everything is perfect. Surfaces gleam, cushions are plumped, ornaments are positioned in all sorts of places where a stray elbow might easily catch them.

'Don't break anything,' I tell Josh and Becky. 'Or if you do make sure it's not something priceless.'

The hotel's owner, Edward, does his best to put me at ease, showing us through the house and explaining how it was once a ruin, and bought for just one euro, then restored painstakingly by him and his husband. Tim is completely enchanted by this story and full of questions. I can tell he is dreaming already about doing something similar.

'The ceilings were collapsing, the shutters were rotten, the whole place was falling apart,' Edward is explaining. 'Our one euro investment ended up costing an awful lot more.'

'Look at it now, though. All that effort has been worth it.' Tim is gazing at the frescoed walls of a large reception room and I suspect that already dreams are starting to form in his head.

'Do we really have this whole palazzo to ourselves for a week?' Becky seems astonished to find herself in such a place.

'You really do,' says Edward, smiling. 'The town is very excited to welcome you all here. I'll be at the cocktail party later with Gino, my husband, so we can introduce you to everyone.'

Edward is warm and reassuring, still I'd rather spend the evening having a quiet dinner with my family. 'None of us understands any Italian,' I tell him. 'Is it going to be a bit awkward?'

'Don't worry, there'll be plenty of people there who speak English.'

I put on the orange dress, as Becky suggested. In the mirror my face looks pinched and pale and, remembering Tim's lie, I suspect it might not be too difficult to believe I've been through an illness. He may have told them that I want to put the whole thing behind me but what if someone mentions it? Will I be forced into lying too? My stomach turns over at the thought.

'You're not really a party person, are you Mum?' Becky smiles at my reflection, as she's pulling my hair into an elaborate up-do she must have learnt from YouTube.

'I'm kind of boring, aren't I?' I say, ruefully.

'No, you're not,' Becky tells me. 'People are into different things, that's all.'

Whenever I go to a party with Tim, I lose him the moment we walk in the door. He is a life and soul person, it energises him to meet new people, and he tends to be the last to leave any social gathering. Meanwhile I'll end up in a kitchen, helping prepare food, or sit alone outside in a garden. We're so different, how did we ever end up spending all those years together?

'I'll need to make an effort this evening,' I say, watching my daughter transform me. 'After all, these people are hosting us.'

'It'll be fun,' says Becky. 'Maybe there'll be champagne.'

The party is in the town hall and the mayor is the first to welcome us. To Becky's delight, we're given glasses of bubbly, and I gulp mine down a little too quickly. Soon Edward is at my elbow and, as promised, he steers me through the room introducing me to people. A very elderly man explains in un-expectedly fluent English that the wedding competition was all his idea. A rather beautiful woman in a bright red dress with a feathered trim tells me that she is looking forward to our lunch in her olive grove. The wedding planner, Elise, comes and introduces herself, wanting to set my mind at rest, because every little detail is organised and I don't need to worry at all.

'Are you nervous?' she asks.

'Do I seem it?'

'Maybe a little. Let me get you some more bubbly.'

As she's flagging down a waiter, I think how pretty she is, with her long fair hair and glowing skin. She's definitely English, but seems to speak fluent Italian.

'It must be overwhelming,' Elise says, furnishing me with a fresh glass. 'But we all want you to have a great time so if there's anything you're not comfortable with or don't like, just let us know.'

'I'm not going to be a nightmare bride,' I promise, taking another gulp of bubbly.

The wedding planner laughs. 'Well, that's a relief.'

'Tim and I have been together so long. It feels a bit silly us getting married. I can't help thinking you should have chosen younger people to win your competition.'

'Often they're the nicest weddings though,' she tells me. 'Couples who have some life behind them, who have survived a few ups and downs. Don't get me wrong, the romantic young couples are gorgeous. But you can't help feeling a little worried for them. What will happen when romance meets up with reality?' Then her tone lightens. 'My job isn't to worry about that, of course. I'm only responsible for making sure the wedding day is perfect. And Skye? If you're in love, getting married is never silly.'

In the end I do reasonably well at the party, helped by lots of bubbly. For a while I'm held in conversation by the elderly man, who reminds me three times that his name is Augusto and he was the mastermind behind the competition. I'm getting a strong sense that he doesn't approve of the bridal gown I've chosen.

'You are a beautiful woman and it is so ... .'

'Simple,' I say, firmly. 'I like simplicity. Best to leave glamour to the young ones like my daughter.'

'But you are not old, Signora,' he is quick to point out, and I suppose compared to him I'm not.

We are joined by another older man who has a medal pinned to his lapel. He proceeds to explain at length and in very broken English why it was awarded to him. Even Augusto's eyes glaze over. Suddenly he grips my arm.

'But Signora, you must meet my new friend Ana.' He steers me away from the medal-wearer and towards a woman who looks vaguely familiar. 'She is English, just like you.'

The woman is somewhere in her fifties, elegant in an unfussy way, with fair hair that curls softly round her face, red lipstick and stormy blue eyes.

'Ana King,' she says, holding out a hand to shake mine, and suddenly I know where I recognise her from, although she doesn't look much like the photographs I've seen.

'You're the editor of *Culinaria* magazine,' I gasp, hand to my mouth.

'Former editor, but yes that's me.'

'I loved that magazine so much. I couldn't believe they folded it.'

'Then you'll be pleased to hear they're bringing it back,' says Ana. 'Not with me at the helm though. I live here now. I'm buying an old farmhouse and have plans to restore it.'

I'm concerned that if Tim meets too many of these people who are living the Italian dream, he'll be unstoppable. 'How amazing,' I say, politely.

'Onwards, right?' says Ana, arm aloft and fist clenched, a strong gesture. 'New challenges lie ahead.'

'Onwards,' I agree, wishing I had a fraction of her courage. Ana King is so impressive.

Ana

Ana had been in two minds about attending the cocktail party but, in the end, talked herself round. It would be a useful opportunity to meet people after all. Besides the *agriturismo* where she was now staying was rundown and evenings spent alone in her room weren't fun.

Worryingly, it seemed like she might be stuck in the dispiriting farm stay for a while as everything to do with her *masseria* was taking far too long. Gathering the documents required before the power could be switched on, having the wiring checked for safety. Patience had never been Ana's greatest strength and she was seriously considering buying a barbecue grill to cook on and moving in anyway. It was time to get on with her new life.

At least the cocktail party might be a short distraction from feeling so frustrated and she was bound to know at least a few of the other guests – Edward and Gino from the hotel; Augusto of course. As Ana struggled to apply make-up in front of the foggy tarnished bathroom mirror, she found herself wondering if Rocco might show up. Her handyman continued to be an enigma. Twice now he had arrived at the *masseria* with food to share for lunch. They had eaten pasta al forno with a creamy sauce of ricotta and tomato. The last time he had managed to uncover a peach tree in the overgrown gardens and together they had devoured the ripe, sun-warmed fruit, juices running down their arms. It was all very lovely, but what Ana really needed was progress and very little had been made.

As the days drifted by and nothing much changed, she wasn't quite sure what to do with herself. This dress she was wearing for the party was a new one, bought when she was trying to distract herself by browsing through the shops of a nearby town, Borgo del Colle. It wasn't really her style, but for some reason she hadn't wanted to leave empty-handed and, given its cost, she had to wear it now. Made from ivory linen, covered in an embroidered pattern in a matching shade, it was floaty and casual. In it, Ana looked far more relaxed than she felt.

Arriving at the party, she found the room already full. Ana had been to enough of these semi-formal functions not to feel fazed at the prospect of walking alone into one. She circled the crowd, scanning faces for someone she recognised. There was Augusto in the centre of the room, chatting to a red-headed woman as well as an old man with a medal pinned to his jacket. Ana was heading in their direction, when Edward stopped her, putting a drink in her hand.

'I didn't realise you were coming,' he said.

'Well, I was invited, although I'm not really sure why.'

'Italian towns love to throw a festa.' Edward told her. 'They're always celebrating something, a cheese, a grape harvest, a saint's day. If you stick around then you'll find yourself invited to a lot of parties.'

'I'm sticking around,' promised Ana, clinking her glass against his. 'But I don't know that I'll be going to lots of parties. This evening I'm here mainly to escape the shitty *agriturismo* I managed to book into. Are you absolutely sure you can't fit me back into your hotel?'

Edward frowned over the rim of his glass. 'Not this week sorry, we're fully booked. There's a possibility I could find you something later next week, but won't you be in your own place by then?'

'I hope so but the way things are going, who would know.'

Ana needed to vent and Edward was right there, a sympathetic ear. Between sips of the dry, yeasty bubbly she told him about her frustrations with the power company.

'Before they'll give me any electricity, I have to supply them with my Italian tax code and getting one of those seems a challenge,' she complained. 'It's driving me crazy.'

'Yeah, I know, but that's Italy; you just have to go with it.'

'Also, the place where I'm staying is in a worse state than the *masseria*,' she continued. 'The toilet doesn't flush properly and don't even start me on how hard the bed is. I keep thinking it's not worth finding somewhere better because I'll be moving into my own place soon.'

'It's definitely worth finding somewhere better,' Edward advised.

'And this handyman of yours? Do you recommend him or is he a bit of a time waster?'

'Handyman?' Edward sounded uncertain. 'I'm sorry but who are you talking about?'

'Rocco.'

'Rocco Cicuzzo?' Edward checked and when Ana nodded, he smiled. 'Well, I suppose he's a man and he is pretty handy.'

Before she could ask exactly what he meant, Ana heard Augusto calling her name. As she glanced over, another woman appeared at Edward's side and it seemed their chat was over. That was the thing about cocktail parties, there was always such a churn of people and you were meant to move on to the next, then the next, never really managing more than a shallow conversation. Ana preferred dinner parties; sitting down, eating well and talking properly. That was more her style.

She could see Augusto beckoning her insistently. He must want her to meet the red-headed woman, and was gripping her elbow, leading her over.

'This is our bride, Skye Olsen, the winner of our competition,' he said, with evident pride.

The red-headed woman was very attractive, although in Ana's opinion the bright orange of the dress she was wearing wasn't her most flattering shade. As she introduced herself, the woman gasped.

'You're the editor of *Culinaria* magazine,' she said, and instantly Ana wished she hadn't bothered coming to the party.

'Former editor, but yes that's me,' she replied, and as Skye launched into how much she had loved the magazine, Ana cut her short, changing the subject, talking about her exciting new life, then actually striking a power pose. 'Onwards,' she said, fist clenched while inwardly she cringed. Who was she kidding?

But Skye seemed to buy it. She wasn't to know that any mention of *Culinaria* magazine still felt like a knife cut to Ana. Or that onwards wasn't really happening right now.

'Of course, it's all progressing very slowly,' Ana felt she had to admit. 'And at the moment I'm staying in this awful *agriturismo*. I really must find somewhere better.'

'Can't you stay in the hotel here in Montenello?' asked Skye. 'It's lovely.'

'Fully booked, unfortunately.'

'But there's loads of room in the palazzo where we're based. So many bedrooms; and we only need three of them.'

'I'd imagine they want you to have that place to yourselves; as a part of your prize,' said Ana, thinking that, tempting as the palazzo sounded, she didn't need any more *Culinaria* conversations.

'They have all these activities planned for us so we'll hardly be there.' Skye seemed set on the idea of Ana staying with them. 'And the place is vast. Why don't we have a word with Edward? I mean, that's if you'd like to stay there.'

'I don't know I ...' Ana summoned thoughts of the *agriturismo*. This evening when she had shut her door, half its frame had collapsed onto the ground.

'There's just one thing,' added Skye. 'Please can you not mention your renovation plans to Tim, my partner? The thing is he's really impressionable and I'm worried that by the time we leave, we'll be buying a *masseria* too.'

Skye smiled nervously, so she might have been joking, but Ana had the impression that she was genuinely concerned.

'May I ask a favour in return? Could we not talk about *Culinaria*? I'm still licking my wounds where that magazine is concerned. It's taking a while to get over what happened.'

Skye's hand flew to her mouth. 'I'm so sorry.'

'No need to apologise,' Ana said, hastily. 'I would very much like to share the palazzo with you. And I promise not to talk your fiancé into buying a ruin.'

'My fiancé ... oh yes Tim. We've been together so long it seems funny to call him that.' Skye finished her drink then stared down at the empty glass. 'I've lost count of how many of these I've had so I guess that means I shouldn't have another.'

'What activity do they have planned for you tomorrow?' Ana wondered.

'A walking tour of Montenello, guided personally by the mayor.'

'Oh dear.'

'I know. I'd much rather just hang out with my family, but I can't really say no.'

'Well actually, you could. The mayor seems like a nice guy but he's *very* passionate about his town. A guided tour could

249

go on for some time. Just tell him you'd rather explore alone.'

'Do you think he'll mind?'

'Probably, but he'll get over it.'

Skye seemed to be considering the idea. Then she nodded. 'OK, but I'm going to need another drink before I do that.'

'Let's talk to Edward first ... and score me a room in your palazzo.'

Skye smiled. 'It'd be good to have you there ... even if I'm not allowed to be a fangirl. We can still talk about food though, right?'

'Definitely,' agreed Ana. 'Food remains my favourite thing to talk about.'

'You wouldn't happen to know if there's anyone that does cooking classes in Montenello?' Skye wondered. 'I'm particularly interested in cakes and pastries.'

'Then you'll be pleased to hear there's an exceptionally good *pasticceria* in the main piazza.' Ana enjoyed a small sense of feeling like a local. 'It might be worth asking there.'

'I'll do that tomorrow,' Skye decided.

'Instead of going on a forced march with the mayor?'

'Exactly.' Skye laughed. 'My kids might be keen on a cooking class too. Not my ... my fiancé though.' Her eyes drifted across the room towards a tall man with lots of curly hair and an animated air. 'It's not his thing at all.'

'I'd be interested in joining you,' said Ana, impulsively. 'I need to distract myself from the joys of dealing with Italian bureaucracy. Did you know that before you can get your power switched on you need an Italian fiscal code ... and for that I need an appointment at the tax office and apparently they're behind with everything because of the pandemic so they're keeping me waiting.'

'We have to get you out of that *agriturismo*.'

'We really do.'

Threading their way through the room filled with over-dressed people, Ana was now very glad she had made the effort to come. A room in the palazzo would be a vast improvement on a farm stay that had looked infinitely nicer online. And having some company for a few days might not be such a bad thing. It would help stop her brooding over all the things she couldn't control.

Edward seemed surprised by their plan but was happy to go along with it. He said there was a room already set up and Ana could move in whenever she liked. With that sorted, Skye set off to tackle the mayor while Ana tracked down Augusto. If anyone knew about cooking classes, she imagined it would be him.

At first, he was nowhere to be seen and she assumed he had grown tired and gone home. Then Ana spotted him, at the far end of the chamber, seated in a throne-like chair that must have been used for mayoral ceremonies.

As Ana approached, he tilted his glass at her. 'Don't tell my son and daughter that this isn't sparkling water.'

'I won't say a word,' Ana promised.

'You are enjoying the party?'

'Actually, I am.'

'There will be speeches soon; lots of speeches,' he added, cheerfully.

'That sounds less enjoyable.'

Augusto nodded. 'This is why I have filled my glass with something more than sparkling water.'

'I ought to follow your example.' Ana cast her eyes around the room, searching for a waiter.

'I think she is very nice, the lady who has won our competition,' Augusto decided.

'I think so too,' said Ana. 'We had a good chat. Both of us are thinking we might like to take a cooking class, learn some authentic regional recipes. Would you know of anyone local who runs them?'

Augusto considered the question, finger and thumb pinching the bridge of his nose, deep in thought. 'No,' he decided.

'What about your daughter, the one who runs the trattoria. Might she consider it?'

'No,' Augusto said again, this time in a tone that was more definite.

'Skye has a particular interest in cakes and pastries,' Ana persisted.

'Then yes, I can help.' Augusto waved his glass triumphantly. 'My granddaughter Cecilia, she has the *pasticceria*, I will talk to her ... for me she will do this.'

Ana wished that she could sort everything in her life so quickly and easily. She suspected even Augusto would be defeated by Italian bureaucracy. There was nothing to be done to speed the process up. Without a tax code Ana couldn't buy the *masseria*, or rent it for any length of time, and she couldn't even open a bank account. To wait was her only option. She could almost feel her blood pressure rising.

'I'm going to slip away before the speeches start,' she decided. 'Do you want to come too? We could eat at whichever food truck is parked in the piazza this evening.'

'I must stay,' Augusto told her. 'I am expected to be here.'

Ana left as the mayor was climbing onto a podium and tapping his microphone to make sure it was working. Walking down the marble-floored corridor towards the exit she heard him begin to speak and wondered how long it might be before he got round to stopping. She didn't envy Skye and her family. It seemed as if their free wedding might be coming at a cost.

Half skipping out of the door, she crossed the piazza towards the bar. She could have one more drink before driving back to spend her final night at the awful farm stay.

Skye

It's fair to say that I'm starstruck. Ana King is a total legend, a foodie icon, and we've just been chatting together like we're friends. None of my family gets why I'm so excited. Becky seems almost put out at having to share the palazzo with an outsider and Josh couldn't care less. Only Tim shows any interest.

'She edits that recipe magazine you collect, right? *Culinaria*? What's she doing in Italy?'

'I think she's taking a sabbatical,' I say, careful not to put any ideas in his head by mentioning the old farmhouse she's planning to restore.

We're back in the palazzo, snacking on a platter of cheese and cured meats. The mayor wanted to take us out for dinner but it was late by the time the party ended and we were all exhausted. Besides I think we've heard enough from him for now.

'That was a very long speech,' Tim remarks.

'Brace yourself, I think there are going to be more speeches,' I tell him.

At least I've managed to get us out of tomorrow's guided tour of the town. The mayor looked a bit crushed when I told him that we'd rather do our own thing, but then rallied when we agreed to have lunch with him at the little trattoria in the main piazza. It's obvious the kids aren't thrilled at the prospect but I point out to them that a lunch can't possibly last more than an hour or two.

'It's the least we can do, given this whole week in Montenello is free.'

'But Mum, the party was so boring,' complains Josh. 'I got stuck with some man who didn't seem to get that I can't understand a word of Italian. He went on and on.'

'Well, I had to talk to the guy with the medal and he did speak some English; that was worse,' says Becky.

'We all have to do things we don't want to do,' I tell them.

For once Tim backs me up. 'Having a good time is just a matter of attitude,' he adds. 'If you decide to enjoy yourself then you will.'

That is the kind of thing he's fond of saying. Often, I find his mindset mantras deeply irritating, but on this occasion, I'm forced to agree.

'Look at this place, how can we have a bad time?' asks Tim, waving his arms around expansively, before going on to tell Becky and Josh how proud he was of them at the party, watching them mix with a roomful of strangers, how confident they seemed, and how grown up. Both of the kids are pinking with pleasure at his words.

'This cheese is insane,' says Becky, tasting a slice from a pure white round that is coated in dried grass. 'It must be goat … or sheep maybe.'

'The salami is really spicy,' Josh tells her. 'Oh, and have some of those wrinkly black olives. They're a taste sensation.'

And there they are back again, our fun, upbeat kids, who love trying new things and going places. For a few moments I forget about everything except how glad I am that we're all here together.

As we're getting ready for bed, Tim is darting around the room picking up objects he's only just noticed; a Murano glass paperweight, a vintage copper shoehorn. Meanwhile I'm taking off the make-up I'm not used to wearing. He turns to me and says, 'I was truly proud of them this evening you know, the way they handled themselves. We made great kids together, you and me.'

'Really?' I pause, cotton wool pad in hand. 'I thought I was bringing them up to have life-limiting beliefs, making them feel like the sky was going to fall on their heads, isn't that what you said that day after our meeting at Bicycle Junction?'

'Did I?' Tim sounds guilty. 'It was just a stupid thing that came out of my mouth in the middle of a fight. I didn't mean it. Just forget whatever I said.'

'I can't though,' I tell him, as I start scrubbing mascara from my lashes again. 'Because it's made me think about you and me, how different we are, how incompatible.'

'Skye, what are you talking about?' Tim is about to climb into bed, and pauses.

'We're polar opposites, that's the problem.'

'That's why it works,' he tells me. 'We balance each other out. When I go too far you reel me back in. And I keep things interesting.'

I look at him, dressed in blue striped pyjamas, his head a mass of greying curls, his skin tanned. He's so familiar to me. I know every inch of Tim, every mole, every scar, often I know what he's going to say before the words come out of his mouth.

'The more I think about what you told me that day, the truer it seems,' I tell him.

'Skye,' he says, his voice very soft.

'We shouldn't be getting married. Sometimes I'm not even

sure whether we should still be together.' As the words leave my mouth, I see Tim's face crumple.

'You don't mean that.' Tim comes over and, taking the damp cotton wool pad, holds my hands in his. 'This is that girl isn't it, the one who hangs on your coat-tails, she's poisoning you against me.'

'You mean Meera?' I pull away, grab another pad and soak it in cleanser.

'Yeah,' he says. 'I do mean Meera. She's judgmental ... she can't stand me ... and now it seems like she's coming between us.'

'No, this has nothing to do with her,' I say, turning my back on him.

In the mirror I watch as Tim climbs into bed, pulling the sheet up to his chest and crossing his arms over it. 'Every marriage goes through ups and downs, this is just one of the downs for you,' he decides.

I shake my head, but Tim forges on, as though he hasn't noticed.

'We'd both be fine on our own, no question about it. But we're better together, Skye.'

I turn and stare at him, waiting, because I know he has more to say.

'The kids will be leaving home before long and then we'll be free to do whatever we like. I want more adventures and to have them with you, before we both grow old together. I've always thought that was what you wanted too.'

'You never asked though,' I point out.

Now Tim is staring at me, his eyes very wide in his narrow face.

'And even if you had asked, you wouldn't have listened to whatever I said in reply,' I tell him.

'Yes, I would,' argues Tim. 'It's you that's uncommunicative.

256

You hardly ever listen. And you don't talk to me, not properly, not anymore.'

Why am I even trying to talk to him now? It must be all the bubbly I drank. Or perhaps it's meeting Ana King, hearing her talk about her life, seeing the way she clenched her fist in such a determined way. Onwards, she said, like a person who knows precisely what direction they are heading in. It has made me question where I am going.

'Anyway, I do listen,' says Tim defensively. 'If there's something you're not happy with, then you only need to tell me. I want you to be happy, Skye.'

'The lies,' I say. 'I'm not happy about them and I've definitely told you.'

'OK, fair enough.' Tim's eyes can't quite meet mine. 'That's an example of me going too far. I mean I did it with the best of intentions, but ...'

'For fuck's sake, Tim.' I shout the words then we both fall silent, concerned Josh or Becky might have heard. Fortunately, the walls of the palazzo are thick and often the kids fall asleep wearing headphones; there are no sounds from them at all.

'I'll make it right,' he promises. 'I'll fix everything. Just give me a chance. Don't do anything hasty.'

We're silent as I change into my nightgown. Silent as I climb into bed beside him, turn off the lights and lie down. Somewhere there's a clock ticking. That's the only thing I can hear.

'It's so dark here,' says Tim. 'So quiet.'

'No darker or quieter than at Lost Cottage,' I point out.

'I never seem to notice it there.'

He falls silent again, but I can hear him breathing. I'm used to the sound of him beside me. It would be strange to fall asleep without it.

'I love you, Skye,' he says, touching my back.

'I know you do,' I tell him.

Ana

The prospect of moving back into the hotel had lifted Ana's spirits. And now she had woken to a message from Rocco that contained more cheering news. Today her furniture was to be delivered to the *masseria*.

Intending to be there to meet the van so she could make sure everything was positioned exactly as she wanted, she checked out of the awful *agriturismo*, threw her bags into her car, and headed off without bothering with breakfast.

It was only a short drive; which was why she had booked into the farm stay in the first place, so Ana arrived well before the van appeared. Waiting for Rocco, she regretted not stopping at least for a coffee.

Then she heard a screech of brakes and the rumble of an engine, and saw the van raising clouds of dust as it came up the driveway, Rocco at the wheel and a young man in the passenger seat beside him. As they climbed out and came towards her, Ana thought she could detect a family resemblance, something about the strength in their faces and bodies.

'Meet Biagio,' said Rocco, and Ana assumed this must be his son. 'He is going to help me carry everything in.'

They didn't waste time. The van doors were flung open and they launched straight into emptying it, the two men carrying the larger items – bed, table, sofa, wardrobe – while Ana followed with dining chairs and lamps, issuing instructions.

'The sofa over there, I think. No, a little to the right so it's facing the window. The table can stay in the kitchen. Can you help me with this lamp, it's a little awkward. Yes, thanks that's great. Oh, and you've brought me some bedside tables too.'

By the time they were finished Rocco had stripped his overalls down to his waist and was sheened with sweat. Ana wasn't entirely satisfied with the position of the sofa, but thought she could probably shift it herself without causing any more damage to the tiles.

'That's done then,' she said, pleased.

Rocco looked around. 'It is a little too minimal,' he decided. 'Do you have many of your own belongings to bring over from England?'

'I got rid of a lot and don't feel as though many of the things I do still own would be right here.' Ana walked into the kitchen and stared at the scarred walls. 'Although wait, I do have an idea. Could you and Biagio help me with one last thing?'

'Sure,' agreed Rocco. 'We are here, so you might as well make use of us.'

Still in her car, was Ana's collection of vintage copper moulds. They had hung in the kitchen of her London apartment and she couldn't bear to leave them behind. It was silly really, driving all over the Italian countryside with them stowed in a box on the back seat, but Ana had liked knowing they were there, even if she hadn't been sure what she would do with them. Now she could see exactly where they belonged.

The box was heavy, but Rocco had no trouble hefting it on one shoulder and carrying it in. He watched as she unpacked, pulling out Victorian copper moulds for jellies, blancmanges and pies, polished and layered with tissue paper all those weeks ago before she left London.

'They are very beautiful,' said Rocco, handling one carefully. 'Do you ever use them?'

'No, they're purely decorative. I inherited my parent's collection and kept adding to it. I should probably wait until I've finished renovating before I hang them.'

'They will look good displayed on the wall and we can always help you take them down again, eh Biagio?'

The boy nodded and mumbled that he would fetch what they needed.

'Your son?' asked Ana.

'My nephew.' Rocco's lips twitched. 'Only Biagio is truly my nephew, not an invented one like Augusto has.'

'Are you absolutely sure there is no family connection with him?' Ana was intrigued. 'He seems to be related to everyone.'

Rocco's smile widened. 'You would have to make one of those graphs with tangled pieces of thread leading in all directions to work out how Augusto is related to people in Montenello but I am almost certain there is no link to my family.'

'Why do what he asks then, and drop all your other work to come here and help me?' she wondered.

'How do you know I have other work?'

'I'm assuming you do.'

Rocco shrugged. 'There was enough time for you. Besides I like Augusto. He is broad-minded, forward-thinking.'

'It's quite something to be forward-thinking at his age,' observed Ana.

'Augusto is a man who is interested in life and living.' Rocco chuckled, a low throaty sound. 'Have you seen how he thinks he must smile to make his phone recognise him? Maybe he is right though, who would know.'

When Biagio returned with a hammer, nails and a measuring tape, Rocco squinted at the wall, and sent him back for a stepladder.

'If we are going to do this then we may as well do it prop-erly,' he told Ana.

She hovered as the two men worked, fighting the urge to give instructions that Rocco didn't seem to need, as he measured and marked the wall where each mould would hang, working accurately and fast.

'You're doing such a lovely job,' said Ana, approvingly, when the copper moulds began to go up.

Rocco looked down on her from his perch on the stepladder. He nodded and she thought he seemed amused. 'I hope so.'

When he had finished, and the rows of copper moulds were glowing on the walls, Rocco climbed down from the ladder, wiped the sweat from his brow with a clean, white handker-chief and handed the hammer to Biagio. 'Coffee?' he asked.

'Unfortunately, I don't have any,' said Ana.

'No but I do ... and also I brought us a little snack. Biagio you know where everything is, yes?'

The boy nodded, and raced off back to the van, while Ana stood back and admired the wall. Her collection looked like it belonged there.

'It does seem more like a home now,' she said, satisfied with the morning's work.

'A little more,' Rocco agreed.

When Biagio returned it was with a Primus stove and a Moka pot already primed with sweetened coffee. As it heated, Rocco opened a paper-wrapped package and produced a flat-bread stuffed with provolone cheese and fennel-spiked sausage, pulling it apart into crusty chunks. To Ana it looked and tasted home-made.

'Does your wife supply us with all this good food,' she won-dered, when they had finished eating.

'No, I live alone,' Rocco told her, shaking his head.

'You're not married?' Ana was surprised.

'Not so far.'

'Then you made that bread yourself?' she checked.

He nodded. 'With my own hands.'

Ana was intrigued enough by her handyman to want to know more. But he was packing up his gear now and saying something in Italian to his nephew. They must have other jobs scheduled. Soon they were gone.

After Rocco left, Ana stayed in the kitchen. It gave her a good feeling to see the wall hung with her vintage copper moulds and she imagined that her father would have approved. Ana wasn't sure if he ever intended to start a collection but, after he and her mother died, she had found several of the moulds among their belongings. She was attracted to the highly polished surfaces and thought the way they glowed, reddish brown, seemed to warm a room. She found herself buying more, seeking out different shapes and soon the collection was a striking feature in the kitchen of her London apartment. They had looked good there and also looked beautiful here, in this new home and life. Ana was pleased that she had held onto them. She snapped a photograph on her phone and sent it to her sister in Australia with a message.

The end of my adventure or perhaps the start of a new one. When the place is finished, I hope you will come.

Skye

My name isn't even Skye. My parents christened me Stacey and that's what people called me right up until Tim came along and gave me a new identity. We'd been out for a picnic and were lying on our backs in the long grass, holding hands and staring up at fluffy white clouds drifting across a sea of blue. It was one of those idyllic little slices of life.

'You're really not a Stacey,' Tim declared, suddenly. 'It doesn't suit you at all.'

'Really? What am I then?' I was probably pleased that he was giving so much thought to the sort of person I was.

Tim rolled over, pressed his mouth to my cheek, then to my lips. 'Hmm I've got it,' he said, when we'd finished kissing. 'I'm going to call you Skye.'

I liked the name more than my own and, much to my surprise, it stuck. Everyone started using it, even my parents although it took them some time. Then the kids came along and it made sense to use Tim's surname too. Skye Olsen. That's who I was.

Could I ever go back to being Stacey Hughes again? I don't feel like that girl anymore. I've been Skye for so long now.

That's what I'm thinking about as the kids and I are standing on top of a semi-ruined old tower, at Montenello's highest

263

point. The view from up here is breathtaking. We can see across a valley filled with vineyards and olive groves, and roads running like ribbons between them, towards mountains that look like smudged shadows in the hazy sunshine. It looks like a picture, and the kids seem captivated. I'm fighting the urge to warn them to step back from the ramparts; there'll only be more eye-rolling. And I'm also wondering what Tim is up to.

This morning I woke to a message on my phone, saying he had gone to sort out a few things and we should carry on and explore without him. So that's what we're doing, although there's not a lot to see in this cluster of time-worn buildings clinging to a hilltop. Just very steep, narrow streets, with lots of steps to climb and a few elderly people sitting outside the open doors of their houses, holding shouted conversations with one another.

I'm fairly sure we're not meant to be on top of this tower, but the door was unlocked and the kids were keen. They urged me up a spiral of worn stone steps, using the light from their phones to guide us, and now they're taking selfies, the view in the background.

'Come on Mum, get in the shot,' Becky urges.

'Move away from the edge then.' I can't help myself; the ramparts are low and disaster looms only a few steps away.

The kids shuffle forwards, with a minimum of eye-rolling, and there's laughter as we try to fit more than my forehead into the frame. Josh has long arms, but not as long as Tim, not yet anyway.

'We'll have to come back up here with your dad,' I say. 'It'd be a shame for him to miss this view.'

'Have you heard from him? Is he going to meet us for lunch?' Becky wants to know. But Tim's not responding to my messages, so I have no answers.

As we walk back down towards the piazza, there are more

elderly folk, wheeling their shopping trolleys behind them over the cobbles, sitting together on low walls, even a cluster of men playing cards beneath the shade of a wind-burnt tree. It's such a classic Italian scene that I stop and watch for a moment, tempted to take a photograph but concerned it might seem intrusive and rude. I'll hold the image in my mind instead. One day perhaps I'll make it into a painting.

'Where are all the young people?' Josh wants to know.

'I guess they have to leave and go to the cities to find work,' I tell him.

'There wouldn't be much to do here anyway,' he observes, 'if you were young.'

It seems to me that there might have been a few parties up on that tower. The stones are blackened where fires have been lit and I could see several dented beer cans lying round. That has to be where the youth of Montenello go for the closest they get to excitement.

'Are you bored?' I ask my kids.

'I preferred Rome,' admits Josh.

'Yeah, me too,' says Becky.

In Rome there was so much going on that I couldn't think properly. Here my head still seems muddled, but I'm appreciating the peace and the clear mountain air. Am I really so different to Tim, Becky and Josh? Am I incompatible with my entire family?

'There's the wedding in a couple of days though. That'll be exciting,' says Becky.

The wedding. How can we go ahead with it? And where is Tim? When we reach the piazza, and the kids are photographing each other in front of the fountain, I send another message.

This time he responds.

Won't make it to lunch sorry. I'll catch you later.

'He's planning one of his surprises, isn't he?' says Josh, as we settle at a table in the trattoria.

'Bound to be,' says Becky, sounding pleased. 'I wonder what it's going to be.'

They play a guessing game, as I try to attract the attention of the woman in the kitchen and get us some menus. It turns out there aren't any. We'll be eating whatever she's decided to cook. I'm fine with that but Josh seems concerned.

'What if it's something awful like liver and onions?'

'Then you don't have to eat it,' I point out. 'But if it tastes as good as it smells in here, I think we'll be OK.'

There's no sign of the mayor. A basket of bread is delivered to the table along with a carafe of red wine, and shortly afterwards a first course of pasta in a soupy sauce of aubergine and tomato. The food is simple, rich in flavour and very comforting. Josh wipes a crust of bread around his plate to catch every drop of the delicious sauce, like a real Italian. And Becky forgets that she's been talking about giving up carbs.

We're waiting for the second course, still wracking our brains to work out what Tim might be planning, when I notice the elderly man who was talking to me at last night's party. He's sort of hovering in the orbit of our table, looking as though he wants to speak to us.

'Augusto,' I say, managing to remember his name.

He comes closer. 'Signora, the mayor sends his apologies, he is unable to join you for lunch today.'

'Oh, that's a pity,' I reply politely, although obviously I didn't want to spend my lunchtime making conversation with someone I barely know, especially without Tim to keep things flowing. 'Perhaps another time.'

'The mayor is very busy.'

'I can imagine,' I say.

The man is still hovering and he's so very old and stooped that I'm sure he would be better off sitting down.

'Would you like to join us?' I ask, nodding towards the spare seat at our table. 'If you're here for lunch that is.'

The kids look faintly horrified but the elderly man beams. 'Of course,' he says. 'I eat lunch here every day. This is my daughter's restaurant.'

His English is very good and he hardly stops talking, although he manages to eat a plate of pasta and move on to tackle a second course of thin slices of beef folded into a parcel filled with cheese, herbs and olives. The kids are interested in his stories and perhaps the old man is lonely because he seems to take great pleasure in having an audience.

'Many people must leave Montenello when they are young,' he is explaining. 'Some come back again, but others don't. In recent years we have done whatever we can to attract new residents, because we don't want our town to slowly die like others have. The weddings have been very important. They have helped change our town and now this is a very lively place, as you can see.'

The thought of weddings silences me, and a knot forms in my stomach. I put down my fork and push the rest of my food aside.

'Don't you want that, Mum?' Josh's own plate is clean, and he reaches for mine, and starts demolishing the leftovers. As he eats, he's listening to Augusto, nodding along, while Becky is asking questions. She's so much Tim's daughter in this moment, with her dark hair and lean frame, and her ease with other people, even strangers.

'What do young people do for fun here, Augusto?' she wants to know.

'They do what they've always done. Drive a Vespa too fast and have parties on top of the old tower, even though they're not meant to.'

'We were just up there,' Josh tells him. 'On that tower.'

'It ought to be closed but the young people, they keep breaking the padlock. When I was their age, I did the same.'

'Isn't it dangerous though?' I ask, struggling to imagine him as a mischievous young man.

Augusto shrugs. 'Of course.'

When I go to pay the bill, no one will accept my money. This lunch is on the mayor they keep insisting. There's a small battle with me waving a handful of euros around, then trying to push them under the bread basket, and Augusto pulling them out to give back to me.

'You are our guest of honour,' he says and I feel terrible, because we've taken so much from this town already and I'm not sure if Tim and I will ever be able to repay them.

I'm sitting there thinking about Tim and wondering if we should send out a search party when Augusto breaks the news that he's organised a cooking class, just like I asked him to. He seems very pleased with himself.

'My granddaughter Cecilia has her *pasticceria* right next door. You can go to her once you are ready,' he tells us.

'Sorry you mean now … this afternoon?' I check, hoping that he doesn't.

'Of course,' says Augusto. 'Ana is coming too. I have already told her.'

I'm about to come up with a polite refusal when I realise that it might be good to sink my hands into some dough. It's only been a few days but I kind of miss baking.

Augusto insists on escorting us next door to the *pasticceria* and making introductions. His granddaughter Cecilia offers an understated welcome and I get the sense that she has been coaxed into this cooking class. She's a small, slim woman with a long plait of hair coiled into a bun and a stern expression.

The kids are enchanted by her shop, with its glassed-in wooden counter filled with pastries and its cellophane bags of biscotti tied with white ribbon. Their enthusiasm seems to thaw her a little.

'What is it you would like to learn?' she asks.

'Could you teach us the Neapolitan pastry, *sfogliatella*?' I ask. '*Frolla* or *riccia*?'

'Oh, I'm not sure. The one that's like a clam shell, with layers and layers of pastry.'

'*Riccia*. It is a little tricky to make but I can show you,' she decides.

The hairnet I'm handed feels like an old friend and I slip it on without complaint. Ana, arriving ten minutes later, isn't so keen.

'Is that really necessary?' she asks, her tone queenly, but Cecilia isn't going to back down.

'We take hygiene very seriously in our kitchen,' she replies, and Ana accepts the hairnet, putting it on and pushing her hair inside.

'Today we are learning *sfogliatella riccia*,' Cecilia continues. 'Do you know it?'

'Yes, of course,' says Ana, not mentioning that she used to be the editor of a renowned food magazine or that she knows a few things about cooking. She must really not want to talk about *Culinaria*, which is a shame as I'm dying to tell her that, before it folded, my cake was being considered for the Christmas cover.

I lose myself in kneading dough, rolling and stretching it into shape, then coaxing it into a cone to hold a ricotta-rich mixture of semolina, spices and candied orange peel. I'm aware Josh is filming and taking close ups of my hands as they are working. Then he focuses on the result which I'm pretty pleased with, for a first go, given that we couldn't rest the dough for long enough, it doesn't look too shabby.

'You've done this before,' says Ana, a little accusingly and I realise she must have been struggling.

'I'm a baker,' I tell her. 'I have a little business, the Lost Cakery.'

I'm hoping she'll recognise the name, but Ana doesn't seem to be listening properly. 'It might help if your son would stop filming us,' she says, testily.

'It's material for my Instagram and Facebook, the kids help me,' I explain.

'I'd prefer not to be on your social media pages. Particularly with this thing on my head.'

Becky steps in, smoothing ruffled feathers, reassuring. She's definitely developing her father's charm. 'He'll edit you out of the footage we use,' she promises. 'But would you like him to share something with you for your own social media?'

'I don't do any of that.' Ana is brusque.

Josh seems staggered. 'None at all? Not even Instagram?'

'People keep asking me that.' She sounds exasperated. 'But I'm a very private person.'

'You're Ana King,' I say, not really getting it. 'You're famous.'

She stares down at her misshapen pastry, then picks it up and tosses it into a large bin beneath the work counter. 'I'm going to have another go at this. No filming, OK?'

Her second attempt is better. It goes into the oven alongside mine and, with evident relief, she strips off her hairnet and uses it to fan herself. 'It's too hot to be around ovens,' she complains.

'You get used to it,' says Cecilia, who is relatively cool and calm.

'Even so I think we all need a long, cold drink.'

Josh prefers to wait with Cecilia and photograph the *sfogliatelle* as they come out of the oven. Becky says she'll stay too.

So, it's just me and Ana heading to the bar for a large bottle of sparkling water and a couple of Aperol Spritzes.

'I'm not sure that was the right amount of fun,' Ana says, claiming an outdoor table in the semi-shade of a parasol. 'But maybe that's because I wasn't very good at it.'

'It's my fault,' I apologise, squinting as the sun hits my eyes. 'I should have requested something less fiddly.'

'No, no it's good to be challenged and learn new things. That's why I'm here, after all.'

As the waiter delivers our drinks, she starts telling me the highlights of her story: moving to Italy, finding a place she wanted to buy, planning a new life.

'What will you do here?' I ask. 'Once you've finished the renovation?'

'The *masseria* is huge,' she says. 'I was thinking of organising cooking classes and gastronomic retreats … that's if enough people are interested.'

'But you're Ana King, of course they'll be interested.'

'In the days when I had a magazine, they might have been, but not now,' she says, dismissively.

'That's why you need social media. Instagram at least. If you start posting about your life in Italy then people will find you.'

She frowns at the idea. 'I've taken a look at it, of course, but I don't really know how to participate.'

'It's not complicated,' I tell her. 'I'll show you.'

We sit outside the bar, sipping our drinks, heads bent over our phones, like a couple of teenagers. I never imagined there would be something I'd be able to teach Ana King; it gives me a bit of a buzz actually. When the kids arrive, bearing our pastries still warm from the oven, Ana takes a photograph and posts it on her newly-created Instagram page.

'Ta-da,' she says. 'And now I'm an influencer.'

There's a vintage pinball machine inside the bar and the kids head inside to order Cokes and see if it works. I watch them through the window. At home they don't spend much time together and it's lovely to see them getting on so well.

'You've got your wedding in a couple of days,' Ana reminds me. 'You must be excited.'

I suppose I could lie and reply with a yes, then change the subject. But I'm not a liar. Also, I need to talk to someone. All those thoughts buzzing round my head, they have to go somewhere.

'Excited,' I say. 'Not really.'

Ana

Ana wasn't accustomed to being bad at things and more than once during the course of the afternoon, as she failed to make a decent *sfogliatella,* she wished she had gone ahead with her original plan and spent the time shopping in Borgo del Colle instead.

Now she was sitting outside the bar, listening to Skye unburdening herself, and again regretting how she had chosen to spend the day. Relationships really weren't something she felt qualified to give advice on.

'I'm sure it's normal to be nervous in the run up to a wedding,' she murmured, feeling she had to say something.

'This is more than nerves though.' Skye's face pinched into a frown. 'I don't really know about Tim and me. We're such different people. Do I want to grow old with him? Do we even belong together?'

Career advice was more Ana's domain. She had always loved mentoring people and guiding them upwards. Fortunately, it seemed like Skye didn't expect a response.

'It's just that Tim never listens.' The words were rushing out of her. 'I'm not sure he even sees me; he's always staring at a screen. And I do everything: housework and shopping, running the business, keeping our kids on track, remembering everyone's appointments, while he gets to be the fun guy that everybody loves ...'

Ana had listened to plenty of friends airing similar complaints. What Skye was describing seemed to be how it went when you'd been living with the same person for a long time. Perhaps it was inevitable.

'I never for a moment thought we'd actually win the competition,' Skye added. 'But here we are. Oh God, what am I going to do?'

Over the years Ana had helped many younger colleagues identify their skills and map out where they wanted to go. Was relationship advice really so different to guiding a career? Surely it shared the same principles? In the end both were about passion; without enough of that, it was pointless doing anything.

'Do you love him?' To Ana that seemed the obvious starting point.

Skye sat back in her chair and considered the question. 'We've been together for half a lifetime, he's the father of my kids and he's a really caring dad ...'

'Yes, but how do you feel?' Now Ana was thinking of this as like career counselling, she felt on safer ground.

'I care about him, of course.'

'I'm sure you care about lots of people, that doesn't mean you want to spend the rest of your life with them. Does he make you happy? You don't have to tell me; you just have to know yourself.'

Skye nodded, thoughtfully. 'OK yes, that's the big question ...'

'There must be reasons why you fell in love in the first place.'

'Tim used to keep me laughing like no one else could,' said Skye. 'We hardly ever seem to laugh anymore. I never thought we'd grow apart like this.'

'Why did you enter the competition?'

'Tim entered it, not me.'

'Then why did you agree to come?' That was what Ana couldn't understand.

'For all sorts of reasons that are probably the wrong ones.' Skye half closed her eyes and sighed.

'Such as?' Ana was still a journalist at heart. She wasn't afraid of asking questions.

'Well for a start I wanted my kids to have this trip. I couldn't bear to disappoint them, to let everyone down.' Skye hesitated. 'I didn't want to be the boring sensible person who's always saying no to things.'

'You're getting married for other people, not yourself.' Now Ana felt like they might be getting somewhere. 'At least that's what I'm hearing.'

'I guess you're right.'

Ana could imagine the fuss it was going to create if this woman backed out of the wedding plans the town had been making. Augusto would be crushed and the mayor disappointed; there would most definitely be a number of awkward conversations. But that was no reason to go ahead, if Skye wasn't happy.

'I never married,' Ana confided. 'I have a great life and always thought that if I was going to let someone in and make them a part of it then I had to be certain they weren't going to make it worse, only better.'

'You can never be certain of that though, can you?' said Skye. 'There wouldn't be such a high divorce rate if you could.'

'Which may be why I've stayed single.'

'You've lived with partners though, right?' asked Skye. 'You've let some people in?'

'Never for very long.' As she spoke, Ana was watching women milling round the piazza and noticing how many of them were one half of a couple. Perhaps she was a rare

275

exception. 'I've always liked living alone, having my own space and making my own decisions, that's what I'm used to. When I look at other people's relationships, I feel like what I've mostly avoided is a lot of stress and heartache.'

'There are good things about sharing your life with another person,' argued Skye, leaning forward now, elbows on the table. 'Doesn't everyone want some support and companionship?'

'We don't need men anymore though, do we?' pointed out Ana, who wasn't convinced that everyone did. 'Not like we did back in the days when women were financially dependent on them. Things have changed. We have other choices. And thank goodness for that.'

Skye was fidgeting now, stirring the straw in her glass, ice cubes clinking. 'Yes, thank goodness,' she agreed.

'So far you haven't given me any compelling reasons to regret staying solo,' added Ana.

'What if you met the right person, that could change everything?'

Most people found it difficult to understand Ana's resolve not to hitch herself to someone else. There seemed a general assumption that happy-ever-after had to mean being in a relationship. If that was what you wanted, then great. But Ana had never wanted it.

As she was thinking how difficult it was to get this across, she saw a large van pulling into the piazza and parking not far from the bar. How did the locals manoeuvre these vehicles down such narrow streets, she wondered distractedly, then realised the van was familiar. Sure enough, it was Rocco that climbed out, raising a hand to wave at her.

'That's my handyman,' explained Ana, waving back as he headed towards them.

When Rocco stood beside the table, he created almost more

shade than the parasol with his burly body and broad shoulders. He smiled at her.

'I was hoping to find you here. I have some good news and wanted to give it to you in person.'

'Oh, yes?' Ana gazed up at him, hopefully. 'I'm keen on good news.'

'Yesterday I talked to the mayor and discovered he has a contact in the tax office. Now he has been in touch and your appointment is being brought forward. You are going to get your fiscal code.'

'Really?' That code was like the magic key that unlocked everything and Ana was almost giddy with elation. She sprang to her feet. 'I could hug you.'

Rocco smiled and, with a slow shrug of his shoulders, opened his arms. '*Va bene*. Why not?'

Ana had imagined he would smell like sawdust and sweat. But as she leant into Rocco, she was enveloped in a fresh, clean scent. Very lightly her body touched his and her face moved to his shoulder. He held her for a moment, until she stepped away. 'Thank you so much for sorting that out,' said Ana, flustered and trying not to show it.

'Now we must find someone who has a friend at the power company,' he told her. 'This is how Italy works.'

'Is that likely to be possible?' It seemed too much to hope for.

'I have a few ideas. Leave it with me.'

Ana felt awkward about the hug and also surprised at herself. She wasn't in the habit of throwing her arms around people that she barely knew.

'I really don't know how to thank you. You haven't even given me a bill yet for the work you've done so far,' she said, trying to regain her composure.

'No problem, we will get to it,' Rocco told her. 'Now though you must excuse me, I have an appointment.'

Ana's eyes followed him as he went striding across the piazza towards the town hall and disappeared inside. Skye was watching too.

'Your handyman?' she confirmed. 'He seems … nice.'

'Yes, he is,' Ana agreed, a little faintly. 'Very nice.'

For dinner Ana ordered room service, planning on an evening alone. As pleasant as Skye seemed, she wasn't interested in being adopted by her family. Every now and then she heard a door slam, but otherwise the palazzo seemed peaceful. And Ana's room, decorated in pale shades, with a vast bed and a crystal chandelier hanging from the ceiling, was an elegant space to relax in.

Not that she was quite ready to relax. First, Ana wanted to explore the world of social media and decide if it was worth her getting involved since everyone seems to be so astonished that she wasn't. Mindlessly scrolling didn't appeal, but perhaps, just as Skye had advised, it might be a useful strategy.

On Instagram she followed a few people that she knew, old colleagues and friends, several chefs, a cookbook writer she particularly liked, several restaurants, rival food magazines and finally even *Culinaria*. Most were posting carefully-curated images. Apparently, every meal they cooked looked like a work of art and no one ever allowed themselves to appear in bad lighting. It was as unreal as magazines had always been. Ana remembered the photo shoots, with food teased and primped to perfection. The hand models brought in for step-by-step guides. The many hundreds of pictures that were shot so she could choose one perfect image. Apparently, nothing had changed.

Ana wasn't a follower; it was why she had stayed away from social media in the first place. If she was going to get involved now, then she would do it her way. She examined the solitary photo she had posted. Her sad, misshapen pastry. What was the point of pretending she had been anything other than useless. More for practice than anything, she added a few more shots. Her copper moulds on the scarred stone wall, the faded tiles in her living room, the damaged fresco, her overgrown garden, rusting metal gates. Ana thought it might serve as a scrapbook of the new life she was creating in Italy, and be something to look back on. She couldn't imagine anyone else bothering with it.

Downstairs there was more slamming of doors. To Ana it sounded as though someone had gone out. Glancing at the clock, she noticed how late it was and wondered what they were up to. Montenello had no nightlife to speak of. There was nowhere to go at this hour.

Putting down her phone, Ana turned out the light and nestled into her bed. As she was drifting off to sleep, her final thoughts were of Rocco. She had actually hugged him. What had she been thinking?

Skye

Tim has been missing all day and only appears shortly before dinner time. Noticing he seems wound up with excitement, I decide the kids must be right and he's been busy planning some surprise.

'Where have you been?' I ask, as I'm trying to decide what to wear. We're booked into the swanky hotel restaurant which calls for something smart. 'What have you been doing?'

'Just ... things,' he says, evasively.

'What things?' I demand, grabbing the green dress and pulling it over my head.

'Let's talk about this later, when there's more time.' Tim is busy changing into a linen shirt and trousers. 'Then we can have a proper conversation.'

The restaurant is actually not too swanky. It has a vibe that I love; plates are mismatched and the napkins seem vintage. The kids order adventurously but I feel too unsettled for anything but plainer food and Tim barely eats, which is generally the way if he's hyped himself up. When we've finished, I assume we'll all wander back to the palazzo and spend the evening together, but Josh and Becky have other ideas. Apparently, they got talking to some locals in the bar earlier when they were playing pinball and they've made plans to hang out in the piazza with them.

'Take your phones,' I tell them, unnecessarily as they're rarely separated from their digital devices.

'Answer your phones,' says Tim, which is actually far better advice.

After they've gone the waitress brings over a bottle of limoncello. I'm waiting for Tim to launch into our proper conversation but it seems that he would rather talk about almost anything else. He's keyed up and jittery, pouring a second glass of the limoncello then insisting on topping me up too.

'I think it's quite alcoholic,' I warn.

'Isn't it meant to aid digestion?' he argues.

Tim has polished off a fair bit of the bottle by the time we get up to leave. He seems steady enough on his feet, though, as we wander back through the piazza.

'No sign of the kids,' I say, looking round, having expected to see them hanging out beside the fountain with a group of local kids.

'Maybe they've gone to the bar for a *gelato*,' suggests Tim, but I peer through the open door and they aren't in there either.

Tim shrugs. 'Probably just headed off for a walk then. They won't have gone far.'

The two of us weave through the maze of narrow streets that lead back to the palazzo.

'Well then,' I say to Tim. 'What's the big mystery? Where have you been all day?'

He shakes his head. 'Let's wait till we get inside. I'll explain everything.'

Even then he has to pour glasses of wine that neither of us want to drink and put out cheese we don't have any appetite for. Finally, we're sitting side by side on an uncomfortable sofa in one of the grand reception rooms and there's no way Tim can avoid telling me what's been going on.

281

He stares at the honey-coloured wine, swirls it in the glass, goes to take a sip, then puts it down. 'I went to see the mayor. They made me wait for ages because I didn't have an appointment and he was in meetings. Anyway, I told him everything.'

'Everything?' I ask, slightly dazed.

'I admitted to lying on the competition entry form, made it clear that you haven't been ill and then I offered to pay for the flights, accommodation, meals we've eaten, wedding costs; the whole thing.'

'Why would you go and do that without telling me first?' I'm reeling at this news.

'You kept saying that you wanted me to be honest. I listened.'

'Yes, but how are we going to afford it?' As I ask the question my mind is jumping from one solution to another. Could we increase our mortgage? Borrow from my parents? Sell something?

'I'll sort it out,' he tells me. 'You don't need to worry.'

'How?' I want to know.

'There's plenty of work out there. I can get back into house-painting or garden maintenance. I'll chip away at the debt.'

Reflexively, I gulp some of my wine. 'What did the mayor have to say when you told him all this?'

'He was pretty unimpressed at first but I managed to talk him round. Once I'd told him why I was so desperate to win the wedding I think he felt a bit sorry for me.'

I can almost imagine the scene, Tim using all his charm to win the mayor over, the two of them almost mates by the end. Now though the sparky, brightly lit Tim has gone, he isn't that version of himself at all.

'It felt like I was losing you,' he says. 'For a while now you've been pulling away. I've blamed Meera and all that scowling she does every time I come anywhere near you. But perhaps it's

282

got nothing to do with her ... maybe you just stopped needing me ... loving me ... that's why I entered the competition. I thought coming here and getting married; it might put us back on track.'

'You told the mayor all this?'

Tim nods. 'It took a while.'

'So, is he going to give us a bill?' My mind is focused on money worries. All I can think is that we'll paying off this debt for years and years.

'Eventually yes, but some things were contra deals and free-bies. We spent the afternoon trying to work through it.'

'Right,' I say, still trying to tot up the worst-case scenario of what we might owe.

'The thing is Skye, what this means is we can choose whether we want the wedding to go ahead.' Tim stretches out a hand and curls it around mine. 'To be clear, I still very much want to marry you, but only if you feel the same.'

He's so still and solemn, his shoulders are hunched and in this vast room, he seems diminished. Looking at him, I'm reminded that there's more than money at stake. Our whole future, mine and Tim's, our family's, that is on the line. Right now, in this moment, is when I have to decide for all of us.

'Tim I ...'

'Take your time, no need to rush,' he tells me. 'Think about it.'

I wish there wasn't any need to think. If only we could continue the way we always have, getting through all those ups and downs, never looking too far ahead or thinking too hard about it. I can't marry this man ... and I can't not marry him. I feel completely stuck.

Outside the sky is darkening. As I'm sitting there, at a loss for words, Tim glances through the window and shifts in his chair. 'Have you heard from the kids?' he wonders.

I pull out my phone and see there are no messages. It concerns me that they weren't in the piazza, which is where I imagined they'd stay, so I call to check exactly where they are and when they're planning to get back. Neither of them answers.

'I hope they're not up on that tower,' I say.

'You mean the ruin at the top of the hill.' Tim frowns. 'Is it safe up there?'

'No, definitely not.'

'Call them back,' he suggests.

Again, the phones ring and go to voicemail, which I know neither of the kids ever bother listening to. I send them a couple of text messages and try not to worry. They're probably busy having a good time.

'A wedding doesn't get a couple back on track,' I tell Tim. 'What gave you the idea that it might?'

'A wedding, a holiday, a break from our normal lives … I thought it had to help.'

I shake my head at him. 'It wouldn't fix anything.'

'What do you need from me? Just say and I'll do it.'

He's gripping my hand more tightly now, and I want to pull away, but I know how much that will hurt him, so I don't.

'It's not really all that complicated Skye,' he says. 'Either you love me … or you don't.'

Do I love Tim? That's the question I really need to answer, just like Ana King said. After all these years, the good times and bad, the moments when we've laughed or cried or driven each other crazy, the holding newborns in our arms, the waking in the night because someone had a nightmare, the cooking and cleaning, the half-remembered dreams and unforgettable disappointments, can it really be as simple as a yes or no?

Tim's phone is ringing and it's Becky so he picks up. As he's listening to whatever she is saying, he pales. 'Stay right where you are,' he tells her. 'I'm coming.'

'What's happened?' I ask anxiously, as he leaps to his feet and scoops up the trainers he kicked off earlier.

'They're up at the tower, like you thought, and Josh is hurt.' Tim is lacing up his shoes. 'She says he can't walk.'

Instantly the worst scenario plays through my head and I panic. 'There's this huge drop, what if he's fallen?'

'I'm going straight up there,' Tim says, already heading for the door.

'In the car?' I ask, remembering how much he had to drink.

'I'll run; it'll be faster.'

The door slams and Tim is gone. I'm left shaking so much I can hardly manage to google emergency medical centres. The nearest hospital is in Borgo del Colle and that's a drive away.

I toss up whether to try for an ambulance or fetch the car. Then I'm the one lacing up my trainers, slamming the door behind me and setting off at a run.

I access the parking garage all right but as I start the car it occurs to me that I've no idea how to get to the tower. There must be a way up, because I saw vehicles parked near it, but when we were walking most of the streets seemed to be steep flights of steps.

I don't care if I dent every panel of the car, I need to get to my family. Crunching the gears, I lurch out of the parking building and point the car in the direction I think I need to head in. There's no one about to ask for directions, and a lack of street lighting. Twice I have to reverse out of a lane that isn't navigable and I smash off a wing mirror halfway up, but I think I'm getting closer.

First, I see the tower, then in my headlights a group of people huddled on the ground. Leaving the engine running, I leap out and that's when I realise that it's Tim who is flat on the ground, with Josh and Becky leaning over him.

'Mum, I think Dad is having a heart attack.' Becky's voice is shrill and scared.

I fling myself down on the ground next to him. By the light of the torches on the kids' phones I can see Tim doesn't look good. He's sweating and trembling, and he seems to be having trouble breathing.

'We need to get him in the car,' I say. 'Quickly.'

Becky helps me support him, easing him into the back seat. Then we have to do the same for Josh, because he's hurt his ankle. I hand my phone to my daughter, telling her to navigate, and then I drive like a maniac. I keep talking to Tim, telling him it's going to be OK, that he just needs to hang on and we'll get him to a doctor.

'My chest hurts,' he gasps.

Once we're over the causeway, I put my foot down, focusing on the white lines down the centre of the road, trying to hold the car steady.

'It's twenty minutes from here,' says Becky sounding panicked.

Josh is behind me and I can tell from his ragged breathing that he's in a panic too. 'What if there's no one who speaks English?'

'It's going to be fine … it's going to be fine,' I repeat, because I have to believe it.

Ahead the sky looks lighter and, speeding towards the brightness, I hope that's the town I'm seeing.

'Turn right here,' says Becky, a little later, and I hear some relief in her voice. 'Then straight ahead at the roundabout. This is it Borgo del Colle.'

We find the hospital without any trouble and I screech to a halt and go tearing inside. Once I've managed to make myself understood, things happen fast. Tim is stretchered inside and Josh follows in a wheelchair.

My mind is racing, but as we're sitting and waiting for news it slows and I start to think properly. That's when I get angry and Becky bears the brunt of it.

'What were you thinking, being on that tower after dark? You knew it wasn't safe.'

'I'm sorry Mum. The local kids said they go up there all the time. We thought it'd be OK.'

'Were you drinking?' I ask, presuming she'll say no because she's never seemed interested in alcohol.

'Everyone was. But we only had a couple of beers, we didn't get drunk.'

'Why did Josh hurt himself then?' I'm even angrier now.

'He was being an idiot, messing about and he slipped going down the steps. The others all took off; they didn't want to get into trouble and Josh was more worried about smashing his phone. Then Dad appeared and he was helping him then suddenly ...' Becky shudders. 'Do you think he's going to be all right?'

'I don't know.' There's no point in lying. 'Heart attacks are serious.'

Becky starts to cry and, putting an arm round her shoulders, I pull her closer. 'He's in the right place though. They're looking after him.'

'It's all our fault,' she says, between sobs.

'No, it's not,' I reply, worrying that if something happens to Tim, they'll always blame themselves. Then I rub my eyes and realise that I'm crying too. What if something happens to Tim?

It's a long and anxious wait, sitting on hard chairs under strip-lighting, sipping hot drinks from a machine. When Josh appears he's on crutches and wearing an ankle brace.

'It's not broken,' he tells me. 'Just a really bad sprain. How's Dad?'

'We still haven't heard,' I tell him.

'I'm so sorry, Mum.' His voice and expression are sombre.

'I know you are.'

There's more waiting, much more. It feels like we've been there forever. At long last a doctor comes to find us and in heavily-accented English he tells us they've run tests and Tim's heart is fine. He says they think it was just a very intense panic attack. The relief is immense; Becky falls into my shoulder and Josh clutches my arm.

'It really seemed like a heart attack,' I say, and the doctor nods.

'Even though it isn't life-threatening we must take this seriously,' he tells me. 'If it happens again your husband should seek treatment. Drugs can be effective, therapy ...'

'He's been under a lot of stress lately,' I admit.

'Then that is something you should address.'

'Why's Dad stressed?' Becky wants to know.

I shake off the question. 'Not now, I'm too tired, we'll talk about it another time.'

The drive back to Montenello is slower and subdued. There's a grey dawn breaking and beside me in the passenger seat, Tim's colour still looks bad although he's claiming he feels better.

'We'll take it very quietly today. All of us need some rest,' I say.

'What about the wedding?' Becky asks. 'Is it still going ahead if Dad's sick and Josh can't walk properly.'

'I'll be fine on crutches,' Josh says, confidently.

'I'll be fine too.' Tim turns to me. 'So, Skye, what do you say? Are we getting married tomorrow?'

I'm driving and my eyes are focused on the road. My hands are gripping the steering wheel. I didn't think I could drive down those narrow streets and on the wrong side of the road, but I coped with it. If I didn't have Tim, then I could manage on my own. I don't need him to survive. But I know that he's right and we're better together. More importantly this long, dark night has answered a question. Sometimes love seems missing in action, somehow it was always there. I don't want to lose him.

I take a deep breath. 'That's why we're here, isn't it?'

Ana

Ana was at the *masseria*, standing in the room she would soon be using as a bedroom, surrounded by pots of paint she had bought in a hurry, staring up at the ceiling. It had seemed such a great idea to transform the dingy yellowing walls with a coat of fresh white then find a blingy chandelier to hang and maybe a large vintage mirror. Inspired by the décor at the palazzo, Ana had launched straight into the plan, arriving in Borgo del Colle first thing and stocking up on paint that seemed a suitable shade without endlessly poring over swatches and trialling samples of colour as she normally would. Her mind was set on cheering up this room before she moved in.

Now Ana was here, all she could see were problems. This ceiling was high and she was still suffering dizzy spells. Was she really going to manage hours on a ladder, looking upwards, to paint it? And when she found a chandelier and mirror, who was going to hang them?

Rocco was the obvious answer to both of these questions. Not that Ana wanted to rely on him too much; but she had to admit she did need some help.

Inconveniently, he hadn't been available to come over until after lunchtime and she decided to make a start rather than waiting. Once everything was well protected with drop cloths,

Ana prised the lid from a paint pot, and got to work with a wide roller covering the walls as fast as possible. With each swipe of paint, it became easier to see how much better the room was going to look, and that encouraged her to keep going.

Listening to music with her earbuds in, working away and singing along, Ana wasn't aware that Rocco had arrived. Suddenly there he was filling the arched entranceway.

'You started without me?'

Ana removed her earbuds, startled by how pleased she was to see him as much as anything else.

'Oh good, now we can really make some progress,' she said.

'No prep? No filling in holes in the walls?' Rocco was examining her work. 'No scraping and sanding down the old paint?'

'This is just a temporary fix up,' Ana explained. 'I'll do everything properly later on once the place is mine. For now, we're going for shabby chic.'

'So long as you don't tell everyone in town that Rocco Cicuzzo decorated your bedroom and look what a bad job he did.'

'No one but me will ever see inside this room,' Ana promised.

'I am going to see it,' he pointed out.

'True,' she conceded. 'And I know this isn't the right way to go about things, but I need to make the room a nicer place to wake up in.'

Looking up at the arched ceiling, Rocco shrugged. '*Allora* I'll get my ladder, shall I?'

As he turned away, Ana's eyes followed. She watched his broad back disappear through the doorway and heard his footsteps echo down the hall. Soon he was back, the ladder balanced over his shoulder and the muscles in his arms tautening with the weight of it. Ana remembered that brief moment of hugging him outside the bar, the hardness of those muscles, the strength in his body, the way he smelt. Then she shivered slightly, despite the warmth of the day.

They worked together almost in silence, Ana focusing on the walls, Rocco tackling the ceiling. Her eyes kept being drawn back to him, she couldn't seem to help taking quick, sly glances. Every now and then she noticed him grimace, as if such shoddy workmanship was causing him actual pain.

'You're a perfectionist,' observed Ana, 'and you are hating doing this aren't you?'

'No, no, I am happy to paint over the cobwebs,' he said, balanced on the ladder, wielding a long-handled roller. 'Perhaps it is not the way I would choose to decorate a room, but if it is what you want.'

'There's a reason why we're not doing a more thorough job,' she pointed out. 'Who knows what will happen with this *masseria*; my bid to buy it might not be accepted; the vendors may change their minds about selling; there's no point in investing too much money and effort until I know for sure it's mine.'

'Please tell me that we are going to put on a second coat of paint. Don't break my heart completely.'

'Two coats,' she agreed. 'So long as you brush away the cobwebs before you paint. Are there many? I can't tell from down here.'

'Generations of spiders have made their homes here,' Rocco told her.

'I should buy some insecticide.' Ana wasn't a fan of bugs in the house, particularly large spiders. 'Are any likely to be dangerous?'

'Out here in the countryside you will encounter lots of wild creatures, snakes and lizards in the grass, pine martens in the trees, many insects and birds.'

'Outside, is fine, but the interior is my space and they'll have to get used to that,' said Ana, firmly.

Rocco was smiling now. 'If only I could let them know what they are up against.'

Ana paused, brush in hand. 'What do you mean by that?'

'You are formidable,' he told her, coming down the ladder, the roller tucked beneath his arm, empty paint tray in hand.

'Formidable makes me sound scary.' Ana watched him bend to fill his bucket with more paint. 'You're not scared of me, are you?'

'Maybe.' Rocco smiled up at her. 'I am doing a terrible job of painting this ceiling because you have instructed me to.'

'It actually doesn't look too bad,' she assured him.

'You won't lie there in bed and stare up at your ceiling, thinking bad thoughts about me.'

'I won't think bad thoughts about you; I promise.'

As he straightened, Rocco towered over her again and Ana sensed a flare of something. Need ... want ... desire. Her whole body came alive with it. For a moment, she felt so unsteady, it seemed like another dizzy spell.

'You have paint on your cheek.' Coming closer, Rocco brushed at it gently with his hand and his touch lit the spark again. 'Ah, now I have made it worse.'

Paint was splashed on her hands and shirt. Ana had tied a scarf over her hair and likely that was spattered too. She brushed her cheek where his fingers had been. 'I'll clean it off later once we're finished for the day,' she managed.

'By then you may be better decorated than your ceiling is.'

Ana had never expected to have this again. Long ago, she had made peace with that, as lovers became less easy to come by, and the men she did meet were bruised by divorce or hoping to be looked after, and the endings started getting messier. She had thought that part of her life was over.

293

Now, as Rocco placed a foot on the lowest rung of his ladder, she took a step closer. Ana wanted to kiss this man, to know what his lips felt like beneath hers and how his mouth tasted, to touch every part of him.

'Rocco?' she asked.

'Yes?' His eyebrows were raised.

'How do you feel about formidable women?'

His laugh was low and throaty. 'I like them, of course I do.'

'Some men don't.'

'Then they are idiots.' Rocco was moving towards her and away from the ladder. 'I like formidable women ... and I like you.'

Their bodies were as near as they could be without touching. In one small shift, Ana stretched upwards and Rocco lowered his head to meet hers, the paint tray still in his hand.

'If we are going to do this, then I had better put it down,' he said, softly. 'Are we going to?'

There were many sensible reasons to say no. Some of them rushed through Ana's mind. He was her handyman, on her payroll, it might be tricky later. But Rocco had set down the paint tray and she was drawn into his wide chest by strong arms circling her waist. He smelt like a man who had worked hard all afternoon, warm and musky. Ana forgot about being sensible.

'We're doing this,' she told him.

Afterwards, twined together on the bed, tangled in a paint-stained drop cloth, Ana sensed that Rocco was drifting off to sleep. Her head was on his chest and, listening to his steady heartbeat, only now did it occur to her that all she knew about this man were the things he wasn't. Definitely not Augusto's nephew. Probably not a plumber or a builder. Not married.

'Who are you, Rocco?' she whispered, but he was breathing deeply and his eyes were closed.

Eventually Ana slept too. When she woke the light had changed and the room smelt of paint fumes. She had made love to her handyman. Stretching along the length of his body, Ana couldn't bring herself to regret it.

'Rocco, wake up.' With her shoulder, she nudged at him, and he stirred. 'I'm hungry, do you have anything we could eat. One of those delicious stuffed breads?'

'I'm hungry too, but no, this time I brought nothing.' Drowsily he rolled to face her, opening his brown eyes, and flashing a quick, bright smile as they met her stormy blue ones. 'There is food at my house, we could go there.'

'Where do you live?' Ana didn't even know that.

'Not far away. We are almost neighbours.'

Ana hesitated. 'But I need a shower.'

'That is fine, I have one of those too.'

He leant in to kiss her again and, feeling the weight of his body against hers, Ana wanted to see what kind of place her handyman lived in. She wanted to know who Rocco was.

The house was not what she expected. Once it must have been a humble cottage, but it had been transformed. Inside the decor was simple with layers of pale shades and furnishings pared down to only what was needed. But every room opened out to a garden: the kitchen to flourishing vegetable beds, the living area to a pool fringed by lush greenery, the bedroom to a riot of red hibiscus.

'You did all this?' asked Ana, taking it in.

'Like your *masseria* it was a ruin when I bought it. And yes, I did everything myself. It is how I relax.'

Ana found that interesting. 'Even after you've spent all week working on other people's places?'

Rocco had his back to her. He was reaching for a basket stored on top of a tall cupboard. 'It feels good to bring a building back to life, as you will discover when you begin to renovate properly.'

'Instead of just slapping on paint without any prep you mean?' asked Ana.

Rocco turned, one hand clutching his heart. 'It is killing me to do that and now you see why.'

'This place is flawless,' she agreed.

'No, not flawless … there is always a list of things to be done.'

'A perfectionist,' Ana murmured.

With the basket over his arm, Rocco led her out to his kitchen garden to pick plump red tomatoes, leafy sheaves of basil and glossy aubergines. Then she sat in a window seat, with a glass of red wine in her hand, as he cooked for her.

For such a large man, he moved lightly, slicing the aubergine into rounds, simmering the tomatoes and basil into a sauce, grating a pyramid of Parmesan from a large wedge. Ana didn't ask if she could help. She liked watching other people at work in a kitchen. It told you a lot about them. She found that she particularly liked watching Rocco.

He was a relaxed cook who knew exactly where to lay his hands on a particular saucepan or wooden spoon and his cupboards were orderly. There was no music playing and he spoke very little as he fried the aubergine in a cast iron skillet and stirred the sputtering sauce.

Once everything was layered in a dish and showered generously with Parmesan, Rocco slid it into the oven and turned his attention to a salad that he dressed with a squeeze of lemon picked from a tree growing outside the window and a swirl of grassy-green olive oil.

'We will eat outside, a sort of picnic,' he said, pulling cloth napkins from a drawer, then gathering tea lights and candles.

Outside there was a long woven-metal table, shaded by a

pergola covered in bougainvillea. Rocco ferried over platters of smoky cured meats and sharp sheep's cheese, he brought out dishes of olives and semi-dried tomatoes, a golden-crusted sourdough loaf so rustic it might have been home-made, the salad and finally his aubergine dish hissing from the oven, blanketed in melted cheese and basil-spiked tomato.

'I have a large family; many nieces and nephews,' he explained, as Ana sat down at one end of the very large table. 'Often this is where we gather for parties and feasts.'

'Do you all cook together?' she asked, picturing the place spilling over with people, noisy conversation, laughter and music.

Rocco was lighting candles down the length of the table. He shook his head at the question. 'The Cicuzzo family know better than to invade my kitchen. I prefer to cook alone; it is more relaxing. And I enjoy watching the people I love eating the food I have made for them.'

'But you like others to cook for you?' checked Ana, unfolding the linen napkin in her lap and noticing that it had been carefully ironed.

'My sisters would tell you, no I do not,' admitted Rocco. 'They all say I am a person who doesn't know how to relax, that I need to be busy and when I come to their homes I pace up and down while they are preparing a meal. Apparently, this drives them crazy.'

Ana watched him tossing the salad so every leaf was evenly coated in lemony dressing. 'How many sisters do you have?'

'Four sisters and three brothers. We are a close family although one of us is always fighting with another, or telling everyone what to do, or demanding something.' He spooned a little salad onto her plate and served a portion of the steaming aubergine. 'I like it when they come here but I also like it when they leave again and I have the place to myself.'

Ana felt a flutter of recognition; wasn't she exactly the same? It was surprising how much they appeared to have in common.

'Some people don't enjoy their own company,' she observed.

'My sisters are like that,' agreed Rocco. 'Always their homes are busy or they are on the phone and shouting over the noise of a television. They can't understand why I need peace and quiet.'

'I understand,' Ana told him. 'I like being alone. Peace and calm are things I value.'

'You will create peace in your *masseria*,' Rocco promised her. 'Just as I have here.'

Dusk had settled and was deepening into night. The moon edged upwards and stars scattered across the sky as they ate their supper in the patch of flickering light.

'Ana?' Rocco's voice was a deep murmur. 'I must ask if you would like to stay here with me tonight or if I should drive you back to your hotel instead?'

Ana took a breath. Here it was already, the conversation that she always needed to have. 'The thing is I don't want a relationship,' she told him. 'I'm not interested in complicating things. I'm very happily single.'

Rocco seemed to stifle a smile. 'I understand that. All I am asking is whether you would like to stay tonight? Because if your answer is yes, I can drink another glass of this very good primitivo wine. If no, then I will keep a clear head.'

In the soft glow of the tea lights his eyes seemed bright. Ana wasn't sure. Spending a night together hadn't been a part of her plan.

'But you said that you like it when people leave and you have this place to yourself,' she countered.

'I was talking about my family who are noisy and create a drama wherever they go. You aren't like that,' Rocco observed.

'Not at all,' Ana agreed.

'I am content to be alone but I would be happy if you stayed … so, what do you think?' His eyes held hers and he smiled.

'Have the wine,' Ana decided, holding out her own glass. 'I could drink a little more of it too.'

With one hand Rocco grasped the wine bottle, with the other he touched her outstretched arm, running his thumb from elbow to wrist, sending a thrill of surprise and longing all the way through her.

Ana had been certain this part of her life was over. For once, she was pleased to be wrong.

Skye

It's the morning of my wedding and I'm still not sure if I feel the way that a bride is meant to. My dress, the party, even the cake; none of it seems exciting.

I'm sitting watching Becky having curls tonged into her hair, waiting for my own turn when I hear the front door open and close, then Ana King appears. She's wearing paint-splattered clothing with her skin shiny and hair in a tangle, and it strikes me as odd that she's been out so early looking like that, but I don't mention it. Instead, I invite her to the wedding.

'I'd love you to come,' I say. 'Your advice the other day really helped.'

'My advice?' Ana's eyes widen, presumably in surprise at the unexpected invitation.

'You asked me if I love Tim and I didn't really give you an answer. Now I can.'

'It's all going ahead then,' she observes.

'Yes, and it would be great if you'd join us,' I say, because what other wedding guests will we have? Town dignitaries, strangers we met at a cocktail party.

Ana murmurs something that I don't catch. 'I'm pleased,' she adds, 'if what I said has helped ... if you've sorted things out.'

I smile at her, although by no means have Tim and I sorted

everything out, and I'm not sure we ever will completely. Yesterday was intense. We spent most of it talking and tearful, as I told Tim the things I'd been holding inside for too long. At first, he didn't want to hear them.

'You need proper help, therapy and maybe medication, you have to see someone,' I kept repeating.

We were in our room, sitting up in bed. Becky had brought a breakfast that neither of us could touch because we were still so churned up from the night before.

'I'm fine, I don't need therapy,' Tim was insisting. 'It would be a waste of time and money.'

'You had a panic attack that was so bad we thought you were dying,' I pointed out. 'And your moods are up and down all the time.'

'Everyone is like that,' he said, defensively. 'It's normal. There's nothing wrong with me.'

'It's impossible to live with,' I told him. 'You can't rely on someone if you never know which version of them that you're going to get. And I need to be able to rely on you.'

Tim has always hated to be criticised. 'You want to turn me into someone else. This is who I am, OK?'

'But it's not OK. That's what I'm telling you.'

He tried all the usual things. Turning what I said back onto me, blaming other people, retreating into silence – his full repertoire. Eventually we broke through some sort of barrier.

'That wasn't the first panic attack, was it?' I asked. 'There have been others?'

Reluctantly, Tim nodded. 'A few.'

'How long for?' I wanted to know.

'A while,' he admitted. 'Never as bad as that one though.'

'Why didn't you tell me?'

He shrugged, and looked away. 'I don't know really. Who

wants to be a person that has panic attacks? It seemed better to ignore them and carry on.'

'You heard what that doctor said. This isn't something to ignore. We have to get you some help. We need to get to the bottom of why they're happening.'

Tim still couldn't meet my eyes. 'Sometimes everything makes sense, other times nothing does. I don't see how anyone can help with that. I've always assumed most other people feel the same way.'

'Maybe you feel it more, though,' I told him, and that was when he started to cry. Tim has always been a demonstrative person but I've never known him sob like that. We stayed beneath the bedcovers, holding onto each other, my body curled into his long, spare frame and for once I wasn't restless or trying to pull away. There was nothing I had to do and no one but Tim who needed me.

Later there were more tears from both of us while we were talking to Becky and Josh, telling them the truth for once, admitting we'd had some problems. Tim said we weren't doing our kids any favours by keeping that from them and I agreed with him.

'Life isn't perfect and neither are relationships, they're old enough to know it,' he pointed out.

All that honesty was exhausting. This morning I'm still so tired that everything feels floaty and dream-like. I swap places with Becky and the hairdresser comes at me with a detangling brush, muttering to herself in Italian. She's still tugging through knots when Tim puts his head round the door. We're not bothering with any of those superstitions about the groom not seeing the bride prior to the ceremony. Both of us are past that.

'Coffee or champagne?' Tim asks.

'Coffee,' we chorus.

'Josh is going out to fetch some pastries,' he adds.

'On crutches?' That seems like a terrible idea. I don't want to be paying another visit to the hospital. 'How's he going to carry everything?'

Tim holds up a finger. 'Stop worrying, he's got his backpack, he'll be fine.'

When Josh returns, swinging in on his crutches, I devour a Nutella-filled pastry, making a sticky chocolatey mess of my fingers. It feels like I need the sugar-hit of energy.

Becky rolls her eyes at me. 'Don't touch your dress till you've washed your hands. Don't ruin anything.'

'As if I would,' I say, eye-rolling right back at her.

The flowers are delivered and we admire our bouquets of roses, amaryllis and delphiniums. The hairdresser helps me into my dress and Becky spends ages trying to choose a lipstick shade. With a lot less fuss, Tim and Josh slip on their suits along with bright pink waistcoats that match the bridesmaid's dress. At last, we're ready.

'A wedding doesn't fix anything.' That's what I keep telling Tim. 'It's not a glue. It won't stick us together.'

'I know all that,' he's been assuring me. 'But still, I want us to get married.'

Now, as I straighten his tie and make sure the spray of white flowers is secure in his buttonhole, I'm nervous. I've never enjoyed being the centre of attention and am trying not to think about standing there, in front of a bunch of strangers.

Even walking the short distance to the town hall, we draw glances. A few people call out to us as we cross the piazza. 'Auguri, auguri.'

'They're wishing us well,' Becky explains, her arm hooked through mine as she navigates the cobbles in her slender heels.

Stepping inside the town hall and hearing a string quartet playing chamber music, my stomach flips.

'Are you OK?' asks Tim, and I can't find my voice, so only manage a nod as our heels clack over the long stretch of marble floor towards the wedding chamber.

It's a grand room hung with a massive chandelier; its walls covered in gilt-framed mirrors. Several people are already gathered and as I scan the faces turned towards us, Ana rushes in and takes a seat in the front row beside the elderly man, Augusto.

The musicians strike up the wedding march and Tim takes my hand. Together we walk down the aisle towards the mayor who is officiating.

As we're standing in front of him, ready to say 'I do', he takes the opportunity to make another speech, switching between Italian and English, and my attention keeps drifting but I think what he's mostly talking about is love. Halfway through Josh knocks over one of his crutches with a loud clatter and Becky starts to giggle. The room is stuffy, and Tim is looking sweaty in his suit. Ana seems bored and Augusto might have fallen asleep. Just like us, this wedding isn't perfect.

Suddenly I realise how happy I am. Happy that Tim and I waited this long, so our kids could be a part of this day. Happy to be here, on the brink of repeating the words I hadn't imagined saying. *For better, for worse, for richer, for poorer, in sickness and in health.* So many brides have spoken the same promises out loud and, as I start, my voice is shaky, but soon it gets stronger. I'm not only saying these things, I mean them.

Tim squeezes my hand and I smile at him. We both look over towards the kids and I know we'll always remember this moment.

Now it makes sense; the exchanging of rings and repeating vows, the bouquets of flowers, even the three-tier cakes. We're together, me and the little band of people I love most. We've made it through all the things that life has thrown at us, and this is our chance to celebrate.

Later, leaving the town hall, we're showered in confetti and the photographer seems intent on capturing our every expression as it settles on our hair and clothes. There are more shots taken as we stand in front of the fountain and I know Tim well enough to see that he's in his element. Becky is like her father, posing confidently like a model. Josh is more me; his grin is fixed and I can tell he wants this part to be over.

There are pictures taken of us with the kids, with the mayor, with what seems like half the town. We're photographed kissing and we're videoed walking hand in hand across the piazza once, twice, three times. I start losing patience and Tim notices.

'You're over this, aren't you?' he says, glancing at my face. 'You hate having your photograph taken.'

'They've got enough shots by now surely?'

'I really think they do.'

Tim takes my hand again, but instead of turning back to strike yet another pose, we walk away together over the cobbled piazza, leaving the photographer behind, faster and faster, half running now and giggling. Once we're out of sight, Tim pulls me close.

'We're married,' he says. 'Can you believe it?'

I stare up at his face, swamped with such a rush of tenderness, wanting to hold onto that feeling for as long as I can.

'I'm not always easy to live with, I know that,' he says. 'I'll change for the better.'

'You wouldn't be you, if you didn't drive me crazy sometimes.'

Tim laughs. 'I drive myself crazy too.'

He's bending to kiss me, when the photographer rounds the corner, and raises his camera to capture the moment. I shake my head in his direction. 'Not now.'

The photographer, a young guy in a sharp suit, doesn't make a move.

'My wife said not now,' Tim tells him, his tone firm. 'I think we should listen to her.'

With a shrug, the photographer lowers his camera. And then we kiss properly, like we did when we were young, a long kiss, hard and urgent, a kiss that goes on for so long that by the time we finish the photographer has given up and walked away.

'Shall we skip the reception?' Tim asks me.

'We can't do that.'

'Together you and me, we can do whatever we want,' he insists.

Right now, he's Tim the rule-breaker, full of bravado and swagger, and so much the man I fell in love with that it almost takes my breath away.

'We don't want to miss it though, do we?' I say, knowing I could never let everyone down. 'The kids will be there by now. And anyway, it might be fun.'

'We'll make it fun,' Tim promises.

'We always do.'

As we start walking to the hotel, where our handful of wedding guests will be waiting, Tim catches hold of my hand again.

'We'll sort it out, this mess I made with my stupid lie,' he promises. 'So don't worry, OK?'

I'm thinking that we'll have to, one way or another, but I don't say anything.

'You're glad aren't you, that we did all this?' Tim is sounding insecure now. 'Came to Italy, got married at last ...'

I lean into him. 'Yes, I'm glad.'

Soon I'll be holding a glass of Prosecco and raising it in a toast, to Tim and me, to our family. I may not feel the way a bride is meant to, but I do feel like a wife. And that seems much more important.

Ana

Wasting a day was frustrating, but Ana hadn't the heart to turn down Skye's invitation. Upstairs getting ready, taking a quick shower and trying to decide what to wear, she found herself wondering if Rocco might be at the wedding, then dismissed the thought of him as soon as it entered her head; because of course he wouldn't.

She put on a pale blue broderie anglaise frock, chosen because it didn't need ironing. Even though she had showered, she could almost still smell Rocco on her skin and thinking about him again, remembering their night together, warmth spread through her body. That feeling was back. The tingling of her nerve-endings. The rush of longing.

Rocco was going to be all she could think about at the wedding ... his skin against hers, his strength wherever she touched him. She would have to sit smiling coolly through vows and speeches, while inside she felt molten.

Ana was almost late to the ceremony, rushing in as the wedding march started and finding a seat next to Augusto moments before the bride and groom walked down the aisle. The whole affair might have dragged, particularly as the mayor made one of his long speeches, but Ana had her own thoughts to get lost in while Augusto closed his eyes, and the mayor talked, and the room grew hotter.

By the time they emerged from the town hall in a hailstorm of confetti, Ana felt almost feverish. She pressed the back of her hand to her forehead; thinking that perhaps she was coming down with something, but her temperature didn't seem unusually warm.

Her best opportunity to escape was while the wedding portraits were being taken. Ana might have seized it except Augusto was beside her and glancing at his narrow face, braided with wrinkles, she couldn't bring herself to leave him. Then the mayor came over, the hoteliers Edward and Gino joined them, and she found herself in the middle of a crowd moving towards the hotel for the reception party, leaving behind the bride and groom, still standing in front of the photographer.

Canapés and bubbles were being served, the room looked lovely and the string quartet had decamped from the town hall and was now playing Neapolitan love songs.

'Romantic enough?' Edward asked her.

'Romance isn't really my specialty, but yes I think so,' Ana replied.

To while away the time, she took a series of quick shots with her phone. Augusto looking especially dapper in a polka dot tie. A table set with green cut-glass vases filled with white hydrangeas. A tray of shot glasses filled with chilled cucumber soup and scattered with nasturtium flowers.

Sipping her sparkling wine, Ana started to load these latest pictures onto Instagram. Already she had posted a number of shots, mostly of her dilapidated *masseria*, even one that she had taken surreptitiously of Rocco painting her bedroom ceiling. They were interspersed with images of meals she had enjoyed and views she had admired, making up a patchwork of her new life that Ana enjoyed adding to. It was unexpectedly addictive.

Glancing at her profile page, she was surprised to see how much her number of followers had jumped up already.

'That's odd,' she said, aloud.

'What is?' asked Edward, who was fiddling with the flower arrangement.

'Do you think twenty thousand followers is a lot to have on Instagram?'

'I suppose that depends on who you are.' He moved one of the vases a few millimetres to the right, then shifted it back again.

'I'm me and I only started this account a couple of days ago.'

'Then yes, it does seem like a lot.' Edward came closer, peering at her screen. 'Make sure you tag in the hotel and the town. Oh, and mention the wedding competition.'

'I'm not an influencer,' Ana told him.

'With twenty thousand people viewing your posts, I think you might be.' Edward pulled out his own phone and his finger flew across the screen. 'Now you have another ... I'm following you too.'

'How did they find me, all those people?' Ana was mystified.

'Look I've got no idea. We have social media for the hotel, of course, but I don't really understand how it all works.' Edward was scrolling through her grid of images. 'Wait, is that Rocco Cicuzzo? He's a good friend of ours.'

'He's my handyman,' said Ana. 'It was Augusto who put me onto him.'

'Your handyman?' Edward gave her a sideways glance. 'I think you said something like that before and I assumed it was a joke.'

'Not a joke.' Ana wondered why Edward seemed so surprised. 'Rocco's been doing a really great job, actually. He can tackle almost anything.'

'Maybe, but he isn't a handyman,' Edward told her.

'No? What is he then?'

'An engineer. Rocco has his own construction company, a fairly big one, building roads and tunnels.'

Ana couldn't believe it. 'Then why is he painting my ceiling?'

'That's what I'm wondering.' Edward scooped up a tray of canapés. 'I guess you'll have to ask him.'

As Edward moved round the room, offering miniature arancini, Ana stared at the photograph of Rocco. She had captured him balanced on top of the ladder, face slightly upturned, one toned arm wielding a roller. Hundreds of people had liked what seemed to be an ordinary shot of a man at work. But no picture could tell the whole story.

'Augusto?'

Throughout the ceremony Ana had been concerned that he didn't seem his usual bright self. Now the older man was sitting at one end of a long divan, his eyes half closing. At the sound of her voice, they opened.

'*Si, cara.*'

'I know I'm not meant to ask this, but are you OK?'

'No need to worry, I am only thinking,' Augusto told her. 'Today I have a lot of thoughts.'

Ana sat down next to him. 'Can I ask you something?'

'Of course.'

'Edward tells me Rocco is an engineer and he owns a large construction company. Is it true?'

'My nephew Rocco? Yes, yes of course.'

'Why has he been helping me then?'

'Because I asked him to,' Augusto's tone implied that it should be obvious.

'He's not really your nephew, is he?' she pressed him.

Augusto threw up his hands. 'Nephew, cousin, friend, what difference does it make? He is family.'

Ana hoped she hadn't offended the old man; that was the last thing she wanted. She stayed beside him, perched on the divan, as the bride and groom arrived and Edward clinked a piece of cutlery against a wine glass, to signal for everyone's attention. Then Skye's children proposed a toast and her husband made a short speech that got everyone laughing. Ana smiled along with them, her mind elsewhere.

Why would Rocco spend his time working as a labourer when he had a business to run? It made no sense.

As they were going into lunch, she took the chance to send him a message.

Where are you?

His reply came as she was contemplating a first course of scampi ravioli in a rich bisque.

I'm at your place putting on the second coat of paint.
Where are you?

Earlier that morning, as they were saying goodbye, she had told Rocco she would see him soon. It was the kind of thing you said very casually after spending a night together and didn't necessarily mean much. She had forgotten the promise of a second coat of paint. Holding her phone beneath the table, Ana started typing again.

I'm at a wedding. I'll come as soon as I can.

He replied with a smiley face, a heart and a bouquet of flowers.

Ana had never been a sender of emojis. She managed a thumbs up in return then put her phone away, wishing she wasn't stranded at the wedding of a couple she hardly knew, making polite conversation. There were other things she needed to do. And so much that she didn't understand. Why hadn't Rocco told her who he was? Why was he spending time checking out her plumbing and painting her ceiling? Didn't he have his own job to do?

As she stored up questions, the lunch went on. Plate after plate tested Ana's patience. A tuna crudo with preserved artichoke and caperberries. Another course of pasta. Beef tagliata served rare and drizzled in balsamic. A creamy concoction for dessert. When it seemed that surely things must be coming to a close, a towering cake was wheeled in and there was a whole ceremony around cutting it.

'A wonderful wedding, a perfect day,' Augusto exclaimed for at least the fourth time, and Ana forced a smile as she nodded in agreement.

Coffee and biscotti were being served by the time she managed a discreet exit. With a whispered goodbye to Augusto and a smile in Skye's direction, Ana slipped out of the door. By now she feared that Rocco might have finished painting and gone. Rushing to retrieve her car from the hotel's parking building, she hoped his perfectionism was holding him up. Otherwise, what excuse would there be for her to see him again?

Driving a little too fast, she shaved a few minutes off her trip and, pulling through the gates of the *masseria*, was in time to see Rocco loading his stepladder into his van.

'Take a look inside and tell me what you think,' he called, as she climbed from her car. 'I'm quite pleased with the result.'

'A professional job then?' she asked, moving towards him rather than the doorway.

'No, I wouldn't say that, but an improvement most definitely.'

Rocco was so much larger than her; taller and wider. Ana straightened her spine. 'Why did you lie to me?' she asked, coolly.

'What? I haven't lied.' He sounded taken aback.

'You let me believe you're a handyman but that's not the truth, is it?'

Rocco studied her face. 'Is not mentioning something to you the same as lying?'

'Yes, I think it is,' Ana's hands were on her hips. It was a power pose she had often used in presentations. 'You have your own construction business to run, so why are you here, helping me?'

'Augusto asked me to.'

Ana refused to believe it. 'You're not doing all this for Augusto?'

Giving the ladder a final shove, Rocco started to pile his painting gear into the van beside it. 'The first time I came, yes, I was doing him a favour. But it is true that Augusto is not the reason that I kept coming back.'

'Why then?'

Rocco's voice softened, as he turned to her. 'I was curious about you, my fiercely independent neighbour making a new life in a strange place. I wanted to know you.'

'You weren't busy, with your job?' Ana stared up into his face.

'I had taken some time off to work on my own place – that list of chores I mentioned – and instead I kept coming here and working on yours.' His softer voice was matched by a slight smile. 'I didn't really mean to … but somehow I did.'

Ana's hands slipped from her hips and hung by her side. She wasn't sure what to say.

Rocco looked away, then back again, his gaze holding hers, a question in his eyes. 'Ana, you know that I like you, yes?'

'Well yes … and I like you too … but Rocco …'

'Are you going to tell me again that you don't want a relationship?'

She nodded, wordlessly, and for a few moments all there was between them was warm air and silence.

'We are both people who value our independence,' said Rocco, at last. 'But perhaps there is still a way to be in each other's lives.'

'Lovers then,' said Ana. 'Friends with benefits, I think that's what they say.'

'Who are *they*?' he asked dismissively. 'And who cares what *they* might say. I am talking about us; what we want. So, tell me, Ana. Do we want the same thing?'

'I want my own life, I need my own house,' she told him. 'It's important for me to have my space.'

He nodded. 'Me too.'

'In the past, my relationships have never worked out. I just don't think I'm very good at them.'

'Me neither,' he admitted.

'Why, should this be any different, you and me?'

'Perhaps it won't be different, but what is the worst that can happen?' Rocco shrugged, his lips twitching into that familiar half-smile. 'You may need to find another handyman.'

'I really like the handyman I've got,' Ana admitted. 'He's useful ... reliable ... he makes a great lunch.'

'You need him then?'

'Need?' She shook her head. 'Not really ... but I want him.'

Rocco touched her gently with his fingertips, stroking down her clavicle and beneath the fabric of her dress, making Ana shiver.

'Then I think we want the same thing,' he told her.

Skye

It was a long, long day and by the time the fireworks display was over it was getting late. Drooping with fatigue, Tim and I had what must have been the least passionate wedding night ever. I fell asleep the moment I curled up in bed, and I'm assuming that he did too.

Waking up this morning, much too early as usual, Tim is still snoring lightly and I shuffle over to his side of the immense bed and lie against his back, curling my legs up around him. Mostly what I'm feeling is relief. We're married, it's done and I don't have to think about it anymore.

I'm not under any illusions. Those vows we repeated weren't a magic spell, they haven't made our problems disappear. But we're going to face them together from now on, and that seems like a good start.

Tim shifts, stretching his long body, then rolls over.

'Good morning,' he says, reaching for me. 'Don't we need to consummate this marriage?'

'I think we might have already consummated things a few times.'

His arm tightens round my waist. 'Not for ages though.'

That part of our relationship was never a problem, even after the kids came along. Lately though, I've been so lost in my resentment and stress, while Tim's had his own stuff going on. No wonder, we've barely touched each other.

As we kiss, I find myself wondering *how many times have we done this*? Thousands, surely. First in Tim's tiny flat where we spent hours finding each other fascinating. Then in cars and tents, hotels and hostels, the many places we've stayed and slept. All those kisses as the years went by and we drifted apart.

When our mouths meet now, it should feel familiar. Pressed to Tim's chest, I sense his heart beating against mine. With one hand, he pushes between my legs and his fingers begin to tease. As I gasp, I feel his lips curve into a smile, then his kisses become harder and more urgent, while his fingers move faster, until I'm on my back, legs apart, and shuddering.

Tim's body covers mine and we begin to move together. There's no need for either of us to say a word. With this at least, we know exactly what the other needs. How many times has it happened? And in how many different places? It should feel completely familiar, but somehow it never does.

Our room in the palazzo is thick-walled and silent. It's easy to imagine we're the only ones here. But when Tim gets up to fetch coffee, we hear the sound of laughter and cheering.

'What's going on out there?' I ask, reaching for my robe.

'I don't know, but it must be fun,' decides Tim, standing by the open door and listening.

As I follow him downstairs, the laughter gets louder. Becky and Josh are finding something very amusing and I assume they're watching TikTok videos but when we reach the ground floor, Becky comes flying down the hallway on Josh's crutches, nearly crashing into us.

'We're having a race,' she says, looking sheepish. 'Josh has set a record and I'm trying to beat it.'

'On crutches?' Tim is instantly engaged. 'Have you marked out a course?'

Becky nods. 'Yes, and there are obstacles.'

Their racecourse covers the whole ground floor: the kitchen and dining chamber, both reception rooms as well as the hallway. There are cushions piled on the floor here and there for them to leap over. My instinct is to beg them not to smash anything and I'm itching to put the cushions back on the chairs where they belong. Instead, I knot the cord of my robe more securely round my waist and hold out my hands.

'Give me those crutches and let me try.'

'Really?' Becky looks like she doesn't believe it.

'Just show me which way I'm meant to be going.'

It's so long since I've done anything silly, and I'm rubbish on crutches, clumsy over the obstacles, and breathless by the time I finish. Becky is a lot faster but can't match her brother's time. Only Tim gets close to beating him. On his final round, as we're whooping and laughing, Ana King appears. It doesn't escape my notice that she's still wearing the same pale blue dress she had on for our wedding yesterday.

'It's a point-to-point race,' I explain, as she stands there looking bemused. 'But on crutches so you can only use one leg.'

'Okaaay.'

'Would you like to have a go?' Tim asks.

'Tempting as the prospect is I have things to do and need to get changed,' Ana replies, picking her way over a pile of cushions and making for the stairs.

Tim and I exchange a glance and I can tell we're both having the same thought. She can't have come back here last night. Not that it's any of our business, but still I'm intrigued.

'We should get changed too,' I realise. 'We've got lunch at the olive grove on our schedule today.'

317

'Yeah, and I need to talk to the mayor, sort some stuff out,' says Tim, his voice heavier now, handing the crutches back to Josh.

'I think you mean *we* need to talk to him,' I say and it's obvious from Tim's face that he's relieved. It must have been weighing heavily, the lie he told on our competition entry and not knowing what we'll have to pay to make amends. No wonder he had that panic attack.

'And so, I retire undefeated,' Josh holds his crutches high. 'The supreme champion.'

'Winner tidies up,' I tell him.

The olive grove is a forty-minute drive along winding hill roads and straight highways. The further we go, the quieter Tim becomes. I understand why he's preoccupied, but the kids don't and this is one thing we don't need to tell them.

'Do you think the mayor will make a speech?' I ask, attempting to lighten the mood.

'I hope it's a really long one,' replies Becky, perhaps picking up on her father's subdued state.

Tim is staring over the top of the steering wheel, his expression strained. If you didn't know him it might be difficult to believe that only a couple of hours ago, he was racing round the palazzo on crutches, laughing his head off. But I've had half a lifetime of his shifting moods. I know that sometimes they're like lightning.

'Today's lunch is the last of the official functions,' I remind everyone. 'After this, we're on our own for the rest of our time here. So, what are we going to do?'

Becky is all for abandoning Montenello and going somewhere more exciting, Josh is keen on heading to the beach. Tim gives a shrug. 'Let's see how things pan out,' he says.

★

The olive grove restaurant is rustic yet still fancy, and mentally I start imagining how much this will add to the bill we're facing. Then I remind myself there's no point in worrying about it. Money is important but it's not everything. Tim and I are ready to work hard, we'll find a way to pay.

I take some encouragement from the friendly smile on the mayor's face as he swoops over to greet us. Hopefully we'll manage a few moments alone with him later so we can start the awkward conversation we need to have. For now, he's introducing us to his mother, who owns the restaurant and is keen to tell us all about the menu she has planned. Then we're shown to a table where Tim and I are seated on either side of Augusto, and surrounded by a group of other people from the same generation, none of whom seems to speak English.

Becky is at the far end of the table using Google Translate, which makes for a slow exchange, but like her father she has the ability to talk to anyone. Beside her Josh is on his phone too, scrolling with his thumb. Normally I'd tell him to put it away, but he's not at ease like his sister, and the screen is another sort of crutch I suppose.

'What a wonderful wedding,' says Augusto, smiling. 'A perfect day.'

'It really was perfect,' I agree.

'Already we have put some photographs on the internet. This publicity will lead to many more bookings for weddings, and that is very good for the whole town.'

'It's why you had the competition in the first place,' I say. 'We know that.'

'And it has been a great success. My friends Edward and Gino at the hotel, my niece the bridal designer, my granddaughter who made the wedding cake, everyone is happy. I am pleased too, because this was my idea. I helped the mayor to plan every part of it and together we picked you as our winners.'

Tim's gaze meets mine and I know both of us are thinking this is the conversation we've been dreading.

'Along with the mayor, I am the only one who saw your competition entry,' Augusto adds, confirming it.

Shame is flooding Tim's face. His cheeks flush and his eyes are slits. 'Then you must be aware of what happened ... what I did ...'

Augusto holds up a hand. 'The mayor's assistant, he is not very efficient,' he confides, lowering his voice. 'Files get lost, they are deleted. When I was running the office there were never such problems. Now this happens all the time; it is re-grettable.'

'We're going to talk to the mayor, make everything right,' I say, and Augusto shakes his head.

'I owe you an apology Signora. Your simple dress was the right choice. Sometimes simple is best.'

Tim and I both stare at him; unsure what he's trying to say in this roundabout way.

'The wedding was wonderful and the publicity is good.' Augusto smiles at me then at Tim. 'We don't want anything to change that.'

'Surely there is a way that I can make up for it?' Tim says, flustered now. 'We're planning to pay everyone back.'

'I have thought about this for many hours.' Augusto pinches the bridge of his nose between his thumb and forefinger, as if re-enacting the effort. 'During your ceremony and reception, I exhausted myself thinking. So many people came together to give you that day. How to even decide what each of them is owed? It is much too complicated. Then I looked at your wife, beautiful in her wedding gown. And that is when I realised, the simple way is the best for everyone.'

'So, are you saying we don't need to worry?' I'm hardly able to believe it.

Augusto studies my face and gives a small shrug of his shoulders. 'There are many things in the world we must worry about, but this is not one of them. I have talked to the mayor and he agrees, there is no need to mention this again.'

Tim looks glassy-eyed. He is overcome and can't seem to say a word, leaving me to stammer out my thanks to Augusto.

'That's unbelievably generous of you.'

'Eat, eat, the food here is very good,' Augusto urges us.

'We can't tell you how sorry Tim is and how grateful we are.'

'This is another lovely day, another wonderful occasion,' Augusto continues. 'Enjoy, enjoy.'

'Thank you so much,' I persist.

The old man raises his glass of bubbly. 'A toast,' he calls down the table. 'To love and to everything we do for it. *Amore.*'

'*Amore,*' his friends echo back, to the sound of clinking glasses.

Lunch goes on for most of the afternoon. Between courses people leave the table and wander through the olive groves then return for another bite. As coffee is served, the mayor does make a speech, but it's quite a short one. He thanks everyone who has played a part in making our dream wedding happen, then we all clink glasses again.

I'm expecting Tim to get up and say something, but today he seems reluctant to step into the spotlight. It's Becky who stands and clears her throat, as all those expectant faces turn towards her.

'The word thank you isn't really enough,' she begins, and I marvel at how poised she is, her voice clear and steady. 'This part of Italy will always be special to our family. The places and the people, the memories we've been making. So even though it isn't enough, from me and my brother, from our parents, thank you is all we can say.'

321

Before sitting down, Becky reads out the Google Translate version of the little speech she must have prepared earlier. She stumbles over the Italian once or twice and most likely there are words mispronounced, still I'm so proud of her. Josh leads the applause as I'm beaming at them both. Tim and I might have got many things wrong in our years together, but we made great kids.

All of us are drowsy after so much good food and sunshine, but Tim especially, and he falls asleep in the passenger seat as I'm driving us back to Montenello.

'Is Dad all right?' Josh wonders, and I hear an edge of anxiety in his voice. 'He's not going to have one of his attacks, is he?'

My eyes are focused on the winding hill road but I spare a glance for Tim. 'I think Dad just needs a good rest.'

'Let's stay in Montenello then,' decides Becky. 'Instead of moving on to somewhere new.'

'Aren't you bored there though?' I ask.

'The beach isn't that far away, we could go for a day,' suggests Josh.

'Oh, and we could have another crutch race, take it outside this time.' Becky sounds keen on the idea. 'The piazza would make a good racecourse.'

'You're dreaming if you think you'll beat me,' Josh teases.

'I've walked over those cobbles in stilettos,' she reminds him.

Tim's head falls back and he lets out a hearty snore. All of us start giggling but even that doesn't wake him. We'll need to have a quiet time together for the next few days, just the four of us. Well, quietish.

'I think you're under-estimating my skills on crutches,' I say. Both of them giggle again.

'I'm sorry Mum, but you were terrible,' says my daughter.

'Yeah,' my son agrees. 'Like the worst.'

Ana

After a painfully long wait, Ana had the key to unlock her future. Her tax code – or *codice fiscale*, as the rather imperious man in the tax office called it – was only a string of letters and numbers, but it meant that she could get the electricity switched on and make a formal offer to buy the *masseria*. She celebrated by going shopping for bright ceramics, vibrant cushions and throw rugs, even a cutlery set with colourful handles, wondering what the London version of herself would make of it all. The Ana who wore tailored clothes and a slash of Ruby Woo lipstick liked everything to be perfect. That woman never would have settled for chipped tiles, crumbling plaster and rotting window frames, or attempted to distract the eye from all of that by layering in lots of colour. Now Ana wondered if she might have been perhaps a little too controlled before.

This evening, she was going to cook a celebration dinner, just a simple pasta dish as she only had a Primus stove, and by necessity the room would be lit by candles. It was a thank you to Rocco for everything he had done and all the meals he had fed her. For now, though she was busy arranging all her bright new things in the few spaces she was planning to use, moving cushions around, adding a throw rug here then there.

323

When her phone rang, she startled at a sound she hardly ever heard these days. Seeing who was calling gave her another jolt. Tammy Wong. Ana hadn't talked to her young digital editor since the *Culinaria* days. She always pictured Tammy sitting at her old desk, directing what was left of her magazine and it seemed easier not to make contact.

She answered now though, her voice upbeat. 'Tammy, how are you?'

'Ana, oh great you do still have your old number, I wasn't sure. How's Italy?'

It took Ana a moment to realise that Tammy must be among her social media followers so knew exactly what was going on in her life. 'It's mostly wonderful, although I'm about to buy a huge pile of old stones that badly needs renovating.'

'Which is why I'm calling.' Tammy explained. 'We ran a news item about you on the website after I saw your Instagram posts and we've had such a huge response that I wondered whether you'd give us a few quotes and maybe even let us use some photos, so we can expand it into a longer feature. The readers are so interested in what you're up to.'

The readers are so interested ... Ana had used the same line repeatedly over the years when lining up interviews with celebrity chefs or to talk them into sharing top secret recipes.

Then she had a thought. 'Wait a minute. Is this why I seem to be getting so many likes on my Instagram?'

'We did link to your page but I'm sure people would have found you anyway. You've got such a following.'

'There's no need to flatter me, Tammy. I'll give you the quotes and the photos.'

'But I mean it.' The younger woman insisted. 'All those dedicated readers. They loved the magazine you made.'

'I hear it's coming back.'

'Yeah, yeah.' Now Tammy's voice flattened.

'How's it going?' asked Ana, walking through to her bedroom with a cushion.

'Honestly? It's turning into a total shit-fight.'

Ana smiled; it was impossible not to. 'Oh dear.'

'I don't suppose you'd come back would you, even short-term? I know there's been some talk about approaching you.'

'Absolutely not.' Ana had never been more certain of anything. 'Please tell them not to bother asking. They should be giving the editor-in-chief's job to you.'

'I couldn't do it, I'm not across everything the way you were, I don't have your talent.'

'All you lack is my experience and there's only one way to get that.' The cushion looked wrong on the bed so Ana picked it up again. 'But Tammy, you can always call if you need my advice. I'm just here, rearranging soft furnishings, and happy to chat. Right now, though, do you want those quotes?'

'Tell me everything,' Tammy said, and Ana could tell she was reaching for a notebook and pen. 'How did you find the place you're buying? And why Italy?'

As they talked, she walked upstairs, still holding the cushion. She had been planning to use the tower room as a place to sit with a glass of wine and enjoy the view, so had placed a single chair in there beside the window. Looking around the large, bare space, Ana decided she ought to bring up another just in case Rocco wanted to join her.

He arrived for dinner at precisely the time they had agreed, bringing with him the ingredients to make her a negroni. For once he wasn't wearing overalls and Ana watched as he stirred the drink and added a twist of orange peel. Even in loose cargo pants and a shirt, Rocco was a mountain of a man.

'Where's your drink?' wondered Ana, accepting her negroni.

'I need to drive home later,' he reminded her.

'Not if you stay here with me.'

'Then in the morning I will open my eyes and see the ceiling that your handyman made such a terribly bad job of,' he complained.

'I'll find a way to distract you,' Ana promised.

'*Va bene.*' Rocco took his penknife and began to pare another strip of peel from the orange. 'Then I will drink a negroni.'

As he was mixing up gin, vermouth and Campari, Ana told him about her day, thinking how great it was to be with someone who actually listened. So many men over the years had only wanted to talk about themselves. No wonder she had never stayed with any of them for long.

'I did an interview earlier for my old magazine,' she explained, now. 'The woman I talked to, Tammy, she's smart and digitally savvy, and she gave me a few ideas. I've made a list.'

'Ah, a list. And what does it say?'

Ana produced her primrose-coloured Moleskine notebook and flicked to the right page. 'Item one, start an email newsletter and build up subscribers.'

'What will you say in this newsletter?' Rocco wanted to know.

'I'll talk about my life here in Italy – renovating the house, the food I eat and cook, the characters I meet. But I'll be real about it. I'm not going to pretend everything is perfect.'

'You are going to write about Augusto?' he asked, as she was filling a pan with water to boil for the pasta.

'Almost certainly.'

'He will love that,' said Rocco, putting down his drink so he could light the Primus stove for her.

'Hey I'm the one who's doing the cooking remember. You're not supposed to be helping.'

'Am I meant to stand here and do nothing?' he asked.

'You're meant to drink your negroni and listen to my plan. No pacing up and down, OK?'

'*Va bene*,' he said, sounding resigned.

'Tammy says people charge for these newsletters. But the main reason for me doing one is when I start my cooking classes, or writing retreats, or food tours ... whatever it is I end up doing here ... I'll have all these people ready and waiting, my readers or followers, whatever you're meant to call them. Anyway, that's my list.'

From the side pocket of his cargo pants Rocco produced a small black Moleskine notebook. 'I have a list also.'

Not for the first time, it struck Ana that she and her former handyman were very alike.

'What does it say?'

'I write down whatever I need to remember or do. But nothing exciting like you.'

'It is exciting, isn't it?' Ana was eager to begin. 'This is definitely my best list ever.'

Rocco put down his drink again but this time he didn't try to help Ana cook, winding his arms round her waist instead. 'You are formidable.'

'So, you keep saying.'

Turning off the Primus stove, she leant into him. Supper could wait.

Candlelight was so flattering. Even once the power was switched on at her *masseria*, Ana thought she would keep tea lights and votives in every room. Now though, in the brighter, less forgiving light of morning, she was hurrying back to Montenello, hoping to catch Skye. The family was leaving today and she wanted to say goodbye.

Somehow, they had managed to spread their belongings through every room of the palazzo. Rolled up socks had found

327

their way beneath chairs, shoes had been abandoned in the middle of the floor and everyone appeared to have lost something.

'Has anyone seen my phone charger?' asked Skye's daughter, wandering through the downstairs rooms. 'Mum, I can't find it anywhere.'

'Let me have a look.' Rushing down, Skye seemed frazzled. 'Oh, Ana hi, have you been out somewhere already?'

'Actually, I just spent my first night at my new home,' Ana told her.

'But I thought you still didn't have any electricity?'

'There were lots of candles so it wasn't so bad.' Ana wasn't planning to mention Rocco. There was no need for other people to know.

'It's in the middle of nowhere, isn't it? Were you on your own in the dark with only candles? You're a braver person than me,' declared Skye, her tone admiring.

'Not on my own, no.' Ana couldn't lie. She couldn't pretend to be someone that she wasn't.

'Oh.' Skye gave her a searching look.

'Rocco, my handyman was there with me,' she admitted.

'So, are you saying that you spent the night together?' Skye checked.

Ana only nodded.

'Well, good on you.' Again, Skye seemed admiring.

'Most likely this won't go anywhere,' Ana added hastily.

'What if it did though?'

Ana gave a casual shrug, as though it wasn't a question she had already asked herself.

'That would be fine.'

Skye gave her a sidelong look. 'Just fine, nothing more?' she wondered.

Ana found herself blushing. 'I suppose it might go further … I hope it does.'

'Is it possible you might have met someone worth letting into your life?'

'It's possible,' Ana conceded.

'Will you let me know? We'll stay in touch?'

Ana hadn't thought to continue the friendship. Now she saw that might be fine too. 'Of course, let's stay in touch.'

'You'll be glad of some peace and quiet, I expect.' Skye was clutching several items to her chest: a pair of reading glasses, a single Adidas trainer, a towel. There were more of her family's belongings strewn around them. 'That's if we ever manage to leave.'

'It's gone so fast, your time here.'

'In some ways it has and in others ... well a lot has happened ...'

'We'll be back,' her husband called, carrying a suitcase downstairs. 'This place is special to us now. We'll come here every year to celebrate our anniversary.'

Skye gave him what Ana could only describe as a sobering look. 'OK maybe not *every* year,' he amended.

'You can come and stay at my *masseria* once it's fixed up,' said Ana, impulsively. 'It would be a thank you for letting me share this place with you.'

'That's such a kind offer.' Skye paused at the foot of the stairs, clearing her throat. 'There is something I've been wanting to ask. I always dreamed of seeing one of my cakes on the cover of *Culinaria*. It very nearly happened but ... well, you know. Anyway, I read on the website that the magazine is coming back and wondered if you're likely to be editing it?'

'Absolutely not.' Ana felt lighter and happier every time she said it. 'I do have some contacts there still but can't promise anything.' She reached behind a cut glass vase and pulled out a phone charger that had been half-hidden behind it. 'I think this may belong to your daughter.'

'Ah, there it is.' Skye said, taking the charger.

'Have a good trip home.' Ana thought of busy airports and crowded planes, she thought of England heading towards its winter and felt glad not to be the one who was leaving.

Skye moved to hug her goodbye, but her hands were too full and she stood back. 'Thanks for coming to the wedding, thanks for everything,' she said.

Ana hesitated, but only for a moment, then she wrapped her arms round Skye's shoulders and managed an awkward hug, the towel and trainer crushed between them.

Skye

As always when I'm working, the air smells of sugar and is spiced with warm cinnamon. Breathing in, it almost feels like I never went away. Baking in the Lost Cakery's oven is my first attempt at Italian pastries. A tray of shell-shaped *sfogliatelle* that I'm going to trial selling at the farm shop down the road. If they're popular then I'll have to get much faster at making them, particularly as I seem to have lost my assistant.

Meera is taking a well-deserved break and when she comes back to work, she'll be busy setting up the new café in Bicycle Junction. As much as I'll miss her, I think Tim is partly right; it's better if she's not always here, making her clear-eyed judgements. Because nothing about life is clear. The older I get, the more I understand that.

For the time being, Tim is doing most of the deliveries. He still drives the van much too fast and I don't trust him with a wedding cake. But without me needing to ask, he always remembers to put on a hairnet.

'This is how much I love you,' Tim says, pointing to it. 'This right here. Incontrovertible proof.'

Honestly, there are still times when it's quite tempting to take to him with my palette knife. Nobody is capable of irritating me quite as much as Tim. Just this morning he came in while I was busy with the pastries and ... well it doesn't matter really. He's making an effort. So am I. Most newlyweds might not find that romantic, but we're not most newlyweds.

Tim is meant to be clearing out one of the sheds. I'm going to set up an art studio. My paintings might be terrible, of course. There's every chance that my talent doesn't extend past creating cake. But meeting Ana King, seeing how she forged ahead and changed her life, helped me realise that it wasn't too late for me to find out.

In the meantime, I need to get on with decorating a cake. No glitter this time because I've decided to ban it. Fake sparkles aren't my thing anymore. I go to the shelf stacked with gel food colouring and select the bottles I need, so everything is close to hand. Beside them, is my new wedding band sitting beside my engagement ring in the small dish where they're kept safe while I'm busy working. I won't forget to slip them back on my finger at the end of the day.

Outside a grey day tells me winter is coming. Soon walking my dog through the woods will mean wading through mud, and Italy's sunshine will only be a memory. A good memory; one I'll hold onto. As I'm getting started on a little girl's pink Barbie doll cake, I think there's something else Tim's not entirely wrong about. We may not go to Montenello every year, but I'll dream of getting back there some day.

Then he appears, rushing as always, in a state of high excitement. As he flies through the doorway Tim pauses, sweeping his hairnet off a shelf.

'Skye, Skye, look,' he cries waving his phone at me whilst also trying to push on the hairnet. 'Check out this competition I just found.'

I had thought this phase was over, but apparently not.

'Aren't you meant to be clearing out that shed?'

'I've done it, I've finished. Everything is in the trailer ready to go. You can start moving in your art stuff.'

'Really?' I can't quite believe it.

'Really,' he promises, holding out his phone again. 'Then I came across this competition. I couldn't believe it.'

'What's the prize?' I ask, assuming it will be an air fryer or a skydive; something I really don't want.

'Win a second honeymoon in Portugal. We have to give it a go.'

'We do,' I agree. 'The chances of winning are tiny, but you never know.'

'I'll enter then, shall I?' he says. 'I'll do it right now.'

I look at my husband, lit up with excitement, curls escaping the hairnet, all windmilling limbs as he turns to dash off again.

'No Tim, hold on,' I call after him. 'Why don't we do it together?'

Ana

Augusto was sitting at his usual table outside the bar in the main piazza. He was wearing a jacket and scarf against the faintest hint of chill in the air. The old man was such a fixture there that Ana couldn't imagine Montenello without him. As she took a seat at his table, he seemed to read her mind.

'They want me to live forever,' he complained, gesturing towards a glass of green liquid. 'Now they are telling me I must drink this every morning. They say it is a healthy smoothie. I say I would rather die than take another sip.'

'You can't die, Augusto, who would run things round here?' Ana thought the smoothie did look unappealing. 'But you can't drink that either. Why don't I fetch you a coffee?'

'A real one?'

She nodded. 'And perhaps a pastry too?'

'A cornetto? Filled with custard?' The old man sighed. 'But they will never allow it.'

'I don't know about that. Rocco says I'm formidable.'

He looked interested now. 'You mean my nephew Rocco?'

Ana nodded. 'We have been spending some time together.'

'Of course.' Augusto treated her to his widest smile.

It wasn't so difficult really to persuade the barman that a little caffeine and sugar wasn't going to finish off Augusto, at least not today. The old man's eyes brightened when Ana appeared with a plate filled with pastries. Sitting outside, the plate on the table between them, they ate together and talked.

'What are your plans now the wedding competition is over?' Ana wondered. 'Have you and the mayor come up with another scheme?'

'Not so far.' Augusto took a sip of his coffee and nodded contentedly. 'But I will think of something; I always do.'

The pastries were rich and sweet. As Ana bit into one, a little creamy custard oozed into her fingers. 'I used to drink a healthy green smoothie every morning when I lived in London,' she told Augusto whose lips were dusted with flakes.

'Did drinking these smoothies make you happy?' he wanted to know.

'I don't think that was really the point of them,' Ana told him.

Augusto threw up his hands. 'What other point is there?'

Italy had changed her, Ana realised as she licked sweet custard from her fingers, and perhaps it was set to change her more. Whiling away the best part of the morning outside a bar, while the sun chased the shadows, was not how she had ever imagined being happy. Still here she was, with an elderly man who was almost certainly her best friend now, watching the life of the piazza. On the wide stretch of cobbles, with a fountain at one end, and a town hall with flags flying at the other, the usual two men were sitting on a bench having a shouted conversation that sounded like an argument but probably wasn't. The same woman was buying vegetables and haggling over the prices and the vendor shaking his head as always. The regular streetsweeper was clearing away confetti before another bridal party came along.

Ana wasn't sure how it had happened, but this was where she belonged now.

Acknowledgments

A while ago, my friend Sarah-Kate Lynch sent me a newspaper article. It was about the British food writer Sophie Grigson, who had packed up her car with pretty much everything she owned and driven to Southern Italy to start a new life. 'Look,' said Sarah-Kate. 'She's behaving like a character in one of your books.' And I thought, *hmm so she is.*

That day, instead of getting on with whatever it was that I should have been doing, I read everything I could find online about Sophie Grigson's Italian adventure. Then I sent for her book on the subject, *A Curious Absence of Chickens*. And finally, I tracked down Sophie herself and she very kindly chatted to me via Zoom.

That's how this story began. Of course, I read more books – *Save Me the Plums* by Ruth Reichl and *Restoring a Home in Italy* by Elizabeth Minchilli. And I'm not a great baker, so I took advice from Jenna Reid of Jenna Maree Cakes. And it's a long time since I was an editor, so I had help from Kelli Brett of *Cuisine* magazine. Thank you to all of them.

One area that didn't need much extra work, because I've been researching it for the past thirty years, is the challenges of a long relationship. Over the period of writing this book, I told my husband twice that I wanted a divorce – actually, he reckons it was four times. Just as Skye says: sometimes love seems to be missing in action, somehow it was always there. So, I'd like to thank Carne Bidwill for riding those highs and lows with me.

Also, thanks to Stacy Gregg. I wouldn't want to do the highs and lows of being a writer without you. Thanks to Justine Johnston for getting lost with me in Tivoli. Huge appreciation to my long-time agent Caroline Sheldon, thanks to my new agent Jon Wood for taking me on and gratitude to everyone who has guided and helped me over the years. This is my fifteenth novel and you can't keep on writing books without support.

A lot of that support has come from my publishers. To everyone at Hachette Aotearoa New Zealand, a very grateful *ngā mihi*. And massive thanks to my editor Charlotte Mursell and her assistant Snigdha Koirala at Orion in the UK for helping make *Marry Me in Italy* everything I wanted it to be.

I've dedicated this book to Clara De Sio, whose home in Maratea has been such an inspiration and a beautiful place to write. Thanks also to her daughter Giusy for her friendship and hospitality, and to all my family and friends in Italy.

In 2024, I'm hosting my first ever tour. I'll be taking a small group to beautiful south-east Sicily, to visit some of the places that have inspired my stories, feast on the flavours and soak up the life and culture of the region's Baroque towns. For information about any future tours, please sign up to my newsletter via my website www.nickypellegrino.com.

And thanks for reading this book … I hope it took you to Italy!

Credits

Nicky Pellegrino and Orion Fiction would like to thank everyone at Orion who worked on the publication of *Marry Me in Italy* in the UK.

Editorial
Charlotte Mursell
Snigdha Koirala

Design
Charlotte Abrams-Simpson
Rose Cooper

Copyeditor
Laura Gerrard

Editorial Management
Charlie Panayiotou
Jane Hughes
Bartley Shaw

Proofreader
Laetitia Grant

Finance
Jasdip Nandra
Nick Gibson
Sue Baker

Audio
Paul Stark
Louise Richardson

Contracts
Dan Herron
Ellie Bowker
Oliver Chacón

Marketing
Sharina Smith

Production
Ruth Sharvell

Sales
Catherine Worsley
Esther Waters
Victoria Laws

Rachael Hum
Anna Egelstaff
Frances Doyle
Georgina Cutler

Operations
Jo Jacobs

Also by Nicky Pellegrino

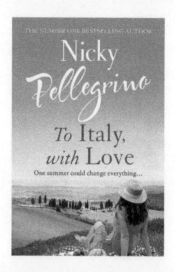

Love happens when you least expect it . . .

Assunta has given up on love. She might run her little *trattoria* in the most romantic mountain town in Italy, but love just seems to have passed her by.

Sarah-Jane is finished with love. She's buying an old convertible and driving around Italy this summer – it's the perfect way to forget all about her hot celebrity ex-boyfriend!

But when Sarah-Jane's car breaks down in Montenello, she has to stay longer than she intended! And the trouble is, love is *everywhere* . . .

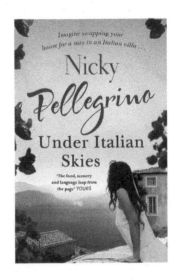

Can you change your life by swapping your home?

'It was a curious sort of feeling, being so cherished by a stranger . . .'

Imagine swapping your house for a stay in an Italian villa . . . and falling in love with the owner's life.

After Stella's boss dies suddenly, she's left with nothing to do apart from clear the studio. It seems as though the life she wanted has vanished. She is lost – until one day she finds a house swap website and sees a beautiful old villa in a southern Italian village. Could she really exchange her poky London flat for that?

But what was just intended as a break becomes much more, as Stella finds herself trying on a stranger's life.

Can Stella overcome her grief and find her way into a new future?

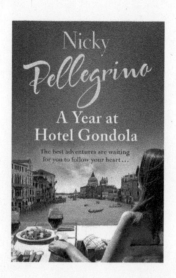

The best adventures are waiting for you to follow your heart . . .

Kat is an adventurer, a food writer who travels the world visiting far-flung places and eating unusual things. Now she is about to embark on her biggest adventure yet – a relationship.

She has fallen in love with an Italian man and is moving to live with him in Venice, where she will help him run his small guesthouse, Hotel Gondola. Kat has lined up a book deal and will write about the first year of her new adventure: the food she eats, the recipes she collects, the people she meets and the man she doesn't really know all that well but is going to make a life with.

But as Kat ought to know by now, the thing about adventures is that they never go exactly the way you expect them to . . .

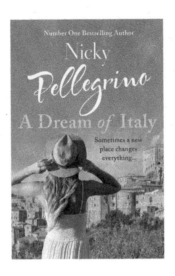

For sale: historic building in the picturesque town of Montenello, southern Italy. Asking price: 1 euro

Cloudless skies, sun-soaked countryside, delicious food . . . In the drowsy heat of an Italian summer, four strangers arrive in a beautiful town nestled in the mountains of Basilicata, dreaming of a new adventure. An innovative scheme by the town's mayor has given them the chance to buy a crumbling historic building for a single euro – on the condition that they renovate their home within three years, and help to bring new life to the close-knit local community.

Elise is desperate to get on the property ladder. Edward wants to escape a life he feels suffocated by. Mimi is determined to start afresh after her divorce. And there's one new arrival whose true motives are yet to be revealed . . .

For each of them, Montenello offers a different promise of happiness. But can they turn their dream of Italy into reality?

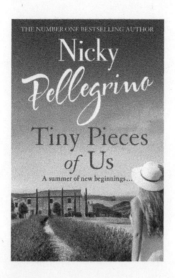

My heart is less than 1% of my body, it weighs hardly anything; it is only a tiny piece of me, yet it is the part everyone finds most interesting.

Vivi Palmer knows what it's like to live life carefully. Born with a heart defect, she was given a second chance after a transplant, but has never quite dared to make the most of it. Until she comes face to face with her donor's mother, Grace, who wants something in return for Vivi's second-hand heart: help to find all the other people who have tiny pieces of her son.

Reluctantly drawn into Grace's mission, Vivi's journalist training takes over as one by one, she tracks down a small group of strangers. As their lives intertwine, Vivi finds herself with a new kind of family, and by finding out more about all the pieces that make up the many parts of her, Vivi might just discover a whole new world waiting for her . . .

Join Vivi as she discovers second chances at life are anything but easy . . .